Praise for Jo Ann Brown and her novels

"The story is rich with relatable…characters."
—*RT Book Reviews* on *Amish Homecoming*

"The characters demonstrate great perseverance."
—*RT Book Reviews* on *An Amish Match*

"Readers will be pleased."
—*RT Book Reviews* on *Her Longed-For Family*

Praise for Debby Giusti and her novels

"The active pace becomes more engaging as the drama intensifies."
—*RT Book Reviews* on *The Agent's Secret Past*

"Plenty of suspense, a captivating mystery and fast pacing make this a great read."
—*RT Book Reviews* on *Protecting Her Child*

"It flows…and the characters' inner struggles are relatable."
—*RT Book Reviews* on *Stranded*

Jo Ann Brown has always loved stories with happy-ever-after endings. A former military officer, she is thrilled to have the chance to write stories about people falling in love. She is also a photographer, and she travels with her husband of more than thirty years to places where she can snap pictures. They live in Nevada with three children and a spoiled cat. Drop her a note at joannbrownbooks.com.

Debby Giusti is an award-winning Christian author who met and married her military husband at Fort Knox, Kentucky. Together they traveled the world, raised three wonderful children and have now settled in Atlanta, Georgia, where Debby spins tales of mystery and suspense that touch the heart and soul. Visit Debby online at debbygiusti.com; blog with her at seekerville.blogspot.com and craftieladiesofromance.blogspot.com; and email her at Debby@DebbyGiusti.com.

JO ANN BROWN

A Ready-Made Amish Family

&

DEBBY GIUSTI

Amish Refuge

HARLEQUIN® LOVE INSPIRED®

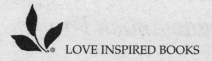

LOVE INSPIRED BOOKS

Recycling programs
for this product may
not exist in your area.

ISBN-13: 978-1-335-08020-2

A Ready-Made Amish Family and Amish Refuge

Copyright © 2018 by Harlequin Books S.A.

The publisher acknowledges the copyright holders of the individual works as follows:

A Ready-Made Amish Family
Copyright © 2017 by Jo Ann Ferguson

Amish Refuge
Copyright © 2017 by Deborah W. Giusti

www.Harlequin.com

Printed in U.S.A.

CONTENTS

A READY-MADE AMISH FAMILY

Jo Ann Brown

For Stephanie Giancola
It's been more years than either of us wants to admit
since you sat down next to me at the first-timers'
orientation (or did I sit down next to you?), and
I've been blessed to enjoy your friendship ever since.
All hail the Queen!

Fear thou not; for I am with thee: be not
dismayed; for I am thy God: I will strengthen thee;
yea, I will help thee; yea, I will uphold thee
with the right hand of My righteousness.
—*Isaiah* 41:10

Chapter One

"You look like you could use help."

When he heard the woman's calm voice, Isaiah Stoltzfus wanted to shout out his thanks to God for sending someone when he'd lost complete control of the situation. One *kind* was using the bellows in his blacksmith's shop to blow cold ashes everywhere, and two others clacked lengths of metal together like ancient knights holding sabers while a fourth *kind* sat on the stone floor and sobbed. In the past fifteen minutes, he'd learned the true meaning of being at his wits' end. He'd never guessed four young *kinder* could make him want to throw his hands into the air and announce he was in over his head. He'd been sure the *kinder* would be interested in visiting his blacksmith shop, but he'd been wrong. After a single glance around the space, they'd been bored and looked for the mischief they seemed able to find anywhere. He needed to take them somewhere else and find a way to divert their energy.

As if he'd given voice to his thoughts, Nettie Mae,

the sobbing three-year-old girl sitting on his left boot, pressed her head against his leg and said, "Wanna go home, *Onkel* Isaiah. Go home now."

Before he could answer either Nettie Mae or the woman, a cloud of dust exploded out of his unlit forge. He sneezed and waved it away. The other three-year-old girl was pumping harder and harder until a wheezing warning sound came out of the leather bellows. He opened his mouth to tell Nettie Mae's twin, Nancy, to stop before she broke something, but one of the five-year-old boys who'd been poking at each other with the metal staffs yelped in pain and began crying.

Isaiah took a lumbering step toward the boys, hobbled by Nettie Mae, who clung like a burr to his trousers. How could he have lost control over four pre-schoolers so quickly?

The task wasn't one for a man who'd never had *kinder* of his own. Maybe if Rose hadn't died soon after they married and they'd had a *boppli*, it would be easier to anticipate what the youngsters might do next. The Beachy *kinder* were active and inquisitive, but every time he thought about scolding them, he recalled how they'd lost their parents two weeks ago. He didn't want to upset them more, yet somehow every situation escalated into pandemonium.

But the woman who had been a silhouette in the doorway didn't seem to have the same qualms. Without a single word, she walked into his smithy as if she'd been there dozens of times. A flash of sunlight danced on her lush, red hair, which was pulled back beneath her black bonnet. Her brown eyes glanced in his direction before she focused on the *kinder*. She plucked the shafts out of the boys' hands and scooped their sister off the cold forge in a single motion, scattering ashes across her own dark blue dress. Placing the metal bars on a nearby table, she settled Nancy on her hip and knelt in front of the boys.

"Where does it hurt?" she asked one twin—Andrew, Isaiah noted—as she wiped tears from his pudgy cheeks and almost dislodged his straw hat.

"Ouch," the towhead said, pointing to his right thumb that was already bright red.

Isaiah watched in amazement as the woman cradled the little boy's hand as she ran a fingertip along his thumb. When the *kind* flinched, she murmured something too low for Isaiah to hear, but Andrew must have understood because he nodded, his eyes wide and filled with more tears.

"I don't think it's broken," the woman said in the same serene voice, but loud enough so Isaiah could hear. "And I suspect as soon as little minds are focused on other things, the bruise will be forgotten. However, just in case, we should watch it over the next couple of days."

"We?" Isaiah asked, his voice rising on the single word.

"You *are* Isaiah Stoltzfus, aren't you?" She looked at the youngsters, then him. No doubt she was thinking there couldn't be another overwhelmed man with two sets of twins wrecking his smithy in Paradise Springs.

"*Ja*. Who are you?"

"Clara Ebersol."

"*You* are Clara Ebersol?" He shouldn't stare, but he couldn't help himself.

As she set Nancy on the floor and came to her feet, he held out his hand to help her. She must not have seen it, because she didn't take it. When she was standing, he was startled to realize he didn't have to look down far to meet her gaze. She was, he noticed for the first time, very tall for an Amish woman, because he wasn't a short man. None of the Stoltzfus brothers were, but her eyes were less than a handbreadth below his. She was also lovely—something he *had* already noticed—possessing a redhead's porcelain complexion. Not a single freckle marred her cheeks or dappled her nose.

He forced his eyes to shift away, glad nobody else was there. If he as much as talked to a woman for more than a minute, someone mentioned she would make him a *gut* wife. Everyone seemed eager to get their widowed minister married. Finding him staring at Clara Ebersol would have given the district's matchmakers cause to start sticking their well-meaning noses into his life again.

"Weren't you expecting me?" Clara stroked Andrew's hair, and the little boy leaned his head against her skirt. "Your brother Daniel learned I was looking for a job, and he asked me if I'd be willing to help you take care of these *kinder*. He said I'd find you here." For the first time, her composure showed a faint crack as she looked at him again. "Didn't he tell you?"

"*Ja*, he told me."

When Daniel had stopped at the Beachys' house on his way home a couple of nights ago, he'd been pleased to tell Isaiah that he'd found someone to help take care of the twins. Isaiah had been grateful when Daniel had said he'd talked to Clara Ebersol himself, and she seemed perfect for the job. Arrangements had been made for her to meet Isaiah at the smithy today, because he'd hoped to finish a few tasks. But what Daniel had failed to mention—and Isaiah had never thought to ask about—was that Clara Ebersol was not a well-experienced *grossmammi* who'd already raised a household of *kinder*. She was a lovely young woman. Was his brother, who'd recently fallen in love and found a family, matchmaking? That was the only reason Isaiah could think of why his brother hadn't mentioned Clara's age. If he had to guess, Isaiah would say she must be close to his thirty years.

Or had Daniel told him?

Isaiah wasn't sure he could recall anything during the past two weeks accurately. Maybe if he got a *gut* night's sleep, he'd be able to think. Every thought had to battle against the appalling memories of his friends' funeral playing over and over through his mind, refusing to be forgotten.

Reaching into the pocket of her black apron, Clara drew out four lollipops. The twins focused on her hand.

"I've got a red, an orange, a yellow and a green." She raised her head and asked, "Do they know their colors?"

Again Isaiah wasn't quick enough to answer, as Ammon, usually the quietest one, shouted, "Want that one!" He pointed to the red lollipop.

She squatted again and made sure each *kind* got the lollipop he or she wanted. Taking the cellophane off each piece of candy, she led the two sets of twins out of the smithy. She looked around, unsure where to have them eat their suckers.

The space between the long, low building that housed the Stoltzfus Family Shops and Isaiah's smithy was more cramped with each passing day. His brother Joshua's buggy shop was outgrowing its space. Last week, Joshua and his two older sons had spent hours setting up a canopy where buggies could be parked out of the weather until Joshua had time to fix them.

"How about over there?" he asked, pointing to the back step of the grocery store his brother Amos ran.

"Perfect." Motioning for the *kinder* to follow, she

waited for each of them to select a spot on the concrete step. Once they were settled, the girls on one side and the boys on the other by unspoken consent, their tears and mischief were momentarily forgotten.

"Let's talk," he said, motioning for her to come back to him.

She hesitated, then walked to where he stood by the smithy's door. For a second, he wondered if she preferred the *kinder*'s company to his. Telling himself not to be foolish, because she didn't know any of them, he recognized he wasn't in any condition to make judgments. He was so tired he had trouble stringing more than three words together.

Quietly so her voice wouldn't reach the *kinder*, Clara said, "Your brother Daniel told me that they're orphans. That's terribly sad."

He nodded, words sticking in his tight throat. It had been only two weeks ago that he'd been roused out of bed in the middle of the night and learned his best friend Melvin Beachy had been killed along with Melvin's wife, Esta. They'd been traveling in an *Englisch* friend's truck coming home from an auction when something went wrong. The truck had gone through a guardrail and rolled, killing all three and leaving four small *kinder* without parents.

Nobody had been prepared for their deaths, but the whole community came together to help with the funeral. In the past two weeks, he hadn't made a single meal for the Beachy twins, because at least one person dropped by each day with casseroles and pies and fresh bread. As they had when his wife had died.

"I heard one of the girls call you '*onkel*,'" Clara went on when he didn't answer.

Relieved to be jerked out of his grim thoughts, he

nodded again. "It's an honorary title. Their *daed* was my best friend, so the twins grew up with me around." He was surprised how *gut* it felt to talk about Melvin instead of avoiding any mention of either him or Esta as he had since their funeral. His family had been trying to tiptoe around the subject. Their efforts not to upset him were a constant reminder of what he'd lost. "Melvin asked me, after the girls were born, to be the *kinder*'s guardian in case something happened to him and Esta."

"They don't have any other family?"

"There are Melvin's parents and Esta's sister. But they are out of the country, working with Mennonite missions. The *kinder*'s grandparents, Melvin's parents, are in Ghana, and Esta's sister is in Chile. It'll take at least a month before they can return to Paradise Springs. Maybe longer for their *aenti* because a recent earthquake along the Chilean coast tore up many of the roads in the area where she's serving."

She smiled. "So you have become their temporary *daed*."

He wished he could smile, but grief weighed too heavily for his lips. "I moved into their house to take care of them until someone from their real family gets here. I figured it'd be easier for them than moving to my house."

He didn't add that disaster had followed disaster while he tried to keep up with the young and confused *kinder* who didn't understand why their parents had failed to come home as they'd promised. It hadn't taken more than a couple of days for Isaiah to realize he couldn't oversee them and run his blacksmithing business and fulfill his duties as a minister in the district. Neighbors and his family had been helping with the chores on the farm and in the house. Now that Clara was going to be at the house, she would tend to those jobs, and he could work in the barn without having the *kinder* out there with him. Keeping an eye on the little kids while trying to milk the family's dozen cows had been close to impossible.

"I should get to know them." She walked to the *kinder* and knelt in front of them.

Isaiah stayed where he was. The soft murmur of her voice drifted to him, but not her words. She seemed uncomfortable with him. If that was so, why had she taken the job? Again, he chided himself. He was in no condition to judge anyone or anything. If she could calm the *kinder* with such ease, then why would he care if she'd rather spend time with the twins?

But he did.

You're not thinking clearly. Be glad you've got help. And he was. Hoping he didn't fall asleep on his feet, he turned to the smithy and the task of cleaning the mess the youngsters had made.

Clara looked from the *kinder* who were enjoying their lollipops to Isaiah Stoltzfus as he walked with slow, heavy steps into the blacksmith's shop. The man was exhausted. He carried a massive burden of fatigue on his shoulders, and, if the half-circles under his eyes got any darker, he would look as if he were part raccoon. She guessed that when he wasn't so tired he was a *gut*-looking man. His brother had mentioned Isaiah was a widower. The beard he had started when he married remained thin in spots, or maybe its white-blond hair was so fine it was invisible at some places along his jaw. Above his snowy brows, the hair dropping over his forehead was several shades darker, a color she'd heard someone describe as tawny.

He seemed like a nice guy, but nice guys weren't always what they seemed. She'd learned that the hardest way. She didn't intend to make the mistake again.

Not getting too close or too involved was her plan. She would help him with the twins, and when their *aenti* or grandparents returned, she'd leave with a smile and her last paycheck. By then, maybe she would have figured out what she wanted to do in the future. It wasn't going to revolve around a man, especially a *gut*-looking one who could twist her heart around his little finger and break it.

A sharp crunch drew Clara's attention to the *kinder*. The two sets of twins looked enough alike to be quads. They had pale blond hair, the girls' crooked braids barely containing their baby fine tresses that floated like bits of fog. Another crunch came, and she realized one boy was chewing on his lollipop.

"Are those candies *gut*?" she asked, already seeing differences between the two boys. The boy with the injured finger had a cowlick that lifted a narrow section of his bangs off his forehead, and the other one had darker freckles.

"Ja," said one of the girls.

"I am Clara." She smiled as she took the empty sticks held out to her. "What are your names?"

The wrong question because the *kinder* all spoke at once. It took her a few moments to sort out that Andrew was the boy with the bruised finger and the other boy was Ammon. The toddler who had been climbing on the forge was Nancy, and her twin was named Nettie Mae.

She led them to a rain barrel at the end of the building and washed their hands and faces. Each one must have given the others a taste of his or her lollipop, because their cheeks had become a crazy quilt of red, orange, yellow and green. She cleaned them as best she could, getting off most of the stickiness.

As she did, first one *kind*, then the next began to yawn. She wondered if they were sleeping any better than Isaiah was. Or maybe they needed a nap.

Clara felt like a mother duck leading her ducklings as she walked to the blacksmith shop. A light breeze rocked the sign by the door that read Blacksmith. Peeking past the door, she saw Isaiah checking the bellows, running his fingers along the ribs. Did he fear Nancy's enthusiasm had damaged them?

Though she didn't say anything and the *kinder* remained silent, he looked up. He attempted a smile, and she realized what a strain it must be when he'd lost two dear friends.

"Is it all right?" she asked. When his forehead threaded with bafflement, she added, "The bellows?"

"They seem to be, but I won't know until I fire the forge."

"If it's okay with you, I'll take the twins home while you do what you need to here."

"I should show you where—"

"I think I can find my way around a plain kitchen," she said. She didn't want him to think she was eager to go, though she was. The fact she'd noticed how handsome he was had alarms ringing in her head. After all, her former fiancé, Lonnie Wickey, had been nice to look at, too.

"I'm sure you can," he said after she'd urged the *kinder* to get in her buggy. "But you should know the pilot light on the stove and the oven isn't working. Do you know how to light one?"

"*Ja*. Our old stove was like that." She lifted Nettie

Mae, the littlest one, into the buggy. "Did you have something planned for supper?"

"We've been eating whatever is in the fridge. I appreciate you coming to help, Clara." He glanced at where the *kinder* were climbing into her buggy and claiming seats. "Can you stay until their grandparents or their *aenti* get here?"

"I can stay for as long as you need me to help with the *kinder*." She didn't add she was glad to get away from her *daed*, who found fault with everything she did. As he had for as long as she could remember. Doing a *gut* job for Isaiah could be the thing to prove to *Daed* she wasn't as flighty and irresponsible as he thought. She had been as a *kind*, but she'd grown up. Her *daed* didn't seem to realize that.

"Gut." His breath came out in a long sigh, and she realized he was more stressed than she'd thought. "If it's okay with you, I'll finish some things here and get to the farm in a couple of hours. You don't have to worry about milking the cows. I'll do that after supper."

"Take your time. I know you haven't had much of it."

He gave her a genuine smile, and her heart did a peculiar little lilt in her chest. She dampened her reaction.

"Danki," he said. "It's late, so getting set up for tomorrow is the best thing I can do. Firing the forge at this time in the afternoon would take too long. With you here to oversee the *kinder*, I'll be able to finish the commission work that needs to be shipped by the end of next week."

Curious what he was making, she nodded and walked to the buggy. She climbed in, pleased he didn't offer her a hand in so that she didn't have to pretend— again—she hadn't seen his fingers almost in her face. She made sure the twins were settled, the girls on the front seat with her and the boys in the back where they could peer out the small rear window. Her two bags sitting on the floor between the seats wouldn't be a problem for their short legs.

Clara drew in a deep breath as she reached for Bella's reins. The bay shook her mane, ready to get to their destination after the hour-long drive from the Ebersol farm south of Paradise Springs. Clara was eager to be gone, too. Every turn of the buggy wheels took her toward her future, though she had no idea what that would be. The decisions would be hers, not some man's who made her a pledge, then broke it a few months later.

She had expected the little ones to fall asleep to the rhythmic song of the horse's iron shoes on the road, but getting into the buggy seemed to have revived them. When she glanced at the twins, she discovered four pairs of bright blue eyes fixed on her.

"You got *kinder*?" asked Nancy.

"No," she said, glad her black bonnet hid her face from them. Try as she might, she hadn't been able to keep her smile from wavering at the innocent question.

She had thought she would have a husband and be starting a family by now, but the man who had asked her to be his wife had married someone else in Montana without having the courtesy of telling her until after she'd found out from the mutual friend who had introduced them. Lonnie had come from Montana to visit Paradise Springs, and he'd courted her. Fool that she was, she'd believed his professions of love. Worse, he'd waited until he was married to write to her and break off their betrothal.

"I like you," said Nettie Mae, leaning her head against Clara's arm.

"I like you, too." Clara was touched by the *kind*'s words. They were what she needed.

"I got a *boppli*." She chewed on the end of her right braid.

"Will you show her to me when we get to your house?" Clara started to reach to pull the braid out of the *kind*'s mouth as she asked another question about Nettie Mae's doll, then stopped herself. There was time enough to help the youngster end a bad habit later. Chiding her wouldn't be a *gut* way to start with these fragile *kinder*.

The little girl nodded.

"Me, too," Nancy announced as she jumped to her feet.

Clara drew the horse to a walk, then looked at the excited little girl. "It's important we sit when we're riding in a buggy."

"Why?" both boys asked at the same time.

Worried that speaking about the dangers on the road might upset the twins and remind them of how their parents had died in a truck accident, she devised an answer she hoped would satisfy them. "Well, you see my horse? Bella is working very, very hard, and we don't want to make it more difficult for her by bouncing around too much in the carriage."

"Oh," said a quartet of awed voices.

"Like horse," Nancy said, sitting on the front seat again. "Pretty horse."

"*Ja*. Bella is a pretty horse." She slapped the reins and steered the carriage along the twisting road, making sure she watched for any vehicles coming over a rise at a reckless speed.

When a squirrel bounced across the road in front of them, the kids were as fascinated as if they'd never seen one before. They chattered about where it might live and what it might eat and if they could have one for a pet.

"It's easy to catch a squirrel," Clara said. "Do you know how?"

"How?" asked Andrew, folding his arms on the top of the front seat.

"Climb a tree and pretend you're a nut." She waited for the *kinder* to laugh at the silly riddle, but they didn't.

Instead they became silent. The boys sat on the rear seat, and the girls clasped hands as Nettie Mae again began to chew on the end of her braid.

What had happened? They were old enough to understand the punch line, and she'd expected them to giggle or maybe groan. Not this unsettling silence.

"Where *Onkel* Isaiah?" Nettie Mae asked.

"Want *Onkel* Isaiah," whined her twin.

"We're going home to make supper for him," Clara said, keeping her tone upbeat.

"*Onkel* Isaiah make supper," Nettie Mae insisted.

"She's right," Andrew added. "*Onkel* Isaiah said he'd make supper until *Grossmammi* and *Grossdawdi* get home from 'freeca."

Glad Isaiah had explained the *kinder*'s grandparents were in Ghana, Clara was able to understand the boy's "'freeca" meant Africa. She struggled to hold on to her smile as she said, "But I offered to make supper tonight. It's nice to share chores sometimes, isn't it? Your *onkel* and I will be sharing the work."

"I'll help," crowed Andrew at the top of his lungs.

"Me, too!" shouted his twin.

Before Clara could ask them to lower their voices, Nettie Mae began to pout. "Me too little."

"Nonsense," Clara replied. "My *grossmammi* says God has work for all his *kinder*, no matter if they're young or old." She turned the buggy at a corner, following the directions Daniel Stoltzfus had given her. "Sometimes it means taking care of the beasts in the fields or making a nice home for our families. Other times, it's letting Him know we love Him. We can sing a song for God. Do you know 'Jesus Loves the Little Children'?"

"Ja!" they shouted.

She put her finger to her lips, but was relieved that they hadn't withdrawn as they had when she told the joke. "Do you know sometimes Jesus hears the song best if we sing quietly?"

"Really?" asked Andrew.

Already she could tell he was the one who spoke for his siblings. She suspected he was also their leader when they got into mischief.

"Ja," she answered. "Jesus listens to what's in our hearts, so when we sing quietly, it helps Him hear our hearts' voices."

Singing along with the youngsters, she watched for the lane leading to the Beachys' farm. Her hopes were high this job would be the perfect way for her to have time to decide what she wanted to do with the rest of her life. The *kinder* were easy to be around...as long as she kept them entertained. Their *onkel* would be busy with work, so she probably wouldn't see him other than at meals.

Driving up the lane toward the large white house with its well-kept barns set behind it, she imagined the first day her parents found money from her in their mailbox. She planned to send her pay home to her parents. Perhaps even *Daed* would be pleased with her efforts and acknowledge she wasn't a silly girl any longer. There was a first time for everything. Wasn't that what the old adage said?

Chapter Two

Clara kept the twins busy once they arrived at the Beachys' house and had put Bella in a stall in the stable out back. The boys' straw hats hung on pegs next to her bonnet by the door. The kitchen was a spacious room with cream walls and white cupboards. A large table was set near a bow window with a *wunderbaar* view of the dark pink blossoms ready to burst on the pair of crabapple trees. Every inch was covered with toys or stacks of dirty dishes.

When she asked the youngsters to pick up their toys and put them in the box in the front room, they kept her busy showing off their dolls and blocks and wooden animals and more trucks and tractors than she had guessed existed. She tried one more time to tell them a silly story, but again they became as silent as a moonless night.

What was she doing wrong? She must mention this to Isaiah when he returned to the house. Maybe after the *kinder* were in bed, though she'd be wiser to talk to him in the morning when the youngsters were focused on breakfast and paid no attention to the conversation.

Help me find the truth, Lord, she prayed as she put

another stack of dishes in the sudsy water and began washing them. The youngsters wanted to help, but she had visions of water splashed everywhere. Instead, she made up a game, and they arranged boots by size beside the door. The weather might be warm, but a good spring rain would turn the yard into mud. It'd be a few weeks before they'd put winter boots away in the cellar.

As the twins debated which boot went where as if it were a matter of the greatest importance, Clara hid her smile and finished the dishes. She took the youngsters upstairs so she could see their rooms after she had swept and mopped the kitchen floor. Once it dried, her shoes wouldn't stick to the wood on every step.

All the *kinder* slept in the same room. It was the breadth of the rear of the house, and she guessed from patches in the wood floor it once had been two rooms. Had their *daed* planned to put the wall up again once the twins were older? She silenced her sigh so she didn't upset her charges. Not that they would have noticed. One after another tugged on her hand, urging her to come and see the dresser and the pegs on the wall where their clothes hung or to look out the windows, both with a view of the fields beyond the barns and a pond. By summer, the frogs living there would sing a lullaby each night to soothe them to sleep.

The sound of the mantel clock downstairs tolling the hour interrupted Andrew, who was eager for Clara to see his coloring book.

"Time to make supper," she said.

"Me help!" Nancy and Nettie Mae cried at the same time.

"Everyone can help." She led the way down the stairs, looking over her shoulder to make sure she was not going too fast for their short legs.

It wasn't easy, but Clara found jobs for each *kind* with setting the table or helping her find the bread, as well as telling her where the pickles were stored in the cellar. The twins were excited when she uncovered a bright red oilcloth in the laundry room and spread it over the table. Using it under the youngsters' plates would make cleaning up afterward simpler and quicker.

Once the twins were carrying spoons and plastic glasses to the table, she went to the refrigerator. As she'd expected, it was full of food brought by caring neighbors. She lifted out a large casserole pan. Peeling back one corner of the foil covering the dish, she discovered it was a mixture of tomato sauce, hamburger and noodles. She hoped the *kinder* and Isaiah would enjoy it. She was sure they would savor the chocolate cake she'd found in an upper cupboard. She lit the oven with matches from a nearby drawer, put the casserole in, set the timer and went to help the youngsters finish setting the table. Several glasses and two spoons hit the floor on the way to the table, but she rinsed them off and handed them back to the twin who'd been carrying them.

Soon a fragrant, spicy scent filled the kitchen. The casserole must contain salsa as well as tomato sauce. Her stomach growled, and the kids kept asking when supper would be served. She reminded them each time that they needed to wait for *Onkel* Isaiah. That satisfied them until they asked the same question thirty seconds later.

Hearing the unmistakable sounds of a horse-drawn buggy coming toward the house, Clara helped the *kinder* wash their hands. She scrubbed their faces clean before urging them to take their seats at the table. As the timer went off, she opened the oven and lifted out the casserole. She was putting it on top of the stove when the kitchen door opened and Isaiah walked in, the twins instantly surrounding him.

He started to speak, but a peculiar choked sound came out of him as he scanned the room as if he couldn't believe his eyes. He set his straw hat on an empty peg next to her bonnet and strode past the long maple table where the twins again sat. He paused between the gas stove and the kitchen sink, turned to look in each direction before his gaze settled on her.

"Am I in the right house?" he asked.

She couldn't help smiling in spite of her determination to keep Isaiah at arm's length. As long as the only thing between them was business, everything should be fine. "I hope so, because this is where your brother said to go, and we've spent the past two hours here."

He shook his head. "But there were dirty dishes everywhere when we left this afternoon, and my boots tried to cement themselves to the floor where the *kinder* had spilled food and milk."

"I know."

"How did you do all this in such a short time?" he asked as if he expected to see dirty dishes piled in a corner.

"Practice." She smiled at the *kinder*. "And plenty of eager hands to help."

He faced her, surprise in his eyes. "Those same hands make anything I try take two or three times longer than if I'd done the job by myself."

"I know a few tricks." She smiled. "I'm glad there are plastic glasses in the cupboard. Otherwise, I would have been sweeping up plenty of glass."

"*Ja.* They sometimes confuse glasses with a volleyball."

Her smile widened. "Wash up, and I'll get the food on the table. It'll be ready when you are."

When he glanced at her in astonishment, heat rushed up her face. She was acting as if she belonged there. It wasn't an impression she wanted to give him or anyone in Paradise Springs. As soon as he went into the bathroom, she busied herself getting milk from the refrigerator and filling each *kind*'s glass halfway. She needed to guard her words and remember she was the hired girl whose duties were to cook and clean and look after the *kinder*.

If Isaiah was bothered by what she'd said, he showed no sign when he walked into the kitchen. As he pulled out a chair, he said, "I'm amazed how fast you cleaned the kitchen. It took two of my sisters-in-law more than a day to set everything to order yesterday."

"The kitchen was cleaned yesterday?" She halted with the casserole halfway between the stove and the table.

"*Ja.* They came over to help."

Clara blurted, "You made such a mess in a single day?"

He arched a pale brow, and she laughed.

Sudden cries of dismay erupted from the twins, and Clara set the casserole on the stove. Had one of them gotten hurt? How? The shrieks threatened to freeze her blood right in her veins.

At the same time Isaiah jumped to his feet and hurried around the table to where the youngsters stood together in a clump as if trying to protect themselves from an unseen monster. Their eyes were huge in their colorless faces.

"What is it?" Isaiah asked, leaning toward them. "What's wrong?"

All four pointed at Clara. Shock riveted her. Were they insulted by her comment about the house becoming a disaster area in a day? No, they were barely more than toddlers. They didn't care about the state of their house.

"No laugh," said Nettie Mae around the end of her braid she'd stuck into her mouth again. She put her finger to her lips and regarded them with big, blue eyes. "Quiet and no laugh."

"No laugh. Quiet." Nancy pointed at Clara. "No laugh. Gotta be quiet."

Clara listened in appalled disbelief. Isaiah's face revealed he was as shocked as she was.

"Not laughing is hard," Andrew lamented. "Really, really hard."

"Squirrel funny, but no laugh," added his twin, his words coming out in an odd mumble. Was he trying not to cry? "Really, really hard no laughing."

"Really, really hard." Nettie Mae's lower lip wobbled, and a single tear slid down her plump cheek.

Clara gasped when Isaiah sat on the floor. He held out his arms, and the *kinder* piled onto his lap. But there was nothing joyous about them as they held onto him like leaves fighting not to be blown away by a storm wind.

"Tell me about the squirrel," Isaiah said. "I like funny stories."

Andrew shook his head, and his brother and sisters did, too. "No laughing. Be quiet."

"Who told you to be quiet?"

"She did." He pointed an accusatory finger at Clara. When Isaiah frowned, she said, "I asked them—"

"It's *gut*," Andrew said. "What Clara told us. To be quiet when we sing so Jesus can hear what's in our hearts."

Again Isaiah's pale brows rose, but his voice became calmer as he replied, "That is true. Clara was very kind to help you learn that. Has anyone else told you to be quiet?"

"You!" Nancy poked one side of his suspenders.

He tapped her nose and smiled. "I've told you that a lot, because you make more noise than a whole field of crows, but you don't listen to me. You keep chattering away."

The twins exchanged glances, and Clara couldn't help wondering if they had some way to know what one another was thinking. She'd heard that twins seemed to be able to communicate without words, but had no idea if it was true.

"Tell me the story about the squirrel," Isaiah urged. "Did he chatter, too?"

Four small bodies stiffened. Nettie Mae chewed frantically on her braid, and Nancy's thumb popped into her mouth. The boys grabbed each other's hand and shook their heads.

"No laughing," Andrew whispered.

Clara squatted beside them and Isaiah. "Who told you that, Andrew?"

The little boy clamped his lips closed as his eyes grew glassy with tears. Beside him, his siblings' lips quivered.

When Isaiah started to speak, she put her hand on his shoulder to halt him. She wasn't sure if she was more astonished at her temerity or at the pulse of sensation rippling up her arm. She didn't want to be attracted to her employer—or any man—until she had sorted out what to do with her life. She wasn't going to make the same mistake of believing a man loved her and then being shown how wrong she was.

Pulling her hand back, she forced a smile. Now wasn't the time to worry about herself. She needed to focus on the *kinder*. "Let's have supper," she urged. "It'll taste better hot than cold." She made shooing motions, and the twins clambered onto their chairs.

She started to stand but wobbled. When Isaiah put a steadying hand on her back, she almost jumped out of her skin at the thud of awareness slamming into her so hard that, for a moment, she thought she'd fallen on the hard floor. She jumped to her feet as the *kinder* had and edged away so he could stand without being too close to her.

He asked quietly, "Do you have any idea what's going on with them?"

"You'd know better than I would. You've been around them their whole lives."

Gritting his teeth so hard she could hear them grind, he said, "My guess is, sometime during the funeral or the days leading up to it, someone they respect enough to listen to must have told them laughing was wrong."

"Who?"

"I don't know. You see how they don't always listen to me, and they love me. I've got no idea who might have told them not to laugh."

Why hadn't she seen the truth for herself? But who could imagine four little *kinder* would believe they shouldn't laugh again? When they'd become silent in the buggy, she'd known something was amiss.

But not this.

Putting her hand over her mouth before the sob bubbling up in her throat could escape, she turned away, not wanting them to see her reaction. "*Kinder* take everything at face value, so if someone told them not to laugh, they couldn't guess it meant only at the…" She gulped back the rest of what she was going to say. She didn't want to speak of their parents' funeral and cause further distress. "How much do they know about what's happened?"

He shrugged. "They attended the…the event."

"*Ja*, I assumed that." She was relieved he didn't say *funeral* or the names of the deceased. It was further proof he cared deeply about the twins.

"Who can guess how much a young *kind* understands?" His mouth grew straight. "I'm an adult, and I find it hard to believe my friends are gone."

"Are we going to eat?" called Andrew, again the spokesman for his siblings.

"Of course." Hoping her smile didn't look hideous, Clara slipped past Isaiah and went to get the casserole. "We don't want supper to get cold, do we?"

She placed the casserole dish in the middle of the table. She reached to pull out an empty chair next to where the girls sat on red and blue booster seats, but moved to another at the sight of the stricken expressions on the twins' faces. Nobody needed to explain the first chair was where their *mamm* used to sit.

Isaiah lifted Andrew out of his chair and moved him over one. Sitting between the two boys, he winked at them before bowing his head. Clara watched as the *kinder* folded their tiny hands on the table and lowered their eyes, as well. They had been well-taught by their parents. Looking from one to the next and at Isaiah, she closed her eyes and, after thanking God for their meal, prayed for Him to enter the Beachy twins' hearts and ease their grief.

And Isaiah's heart, too, she added when he cleared his throat to signal the time for silent grace was over.

The *kinder* dug into their meal with enthusiasm.

Clara was sure it was delicious, because it'd smelled that way while heating. In her mouth, the meat and noodles tasted as dry and flavorless as the ashes on Isaiah's forge would have. She saw Isaiah toying with his food as well before scraping it onto the boys' plates when they asked for seconds.

He raised his eyes, and his gaze locked with hers across the table. In that instant, she knew what he was thinking. They needed to help the *kinder*. She agreed, but couldn't ignore how uneasy she was that she and Isaiah were of a mind. It suggested a connection she wasn't ready to make with a man again. She wasn't sure when she would be.

Maybe never.

Isaiah smiled, hoping the youngsters wouldn't guess he was forcing it. *Kinder* were experts at seeing through a ploy, so he tried to be honest with them. When Clara gave a slight nod, he hoped she shared his belief they had to help the twins laugh again.

He was astonished when she pushed back her chair and rose. She opened a cupboard and took down the chocolate cake Fannie Beiler had brought over yesterday. The Beilers lived next door to his *mamm*, and Fannie's daughter Leah was married to his brother Ezra. He'd stashed the cake away so the *kinder* didn't tease for it before they ate.

And then he forgot about it.

As Clara carried the cake to the table, the twins began squirming with anticipation of chocolate and peanut butter frosting. "Who wants a piece?"

"Me! Me! Me! Me!" echoed through the kitchen.

She smiled and took six small plates out of a lower cupboard. Setting them on the table, she cut the cake.

She sliced four small servings and then put a plate in front of each *kind*. The piece she put in front of him was much bigger.

"Is that enough, Isaiah?" she asked. "Or do you want more?"

"How about if I say I want less?" he asked.

"I wouldn't believe you."

"And you'd be right." He fought not to chuckle, not wanting to distress the twins again.

"Don't wait for me," she said. "Try it."

The *kinder* needed no further urging. Within seconds, they were covered with chocolate crumbs and wearing broad smiles.

Though he was as eager as the twins to sample the cake, Isaiah waited for Clara to cut herself a small slice. He watched as she ate and glanced at the *kinder*, smiling at their silliness.

She was *gut* with them. He'd seen that from the moment she walked into his blacksmith shop and took control of the chaos. She had an intangible air of calm around her that seemed to draw the *kinder*'s attention so they listened to what she said.

And with her face not half-hidden beneath her bonnet, her hair rivaled the colors of the sunset. Somehow, her red strands weren't garish but more a reflection of the glow that transformed her face when she smiled. Really smiled, not a lukewarm one aimed at hiding her true feelings.

"Wasn't the cake *gut*?" Isaiah asked and was rewarded with four towheads bobbing together, though Ammon wasn't as enthusiastic at first. The youngsters must be exhausted. "Next time we see Fannie Beiler, you must tell her how much you enjoyed this cake."

"Yummy!" Nettie Mae said, patting her stomach. "Yummy in my tummy!"

A laugh, quickly squelched, came from where Clara sat beside the girls. She had her hand over her mouth and a horrified expression on her face.

He put hands on the boys' shoulders to keep them from running away from the table again. Clara had slipped her arm around the girls and started to apologize to them.

"No, don't say you're sorry," he hurried to say. "There's nothing wrong with laughing, right?" He looked at the boys.

Andrew nodded. "Clara can laugh, I guess."

"But not you?" she asked.

When the *kinder* remained silent, Isaiah pushed his plate away, though he hadn't finished the delicious cake. He folded his arms on the table.

"God wants us to be happy," he said as he looked from one young face to the next. "He loves it when we sing and when we pray together. Do you believe that?"

They nodded.

"And when we laugh together, too," he added.

The boys ran into the front room. When Nancy let out a cry, Clara drew her arm back from the girls who chased after their brothers and huddled with them by the sofa.

He wanted to go and comfort them, but wasn't sure what to say. He couldn't tell them they should accept the hurts in their lives because God had a plan for them to be happy in the future. He couldn't say that because he wasn't sure he believed it himself any longer. Since he'd learned of Melvin's and Esta's deaths, the uneasiness that had begun inside him after Rose's death had hardened his heart like iron taken from the forge. Every heartbeat hurt.

He struggled with his faith more each day. He believed in God, but it wasn't easy to accept a loving God would watch such grieving and do nothing. More than once, he'd considered seeking advice from his bishop, because he trusted Reuben Lapp as a man of God. But he knew what Reuben would say. Trust in God and be willing to accept the path God had given him to walk. Once he'd been happy to follow, but that was before Rose died from a severe asthma attack and then his friends' lives came to an end, leaving behind hurt and bewildered *kinder* who couldn't understand why the most important persons in their lives had gone away.

"Don't push them," Clara said from the other side of the table. "There's got to be a way to persuade them it's okay to laugh again like normal kids. I know there is."

"I wish I could be as sure."

When she stared at him, shocked a minister would speak so, he rose and went to the back door. He grasped his straw hat, put it on his head and said, "I've got to milk the cows. I'll be back in an hour or so."

He didn't give her time to answer. Striding across the yard to the big barn where the cows were waiting, he knew he needed to have an explanation for her when he returned.

He didn't know what it would be.

Chapter Three

When Isaiah came in after finishing the barn chores, the kitchen looked as neat as it had before supper. The room was empty, so he glanced toward the front room.

The twins were stretched out on the floor, coloring, while Clara sat on the sofa facing the wood stove and the rocking chair Melvin had bought for his wife when they first learned they were going to have a *boppli*. At that time, nobody had guessed Esta was carrying two *bopplin*.

He didn't move as Andrew got up and went to show Clara the picture he'd been working on. While she listened to the boy's excitement with the colors he'd chosen, she curved her hand across his narrow back, making a connection to the *kind*. Andrew was grinning when he dropped beside his sisters and brother. Clara returned to stitching a button on a shirt that must be from the pile of mending Esta kept in the front room.

It was the perfect domestic scene, one he'd believed he and Rose would one day share. The troubles they'd had in the first couple of months of their marriage had been behind them, and he'd been looking forward to building a family with her in the days before she died.

Alone.

Thinking of that single word was like swallowing a lit torch. There must have been a sign he'd missed, a wheezing sound when she breathed or a cough that went on and on or blueness around her lips. Something he should have seen and known not to go to work as if it were any other day. Something to tell him to stay home and comfort her and call 911.

He'd failed in his responsibility to her, and he couldn't make the same mistake with these youngsters. He owed that to his friends who had trusted him with their precious *kinder*.

Crossing the kitchen, Isaiah was surprised when the *kinder* were so focused on their coloring that they didn't raise their heads until Clara greeted him. She continued sewing, and he was astounded to see it was the shirt he'd lost a button on the other day.

"You don't have to do my mending." His voice sounded strained.

"I don't mind. I like staying busy." She looked at the *kinder*. "They've been coloring pictures for you."

"For me?"

She nodded, and he saw Andrew was coloring a bright red cow while his twin was using the same shade for a tractor. Nancy had been working on a blue bird with most of the strokes inside the lines, but Nettie Mae's page was covered with green with no regard for the picture of a dog in the middle of it. The little girl had her nose an inch from the coloring book.

When Nettie Mae paused to try to stifle a yawn, he had to wonder if she was half-asleep already. It had been a long day for the twins and an upsetting one, as well.

Clara stood and set his shirt on a table beside the sofa. "Time for baths."

The youngsters groaned, but gathered their crayons and put them in the metal box. She snapped the lid closed and picked up their coloring books while the twins asked what he thought of their pictures.

His answers must have satisfied them, though he couldn't recall a moment later what he'd said. His gaze remained on Clara as she set the books and crayon box on the lower shelf of a bookcase. The thin organdy of her *kapp* was warmed by her red hair. Every motion of her slender fingers seemed to be accompanied by unheard music.

When she turned, he didn't shift his eyes quickly enough. She caught him watching her, and the faint pink in her cheeks vanished. Was that dismay in her eyes? Dismay and another stronger emotion, but he couldn't discern what. As she had before, she lowered her eyes.

She remained on the other side of the room while she said, "Isaiah, I must get the *kinder* ready for bed."

"I'll give the boys their bath," he said, trying to lighten the situation. "I'll check behind all four ears."

His hope the twins would forget themselves and giggle was dashed, because they had become silent again. Did they sense the tension in the room? They couldn't know why. He didn't. He couldn't have said anything wrong, because he'd said less than a dozen words since he returned to the house.

But how was he going to convince the *kinder* it was okay to laugh? Though he and Clara had assured the twins a *gut* giggle would be all right, the twins continued to limit themselves to smiles.

I know I should be grateful they can smile, God, but a kind *without a laugh seems wrong. You know what's in their hearts. Help me find a way into them, too, so their laughter can be freed.*

He understood why the youngsters might not trust Clara to release them from their promise not to laugh. They hardly knew her, though they seemed to like her.

And why wouldn't they like her? She was gentle and showed an interest in what mattered to them, acting as if each toy they showed her was the most amazing thing she'd ever seen. They wolfed down the food she put in front of them as if they hadn't eaten since birth.

But that didn't explain why the twins didn't heed *him*. He'd loved them before they were born. They called him *onkel*, and they were as close to his heart as his true nieces and nephews. Why didn't they trust him when he told them it was okay to laugh?

"I'll give the girls a bath," Clara said, "and checking behind ears sounds like a *gut* idea." She took a single step toward him, then paused. "Are there two bathrooms in the house?"

"We'll use the bathroom in the *dawdi haus*." He took the boys' hands. "Don't worry. My sisters-in-law cleaned it yesterday, and I moved my stuff over there."

"You're staying in the *dawdi haus*?"

"Is that a problem?"

For a moment, he thought she was going to say *ja*, but she replied, "I assumed you would stay at your house."

He let go of the boys' hands and crossed the room so he could lower his voice to keep the *kinder* from overhearing. "Clara, you've got to understand. Melvin and Esta expected me to take care of their family, and I won't let them down. When Daniel told me you'd agreed to come and help, I decided I'd use the *dawdi haus*. With the door between us and four very nosy chaperones—" He made a silly face at the twins who'd tiptoed over to listen.

Again they didn't giggle, though they smiled. It seemed bizarre to have young *kinder* acting restrained.

"You think," Clara finished for him, "that will keep tongues from wagging."

"These are extraordinary circumstances as well as temporary ones. Everyone knows that. However, if you're uncomfortable, I won't ask you to stay."

"Stay, Clara!" shouted Andrew, bouncing from one foot to the other. "You said we can make cookies tomorrow."

"I can ask *Mamm* to come while we look for someone else," Isaiah continued as if the little boy hadn't spoken. "She planned to help, but she had a bout with pneumonia last month. She's not completely recovered. That's why my brothers and I thought it was better to hire someone."

"You need my help, and I'm here." She held out her hands to the girls. "Let's get you fresh and clean."

As she started to walk past him, Isaiah said, "*Danki*, Clara." He pointed toward a door between the refrigerator and the stove. "Just so you know, the *dawdi haus* is through there. You're welcome to use the downstairs bedroom by the bathroom."

"I'm sorry to take it from you."

"I didn't use it."

Her earth-brown eyes grew round. "Because it was where…" She glanced at the girls who were listening to every word. "It was where your friends slept?" She gave him a sad smile. "Aren't there more bedrooms upstairs?"

"*Ja*, two, but they're used for storage."

"Is there a bed in one?"

"*Ja*, in both."

"Then I'll use the one close to the *kinder*'s bedroom

door. I think it'd be better for me to be on the same floor with them."

He glanced at the boys, who had gotten bored and were pulling blocks out of the toy box. "That's a *gut* idea. I slept on the sofa, and I was up there most nights several times."

"Nightmares?"

"Either that, or they couldn't sleep." He grimaced. "I hate that you'll be taking care of them while I'm sleeping in the *dawdi haus*."

"It's what you're paying me for." She spoke the words without any emotion and walked with the girls toward the bathroom.

He wasn't sure what he would have said if she hadn't left him standing in the middle of the front room.

After he'd finished cleaning the puddles in the *dawdi haus* bathroom left by two little boys, Isaiah returned to the main house. He went upstairs and waited by the twins' bedroom door. He said nothing as Clara finished reading a story. The *kinder* listened, rapt, to the tale of a naughty bunny who learned a lesson through misadventures. He held his breath each time a little one raised a hand to an eye. Each time, the *kind* was trying to rub away any sleep catching up with him or her before the charming story was over.

He forced his shoulders to relax. He needed to stop overreacting to everything the twins did, assuming their tears had to do with grief instead of a bumped knee and being sleepy. He needed to be more like Clara, who kept them entertained but allowed for quiet moments, as well. He could see he'd been winding them up tight in an effort to prevent them from thinking about their parents. He shouldn't have been surprised they'd acted badly at his blacksmith's shop.

Being too busy to think hadn't worked for him either. No matter how many tasks he tried to concentrate on, he couldn't forget the gigantic hole in his life. How many times in the past couple of weeks had he thought of something he wanted to tell Melvin? Each time, renewed anguish threatened to suffocate him.

"Do you want to *komm* in and say a prayer with us?" Clara called as she knelt with the *kinder* by one of the small beds.

Joining them, Isaiah listened to their young voices saying the prayer they spoke every night. Clara asked if they wanted to ask for God's blessing on anyone special.

Andrew, always the leader, said, "*Onkel* Isaiah."

"Clara," added Nettie Mae, smiling at her.

But the smiles vanished when her twin said, "*Mamm* and *Daed* in heaven with You."

The pressure of tears filled his eyes, but he blinked them away as he lifted Ammon and set him on his bed before doing the same with Andrew. He tucked them in after they kissed him *gut nacht*. He turned to check on the girls. They were already beneath their covers, but he leaned over to collect kisses from them. All four insisted on giving Clara a kiss, too.

"Sleep well and have pretty dreams," she said as she turned down the propane lamp so a faint glow came from it.

He walked out with her, and she left the door open a finger's breadth. "That was a cute story," he said. "The twins were enthralled, though they've probably heard it a dozen times."

"No, they haven't. I brought the book with me." She glanced at the door, then followed him down the stairs.

"I brought several along. Reading them a story that their *mamm* or *daed* read could be too painful for them."

He relaxed his shoulders, letting some of his worry slide away. Maybe this would work out. Clara was tender with the *kinder*, thinking of their needs and trying to keep them from more pain.

He urged her to contact him if she needed anything, then said, "*Gut nacht*, Clara."

"*Gut nacht*," she replied before she went into the bathroom. She didn't close the door, and he guessed she was gathering the wet towels left from the girls' bath.

Going into the *dawdi haus*, he shut the door to the kitchen behind him. He faltered, then threw the sliding lock closed. Anyone seeing it would realize he and Clara intended on maintaining propriety.

Isaiah lit a lamp in the small living room that had two other doors opening off it. One was to the bathroom, the other to the cozy bedroom. Picking up his extra boots, he set them by the door he'd be using except when he went to the main house for meals or to spend time with the twins.

A light flickered outside the living-room window, startling him until he recognized the easy stride of Marlin Wagler, the district's deacon. If Marlin went to the main house, he could disturb the *kinder* whom Isaiah hoped were asleep. He grabbed a flashlight and hurried outside. He waved the light, catching the deacon's eye.

He wondered why the deacon was calling tonight. The deacon's duties revolved around making sure the *Leit* followed the district's *Ordnung* as well as handling money issues, helping any member of the community pay medical bills or appointing people to arrange fundraisers to provide for those who needed extra assistance. He hoped the problem was a simple one, because he didn't know how long he'd be able to focus on anything complicated tonight.

"*Komm* in," he said with a smile.

"I didn't expect to see you in the *dawdi haus*," Marlin said as he switched off his flashlight and walked in.

The deacon was a squat man, almost as wide as he was tall. Since he'd handed over the day-to-day running of his farm to his youngest son, Marlin had gained more weight. He was about the same age as Isaiah's late *daed* would have been. What hair remained on his head clung in a horseshoe shape from one ear to the other. It had turned gray years ago.

"Let's sit," Isaiah answered, "and you can tell me why you're here."

Marlin sat with a satisfied sigh in the overstuffed chair closer to the door. Once Isaiah had taken the other seat, Marlin began speaking of news from throughout the district and beyond. After he finished farming, he'd taken a job giving tourists buggy rides to his family's farm. He had amusing tales to share about the outrageous questions visitors asked.

"I've got to explain over and over," the deacon said with a chuckle that shook his broad belly, "we're not part of a living museum. We're just living our lives. However, I've recently driven people who seem to understand that. It's a blessing to be able to answer sensible questions."

"But those tourists don't make for *gut* stories."

"No, but they make for a pleasant day."

"I'm sure." Isaiah intended to add more, but a knock on the connecting door brought him to his feet. Sliding the lock aside, he opened it. Belatedly he realized he should have explained the situation to Marlin already.

Dear Lord, give me a gut *night's sleep tonight. I'm no longer thinking straight.*

"Excuse me." Clara clasped her hands in front of her. "I didn't mean to interrupt. I was wondering what time you wanted breakfast, Isaiah."

"*Komm* in." He motioned toward his other guest. "This is Marlin Wagler, our district's deacon. Marlin, this is Clara Ebersol."

"Oh," Marlin said, "I thought you might be the *kinder*'s *aenti* Debra. I've been looking forward to meeting her."

"It'll be several weeks, maybe as much as a month, before Debra will be able to get here from Chile." He'd never met Debra Wittmer whose home was in California when she wasn't away on mission work.

"Meanwhile," Clara said with a smile, "I'm here as a nanny for the *kinder*."

Marlin smiled. "*Gut.* They need a stable home. What a blessing your family and your young man don't mind you being away."

"I don't have a young man," Clara said, blushing so brightly her face was almost the color of her hair.

"No?" Marlin glanced at Isaiah and arched a brow.

"Will five be too early for breakfast?" Isaiah asked before the deacon could add anything else. He hadn't expected Marlin to start quizzing Clara about her personal life. It was, Isaiah was sure, an attempt at matchmaking.

"Five will be fine. I'll have breakfast ready then. *Gut nacht.*" She shut the door, not hiding her yearning to escape before she embarrassed herself again.

He heard her fading footsteps. Taking a deep breath, because Marlin was sure to have questions, Isaiah said, "Before you say anything, I'm living in the *dawdi haus*, as you can see." He hooked a thumb toward the stacks of clothing he'd brought from the main house. "With four very young *kinder*, I'm staying nearby in case Clara needs help with something. Though she's already shown she can take care of the household better than I could."

"I assume Reuben approves of this plan."

"Ja," he replied. As soon as his brother had told him about Clara, Isaiah had gone to the bishop and shared the plan with him. Of course, at that time, he hadn't known Clara Ebersol was a beautiful young woman.

It doesn't matter, he told himself. He wasn't looking for someone to court, and Clara was at the house for one reason: to take care of the *kinder*.

"Gut," Marlin said, his smile widening.

Isaiah wanted to groan aloud. He recognized the twinkle in the deacon's eye. Marlin and Atlee Bender, the other minister in their district, had been getting less and less subtle in their pressuring for Isaiah to choose another wife. They believed an ordained man should be married. It was a requirement for one's name to be put into the lot when a new minister was chosen, but nobody could have guessed Rose would die so soon after Isaiah was selected. Both men had told him that he'd had enough time to mourn, and finding a wife should be a high priority for him. They seemed to think it was as easy as going to his brother's grocery store and selecting one off the shelf.

Even if it was that simple, he wasn't interested in risking his heart and the devastating pain of loss again.

Clara slipped into the front bedroom across from the twins' bedroom door. It was crowded with boxes and cast-off furniture as Isaiah had warned. Trying to be quiet, she moved quilts and unused material from the bed. The mattress was clean, and she found sheets and a pillow in a cupboard in the hallway.

She made the bed, covering it with the topmost quilt from the pile. After braiding her hair, she went to the bed. Pulling back the bright red, blue and purple nine-patch quilt and the sheet beneath it, she sat on the edge of the bed and plumped the pillow.

Lying down, she watched the moonlight filtered by the leaves of the tree outside the window. It danced, making new patterns with every shift in the breeze.

The day had not gone badly, other than the shocking revelation by the *kinder* that they'd been told not to laugh. The twins seemed to accept her as part of their lives...so far. And she hadn't insulted Isaiah—or she thought she hadn't—so far. She must keep everything impersonal between them, as she would with anyone who hired her. Though he'd been puzzled when she spoke to him from the other side of the front room, he hadn't said anything.

Thank You, Lord, for keeping Isaiah from asking questions. She started to add to her prayer, but paused when she heard something. The noise was so soft she wasn't sure if she'd heard it. Then it came again.

A sob.

One of the *kinder* was crying.

Kicking aside her covers, Clara leaped out of bed. She grabbed the flashlight she'd left on the windowsill. She bumped into a stack of boxes, but kept them from tumbling to the floor. The big toe on her right foot hit the frame around the door, and she bit her lower lip to keep from making a sound. Limping across the hall, she aimed the flashlight against her palm and switched it on. Its glow gave her enough light to see without being so bright it woke any *kinder* who were asleep.

Her aching toe was forgotten when she heard another sob. It led her to where Ammon was lying on his left side with his knees drawn up to his chest as if in grave pain. She leaned over and spoke gently. He didn't respond, just kept sobbing.

Wanting to soothe him, she lifted Ammon off the bed and carried him out of the room before he woke his brother and sisters. She kept the flashlight pointed at the floor as she eased down the unfamiliar stairs and into the living room. Lighting the propane lamp while she held him took twice as long as it normally would, but she didn't want to release the *kind*. Not when he was sobbing as if he believed nothing in his life would ever get better.

She went to the rocking chair in front of the unlit wood stove. Sitting, she began to rock as she settled Ammon's left cheek over her heart. She spoke to him, but when her words seemed to offer him no comfort, she began humming the song she'd sung with the *kinder* in the buggy. She meant it as a prayer, wanting Jesus to fill Ammon's heart with His love and reassurance. Slowly the little boy's body relaxed, molding to her. She kept rocking as he closed his eyes, a longer time coming between each sob.

Hearing a soft click from the kitchen, Clara looked over her shoulder. Isaiah walked toward her, his face lengthening when he saw the *kind* in her arms.

"I saw the light," he whispered. "Is everything all right?"

"It will be." She glanced at the *kind* cuddling close to her. Ammon had fallen asleep. "I thought he'd had a bad dream. I heard him crying and went to check. He wasn't asleep. I think he's missing...." As she had before, she chose her words with care, knowing if she said "*mamm*" and "*daed*," she might rouse the little boy. "He wants those who aren't here."

"What about the others?"

"Asleep when we came down."

"That's a blessing." He turned a chair around and sat, facing her. "They went to bed tonight for you better than they have for me."

"They're exhausted." She didn't pause as she added, "You are, too. You should get some sleep while you can."

"A few more minutes won't matter, and that guy is pretty heavy for you to tote upstairs. I don't want you stumbling and getting hurt."

"I appreciate that."

Standing, he held out his arms. "Let me take him."

As Isaiah leaned toward her, Clara realized her mistake. When he lifted Ammon out of her arms, Isaiah's face was a finger's breadth from hers. She held her breath and kept her eyes lowered while they made the transfer. Isaiah's work-roughened fingers brushed against her skin, sending heat along it.

As soon as he took Ammon upstairs, she pushed out of the rocker. She gripped the top of it, her knuckles turning white, as she fought for equilibrium. She couldn't react like this every time a casual touch brought her into contact with Isaiah. She gripped the chair and was trying to slow her heart's frenzied rhythm when he came back down the stairs.

Her hope that Isaiah wouldn't notice her bleached fingers was dashed when he said, "I'm sorry, Clara, for Marlin asking you if you're walking out with someone. He can't seem to help himself sticking his nose into matters he believes are his responsibility."

"That's a deacon's job," she said, not wanting to

speak of how she scurried away like a frightened rabbit in a hedgerow.

"*This* deacon's job seems to be focused on finding me another wife." With the cockeyed grin Isaiah seemed to wear whenever he was trying to be self-deprecating, he sighed. "I'm sorry. I know you didn't figure on being the subject of matchmaking when you took this job."

"I don't like matchmaking."

"I agree. One hundred percent."

She appreciated his blunt answer and that he hadn't asked her to explain her comment. She didn't want to tell him that she was too well acquainted with matchmaking and the heartbreak it could cause.

"Clara, don't worry. We'll ignore everyone's matchmaking." He walked toward the door to the *dawdi haus* before facing her again. "In a way, we should be grateful to Marlin for bringing the subject out in the open, so neither of us has to act like we need to hide something."

"*Ja,*" she said, as he urged her to try to have a *gut* night's sleep.

He closed the door, and she heard the lock slide into place. She reached for her flashlight. Her fingers trembled as she picked it up and turned off the lamp. She hadn't been honest with Isaiah. She already was hiding something from him. The way her heart took a lilting leap whenever he touched her.

"You can jump about all you want," she whispered to her traitorous heart while she climbed the stairs. "There's nothing you or anyone else can do to change my mind. I won't be made a fool of by another man. Not ever again."

Chapter Four

As the sun rose the next morning, Isaiah finished his second cup of *kaffi* and put the empty cup beside his plate with a regretful sigh. Clara brewed *kaffi* strong, as he liked it when he had a long day ahead of him. He'd already finished milking the cows and let them out in the meadow as well as feeding the chickens and the horses. He wanted to finish the final upright for a double gate ordered by an *Englisch* horse breeder in Maryland. He needed to make a few curled pieces and a half dozen twisted lengths to complete the pattern. When the gates were finished, they would be shipped to the man's farm to be hung on either side of a driveway. A truck was collecting it at the end of next week.

With Clara's arrival, he should be able to finish the job on time. He couldn't let her delicious French toast tempt him to have another serving and linger at the table with her and the Beachy twins. The *kinder* were eating their second servings, dripping maple syrup and melted butter on the oilcloth Clara had spread across the table before serving breakfast. Seeing Nettie Mae dipping her fingers in the syrup and then licking them, he smiled. She caught him looking at her and grinned.

"Yummy, isn't it?" he asked.

"Yummy, yummy, yummy in my tummy, tummy, tummy."

"Is that your new saying, Nettie Mae?"

"*Ja*. Yummy in my tummy." She turned the phrase into a little song.

"I see happy faces. What did I miss?" Clara asked as she brought a new stack of steaming, eggy toast from the stove. She set the platter next to him.

"Nettie Mae said the toast is yummy in her tummy," Isaiah replied. "And she's singing about it."

"And a fun tune it is, too. More *kaffi*?"

He pushed back his chair and stood. "*Danki*, but I need to get to work."

"Do you come home for dinner at midday?" Clara asked, sitting where she had the night before.

"I've been since…" He glanced at the *kinder* who were too intent on their French toast to pay attention to the conversation.

"I can move the main meal to the evening if it's easier for you."

"I appreciate that. Once the forge is at the right temperature, I don't want to cool it down and have to wait to reheat it again. I appreciate your flexibility, Clara."

She shrugged off his compliment. "Anything else I should know about your work schedule?"

"Usually I am done around four. That allows me time to milk the cows and get cleaned up before the evening meal."

"I'll have dinner ready around six."

"*Gut.*" He stamped down the thought that Clara had avoided joining them at the table until he got up to leave. That wasn't fair to her. She'd been busy preparing breakfast and trying to stay ahead of four enthusiastic youngsters who seemed to have bottomless stomachs. But he couldn't ignore how, when he looked at her, it was as if he faced a closed door.

"Will you need a lunch packed for today?"

He motioned for her to stay where she was. "I'll get something at Amos's store today. You finish your breakfast before it's cold."

Going to the door, he took his straw hat off the peg above the low row where smaller hats and bonnets waited for the *kinder*. He put it on his head and reached for the doorknob.

"*Onkel* Isaiah!" cried Nancy as she jumped up.

Her booster seat slid forward, pushing her toward the table. Her elbow hit her plate, and everything seemed to move in slow motion. The plate flipped into the air, spraying maple syrup everywhere. Her unfinished slice of toast struck her glass and knocked it into her sister's. Both glasses bounced and rolled onto Andrew's plate before coming to a stop in the middle of Ammon's. More syrup and melted butter flew across the table.

Clara grabbed the boys' glasses and kept them from falling over and spilling more milk on the table. The *kinder* tried to help, but ended up with more food on them and across the chairs. A plate fell off the table and clattered on the floor. It landed upside down, one corner of toast peeking out from beneath it.

Silence settled on the kitchen as they stared at the mess. He heard a muffled sound and glanced at Clara. She was biting her lower lip to keep from laughing.

"Now I understand how the kitchen could get messy in a single day," she said. "Maybe I should have put the oilcloth on the floor instead of on the table."

Isaiah had to put his hand over his mouth to stifle his laugh. The *kinder* were smiling, but exchanging the uneasy looks he realized were their way of reminding each other not to laugh. He lost any desire to give into the humor of the situation. There was nothing funny when four little kids refused to let themselves act as *kinder* should.

Who'd told them not to laugh? Once he found out, he was going to have that person explain to the twins he or she had made a big mistake. It was *gut* for them to laugh. They needed to express their happy emotions as well as their sad ones.

But they aren't showing those either. That thought unsettled him more. How could he have failed to notice? Caught up in the day-to-day struggle to balance taking care of them with his work at the forge, he'd been too focused on each passing minute to look at the bigger picture.

Hanging his hat on the peg, he ran to the sink and grabbed the dishrag. He wet it, wrung it out and began pushing the puddles of syrup from the edge of the table. The cloth became a sticky mess within seconds. Tossing it into the sink, he grabbed the roll of paper towels.

"*Komm*, and let's get cleaned up." Clara motioned for the *kinder* to follow her toward the bathroom.

Placing paper towels over the puddle of milk and syrup, Isaiah started to dab it up.

"Leave it," Clara said. "We'll clean it once there are a few less layers of syrup on us."

"Let me get started so no more hits the floor."

"*Danki.*" Her smile warmed him more than another cup of her delicious *kaffi*. Before he could smile back, she'd turned to the wide-eyed twins. "Pick up your plates and put them in the sink on your way to the bathroom. Don't touch anything else!"

The abashed *kinder* obeyed without a peep, astonishing Isaiah anew. They'd done as he asked, though not always as he'd hoped. And the results had often been another disaster on top of the one he was trying to get put to rights.

Isaiah went to work cleaning the table and the floor while he listened to Clara helping the twins wash in the bathroom. Later, when the youngsters were in bed and couldn't hear, he needed to ask her how she persuaded them to obey her.

He finished catching the last drip of butter off the oilcloth as the door opened. Assuming it was one of his brothers, stopping on the way to work, he gasped out loud when he saw a petite woman stepping into the kitchen.

"*Gute mariye*, Isaiah. I'm here to help you and…" She glanced around the kitchen, and her eyes widened. "It's clean! Except for the mess at the table, I mean."

"*Ja*, it's mostly clean." It took every bit of his strength to keep his smile in place. It wasn't Orpha Mast's fault her voice was too much like her sister Rose's. Putting his finger to his lips, he grimaced as he tasted syrup. "And please not so loud. The *kinder* went to wash their hands, and if they realize someone's visiting, they'll come running and drip water all the way."

"The little ones are washing their hands by themselves?" Orpha waved aside his answer. "Never mind. It won't take long to wipe up the bathroom. It's only soap and water, ain't so?"

"They aren't—"

Not allowing him to explain, she gave him a sympathetic smile. "You look better than the last time I saw you."

"I'd just finished speaking over the graves of my best friend and his wife."

She tilted her head so she could eye him with a sad smile. "You have such a burden to carry, Isaiah. Your work, your obligations to the district and four little ones. You don't have to do it on your own, you know."

"I know. I—"

"You know you can ask for help," she said, not letting him finish again.

"I know. I—"

"Those who want to help are right in front of you." The hint of a smile curved along her perfect lips. "Let me help you, Isaiah. I would do anything for you. Ask me, and I'll be by your side to take care of these *kinder*."

He was saved from having to answer the unanswerable when the twins poured out of the bathroom, holding up their hands to show him they were clean. He had his back to the bathroom door, but he knew the moment Clara stepped into the room because Orpha's smile became brittle.

"Who is *she*?" his sister-in-law asked so crisply the twins halted and stared.

Pretending not to hear the venom in Orpha's voice, Isaiah said, "Orpha, this is Clara Ebersol. She's here to take care of the *kinder*. Clara, this is my sister-in-law, Orpha Mast."

"How kind of you to come and check on Isaiah and the *kinder*," Clara said with a smile.

Had she missed Orpha's tone? Unlikely. Clara already seemed able to discern what he was thinking far too often. She was being nice, he realized, and trying to defuse the situation. Why didn't Orpha see that her sharp words were upsetting the twins?

"I guess I don't need to check on them if you're here," Orpha replied in the same clipped tone. "Are you related to the Beachys?"

"No." Clara folded a damp towel over her arm. "We're about to sit back down for the rest of our breakfast. Would you like to join us?"

Say no, Isaiah begged in his thoughts.

"No." Orpha glared at all of them. "It would appear I'm not needed here." Without another word, she left, closing the door harder than necessary.

"Why was her face like a duck's bill?" asked Andrew as he stuck out his lips in an imitation of Orpha's exasperated expression. "Did she taste something bad?"

"We'll never know, will we?" Clara steered the youngsters to the table. "Who would like more French toast?"

The twins climbed into their chairs and booster seats. They began chattering as if there hadn't been any interruption, and Clara went to the stove. Isaiah put the paper towels he was holding in the trash.

"I'm sorry," he said. "Orpha was surprised to see you here."

"She was." Clara didn't look at him. "Don't worry about it. I know you've got a lot to do at the blacksmith shop."

"I do, but…" He raked his fingers through his hair, then grimaced when he realized syrup still stuck to them. Too late to worry now. "The folks around here are pretty friendly."

"I'm sure they are," she said in the same calm tone as she set two slices of bread on the griddle. She stepped back as egg sizzled and snapped. "Your sister-in-law isn't happy with me being here."

"You don't have to put it politely. Orpha wants me to walk out with her. I don't know how many times she's mentioned being a minister's wife must be interesting." He grimaced. "Her description, not mine."

"Perhaps you should go after her and tell her she doesn't have to worry about me being her competition." She arched a single brow.

Fascinated, because he'd never been able to make that motion, he replied, "That would begin a conversation I'd prefer to avoid."

"And more matchmaking?"

"I hope not." He gave her a wry smile. "There's already enough of that going on because her *mamm* likes to arrange marriages for her daughters."

She started to smile back, then looked toward where the *kinder* were eating with enthusiasm. Turning to the stove, she didn't say anything.

He didn't either. The problem of unwanted matchmakers was nothing compared to what the twins faced growing up without their loving parents. He needed to remember that. Matchmaking was an annoying irritant that he could—that he *must*—ignore. Everything he did and everything he thought about should be focused on four small *kinder* who now depended on him and Clara.

The *kinder* were upset when Isaiah didn't come home for lunch as he had every day since the funeral, but Clara distracted them by letting them help her make church spread sandwiches for their midday meal. Soon peanut butter and marshmallow whip stuck to their hands, their faces and the table. She kept it from their clothes by tying aprons around their necks.

Serving potato chips and milk to them and getting fresh ice tea for herself, she joined the *kinder* at the table. They yawned while they gobbled their food as if they hadn't had breakfast a few hours before. A morning spent picking up the mess in their shared bedroom had tired the youngsters...as she hoped. A *gut* nap this afternoon would allow her time to check the cellar and see what food was stored there. The dishes left in the freezer could be part of a meal, not the whole thing.

The twins' naptime seemed to fly by, and she'd finished inventorying about half of the canned fruit, vegetables and meat in the cool cellar. Tomorrow, she would count the rest, but she was relieved to see there was plenty of food for the next four to five weeks until their family came to get the twins. She'd also found bottles of root beer with no date on them. Maybe Isaiah would know when Esta had bottled it. If it was *gut* to drink, the *kinder* would enjoy the treat.

Clara was coming down the stairs with the twins when she heard the door open. Sending up a prayer Orpha Mast hadn't decided to return, Clara hurried through the living room to see who was calling.

A short woman with gray lacing through her brown hair stood next to a gray-haired man with the bushiest eyebrows Clara had ever seen.

"Are you Clara?" asked the woman.

"I am."

"I'm Wanda Stoltzfus. Isaiah's *mamm*. I wanted to stop by and see how you're doing." Her round face split with her smile. "And I brought chocolate chip cookies."

The *kinder* cheered and danced around her. When Clara reached to grab little hands, the man grinned.

"They're fine," he said in a deep voice that resembled distant thunder. "Trying to catch them is like trying to capture a clutch of chicks. Oh, I guess I should introduce myself. I'm Reuben Lapp."

She recognized the name of the local bishop. "I'm glad to meet you. Let me put on the kettle. Or would you rather have *kaffi*?"

"Tea would be *gut*," the bishop said. "Ice tea if you have it."

"I made some this morning when it appeared the day was going to be hot."

"Summer is early this year." Wanda gestured with her plate of cookies. "Shall we enjoy these outside? Then the birds can have the crumbs instead of giving Clara another reason to sweep the floor." She smiled over the youngsters' heads. "I assume you've already swept at least twice today."

"Three times, but who's counting?" She regretted the words as soon as she spoke them, because Reuben let out a guffaw.

The *kinder* stared at him, not sure if the sound had been a laugh or a cough or a sneeze. Before they had time to react further, Clara shooed them and her guests out the front door. She would explain to the bishop and Wanda about the twins and their fear of laughter, but she didn't want to when the youngsters could overhear.

Diverted by the cookies, the twins followed Wanda and Reuben onto the porch. The sound of their voices drifted to Clara as she filled glasses with ice tea for the adults and cool water for the *kinder*. There were enough plastic ones for everyone, which was a relief. She didn't want one of the barefoot twins bumping a glass and leaving shards on the porch.

She brought the glasses out on a tray. Wanda and the bishop were seated on the porch. The twins were kicking a ball around the front yard under their watchful eyes.

Serving the ice tea to her guests and setting the tray on a small table beside the cookies, Clara sat on the glider at the far end of the porch. She took a grateful sip as she realized it was the first time she'd been off her feet since breakfast. During lunch, she'd been too busy to sit for more than a few seconds.

She wanted to make her guests comfortable, so she began talking about her impressions of Paradise Springs. While they asked questions in return, she waited for the opportunity to tell them about the odd situation with the twins. She avoided speaking of Isaiah other than to express how concerned he was about the youngsters. And she didn't mention Orpha Mast's call.

Reuben asked where she lived, and she told him. He smiled. "I know your bishop well, and we often meet on a Saturday halfway between his districts and mine for a cup of *kaffi*. If you've got a message you want to get to your family quickly, let me know, and I'll pass it along."

"Danki."

"If you can trust me with a letter, you can trust me with what's troubling you."

Clara wasn't surprised the bishop had guessed at her uneasiness by how she prattled like Andrew one minute and was almost as silent as Ammon the next. Setting her empty glass on the floor by her feet, she folded her hands in her lap.

"Isaiah and I," she said, "are concerned because the twins tell us someone told them not to laugh. We're assuming it happened during the funeral."

"They don't laugh?" Wanda's eyes grew round as dismay lengthened her face.

She shook her head. "When I laughed, they were distressed until they decided the order wasn't for me. Just for them. But Isaiah and I've been trying not to laugh when they can hear."

Reuben began, "But they didn't react when I...?"

Wanda reached across the space between them and patted his hand. "Reuben, I've told you more than once you sound like an old mule braying. They probably weren't sure if that sound was a laugh." Looking back at Clara, she said, "Let me think and pray on this. There has to be something we can do."

Clara nodded but said nothing more about the problem. Instead, she welcomed the *kinder* onto the porch for more cookies and cool water. It was *gut* to see Isaiah had been right when he said the people of Paradise Springs were nice. She hoped so. She didn't want to meet more like his sister-in-law.

Dear Lord, help me find the words to explain to Orpha I'm the last person she needs to worry about interfering with her plans to marry Isaiah. She meant the prayer with all her heart.

Chapter Five

Isaiah arrived home in time to see his *mamm* and Reuben getting into their buggy. From where Clara stood, she could hear him talking to them. He was pleased they'd come to check on her and the *kinder*. He gave her a wave before he went into the barn to do chores. She hoped he didn't hurry, because she needed extra time to prepare their dinner after having company that afternoon.

When he came into the house after changing his clothes and his hair damp and smelling of strong soap, no remnants of smoke from his forge arrived with him. She appreciated that, because the odor would be tough to get out of the house.

"Wow! The chicken and parsley smell good," he said as he put his straw hat on the peg by the door.

"Perfect timing," she replied. The *kinder* were in their seats, because they'd been watching out the window to see when he emerged from the barn.

Isaiah reached the table as Clara put two plates containing freshly baked baking powder biscuits topped with gravy mixed with chunks of chicken in front of the girls. She gave him a smile before going to collect the boys' meals. On the table were bowls of cranberry sauce and corn.

As she placed a plate with three biscuits and chicken gravy in front of him, Clara said, "Don't worry. I saved a couple of your *mamm*'s cookies for you."

"More cookies?" asked Andrew, his eyes lighting up.

"Once we eat our dinner." She added as the twins reached for their forks, "And we'll eat after Isaiah leads us in saying grace."

Waiting until Clara had served herself and was sitting with the girls, Isaiah bowed his head. Again she watched the youngsters do the same, and grief pulsed through her. Their parents had taught their *kinder* to be grateful to God. She hoped Isaiah would make sure they didn't forget those lessons.

With the first bite he took, Isaiah turned to her with an astounded look. "This is amazing. You had only a few minutes to prepare the meal."

"It's a quick one."

"These biscuits are so light they would float away if they weren't weighed down with the chicken and gravy."

"Danki." She hoped her face wasn't red at his compliment. She shouldn't take pleasure in his praise, but she couldn't remember the last time anyone had complimented her cooking.

"Did you enjoy *Mamm*'s and Reuben's visit?" Isaiah asked once he'd cleaned his plate.

"We did." Clara smiled as she placed a cookie beside each *kind*'s plate. "They're an adorable couple." She set the last two cookies in front of him.

Again he regarded her with astonishment. "My *mamm* and the bishop aren't a couple. Just *gut* friends who have known each other for years."

"Are you sure?" She took her seat again and picked

up her cookie. Her smile broadened as she took a delicate bite.

"Very sure. Don't start playing the matchmaker, too."

"No, no." She shook her head. "I don't have any interest in that. I was remarking on what my eyes showed me."

He paused, not answering for a long minute. When he did, incredulity remained in his voice. "I want to say your eyes are mistaken, but I can't help thinking of the number of times *Mamm* and Reuben have been in each other's company the past six or eight months. Reuben has joined us for dinner at least a couple of times each month, and I've seen her talking with him on church Sundays while the two of them walked alone together. I guess I should take a closer look myself next time."

Clara was grateful when Andrew started talking about what the *kinder* had done that day. Isaiah must have been, too, because he listened and asked questions and kept the twins chattering about their games and their chores and how Clara had taught them a fun way to bring their dirty laundry downstairs while they sang a silly song.

A quick glance told her he was well aware of what he was doing, but she didn't attempt to turn the conversation to the subject of his *mamm* and Reuben. Probably he wanted to avoid talking about anything to do with matchmaking, too.

As far as she was concerned, that was the best plan ever!

When, after dinner, Clara had the twins help her clear the table and do the dishes, Isaiah went out to do the last of the chores. He'd noticed his buggy horse, Chocolate Chip—or Chip for short—had been favoring his front right leg on the way home. A quick check showed no signs of damage, but he wondered if the horse had strained the leg. Perhaps Clara would be willing for him to use her Bella tomorrow.

His mind was reeling about Clara's comments about *Mamm* and Reuben. What if Clara was right? How could he have failed to notice his *mamm*'s interest in Reuben? They'd lost their spouses at least five years ago. He almost groaned aloud. If Reuben married *Mamm*, the pressure would increase for Isaiah to find another wife. On the other hand, he wished the bishop and his *mamm* every happiness, so maybe he could find a way to turn Marlin's attention from Isaiah to the fact their bishop was getting remarried. No, Marlin was like a hound dog with a scent. He wasn't going to let up until after Isaiah's wedding supper.

Isaiah walked from the stable to the house, hurrying to put his thoughts behind him. When he came inside, he saw the *kinder* had gathered around Clara, who sat on the rocking chair. Andrew leaned his elbow on the arm and watched what she was doing. The others stretched out on the floor with their coloring books.

As he came into the living room, Andrew grinned at him. "Guess what, *Onkel* Isaiah?"

"What, kiddo?" he asked, as he did each time one of the twins asked him that question.

"We're writing to *Aenti* Debra," crowed Andrew. "Next we're gonna write to *Grossdawdi* and *Grossmammi*."

"Here's my picture," said Nancy, holding up a page she'd torn from her coloring book. She edged around him and held it out to Clara. "Give to *Aenti* Debra? She see how *gut* I color."

Clara smiled. "You asked first, so you can put your

picture in to your *aenti*. Nettie Mae, why don't you color one for your grandparents? Then tomorrow night, it'll be the boys' turn. That way, it'll be easy to keep track of whose turn it is each day."

"You're writing to their grandparents?" Isaiah asked, shocked.

"I will be," she said without looking up again or pausing as she filled the page with her neat penmanship. "After I finish this letter to their *aenti*. I found their addresses in a book in a kitchen drawer, and the twins were willing to share stories about their day." She smiled at them before raising her eyes toward him.

Her smile faded, and he knew he'd failed to keep his thoughts hidden. When she asked what was wrong, he didn't answer. Instead, he asked a question of his own. "Can we talk about this after they're in bed?"

She nodded, and he saw her bafflement. He couldn't blame her. His voice had been sharper than he'd intended, but to apologize in front of the *kinder* was guaranteed to bring question after question from them. He couldn't explain to them when he wasn't able to explain to himself why seeing Clara write the letter bothered him.

But his request put a damper on the twins' excitement. Their voices were subdued, and they glanced uneasily at him while Clara wrote to their grandparents. She promised she would take the *kinder* to the post office tomorrow to buy stamps and send the letters.

"I'd be glad to do that," Isaiah said, as she put the letters on the table beside her chair.

"We can do it." Her voice was prim and cool. "I know how pressured you are to get your job completed."

"True." Why did he sense that a scold underlined her sympathetic words? Maybe because his old companion—guilt—was rearing its head again. How many times had he said the wrong thing and upset Rose? For a man who'd been ordained as a minister and who should know the weight words possessed, he spoke too many times without considering which ones he chose.

When he asked if he could use her horse tomorrow, she agreed and didn't ask why he needed Bella. Instead, she herded the *kinder* upstairs. He followed, feeling like an outsider in the house he'd considered as much his home as his less than a mile down the road.

Isaiah went back downstairs as soon as the kids were tucked in their beds. He'd seen the glances they aimed at him and Clara. They sensed the wall she'd thrown up in the wake of his unthinking question.

Going outside to get a breath of fresh air, he glanced at the sky. He'd been sticking his foot in his mouth a lot lately. Was it because he'd put distance between him and God since Rose's death? He'd guarded his prayers as he'd tried to figure out why a loving Father would let his wife die alone. Couldn't God have given him a hint to stay home that day? What other mistakes was Isaiah going to make as he bumbled forward?

He didn't know, and he didn't want to guess.

The door opened behind him, and Clara stepped onto the porch. The moonlight washed out her ginger hair, but his mind recreated the vibrant color. He shouldn't be thinking about how pretty she was, but he couldn't deny what his eyes showed him.

"I thought you might like something cool to drink." She held out a glass to him. When he took it and peered into the glass, trying to figure out its contents, she added, "It's ice tea."

She sat on the glider, right in the middle, in an unspoken warning she didn't want him beside her. He often sat on it because he liked its easy motion, but a glance at the road passing by the house warned him that anyone driving by would have a clear view of the porch. Besides, he couldn't blame her for making it clear she was perturbed with him.

Leaning against the rail, he stared across the yard. If she were only perturbed, he'd be relieved.

"What's bothering you, Isaiah?" she asked when he remained silent.

"I assumed you'd talk to me before you made any decisions for the *kinder*." As soon as the words left his lips, he realized how petty they sounded.

"I will if that's what you want." Her voice became as icy as the cubes in his tea. "But you hired me to take care of them. I can't do that if I have to wait to talk to you about everything."

He grimaced. "I know. Forget I said that."

"What's bothering you, Isaiah?" she asked again. "What's *really* bothering you?"

"If I tell you I don't know, please don't think I'm trying to be evasive." He sighed. "I'd like to blame it on stress."

"Why don't we?" She gave him a faint smile. "We're trying to help the twins, and there are bound to be times when we rub each other the wrong way."

"I appreciate it." He did. She could have quit; then what would he have done? Finding someone else and disrupting the *kinder* who were already close to her would be difficult. Unless he asked Orpha, and he didn't want *that* trouble. "Why don't you tell me about these letters you and the twins were writing?"

"They are a sort of circle letter with their family. From what they told me earlier, they don't know any of them well, and I doubt their *aenti* and grandparents know much about them. This way, they can get acquainted so when the *kinder* go to live with whomever will be taking them, they won't feel as if they're living with strangers."

He was astonished at her foresight. He'd been busy trying to get through each day, dealing with his sorrow and trying not to upset the grieving *kinder*. He hadn't given the future much thought. Or maybe he didn't want to admit that one day soon the youngsters would leave Paradise Springs. His last connection to his best friend would be severed. No doubt, the twins would stay in contact with him at Christmas or maybe on their birthdays, but he wasn't sure if he'd ever see them again once they moved to California or Florida or the *gut* Lord knew where with their family.

The thought pierced his heart, and he turned and put his hands on the porch railing as his stomach twisted. The moon was rising, its cool light unable to ease the hot pain within him. His hands tightened on the wood, driving chips of paint into his palms.

Clara said, "If you'd rather I didn't send out the letters—"

"Send them," he interrupted and saw shock widening her eyes. "I'm sorry. I didn't mean to sound upset."

"But you are."

He nodded. "Upset and guilty."

"Don't feel guilty you have to work and can't spend every minute with them." She gave him another whisper of a smile. "I don't spend every minute with them, though I don't let them out of my sight. They're young, and they don't want to be shadowed by an adult."

"Everything you say makes sense."

"But?"

"I can't help believing that I'm shunting my responsibilities off on someone else."

"Esta must have used a babysitter sometimes. The *kinder* didn't go to the auction with her and Melvin."

"Thank the *gut* Lord they didn't." He let his sigh sift through his clenched teeth. "Like I said, everything you're saying makes sense, but I want to make sure Melvin's faith in me as a substitute *daed* wasn't misplaced. The twins deserve a *gut daed*, but all they have is me."

"You're doing fine under the circumstances."

"You mean when the funeral was such a short time ago?"

"No, I mean when every single woman in the district is determined to be your next wife, and your deacon is egging them on."

In spite of himself, Isaiah chuckled quietly. He didn't want the sound of his laughter to reach the *kinder* upstairs. Clara's teasing was exactly what he needed. Her comments put the silliness into perspective. If he could remember that the next time Marlin or someone else brought up the topic of him marrying, maybe he could stop making a mess of everything. He hoped so.

Chapter Six

As he reentered the front room of his brother Joshua's house where the worship service was already underway, Isaiah tried to convince himself this day was like every other church Sunday since he'd become one of the district's two ministers. Earlier, he'd greeted the members of the *Leit* as they gathered outside the barn before the worship service started. The men entered, followed by the women, both accompanied by the younger *kinder*. Next came the older girls with unmarried women. At the end were the unmarried men and the boys who no longer had to sit with their parents. While the *Leit* began the first hymn, he'd joined Reuben, Marlin and Atlee in a separate room to pray and plan the three-hour-long service. Isaiah was chosen to give the first sermon, the shorter one that lasted about a half hour.

Exactly like many other church Sundays since he was ordained.

But nothing was as it'd been before.

The Beachy twins were with Clara instead of their parents, and he wouldn't be able to look over at the men's side and see his best friend, who'd been encouraging when Isaiah was first chosen as a minister. Melvin had listened while Isaiah poured out his worries with his Rose's dismay at having the lot fall on him.

Dear Rose. As fragile as the blossoms of the flower that shared her name. She'd come to see the selection as part of the path God had set out for them.

Far better than Isaiah had accepted her death as God's will. He didn't understand how God could take Rose when everything was beginning to go well for them. Every way he looked at it told him submitting to God's will was the sole way to comprehend what had happened. It should be simple for him, as a minister in their district, to take the path laid out in front of him. It should be, but it wasn't.

When *Das Loblied*, their second hymn, was finished, Isaiah didn't sit like the rest of the worshippers. He moved to the front and greeted the congregation before he began to speak. The thoughts he'd organized during the long, slow singing of the hymn tumbled out of his head when his gaze collided with Clara's. Somehow, in the past hour, he'd forgotten how remarkable her brown eyes were. They were filled with anticipation for what he was about to say.

He opened his mouth, ready to give voice to his thoughts, but what came out was, "I—I—I…th-that is, I—I—I wa-wa-wanted to s-s-say…"

Astonishment filled the faces looking at him, but nobody was more surprised than he was. Not once, not even the first time when he'd stood to give a sermon after the lot fell upon him, had he stuttered over his opening words. Each time, he'd easily shared his faith with those who sat in front of him.

Shock raced through him. Had inspiration left him because he'd been fighting the path God had set out before him? Or was it something far simpler—and far more complicated at the same time? Was it because Clara Ebersol sat among the women?

He glanced at her as he struggled to fight off panic. When her gaze met his, she gave him a half smile and a slight nod before her eyes led his to the twins sitting on either side of her. They were watching him with eager expressions. What could he say that would touch their hearts as well as the adults'?

For a moment, he almost asked God for help but halted himself. Until he was willing to accept the Lord's plan for him, he shouldn't ask. Instead, he gathered the sight of Clara and the *kinder* close. A sense of calm settled over him like a warm blanket on a wintry night. He couldn't let his grief keep him from helping Melvin's boys and girls. With that thought to guide him, he started, speaking of *kinder* and how blessed those were who loved them and were given the sacred duty of raising them to know and love God. Later, when he'd resumed his place with Reuben and Atlee, he couldn't recall a word of what he'd said, but several women had tears running down their cheeks. A few men were dabbing at their cheeks with white handkerchiefs. He'd spoken from the heart, and he'd touched theirs. Not him. It'd been the word of God coming through him.

Bowing his head, he praised God for using him as a conduit when Isaiah was resisting God's will. And he thanked the Lord for sending Clara as an inspiration. He couldn't ignore the fact that her being at the service had helped to shape his words in a way nothing had since his mourning began. Not only her presence, but what he'd observed for the past week while she'd worked to keep the Beachy *kinder* happy and prevent them from falling into the chasm of grief he knew too well.

The rest of the three-hour-long service passed so

quickly he was startled. After singing the closing hymn in the slow unison style of their tradition, he watched the congregation exit, the youngest first. He walked out with the men and smiled at those who smiled in his direction. Nobody would tell him he'd done a *gut* job. A preacher must never have too much pride.

"Isaiah!"

At the call of his name, Isaiah tensed and turned to face the members of the Mast family, who were closing in on him like a pack of coydogs ready to pounce on a rooster. Curtis Mast, a man shaped like a bull with massive shoulders, led the way.

Isaiah dreaded this part of Sunday. His late wife's parents didn't seem to care if they were in the midst of the rest of the *Leit* when they cornered him. They found a way to remind him that they believed he should be married, and marrying another of their other daughters would be the best solution.

"*Gute mariye*, Curtis," he said to Rose's *daed*. Looking at her *mamm*, a slight woman who was as pretty as her four surviving daughters who followed behind them, he added, "*Gute mariye*, Ida Mae."

For a moment, when they nodded in his direction, he thought they'd walk right past him without matchmaking, in spite of calling out to him. Instead, they stopped and stared at him. He fought not to squirm under their regard. He wasn't a *kind* who'd gotten caught trying to steal a few extra cookies. He was a man suffering the same grief they did.

"An interesting topic for your sermon today," Curtis said as if they'd already been chatting. It was like Curtis to get to the point. He had opinions, and he shared them. Too readily, some people said, but Isaiah appreciated knowing where he stood with his father-in-law. Except on the remarrying issue!

"Ja," added his wife, "a man who has no *kinder* preaching to those of us who do." Her voice cracked as she added, "And to those who have lost a precious *kind*."

"Don't be silly, Ida Mae," Rose's *daed* added with a narrow-eyed frown at his wife. "Isaiah is gaining a lot of experience. Don't forget. He's a temporary *daed* at the moment." He gave Isaiah a companionable elbow in the side. *"Gut* practice for when you have *kinder* of your own. My girls love *kinder,* don't you, girls?"

Orpha twittered a soft laugh. *"Ja.* Love them." She edged closer to him. "I can't wait to have a family. That's every Amish girl's dream, ain't so?"

Isaiah kept his sigh silent. He'd tried everything to persuade Rose's parents and her sisters that he'd marry again when the time—and the woman—was right. He'd tried agreeing with them to put an end to these conversations, but that made them more persistent about him courting Orpha or one of the other girls. Curtis and Ida Mae didn't seem to care which he married as long as it was one of their daughters. He'd tried being honest with them, but they'd acted as if they didn't hear a single word he said.

"Ja," came a voice from behind him. "And perhaps that's why Isaiah's sermon this morning was interesting." Clara stepped forward and smiled at the whole Mast family. "I'm Clara Ebersol. I don't think we've met."

He was relieved she'd halted the Masts before they could say something else to twist his arm into proposing to Orpha right on his brother's lawn. *Judge not, and ye shall not be judged: condemn not, and ye shall not be condemned: forgive, and ye shall be forgiven.* How many times had he repeated that verse from Luke in his mind to remind himself the Masts were grieving, too?

Then he realized how he'd misjudged the abrupt silence after Clara introduced herself to the family. A silent message he couldn't read passed between the members of the Mast family, and then six pairs of eyes riveted on Clara. They saw her as an unwanted intruder, competition in their determination to have him marry a Mast girl. He resisted the instinct to step between her and them. Why would they see this as a contest with a proposal from him as the trophy? He was no prize as a husband.

"*You* are Clara Ebersol?" asked Ida Mae with unconcealed dismay. Turning to her oldest, she said, "You didn't say she was a redhead."

Isaiah had no idea why the color of Clara's hair mattered to Ida Mae. He said nothing while the Masts introduced themselves to Clara with tight smiles. Holding his breath, he waited for what they might say next.

Clara ignored the glowers aimed at her by Orpha and her younger sisters. Instead, she spoke warmly with the Masts, talking about the Beachy twins as if his in-laws had asked about them. When she told a story of the boys' latest escapade that had left them covered with mud, she laughed without a hint of anything but amusement.

The Masts laughed with her, though it sounded strained in Isaiah's ears. Maybe he was too sensitive, looking for trouble where none existed. Just because Orpha had been cold to Clara the other morning wasn't any reason to believe the rest of her family wished anyone ill.

Turning to him, Clara said, "Reuben has been looking for you, Isaiah. I told him I'd deliver the message."

As she motioned him to follow her, she paused and looked at the dumbfounded Masts. "It's been nice to meet you. I look forward to getting to know you better during my time here."

Isaiah went with her. His farewell to the Masts wasn't returned. They looked stunned by Clara's sunny smile and kindness. He wondered how long ago it'd been since anyone in the district had spoken with warmth and hope to them instead of focusing on their grief.

As others did to him.

Sympathy surged through him. He needed to reconsider how he talked to them next time he encountered them. He would pray for God's guidance in finding the right words to rebuild the bridge that had collapsed with Rose's death. It was his duty as their minister and their son-in-law to help them—and himself—to climb out of the deep, dark pit of grief.

He hoped there was a way, other than proposing to one of their daughters, for them to heed him.

"So that's the Mast family," Clara said as she walked with Isaiah around the far side of the house. "Your in-laws."

"Ja." He didn't say anything more.

She started to speak, then thought better of it. Isaiah was stressed enough already. He didn't need her warnings that Orpha wasn't the only one who wanted him remarried to a Mast girl. At least two of the other three had given her ill-concealed scowls. Instead, she asked, "How are you?"

His mouth worked, then he spat in candid frustration, "Could they be any more obvious?"

She couldn't keep from smiling. "Don't you think

it's better the matchmakers are obvious rather than sneaky?"

"Better maybe, but not easier." He looked at her with a sheepish grin. "I'm sorry, Clara. I know none of this matchmaking was what you expected when you took this job."

"I didn't. That's why I'm extra grateful you were honest with me right from the beginning about the district's matchmakers." She grinned. "Though I have to admit I already had a very *gut* idea of what was on Orpha's mind when she stopped by the first morning I was here."

"I wish the Masts would show as much common sense as you do."

"Did you consider they care about you enough that they want to keep you as a son-in-law and having you marry one of their daughters would be the best way to ensure that?"

He halted and stared at her as if she'd announced a cow had jumped over the moon. She almost laughed at the thought. Spending time with young *kinder* was leaving her with nursery rhymes on the brain. She pushed the silly thoughts aside. Her question had stunned him, and she wondered why he'd never considered the idea before.

"You have a kindhearted way of looking at people," Isaiah said as they came around the corner of the house and saw Reuben talking with two men by the clothesline. "Sometimes it's easier to give into suspicion."

"Suspicion leads to making me think I'm different from others. That way can lead to *hochmut*." She lowered her eyes and shut her lips before she could say more.

Her *daed* lectured her often on the sin of *hochmut*,

but he was the proudest person she knew. When she was younger, she hadn't understood his resolve for them to look like the perfect family around other families in their district. Even making a single mistake would reflect poorly on the family and on him. To be jilted by a young man her *daed* had bragged about marrying his daughter was the worst thing she could have done, in *Daed*'s estimation.

She was glad when Isaiah excused himself and went to speak with the bishop. As unsettled as thoughts of her *daed* and of Lonnie made her, she'd be wise to keep silent.

Clara collected the Beachy twins, who were playing with the other youngsters, and made sure they got something to eat after the men had finished with the midday meal. She didn't have to worry about them being finicky, though she noticed Nettie Mae holding her fork at a strange angle once or twice and examining the food before she popped it into her mouth.

As soon as they were finished, she joined other women in the kitchen washing up. The twins went to play tag with *kinder* their ages, and Clara kept an eye on them out the kitchen window.

She emerged from the kitchen with the women who'd welcomed her as if they'd known her all their lives to see Isaiah walking toward her. She heard whispers behind her, but she paid them no attention as he asked where the *kinder* were.

"Over there." She pointed to where they were running away from a little girl who was It. "Are you ready to head home?"

"Not yet." He glanced past her at the other women as he added, "Just trying to keep track of them."

"You don't need to worry," said an older woman

whose name Clara remembered was Fannie Beiler. "Your Clara has been checking on them every minute."

Isaiah struggled not to react to Fannie calling her "your Clara." She wanted to reassure him that Fannie meant nothing by her words. It was just a way of speaking.

"Let me know when you're ready to leave," Clara said quickly. "I'll have the twins ready to go."

"Danki." He glanced past her with abrupt puzzlement. "Odd."

She looked over her shoulder and saw the other women had moved away.

"Not odd. They're being nice to allow us time to discuss the *kinder.*"

"Or whatever we might have on our minds."

Refusing to let him bring up the subject of matchmaking again, because this time she believed he was mistaken, she said, "Fannie Beiler has been very welcoming to me."

"Fannie is my older brother Ezra's mother-in-law. She's not interested in matchmaking, but it seems to be everywhere."

"Ignore it. If your friends see you bothered by their comments, they're sure to tease you more."

"True, especially my brothers."

Annoyed the subject had once again turned to matchmaking, she wished they could talk of something else. The topic seemed to make her notice how *gut*-looking Isaiah was, and her mind wandered to wondering about having him take her home in his courting buggy. Just the two of them without the twins tossing question after question from the rear of the family buggy.

"How is Reuben?" she asked, grasping on to the first thought she had of something other than walking out with Isaiah. "He appeared on edge when he asked me to find you."

"He's worried about his oldest. Katie Kay has been pushing the limits of our *Ordnung* for over a year."

"It isn't easy to be in a bishop's family and be held up to be a role model for everyone in two districts. The son of my bishop went out and bought himself a sporty car and parked it right in front of his family's house for a few months." She hesitated, then said, "If the Beachy *kinder* were a bit older, they'd find themselves put into that position, too, because you're one of the ministers."

"I'm glad they aren't older. They have enough to distress them."

Again Clara hesitated, but she couldn't keep her concerns silent any longer. "I wish they would act more distressed. They seem to take their parents' deaths in stride during the day. At night, it's a whole other thing, because every night one or the other of them has a nightmare. Sometimes more than one. Don't you think they should be showing more grief?"

"We each show grief in a unique way."

"Don't try to placate me with platitudes, Isaiah. I'm not saying this to you because you're their minister. I'm saying this to you because you're the only *daed* they have. Doesn't it bother you, too?"

"It does, but I can't bring myself to do anything that would make them more unhappy."

Clara gave him a sad smile and reached out to pat his arm. The moment her fingers brushed the skin below his shirtsleeve, a flurry of sensation sped through her like a fiery storm wind. His gaze darted toward her, and she saw his astonishment as well. Astonishment and more, as deeper, stronger emotions burned in the depths of his eyes. She should move her fingers, but they seemed soldered to his arm by the strength of the feelings she couldn't name because they changed like a kaleidoscope being twirled at top speed.

Did he murmur her name? She couldn't tell because her heart was setting off explosion after explosion inside her. When his fingers slid atop hers, the warmth of his skin above her hand and below was more *wunderbaar* than anything she'd experienced before. But how could that be?

She'd had her hand held before. She'd been kissed before, but nothing had overwhelmed her like this. When Lonnie—

The thought of her ex-fiancé's name broke the hold Isaiah had over her. It was as if she'd stepped from a heated kitchen into a predawn winter freeze. With a shiver, she yanked her hand away. She had let her emotions run away with her.

Again.

She was making foolish decisions.

Again.

Before Clara could come up with an excuse that would allow her to walk away without insulting him, she heard, "Isaiah! Clara! *Komm* and sit with us!"

She looked across the yard to where two people sat on a bench facing Wanda Stoltzfus, who was rocking on the front porch. The man, though his hair was a few shades darker, looked enough like Isaiah that she guessed the two men must be related. Beside him sat a pretty blonde. His arm was stretched across the back of the bench behind her in a rare suggestion of intimacy among the plain folk. Was she his wife? No courting couple would be that obvious about the affection between them.

Her conjecture was confirmed when Isaiah introduced the two as his older brother Ezra and Ezra's wife, Leah. As she greeted them, she was relieved nobody mentioned her and Isaiah standing together.

Isaiah brought two lawn chairs onto the porch so they could sit and chat. He gave her a glance she guessed was intended to tell her something. He was wasting his time. She was so discombobulated she had to focus on acting normal.

Within a few minutes, the uneasiness ebbed, and Clara was drawn into a conversation with Isaiah's sister-in-law. Clara enjoyed Leah's enthusiastic discussion of the best fabrics for quilting. Clara wasn't surprised to hear Leah's quilts were prized by *Englisch* tourists who stopped at the family's grocery store. Wanda told her that they sold as soon as they were placed on display.

Clara looked again and again at the twins to make sure they were all right, and she listened to the conversations swirling around her as the Stoltzfus family talked about their plans for the upcoming week. It was as she'd imagined a loving family would be.

Too bad she'd be in Paradise Springs for only a month or so. Once the twins' grandparents or *aenti* came to collect them, she would have to return home. A sigh of regret surged through her because, though she could take with her *wunderbaar* memories of the Stoltzfus family and the Beachy twins, she had to wonder if knowing how families *could* be would make it more difficult to live with her exacting *daed*.

Chapter Seven

Clara draped the wet dish towel over the rack connected to the cabinet. She adjusted the arm so any drips fell into the sink. While she listened to water go down the drain, she gazed out the window over the sink and smiled. It felt *gut* to smile as she'd been up most of the night with the twins as one after another was caught in the throes of a nightmare. They couldn't tell her what scared them, but she suspected the bad dreams were caused by the grief they refused to speak about during the day. Every night, one or more of them woke her and each other with shrieks of terror. It had become a ritual in the morning for Isaiah to ask who had managed to sleep through the night. He'd offered to trade off with her and tend to them at night, but she reminded him that he'd hired her because he couldn't be with the twins night and day.

Otherwise each day unfolded into the next. In the past four days, the weather had been splendid. The *kinder* preferred to be outside, and she'd smiled at their cheers when she told them they didn't have to wear shoes any longer. She'd removed hers for working in the house and the yard. The grass was silken soft, and, when she checked out the vegetable plants growing among the weeds in the garden, the cool, damp earth had been delightful between her toes.

Each day, she worked on the garden. She guessed Esta had kept the garden neat, but in the three weeks since her death, nobody had spent time on the garden. The early peas were ready to harvest, or they would have been if not choked by weeds. She'd spent the morning pulling weeds before the twins' noon meal.

Now they were fed and playing in the sandbox beneath the large maple. She wanted to give them time to tire themselves out more before their naps. She was surprised when the older twins fell asleep every afternoon, but guessed they were exhausted from night terrors and other bad dreams. The boys pushed trucks and tractors around, making roads and furrows in the sand. Both girls shoveled sand into a pail and tipped it over to build temporary mountains for the boys' vehicles. As the sand sifted down the piles, they scooped it up and started over again.

Her one attempt this week to discuss their parents with them had been useless. She'd asked what was their favorite meal made by their *mamm*. A simple question, but none of them answered. Instead, they edged closer together as they had when she and Isaiah asked about why they wouldn't laugh. They'd watched her with guarded expressions until she urged them to go out and play.

What else had been said to them other than not to laugh? They'd taken her urging to sing quietly to heart, so had someone else told them not to talk about their parents? That made no sense, but neither did telling youngsters who were mourning their *mamm* and *daed* to stop laughing.

She needed to talk to Isaiah. Maybe tonight. For now, with the twins busy, she should check the answering machine in the phone shack. Isaiah had mentioned that morning at breakfast how it needed to be done, and she'd offered to do it. She'd wondered if he'd be as annoyed as he'd been about the letter writing last week, but he nodded with a grateful smile.

Each evening, he arrived home wiped out from his long hours of working at his forge. He hadn't said much, but even the youngsters knew his important job needed to be done by the week's end. He'd skipped breakfast the past two days, and she wondered how much he ate while he pushed to finish his project. At dinner, he barely kept his eyes open and didn't eat much. Even the chicken and biscuits he'd raved about hadn't convinced him to do more than pick at his food.

Clara put on her black bonnet before, with a final glance at the youngsters, she went out the front door. Though she was worried Isaiah was trying to do too much, she couldn't nag him. He was her employer. If she were sent home early, her *daed* would believe she'd shamed her family again.

"And in this case, it'd be true," she said as she crossed the yard to the farm lane that ran as straight as a ruler between the house and the road.

But she was worrying unnecessarily. Isaiah needed her at the house. Otherwise, he wouldn't finish his commission on time. She wondered what he was creating. He never spoke of the project other than he must have it done before the arrival of the truck taking it to Maryland.

If he didn't go into the *dawdi haus* as soon as the *kinder* were in bed each night, she might have had the opportunity to ask about what he was making. Tonight, she must speak with him about how to reach the youngsters and urge them to mourn as they should.

At the end of the lane, the phone shack looked like an abandoned outhouse, stuck as it was out by the mailbox. Clara opened the door. Her nose wrinkled at the smell of air cooped up too long. The small building held an uncomfortable bench and a counter stuck in a corner. The single window allowed in light, but was shut tight and edged with spiderwebs littered with white egg sacs. A dusty phone sat on the counter between an answering machine and pencil and a notepad. A list of numbers in a plastic sleeve had been nailed to the wall. They were for the local medical clinic, as well as other phone numbers that might be needed in an emergency.

She wasn't surprised to see the answering machine blinking. When had it last been checked?

Picking up the pencil, she shifted the notepad so she could write any messages. She wasn't sure if the Beachys were the only family who used the phone shack or if it was shared with Amish neighbors. If the latter, she'd deliver any messages right away.

Clara pushed the blinking red light, and a disembodied voice announced there were five messages on the machine. The first was a hang-up, and the second had a message of, "Sorry. Wrong number." She deleted both.

The third call was different. A woman said in a pleasant voice, "Good afternoon. I'm calling from Paradise Springs Optical, and this message is for Esta Beachy. Esta, the glasses you ordered for Nettie Mae are in. We look forward to seeing you at your earliest convenience."

She let the rest of the message play. Blinking back tears, she was glad she hadn't brought the *kinder* with her. To hear the message meant for their *mamm* would have upset them. Look how it was distressing her, and she'd never met Esta Beachy.

But in a way she had. She'd met Esta and Melvin through their twins, who were bright and curious and helpful and loving. The couple had been training up their family well. She recalled the proverb she'd often heard *Mamm* repeat: *Train up a child in the way he should go: and when he is old, he will not depart from it.* The Beachys had started their youngsters off on the right foot.

Listening to the message again, she wrote down the phone number the caller had left. She listened to the final two calls, but both were for political candidates. Those she deleted before she made a call to confirm the glasses ordered for Nettie Mae were still at the shop.

The woman who answered at the shop expressed her sympathy for what the Beachy family had suffered before confirming that the glasses were waiting for Nettie Mae to have them fitted. She gave Clara the address and the times the store was open.

"I'll bring her in later this afternoon," Clara said before thanking the woman and ending the call.

At least once a day, Isaiah mentioned something about how he and Melvin had been best friends and how often he'd joined the family for the evening meal. He must have known about the little girl's eye exam. Why hadn't he mentioned anything to her about Nettie Mae getting glasses?

No matter, she knew now.

Hurrying to the sandbox, she asked the twins if they wanted to go to town with her. When they scrambled out of the box, she smiled and motioned for them to shake sand off their clothes. She brushed as much out of their hair as she could. There wasn't time to give them baths before they drove into Paradise Springs.

The twins ran into the house to collect their shoes. She followed and pulled on her black sneakers before she went into the stable next to the barn to hitch Bella to the Beachys' family buggy. It was less cramped than hers.

Once shoes were on the correct feet and tied, she watched the youngsters climb into the buggy. The boys again chose the back, and the two girls sat on the front seat. Checking the house was secure and she hadn't left anything on, she got in.

"Let's go, Bella," she called.

The *kinder* copied her words, and the horse tilted her head as if wondering why she was getting the same command from different people.

The twins pelted Clara with questions. Where were they going? Who would they see? What would they do? When would they get home? Could they order pizza to bring home for dinner?

She faltered on the last question. She doubted she had enough money in her purse to pay for pizza for the six of them.

"Oh, dear!" she gasped.

Eyeglasses would be far more expensive than two large pizzas. She'd never given any thought to how the glasses would be paid for. Seeing the sign for the Stoltzfus Family Shops ahead, she turned Bella into the parking lot. She drew in the horse when a man waved to her from the general store.

She recognized him as Isaiah's brother Amos. He had reddish-brown hair, but he and Isaiah had the same shaped face and height. As she stopped in front of him, she saw Amos's hands, like Isaiah's, showed he was accustomed to hard work.

Greeting her, he smiled and asked what she and the *kinder* were up to.

"We've got errands to run this afternoon," she replied, "but I need to check a couple of things with Isaiah first."

Amos smiled at the twins. "Why don't I take them in the store while you two talk?"

"They can be boisterous."

"Don't worry. I'm accustomed to little ones." Waving his hand, he said, "C'mon, kids." As they poured out of the buggy, he added, "Let's see what *Onkel* Amos can find for you in the store." He led them like the Pied Piper into his shop.

Clara smiled. *Onkel* Amos? No wonder Melvin had asked Isaiah to be the guardian of his *kinder*. The whole Stoltzfus family welcomed her and the Beachy twins. She was never going to take a moment of her time with them for granted.

Isaiah looked up in surprise when a familiar silhouette walked toward his smithy. What was Clara doing here at this hour? And where were the twins?

She paused in the doorway as she'd done the first time and said as if he'd asked his second question aloud, "The *kinder* are with Amos. He offered to let them pick out a treat."

"He loves doing that for all his nieces and nephews. He makes sure he has plenty of ice cream and candy for them to choose from." He lowered the hammer he'd been using to pound the heated metal thin enough so he could twist it. "Are you in town for something specific?"

She explained the message from the optician on the answering machine. "I'll try to check it more often."

"I didn't know Nettie Mae had been taken to be examined for glasses," he said. He'd thought it would be simple for him to step in as surrogate *daed* until the *kinder*'s family returned. How silly that seemed now!

He was relieved Clara had taken over disciplining the *kinder*. He'd been the fun *onkel*, the one who played with them and tickled them and taught them how to do fun things like skip stones and feed chickens. To become their *daed* and raise them to be *gut* members of their community was a completely different role, and he hadn't been prepared for the responsibilities.

"I'm sure the glasses are strong enough to put up with a three-year-old's antics," Clara said, and he realized she'd misunderstood his silence. One of the few times that had happened.

He latched on to her change of subject as if it were a lifeline. "Esta would have made sure. She wouldn't have wanted to bring the glasses in for repairs all the time. Too costly."

Color rose up Clara's cheeks, astonishing him until she said, "I should have asked if there was an unpaid balance for the glasses."

"Don't worry. What's owed is what's owed."

"I can't argue with that." She chuckled. "Oh, it feels *gut* to laugh."

"Any clues as to who told the kids not to laugh?"

"None," she replied sadly.

He wished he hadn't asked the question. He liked her laugh when she didn't have to restrain herself. It was genuine and hearty and invited him to join in.

"How much do you think glasses for a three-year-old cost?" he asked.

"My *mamm* complained about the high cost when she picked up hers a few months ago. They were almost four hundred dollars."

He grimaced. "I had no idea glasses were that expensive." He tapped the pair hanging around his neck. "My safety glasses cost between ten and twenty bucks, depending on what I buy. The face shield I use for welding is two or three times as much."

"The glasses my *mamm* got were bifocals, so I assume Nettie Mae's should be cheaper."

"Unless she needs bifocals."

Clara considered that, then shook her head. "I've noticed her getting very close and then pulling back when she's holding something or when she's coloring. But she seems to see fine at a distance. She was the first one to point out three deer in a field on our way here."

He went to a table and yanked a drawer open. Reaching in, he lifted out a checkbook. "What's the name of the optician?"

"Paradise Springs Optical... I think. I left the page with it at the house."

"That's okay." He shoved aside his apron and pulled out a pen. Scribbling his name at the bottom of the check, he tore it out of the book and handed it to her.

"You're giving me a blank check?"

He smiled. "I trust you with the twins, who are far more important to me than my bank account, so why wouldn't I trust you with a check?"

She was touched by his words. He wondered why. She should have realized the truth. No amount of money could recompense him if something happened to one of the *kinder*.

"*Danki,*" she said at last. She folded the check and put it in the black purse hanging over her right shoulder. Looking past him, she asked, "Are those what you need to get done before the week is out?"

"Ja." He motioned for her to come closer to the great gates that were almost completed. They were more than twelve feet high and almost as wide, too big to fit in the shop.

As she stepped past him, he drew in a deep breath of the faint scent from her shampoo. It was out of place among the odors of heated metal and coal. Apple, if he wasn't mistaken. An aroma that suited her well because apples could be tart or sweet.

She gazed at the two gates. The arched tops were accented by twisted posts, leading the eye to the huge metal medallions in the center of each section.

"They're beautiful." She ran a finger along the medallion with the large *T* in the center. "Does this stand for something?"

"The first word in the name of my client's horse farm. Look at the other one. It has an *S* on it. Taggart Stables."

"These are stunning, Isaiah."

He turned away and set the rod he'd been working on into the fire. He shouldn't be pleased with her compliment. It was a challenge to be creative and not take pride in his work. The elegant gates weren't anything he'd want on his property, but he'd followed the design the *Englischer* wanted. Checking the brightness of the heated point, he placed it on the anvil where he hammered it with easy, efficient motions.

"It's been nice to make something like that," he said, "after almost a full year of making pot hooks and hinges for tourist shops in Intercourse. Not that I'm complaining. Working here is when I feel closest to God." He was startled when those words came out of his mouth.

Sensing any closeness with his Lord had been impossible for months.

She faced him. "How so? Because you're using the talents He gave you?"

"Partly." He fell back on the words he would have used before sorrow shadowed his days. "Also, it's because everything here from the coals on the forge to the iron to the stones on the floor beneath my feet was created by God. I'm using them to make something, too. Not that I can achieve the perfection of His creation, but I can praise Him for what He gave us for our use."

"I understand. I feel that way when I'm sewing, whether it's a garment or a quilt top or joining others in making a complete quilt."

Until he'd heard Clara talking with Leah on Sunday, he hadn't realized she was as knowledgeable about quilting as his sister-in-law was. But why should he? They hadn't spoken of much other than the Beachy twins.

As if he'd called their names, he saw the rear door of Amos's store open and the *kinder* rush out. They ran toward the forge, excited about the treats his brother had given them. When Clara moved to stand between the youngsters and the forge, he looked at Nettie Mae, who was smiling as she held up the candy bar she'd selected. How could he have failed to see she needed glasses?

He waved to them when Clara herded the *kinder* around the side of the building. Lowering his hand, he let his breath sift out past his taut lips. If anyone had asked him, he would have said—without a hint of doubt—he knew as much about the twins as their parents did.

But he'd been wrong.

That Nettie Mae was getting glasses was a pointed

reminder he had to pay more attention to them. He should be relieved that he'd missed something as simple and innocuous as eyeglasses. He should be, but he wasn't.

What else didn't he know about Clara and the twins? Whatever he might learn, he'd better do it fast. The *kinder*'s family members could be arriving any day. The familiar pain rushed through him at the thought of never seeing them—or Clara—again. Maybe he'd be better off not knowing anything else, because when they left, knowing even a little bit more about them could make saying goodbye harder.

If possible.

Chapter Eight

Rain battered the windshield of his buggy as Isaiah reached the lane leading to the Beachys' house that evening. When lightning flashed followed by the slow, faraway rumble of thunder, a sure signal the storm was receding to the east, he hoped Clara had gotten home before it began. Though he'd thought she'd stop at the shop so he could see Nettie Mae's new glasses, she must have returned to get dinner started.

Or work in the garden, he corrected himself when he saw an abandoned basket of weeds beside the overgrown vegetable patch. The rain must have caught her and the youngsters unaware. Otherwise, Clara wouldn't have left the basket in the rain. After he finished his chores, he'd empty it on the compost pile and put the wooden slat basket in the mudroom to dry.

Bringing the buggy to a stop, he jumped out and went to unhitch Chip. The black horse didn't mind snow but hated rain.

"Let's go, boy," Isaiah said. "It's nice and dry in the stable." He glanced at the house. It would be pleasant in there as well, and he wondered what delicious meal Clara had prepared tonight.

He was no cook, but no matter how burned it was, he'd eaten every bite of the meals he'd made for himself when he lived alone in the small house he'd bought after his wedding. He'd counted himself blessed when he was asked to eat with his family or the Beachys. Either Esta or *Mamm* would have welcomed him every night, but often he'd worked late at his forge and didn't want to inconvenience anyone. *Mamm* was a great cook, and Esta had been less skilled, but much better than his fumbling attempts.

Clara, however, was a talented cook. Even something like her potato salad had an unexpected burst of flavor. She'd revealed that she added barbecue sauce and bacon to the usual ingredients.

Suddenly the door burst open. Andrew ran through the rain to fling his arms around Isaiah. "You're here!" the boy cried.

"*Ja*, I am, but are you supposed to be outside now?"

Instead of answering, the little boy asked, "Where have you been? *Aenti* Clara has had supper ready for a long, long time."

Isaiah flinched. What had Andrew called Clara? Pushing down a sudden rush of dismay, he said, "I'm sorry if you're hungry." He ruffled the *kind*'s wet hair. "Run inside and let her know I'll be in soon."

As the little boy raced away, Isaiah stood still. The rain fell around him and bounced off the brim of his hat. *Aenti* Clara? When had the *kinder* started calling her that? Had she asked them to?

He took the questions with him into the barn. They repeated in his mind in rhythm with the milker and followed him into the tank room where a diesel engine kept the milk cool until it could be pumped into the truck that collected it every day after he left for work.

One of the cows regarded him as she chewed on the hay in front of her stanchion. Her unblinking gaze seemed to ask him why he was upset. That the twins were comfortable with Clara should make him happy, so why was he questioning it? He hadn't been bothered when Amos had told him that the Beachy youngsters now called him *Onkel* Amos.

"They hope they can sweet-talk extra treats out of me," his brother had said with a laugh. "I don't know what you would have done if you hadn't found Clara to corral those youngsters. They've got so much energy."

Isaiah had agreed then, and he still agreed with his brother. So why did having the kids call Clara *aenti* set him on edge?

He dumped the last of the fresh milk through the filter and leaned one elbow on the stainless-steel milk tank. Looking across the small room, he knew he could keep on trying to ignore the truth, or he could start acknowledging it.

He envied the *kinder* who had let Clara into their lives. They didn't worry about what anyone else thought or how calling her *aenti* might complicate their lives. They accepted her kindnesses and her loving attempts to keep their days moving along without too much drama. She asked nothing of them other than to try to behave. If they didn't want to laugh, she wouldn't push them, though she was bothered by the situation. He needed to follow her example.

When Isaiah entered the house, Clara was busy at the stove. He greeted her and quelled his questions. There would be time later. After the twins were in bed. Tonight, somehow, he was going to make the effort to stay awake.

"Where are your glasses, Nettie Mae?" he asked as he sat at the table beside the little girl, who was pouting.

Her lower lip stuck out far beyond her top one, which she had sucked in close to her teeth. She must have been holding the glasses in her lap, because she tossed them on the table. Her siblings glanced at her, then away. They didn't want to be the target of her frustration.

"Those are cute, Nettie Mae," he said, as if he was oblivious to her mood.

"Ugly."

He was startled by her vehemence. Looking over her head to where Clara was placing sliced ham on the other end of the table, he said, "I think your glasses are cute, and I know you're cute, Nettie Mae. Why don't you put them on so I can see how cute you look with them?"

"No! Ugly." The little girl's nose wrinkled. "I no *grossmammi.*"

"Not yet, you're not."

"*Grossmammi* wears eyeglasses. Not me."

Clara glanced at them with concern. She was worried he wasn't going to change the little girl's mind with logic. He needed to try something else.

"Can I see them?" he asked.

Nettie Mae slid them across the table to him. When he picked them up, he saw they were simple gold frames. The sides had been extended and curved so they went behind Nettie Mae's ears instead of on top of them. He guessed that would keep the glasses from flying off an active little girl's face.

Holding them in front of her, he said, "Please put them on so I can see them."

She knocked them out of his hand and onto the floor. "No!"

Everyone froze in the kitchen, including Isaiah. He wasn't quite sure what to do. He looked again at Clara. Did she have any idea?

* * *

Clara wished she knew what to say to stave off the angry words that could be coming next. Her *daed* would never allow her to defy him. The one time she'd been foolish enough to try, *Daed* had punished her severely. The pain from being lashed with his belt had worn off long before her fear of what would happen if she angered him again.

How would Isaiah react to Nettie Mae's blatant disrespect? She shuddered as she imagined him trying to bend the *kind*'s will as her *daed* had struggled to subdue hers. Nettie Mae's frustration wasn't aimed at him. She'd been uncooperative at the optician's, which was why Clara had brought the twins straight home.

Clara needed to act before the situation spiraled out of control, and little Nettie Mae paid the cost of her rebellion as Clara had. Picking up the gold-rimmed glasses, she blew on the lenses to dislodge any dust. She held them to her face as if she intended to try them on. Smiling, she offered them to the little girl.

Nettie Mae ignored her, turning her back and folding her arms across her chest.

Swallowing her gasp of shock, because to act so in her house would have meant a terrible punishment, Clara said, "Nettie Mae, Isaiah hasn't seen you wearing your glasses. Why don't you show him?"

She shook her head.

"*Mamm* wouldn't make her wear them!" Andrew said stoutly.

Bless him! He'd given Clara the opening she needed to defuse the situation. With a smile, she said, "Your *mamm* helped Nettie Mae pick them out and placed the order for them."

The little boy's eyes grew so big, white circled the bright blue in their center. "*Mamm* did?"

"*Ja.*" Clara didn't add anything more. She waited to see how Andrew and Nettie Mae responded.

The two looked at each other, and she could see their certainty crumbling. Isaiah's shoulders relaxed. Had the despair lessened in his expression?

She squatted next to Nettie Mae's chair and placed the eyeglasses in the little girl's hand. She held her breath, hoping Nettie Mae wouldn't drop them again. When the *kind* hesitated, Clara gave her a bolstering smile.

Her eyes swimming in tears, the little girl set the glasses on her nose and settled the curved sides over her ears. A sob caught in the three-year-old's throat as she whispered, "I no *grossmammi*."

"No, but you're a very pretty young lady," Isaiah said as he leaned toward her and rested his elbow on the table. "Don't you think so, kids?"

"But you say, *Onkel* Isaiah," argued Ammon, jumping into the conversation for the first time, "the prettiest thing is a smile."

"And when Nettie Mae smiles, you'll see it's true." He winked at the *kind*, who gave up her attempt to keep her smile off her face.

As her siblings began to smile, too, he turned to Clara. His gaze held hers, and his grin broadened. They were becoming an excellent team in dealing with the *kinder*. The thought should have filled her with joy—and it did, but also sent a shiver of disquiet along her as she wondered how she was going to say goodbye to all of them.

* * *

"Whew!" Isaiah dropped heavily onto the sofa and leaned his head back, closing his eyes. "How can they have so much energy at the end of the day?"

Clara looked up from the letter she was folding and putting in an envelope. Like every other night, she and the *kinder* had spent time writing to their grandparents and *Aenti* Debra. It had become as much a bedtime ritual for them as brushing their teeth and saying their prayers. "Maybe they aren't tired because they don't have to chase themselves to make sure they stay out of trouble."

He smiled. "Not quite true. They do chase each other around, but in an effort to *find* mischief. I wonder what got them agitated tonight after Nettie Mae calmed down about her new glasses."

She shrugged. "They had an exciting day with the trip into town and the thunderstorm." She set the envelope with the other and the stamps on the table beside her. "I didn't realize how frightened they are of thunderstorms. All except Ammon, who seemed to take the loud crashes of thunder in his stride." Her eyes narrowed as she looked at where he was sprawled on the sofa. "What's wrong, Isaiah?"

"Nothing is wrong. Why do you ask?"

"You're here instead of heading to the *dawdi haus* as you've been doing every night this week, so I'm assuming you waited for the twins to go to bed to discuss something with me."

"Did anyone ever tell you that you've got too much insight into people?" He meant the question as a joke, but her face closed up as if she'd slammed a door between them.

"I learned as a *kind* to be aware of what other people

were thinking so I'd know what they'd do." She ran her fingers over the envelopes. A nervous gesture, and he wondered why she was uneasy.

Maybe the best thing would be to end the conversation, but he needed one answer before he went into the *dawdi haus*, which had become a sanctuary where he didn't risk seeing Clara each time he turned around. "Can you tell me something? I'm curious how long the twins have been calling you *Aenti* Clara."

"Did one of them call me that?"

He couldn't doubt her surprise was genuine. "Andrew did tonight."

"I'll ask him not to, if it's bothering you. People might get the wrong idea." She chuckled. "*Onkel* Isaiah and *Aenti* Clara? You might as well put a target on your back for the matchmakers."

"That's not why I mentioned it."

"Oh?" Her wide eyes told him that he'd startled her again.

He leaned forward, resting his elbows on his knees. "It's clear to me that the *kinder* consider you part of their lives."

"But a temporary part."

"*Ja.*"

Coming to her feet, she clasped her hands in front of her. "Isaiah, what would you have me do? Treat the twins as if they're my job and nothing more?" She shook her head with a regretful smile. "I can't. *You* can't either. You were *wunderbaar* with Nettie Mae tonight, convincing her the glasses made her special."

"I think she's special, so why shouldn't she?"

"And that is what makes you special, Isaiah Stoltzfus."

"What? Helping a little girl realize she doesn't need

to be a *grossmammi* to wear glasses?" He waved to dismiss her words. "Anyone would have done that."

"No." Her smile had vanished and regret remained. "Not everybody. I'm going to say something that you probably don't want to hear, but, Isaiah, your friends are right. You need to think of marrying because you're a very *gut daed*."

"That's not the reason to get married." He rolled his eyes. "Don't you dare mention this conversation to the Mast girls."

His attempt at teasing her fell flat because she remained serious. "You're a gift to these *kinder*. They know it, too. I'm beginning to wonder if that's why they're not as grief-stricken by their parents' deaths. They have you, and they know you'll take care of them as Melvin and Esta would have."

"But I'm not their *daed*."

"You are. At least temporarily."

Coming to his feet, he knew he needed to put an end to this conversation before it wandered from the twins to him and Clara. It would be such a small step, and one his heart was pushing him to take. No, he couldn't. Not when he knew how temporary this situation was. The *kinder*'s family should be arriving soon.

And what if he did listen to his heart? How could he be certain he wouldn't make a mess of everything with Clara as he had with Rose? He'd let his wife down by not being there when she needed him most. He could do the same with Clara, being so focused on his work he'd fail her when she depended on him to be there.

Look at how you've left her with all the work with the twins this past week, he reminded himself. *You didn't even have time to check the answering machine, and you drive by it twice a day.* He halted the thoughts.

The gates would be on their way by week's end. In the meantime…

"Don't say anything to the twins about what they call you," he said.

"Are you sure?"

"*Ja.* If someone gets the wrong impression, that's their problem. I'd rather have the *kinder* comfortable with you."

She sat in the rocking chair again. "I agree."

"*Gut.* They are what's most important."

"Something else I can agree with."

He nodded. He doubted Clara did much without her heart being involved.

As she reached for the envelope and began writing on it, he asked, "Have you memorized their addresses already?"

"*Ja.*" Looking up, she smiled, and his insides seemed to be jumping for joy. "The words in their street addresses are unusual. They stick in my mind."

He urged her to have a *gut* night's sleep and hurried toward the kitchen and the door to the *dawdi haus*. He wanted to get out of the main house before he said something stupid like saying how *she* stuck in his mind.

Chapter Nine

"Are you set for tomorrow?" asked Reuben as he reached for another slice of Wanda's delicious *snitz* pie.

Clara had been delighted with the invitation to the Stoltzfus farm for supper. She'd spent the day, while trying to do the household chores, watching Nettie Mae to see where the little girl stashed her glasses when she wasn't wearing them. Like in the center of the kitchen table or on the bathroom sink or in the middle of the living-room floor when she was showing off a picture she'd colored. So far, Clara had been able to keep them from getting broken. She'd been glad when Nettie Mae gave her the glasses to put in her pocket while they drove to Isaiah's family's farm a couple of miles along the twisting road.

She now joined in the celebration that Isaiah had finished the massive gates in time. The flatbed truck had come that morning.

The twins had been excited about seeing Isaiah's *mamm* whom they called *Grossmammi* Wanda. Or to be more accurate, Clara thought as she glanced out the window to where they were playing under the watchful eye of Leah's niece Mandy, to sample Wanda's desserts.

At the bishop's question, Isaiah sat straighter and frowned. "Oh, no! I forgot about tomorrow."

"What's tomorrow?" she asked as she picked up her sweating glass of ice tea.

"Saturday," Ezra said with a smile. He was Isaiah's next older brother, and he ran the dairy farm and oversaw its cheesemaking.

Leah slapped his arm. "Be polite."

"I'm always polite."

That brought a snort from Isaiah. "*Always* covers a lot of time and space, big brother." Without a pause, he turned to Reuben. "Do you think we can find someone else to go at this late date?"

Clara looked from one face to the other around the table. Isaiah was annoyed with himself for not planning for whatever was going to happen tomorrow, but nobody else seemed perturbed. She wanted to ask again what was going on and tried to be patient. The others would let her know if it was any of her business.

But Isaiah is *my business*, her thoughts insisted. *If something is upsetting him, it's bound to upset the* kinder, *and I need to be prepared.*

That was equivocating. She would be bothered whether or not Isaiah's problem with whatever was happening the next day disturbed the twins. After the tough times he'd faced the past month, he deserved a stress-free day or two.

Wanda came to her rescue by saying, "Clara, tomorrow is the annual youth trip to Hersheypark. Several months ago, Isaiah agreed to be a chaperone this year." Without a pause, she asked, "Why don't you go with them, Clara?"

"Me?" She couldn't hide her astonishment.

"We'll watch the *kinder*." Wanda smiled. "Then you

can do as you promised, Isaiah, and Clara can have a day off, too."

"But taking care of the twins is my job," she protested.

"Everyone should have a day off from their job once in a while." Reuben chuckled. "Even the *gut* Lord took a day off after creating the heavens and the earth."

"I can't argue with that."

"I told you that she has a lot of common sense," Isaiah said with a grin.

Wanda wagged a teasing finger at him. "You're saying that because you don't want to have to watch a bunch of teenagers by yourself."

"We won't be the only two chaperones, will we?" asked Clara.

Isaiah laughed, and she knew he was glad the *kinder* weren't there so he had to stifle his amusement. "No, there will be a couple more. Why are you uneasy about being with teenagers when you're outnumbered every day by *kinder*?"

"Because, as you said, I've got a lot of common sense. I know teenagers can think up mischief faster than preschoolers."

"That's *gut* to hear," Reuben said, "for this old man who'll be looking after little ones."

"You're going to help?" Clara asked, surprised. She'd assumed the twins would be cared for by Wanda and her daughter-in-law.

"Why not? It'll be *gut* practice for a man who hopes one of these days to be bouncing more *kins-kinder* on his knee." He sighed. "If one of my younger daughters would pick a young man and settle down…"

Wanda's secretive smile matched the twinkle in her

eyes. "Let's talk later, Reuben. I might have a suggestion to help."

Isaiah grinned, and Clara could hear his thoughts as if he'd spoken aloud. He was pleased to have his *mamm* busy matchmaking for someone else. She lowered her gaze to the table, hoping to hide her delighted smile. It would be fun to spend time with Isaiah. Maybe they'd have time to talk about concerns she didn't want to discuss when the twins were around.

The past few nights, the *kinder* hadn't been as enthusiastic about writing to their grandparents and *aenti*. Their reluctance had begun after they asked her about leaving the only home they'd ever known to live with extended family. She'd told them the decision would be made by adults, and she'd seen the glances they'd exchanged. From then on, they'd come up with excuse after excuse not to include a drawing or colored picture with the letter. In fact, she'd written almost everything in the most recent letters.

She wanted Isaiah's opinion about how to handle the touchy situation. She wouldn't lie to the *kinder*, but she didn't want them to worry all the time.

Reuben cleared his throat, drawing her attention to the bishop. He dampened his lips before he asked, "Do the *kinder* speak of their parents?"

"Never," Clara replied.

"It's not right. Do you talk about Melvin and Esta with them?"

Isaiah shook his head. "Not very often, because we don't want to make them sad."

"My dear boy, nobody on God's green earth could make them sadder than they are." The bishop sighed.

"When I mention their parents," Clara said, "I let

them take the lead in the conversation, but I urge them to talk."

"You do?" asked Isaiah.

She nodded. "Not that it matters. They change the subject. I get the feeling that sometimes one of them slips and breaks whatever agreement they've made not to speak of their parents. They immediately turn the conversation away from Melvin and Esta."

"Agreement?" Wanda frowned. "I don't like the sound of that. It's bad enough someone told them not to laugh. Did someone tell them to stay quiet about their parents?"

"Maybe." Isaiah scraped his palms on the edge of the table. "Who knows?"

"The *gut* Lord." His *mamm* patted his hands. "We need to let God guide the *kinder* and us."

Clara watched Isaiah as the others nodded. He copied the motion, but she could see he was having trouble agreeing. It confirmed what she'd suspected. Something stood between Isaiah and God. His friends' deaths? The tragic loss of his wife? A shadow hung over him, so dark and deep it was almost visible.

She didn't have the slightest idea how to ask him if she could help him. Or if she should. Knowing the truth would bring them closer, and she couldn't risk that.

The next day dawned warm and sunny. Not a cloud marred the perfect blue sky, and the humidity had been washed away by the night's rain. The *kinder* were picked up by Isaiah's younger brother Daniel, who planned to take them to the Stoltzfus farm. His betrothed, Hannah, her great-grandmother and her little sister Shelby, almost two years old, lived nearby in a house Daniel had built to showcase his talents as a carpenter.

"We're glad to have the twins join us," Daniel said with a broad smile that crinkled his eyes. "I was thinking of taking the *kinder* fishing."

"I hope you don't plan on catching anything." Isaiah clapped his brother on the shoulder.

"As long as I don't have to fish them out of the water, I'll consider it a successful day. Hannah and *Grossmammi* Ella will be joining us for a picnic along with *Mamm* and Reuben, so they'll have plenty of eyes on them, too. They'll have a great time with us."

"About telling them a joke—"

Daniel became serious. "*Mamm* warned me. Who would have told those cute kids not to laugh?"

"I'm hoping we can find out, so we can have him or her tell them it's okay to laugh now. If they smile, consider it a *gut* day for them."

"We'll have a *wunderbaar* day. Hope you will, too." He paused as his mouth twisted. "By the way, I know Katie Kay was supposed to go along on this trip…"

"Who's Katie Kay?" Clara asked.

"One of Reuben's daughters," Isaiah said at the same time Daniel replied, "Reuben's problem *kind*. She's run away."

"Reuben didn't say anything about that last night," she said.

"When he got home, he found out she was gone." Daniel sighed. "From what I was told, she's staying with an *Englisch* friend, and nobody knows when she'll come back home."

"Does Micah know?" Isaiah asked. "Clara, in case nobody's told you already, our brother Micah has had a gigantic crush on Katie Kay for a long time. Not that he's asked her if he could take her home. He doesn't talk to her because he's in awe of her."

"I'm not sure that's the case any longer," his brother said with a sigh. "Micah was pretty disgusted when he heard she'd argued with Reuben a couple of days ago. According to her sisters, she left in a huff last night, saying she wouldn't return until she was *gut* and ready."

Isaiah helped Clara get the *kinder* into his brother's buggy along with the plates of cookies and the ready-to-bake casserole she was sending along for their midday meal. Tomorrow, if Katie Kay hadn't come to her senses, he'd make sure to talk with Micah and Reuben. Especially Reuben, because in the past month, Isaiah had come to understand the depth of joy and pain a *kind* could bring to a *daed*'s life. Even a temporary *daed*'s.

He waited until Daniel's buggy had disappeared over a hill before he went into the house. Clara was checking the stove was off and no water dripped in the sink.

"Clara?"

She faced him.

"*Danki* for agreeing to come with me. Again I know it wasn't what you expected when you accepted the job of taking care of the twins."

"Why do you keep saying that?" Puzzlement filled her voice and expressive eyes.

"Saying what?"

"That this or that thing must not be what I expected when I took this job."

"Well, it couldn't have been."

She smiled. "Maybe not a trip to the amusement park, but I didn't come here with any assumptions. I've been surprised every day by big things and small."

"We didn't try to mislead you."

"Of course you didn't. Many of the surprises have been lovely ones like rediscovering how far a grasshopper can jump when trying to get away from youngsters intent on capturing it." Her smile faded. "Isaiah, you worry too much about things that can't be changed. Maybe shouldn't be changed."

He crossed the kitchen to close the distance between them. "Mostly I'm worried about one thing."

"What's that?" Her voice dropped to a husky whisper as she tilted her head to meet his gaze.

His heart halted in midbeat as he gazed into her brown eyes. They were delightfully close to his. A single lock of red hair had escaped her *kapp*, and he had to force his hand to remain by his side so he didn't reach out and twirl it around his finger. Its vibrant color was a tease as he envisioned loosening her hair and seeing it become a fiery fall down her back.

Then she took a step away. A single step, but the motion was enough to break the connection between them and let him escape from his imagination. Nothing had changed. He didn't trust himself to be there for another woman, so how could he ask this very special one to trust him?

"What are you worried about, Isaiah?" she asked, her words as shaky as his knees.

"Having you leave because you decide you don't want to put up with any more of the hassles you've faced since you've gotten here."

Startled, she repeated, "Leave?"

"If you go, Clara, I'm not sure what the twins and I would do. You've brought a serenity into the midst of the chaos exploding around us."

"What makes you think I'm going anywhere? I told you I'd be here, God willing, until the *kinder*'s family comes to collect them."

"I'm glad to hear that." He was. On many different

levels in his heart, including ones he'd thought sealed forever.

"We need to get going, or we'll miss the bus," she said.

"Let's go." He closed the door behind him as he needed to shut out these yearnings. He cared too much about Clara to put her through the hard lessons of discovering how he could let her down.

An hour later, Isaiah was spending more time watching Clara than the five teenagers they were supposed to be chaperoning. The kids were looking around with interest, but she was gaping at the rides and the crowds inside the entrance. When she exclaimed over the bright colors and the delicious smells, the three boys and two girls with them giggled.

"You've never been to Hersheypark before, Clara?" Isaiah asked.

"Never. I know it's a tradition in your district for the teenagers to take this trip at least once every summer, but it wasn't in mine."

"Did you have any traditions?" He paused as the teens discussed whether they wanted to stop for funnel cakes or frozen yogurt first. The idea of either in the midmorning made his stomach protest.

"Of course! My favorite was when the youth groups had a picnic and went canoeing."

"Did you get dunked?"

"More than once, but everyone expected it, so we brought extra clothes with us. Have you ever been out in a canoe?"

"A few times. The creeks around Paradise Springs get high enough in the spring to let us canoe, but by summer, they're trickles."

"I wonder if the twins would enjoy going out in a canoe. I could—"

He halted her by putting a finger to her lips. "Now, none of that." As the teens laughed, he lowered his voice while following them toward the first rides. "It's your day off, Clara. Remember what Reuben said. You don't have to think about the *kinder* today. They're in *gut* hands with my family. My *mamm* has raised nine of us, and Reuben has four daughters of his own as well as a son. Between them, they can handle two sets of mischievous twins."

"I know." She stopped again as the teens decided on hot dogs. When a boy asked if she wanted one, Isaiah was surprised when she nodded and ordered one with ketchup and relish. "But it's difficult *not* to think about them."

He grinned and said as she had, "I know. They're a part of my life." His smile faded. "I don't like to think of a time when they won't be."

"Their *aenti* lives in California, right?"

"When she's not on mission work." He sighed, wishing the conversation hadn't taken this turn. He'd looked forward to having a day with Clara and getting to know her better. "And the twins' grandparents live in Pinecraft, Florida. They belong to a Mennonite church there. When Esta fell in love with Melvin, she accepted our way of life and was baptized before they married."

"Having someone, even a conservative Mennonite, join our church doesn't happen often."

"As you may have noticed, each of the twins has a stubborn streak a mile wide. They got that from Esta." His smile returned when the boys brought over one hot dog for Clara and two for him. "And a little bit more from Melvin."

"And a little bit from you, too."

"Bad habits—as well as *gut* ones—tend to rub off on people."

The teenagers led them from ride to ride, each one more outrageous than the one before it. They laughed as they rode the inanimate horses of the carousel and squealed with excitement on the more adventurous rides. It was a toss-up who enjoyed it more: the teenagers or the chaperones.

The day passed quickly, and too soon one of the teenagers with a cell phone told them that they had one hour before they had to leave. That set off a debate among the boys about which rides they should go on. Isaiah stayed out of the discussion while Clara and the girls went to get sodas for everyone.

At the call of his name, he took a deep breath. He'd seen Orpha Mast get on and off the bus ahead of him and Clara. Someone on the bus must have mentioned he was chaperone. Most likely Larry Nissley, one of the biggest gossips in Paradise Springs, who'd stepped off the bus right after Orpha.

Orpha, wearing a bright cranberry dress, smiled. "Are you having a fun day, Isaiah?"

"I can't imagine anyone not having fun at Hersheypark." He resisted glancing toward the restaurant where Clara had gone with the girls. When he saw Larry hanging by its door, he had to fight not to frown. Was Larry watching them? Or just Orpha? "You'd have to try hard in order *not* to have fun."

"True." She stepped closer, seeming oblivious to the looks the boys—and Larry—shot in their direction. "But it's seldom I get to do anything fun. You don't know how it is in our house."

"I know your family is very close."

Her eyes narrowed as she frowned. "I thought you were insightful. At least, that's what Rose told me. She said you'd guessed the truth of why she married you."

"She married him," said Clara as she came to stand next to them, "because she loved him. That's what everyone has told me."

"*Everyone* doesn't know the truth." Orpha tapped the center of her chest. "I do. She married you, Isaiah, because *Daed* has ordered us to marry before our twenty-first birthday. You were available, so she married you."

Clara stiffened, but her face remained serene as she looked at Orpha as if the other woman were as young as the twins. Her voice remained calm when she said, "That's enough of your vitriol, Orpha. I'm sorry if your *daed* insists you marry by a certain date. Many parents do, but you don't see the rest of us venting our annoyance." Not letting the other woman answer, she added, "Don't listen to her, Isaiah. She's trying to hurt you. You don't have to believe her—"

"No, you don't have to believe me," Orpha snapped, "but you'll believe Leah, ain't so? Rose said she told Leah the truth one day. Ask Leah!"

"What's in the past is in the past." Isaiah appreciated Clara coming to his defense, but it was unnecessary. "Nothing we say or do can change what's happened." He looked from one teenager to the next and saw none of them were surprised by Orpha's outburst. They knew her too well. "We've got time for one more ride. What'll it be?"

He walked away with their group, letting the teens take the lead. Though he kept a handbreadth between him and Clara, he was as aware of her vexation as if it were his.

"Don't dwell on Orpha's words," he said.

"How can you let her say such hateful things to you?" Clara asked, her tone taut.

"How could I stop her?"

She sputtered for a moment, then said, "You're right."

"Clara, no matter what reason Rose had for marrying me, she came to love me. More than I deserved, to be honest."

"Why do you say that?"

He hesitated on his answer, not wanting to darken the day with a litany of his mistakes. But wasn't saying nothing almost as bad as lying?

When one of the boys turned and called that they wanted to ride the Kissing Tower, a round observation tower decorated on the outside by gigantic candy Kisses, Isaiah was grateful he didn't have to answer Clara's question. The five teenagers bounced around them like a mob of kangaroos.

They waited in line at the tall tower. When it was their turn, he motioned for Clara to precede him onto the ride. Entering the circular cabin that moved up and down a cylinder as wide as a silo and twice as tall, she waited for him before she moved toward the teens who were looking out the windows, trying to determine which one would give them the best view.

Clara gazed out, too, as the ride started to rise and then begin to turn to offer vistas of the park and the countryside around it, but Isaiah couldn't take his eyes off her. She was a fascinating collection of contrasts. She showed many of her emotions, but hid others so deeply he couldn't guess what they might be. She was loving with the *kinder*, and, at the same time, she taught them to do what was right. She spent at least an hour each night writing to the youngsters' family, but seldom spoke of hers.

And the one aspect of her that puzzled him most was how she could be alluring without being flirtatious. In fact, it was the opposite. She treated him as a partner in caring for the *kinder*, and she'd agreed to let the matchmakers have their fun without it meaning anything. The few times his resolve had slipped and he'd considered drawing her to him, she'd found a way to edge away.

He grimaced when he thought of how different the day would have gone if Orpha had been with him instead of Clara. She would have hung on his every word and on his arm whenever she could manage it. Rather than enjoying the rides, she would have seen them as an opportunity to nestle up to him.

He would have liked Clara to cuddle close on one of the rides. She'd slid across the seat and bumped into him on the Tilt-A-Whirl, but pushed herself to her side as she laughed. He should have gathered her to him while they enjoyed the ride together.

Stop it! he warned himself. That he liked spending time with Clara was no reason to think of her as anyone other than the woman hired to help him take care of the Beachy twins. Within a few weeks, she'd be back at her family's farm and the *kinder* gone. He'd again be concentrating on work at the blacksmith shop and as a minister. Hadn't he learned how painful it was to imagine a future that could be snatched away?

His gaze went again to Clara. It would hurt her, too, to be separated from the twins. Would she miss him, as well?

The Kissing Tower reached its apex over two hundred feet from the ground, and he saw a few of the *Englisch* riders kissing. Though he considered it an excellent idea, he stood beside Clara and pretended he didn't see the public displays around them.

"Isn't it beautiful?" she asked, as her fingers squeezed his before releasing his hand.

"Beautiful," he agreed, his gaze focused on her.

"I've had a great time today, Isaiah."

"I'm glad I got to spend your first day at Hersheypark with you."

"I am, too."

He wanted to grab her hand and hold on to it, but he was here to keep an eye on the teenagers, not expect them to chaperone him and Clara. Yet, after spending these *wunderbaar* hours with her at the theme park, he was unsure how he'd recover from her departure. In some ways, Clara's leave-taking would be harder to endure than Rose's. He'd loved Rose. He'd married her and dreamed of them starting a family. He'd known from the beginning that Clara was in Paradise Springs a short time. So why would her leaving shred his scarred soul?

Clarity struck him as the circular ride neared its base again. Rose hadn't chosen to leave. Clara would. Once the twins were settled with their extended family, she would pack her buggy and drive away.

And he'd be alone again.

More alone than after Rose's death, because nobody would know he was enduring another loss. He wouldn't have Melvin, who had stood by him in his darkest hours when living had seemed like too great a burden.

Clara didn't notice his silence on the trip home. She was kept too busy chatting with the girls they'd spent time with at the park. Then they picked up the *kinder* from the farm, and the twins spent every minute of the ride home talking about playing with Mandy and Shelby and the fish they hadn't caught.

As soon as the buggy stopped, Clara said, "Let's write a letter to your *grossdawdi* and *grossmammi* after dinner, and I'll tell them about my day at the same time I'm telling you. And you can tell me about your day so we can put it in the letter, too. How does that sound?"

The *kinder* all nodded at the same time.

Isaiah asked, "Would you boys like to help me get the grill going? We'll have hamburgers."

"Ja!" shouted Andrew.

Ammon echoed him a moment later as both boys ran to the storage barn where the grill was kept.

"Leave the charcoal alone!" Isaiah called after them. "I'll get it!" Lowering his voice, he said, "The last time they *helped*, their clothes needed to be washed twice to get the grit out of them."

She smiled as she held her hands out to the girls. Each took one, and he watched them walk into the house. The girls leaned their heads against her, and she put an arm around each *kind*'s shoulders. Anyone driving by who didn't know better would think the three were the perfect image of a *mamm* and her *kinder*.

How easy it'd been to say the past was in the past. It was much more complicated to think of the future. Anything was possible in the days and weeks and months and years ahead of them.

He walked away before the sight tempted him toward thoughts he must not have.

Yet he did. Far too often.

Chapter Ten

Three days later, Clara was astonished to see Isaiah waiting in the kitchen when she came downstairs to start breakfast. Usually, at this hour just before dawn, he'd be out to the barn doing chores. She was about to ask him if everything was okay when the stern expression on his face told her it wasn't.

"There's been a death at the Gingerich house. Henry Gingerich," he said without a preamble. "A heart attack in his sleep. I need to get over there to help the family."

"I'm sorry to hear that. Do you want me to pack food for you to take with you?"

He shook his head. "No. There will be plenty there. You know how plain folks make sure the grieving family has more to eat than they need." His eyes shifted toward the freezer compartment on the refrigerator. He swallowed so hard she could see the motion.

Though the last of the food brought for Melvin and Esta's funeral had been used up, she guessed he couldn't get the picture of the stuffed freezer out of his mind. It was a lingering reminder of his loss.

"Is there anything else I can do?" she asked.

"Will you explain to the kids that I may not be able to

get to their picnic at school?" He raked his hand through his pale hair, leaving it spiked across the top of his head.

She resisted the temptation to smooth those strands. "Don't worry. I'll make sure the boys see everything at school."

"I promised Andrew and Ammon I would attend with them."

"I know."

The older twins had been excited last night about visiting the school they'd attend in the fall. Neva Fry had taken over the school when Isaiah's younger sister, Esther, married, and, as the new teacher, Neva had decided to ask next year's first-time students to attend school for a fun day so the building and scholars would be familiar to them on their first day. In addition, she asked the parents to join in a frolic of cleaning the school building and yard.

With the gates done, Isaiah had looked forward to spending time with the twins at the school gathering. He'd volunteered to help paint the small outhouses used by the scholars. The buckets of white paint were already in the family buggy. Neither Isaiah nor Clara had mentioned that the twins might not be in Paradise Springs in the fall. Until they knew for sure who was going to take them and where, there was no reason to disrupt the *kinder* further.

"The twins will understand," she said, though she wasn't sure.

"If you tell them I've gone to oversee plans for a funeral." His face lost what little color it'd had. "But I don't want them to know that. Not on such a special day."

She put her hand on his arm. "Go and be with the Gingerich family. They need you more than the *kinder* do."

"I'm not sure about that."

"I am. Let me do what you hired me to do."

He put his hand over hers, and she found herself sinking into the depths of his blue-gray eyes. She wished she knew how to answer the questions she saw within them. If she tried, everything would change between them. She couldn't risk her heart again. The cracks in it were welded together by the heat of the tears she'd cried.

"I hate dumping this on you," he said in a whisper.

"Don't you think I know? I'll try to keep them from hearing about Henry for as long as I can."

He nodded. "The boys have looked forward to this day."

"Nettie Mae and Nancy, too."

"I don't want it ruined for them."

"It won't be. Nobody is going to want to upset the scholars today." She hesitated, then asked, "Do you think you'll be able to get there later?"

"I don't know at this point."

There was so much regret in his voice her hand rose and curved along his smoothly shaven cheek above his wispy beard. "I'm sorry *you* have to miss today, Isaiah. After your hard work on those gates, you were due time to have fun with the twins."

He put his fingers over hers and gave her a sad smile. "We'll have to find another way to enjoy a fun day with them." Drawing her hand away from his face, he gave it a squeeze before he walked to the door. "I'll definitely be home in time for milking tonight."

She nodded, holding her lower lip between her teeth. If she spoke, she wasn't sure she could silence the words she wanted to say. Words to tell him again how sorry she was he couldn't join them for the day as well as words to let him know how important he was becoming to her. She couldn't say *that*! It would mean putting her heart on the line again, and she wouldn't, especially when her time with him and the *kinder* was going to end too soon.

"We're going to school! We're going to school!" Andrew had turned the words into a song, which he sang at the top of his lungs, as he led the way out of the house.

When the other youngsters joined in, Clara made a big show of raising her hands as if to put them over her ears. Instead, she joined in, shocking the kids. They grinned, but she didn't hear the laughter she'd hoped for. She had to believe it would come one day.

She skipped with them to the buggy and, after cautioning them not to tip over the plates on the seats, motioned for them to climb in. She handed one plate to each *kind*.

"*Onkel* Isaiah isn't coming?" asked Andrew as he settled his covered plate on his lap, holding it with both hands.

She shook her head as she gave Nettie Mae a box containing the flatware they'd use. "He's meeting with Reuben today." It wasn't a lie, because the bishop would be at Henry Gingerich's house, too.

"But he said he was coming." Andrew stuck out his lower lip. "He told me last night he'd let me help paint."

"The paint is in the back of the buggy, and I'm sure, if you ask, the men painting the outhouses will let you help."

Nancy interjected, "*Onkel* Isaiah gonna push me on the swings till I kick the clouds."

"The next time you see him, ask him to take you there and give you a ride on the swings." To ward off more questions, she said, "Don't forget. Your *onkel* Isaiah knows the school well. He went there when he was a boy."

The *kinder* looked at her with astonishment. She couldn't tell if they were more surprised about Isaiah attending the same school they would or the fact he'd once been as young as they were.

Driving the buggy to the end of the farm lane, Clara asked, "Whose turn is it to get the mail today?"

"Mine!" Nancy jumped down from the buggy and ran to the metal mailbox where the letters spelling the family's last name were hardly visible. The door on the front had rusted away. Standing on tiptoe, she reached in. "A letter!" She waved it in the air as she rushed to the buggy. "For me?"

Clara took the envelope and turned it over to read the return address. "It's from your *aenti* Debra. Shall we read it now or after we go to school?"

"Now!" Nancy, Nettie Mae and Andrew shouted at the same time. Ammon chimed in a moment later…as he often did.

Too often did, Clara realized. He didn't wait for Andrew to speak for the twins, but let the younger girls also answer first. She'd thought he was shy but didn't believe that any longer. Once he joined in, he could be louder than the other three put together. Why was he the last one to answer any question she asked? And not only her questions, but everyone's.

She opened the thin envelope and pulled out a single piece of lined paper. The words were in such tiny handwriting she was tempted to borrow Nettie Mae's glasses.

"What does she say?" asked Andrew.

"Let's see," she said to buy herself time. Much of what Debra Wittmer had written wasn't suitable for the *kinder*. They didn't need to know about the num-

ber of deaths from recent earthquakes and the depriva-
tions being prevented by the Mennonite mission. She
began to read aloud the sections that were appropriate for the twins, the parts where Debra described the
soaring landscapes and the nice people she'd met and
worked with.

"Does she have a llama?" asked Nettie Mae when
Clara paused to take a breath.

Pretending to check, Clara said, "She says the local
people do and that the llamas carry goods for them
when they shop in the village."

"I like llamas," the little girl said with a smile. "Can
we ask *Aenti* Debra to bring one home?"

"Llamas live in herds like cows do. A llama by itself
would be very lonely."

"But we'd love it!"

"I know, but a llama wants to be with other llamas,
and you wouldn't want it to be lonely, would you?"
Going back to "reading" the letter, Clara finished with,
"It's signed with your *aenti* Debra's name."

"Right there," Ammon said, leaning over the seat
to point at the letters. "*D-e-b-r-a*. That spells Debra."

"It does." She smiled at him. "Are you sure you
haven't already been going to school? You know your
ABC's, ain't so?"

"*Mamm* helped me," he whispered before he sat on
the back bench.

Andrew sniffed and rubbed his hand against his nose
as he dropped next to his brother.

"You learned very well," Clara said, not wanting
to let silence settle on the buggy. Her heart ached for
the *kinder*.

If she'd had any doubt, the broken expressions on
their young faces would have confirmed—for once and

for all—that the twins were suffused with grief. She wanted to gather them into her arms and hold them until they let down the walls that must take an untold amount of will to keep in place.

Who were you who told them not to laugh and not to grieve? Why did you deny them the very tools that could allow them to heal?

By the time she reached the schoolhouse, Clara had gotten her unsteady emotions under control. She helped the *kinder* carry the food and supplies to the porch. They put the plates next to what others brought. She'd thought the twins would rush off to join the other kids, but they clung close to her. Another sign of how ragged their feelings were.

A young woman with a warm smile approached them. "I'm Neva Fry, the teacher here. I saw you at the most recent church Sunday, Clara."

"Andrew and Ammon will be joining you in the fall." *If their family doesn't move them away from Paradise Springs*, she added silently as she put one hand on each boy and gave them a gentle shove forward.

Neva asked, "Would you like to see inside the school? *Komm*. I'll show you."

The boys' enthusiasm returned, though they didn't budge far from Clara, as the teacher pointed out where they'd be sitting in the front row with the other youngest scholars. She urged them to sit at the desks and page through the books they'd be using. Andrew seemed more interested in the desk itself, but Ammon ran his finger along the words in the primer and mouthed each letter to himself.

It was the last time either of them sat all morning. While Clara helped the scholars' *mamms* give the classroom a *gut* cleaning, including every hidden space in the desks, the youngsters played outside under the supervision of Neva's assistant teacher.

Clara was pleased to discover Leah among the other volunteers. They worked together washing the windows with vinegar and water until the glass sparkled.

When it was time for their picnic meal, adults had arranged the food, making sure there were serving utensils with each dish. Neva called to her scholars who were waiting to eat. A girl and boy came over and smiled at her when she asked if they'd share their blankets, spread on the grass, with the older twins. They nodded and offered their hands to Andrew and Ammon.

Andrew grabbed the boy's hand, leaving the girl to his brother. Ammon hesitated before grasping the girl's hand, but both boys were grinning as the older *kinder* chatted with them about school.

"He's too young to think girls have cooties," Neva said, as she smiled at Clara. "Most of the girls and boys play with each other until they're around ten or eleven years old."

Clara returned the smile to be polite, but her gaze followed the twins. Again and again, Ammon glanced at his brother before acting. It was as if he sought a clue to what he should do next. Ammon followed his brother's lead. There must be a reason why the little boy was dependent on his twin.

Helping the little girls select what food they wanted from the vast variety on the porch, Clara led them to where Leah was sitting beside her niece. Mandy began talking with the twins who hung on every word. Several times, Clara had to remind them to eat.

"They're adorable," Leah said. "It seems like such a short time ago Mandy was no older than they are. Enjoy them, Clara."

"I do."

"Do you know when their grandparents are returning?"

"I haven't heard from them, but the missionary board said it'd be at least another week or two before they could get home. At the earliest."

"Isaiah is going to miss the *kinder* if they leave."

"I know. We all will."

Leah put her fork on her plate and set both beside her on the grass. "I worry about Isaiah. To lose them on top of losing their parents so soon after Rose died… It would break a weaker man."

Clara jumped in to ask before she could stop herself, "Did Rose tell you that she married him because her parents insisted?"

"Who told you that?" She held up her hands. "No, I know who did, and I'm sure it was when Isaiah could hear, too. I don't know how Orpha thinks she can persuade Isaiah to marry her when she acts spiteful."

"Rose didn't tell you that her parents insisted she get married?"

"She told me, but she also said she married Isaiah because she loved him. I wasn't in Paradise Springs when they courted. I was here during the short time they were married, however. I never doubted she loved him. It's true she was horrified when the lot fell on him, because she didn't believe she would make a *gut* minister's wife. She tried her best before she died."

"Will you tell Isaiah that? He's filled with a terrible guilt about his marriage."

Leah put her hands on Clara's arms. "I've told him that Rose loved him. Over and over. Help him, Clara. After seeing him with you, I think you may be the only one who can."

Clara rolled her eyes. "Please. No matchmaking."

"I'm not talking about you marrying him. I'm talking about you *helping* him lay his past to rest along with whatever guilt he's carrying around with him."

"I want to, but I don't know how."

"I think you do." Leah's smile softened. "I think your heart does. All you need to do is listen to it."

Was it that simple? Even if it was, doing so meant giving her heart free rein. It already yearned to lead her to Isaiah. Yet, how could she *not* help him?

Her thoughts spun around in her head until she heard Neva call, "Who wants to play softball? Andrew? Ammon? Do you want to play?"

Andrew's head whipped around the moment the teacher spoke his name, but Ammon continued to watch the other *kinder* rushing to the spot where teams could be chosen. Jumping to his feet, Andrew gave his brother's arm a gentle slap. Ammon looked at him. When Andrew motioned for his twin to follow him, he did.

Clara stared after them as the truth battered her. Ammon couldn't hear everything said by her or anyone else. He was taking his signals from his siblings, going along and trusting them that they would clue him in on what was happening.

Had Isaiah noticed? She had to tell him about her suspicions as soon as possible.

As he stopped his buggy behind others parked in front of the schoolhouse, Isaiah heard the scholars cheering. Their excitement was what he needed to lift his heart. Preparations for a funeral were never easy, even when the person who'd died was old and in pain.

He'd known Henry Gingerich all of his life. The elderly farmer had been part of the lives of almost everyone in the district because he always helped his neighbors and family. By the next day, vans would be arriving at the Gingerich house, bringing family members who lived too far away to come by buggy.

Tomorrow he'd take each twin aside and tell them what had happened. He doubted they'd know who Henry Gingerich was, though they'd seen him almost every church Sunday of their lives.

As he stepped out of the buggy, a pair of small blurs rushed toward him.

"*Onkel* Isaiah!" shouted Nancy.

Nettie Mae threw her arms around him as if she hadn't seen him in weeks rather than a few hours.

He stopped and gave the little girls each a hug. Tapping Nettie Mae's nose beyond her glasses, he grinned. "Have you been coloring?"

"*Ja! Komm* and see. My dog! Want one."

"A dog?"

"Like Shelby's."

Having no idea what the little girl was talking about, he knew he'd have to ask Daniel what sort of dog—and if it was real or stuffed—the toddler had.

"You here!" Nancy cried. "Me glad!"

"*Ja*, me too." He looked past her. Clara was walking toward them. What would she do if he held out his arms to her as he had to the *kinder*? It was sweet to imagine her stepping into them, because her head was at the perfect height to lean against his shoulder.

"Go and get a ladle of cold water for your *onkel* Isaiah," Clara said. As soon as the girls had sped away, she turned to him. "You look exhausted."

"I feel like I've been carrying an elephant around."

"How's the family doing?"

"There's sadness, but knowing he went in his sleep is

a blessing for the whole family. I—" He was struck from behind twice, hitting him hard enough to knock the breath out of him. Expecting the girls, he was surprised to see the boys throwing their short arms around him.

"You're here! You're here!" Andrew cried.

Beside him, Ammon nodded, his eyes glistening with tears.

Tears? Why would the little boy cry at the sight of a man he called his *onkel*?

As if he'd asked that question aloud, Clara said, "They've been anxious that you wouldn't come…" She pressed her fingers to her lips as her eyes widened.

At the motion, comprehension burst through him as it must have through her. He realized what the *kinder* meant. They hadn't been concerned he wouldn't come to the picnic. They were concerned he wouldn't come home at all.

As their parents hadn't.

With stark dismay, he recalled how one often clung to him when he left for work. They were as excited when he arrived at day's end as if he'd been gone for days instead of hours.

He couldn't promise he'd always make his way home to them. Life changed without warning, as they knew too well.

Soon, the *kinder* would be with their real family. How long would it take for them to forget him? He knew how long it would take him to forget them. Forever and a day. They were as much a part of him as his next breath. And within a couple of weeks, they'd be gone. Just as Melvin and Esta were.

The grief striking him was like a fist to the gut. He turned away so none of them could see his face.

Andrew's name was called, and he looked over to

where the other *kinder* were waiting for him to take his place as the batter. When Isaiah motioned for him to go and play, both boys ran to the game.

"How do we get through to them that they'll never be alone?" asked Isaiah with a sigh.

"I don't know," Clara said, "but I think it's important they learn to be happy again."

He clasped his hands behind him so he wouldn't reach out to take hers. "I keep trying to remind myself that, but then I see the emptiness of my life without them, and my heart breaks again."

"Put them in God's hands, Isaiah, and trust He'll watch over them." She gave a nervous half laugh. "Sorry. I shouldn't be telling a minister to have faith."

"Why not? A minister is a man like any other. Having doubts or needing to reexamine one's faith is part of being human."

"You don't believe...?"

"*Ja*, I believe. That won't change."

"But?"

He shrugged. "Sometimes I'm not as close to God as I'd like to be."

"Are you angry with Him?"

He was about to give her a quick answer, but then he paused. Anger? Was that what he felt? Or was it disappointment or betrayal? He wouldn't be less than honest with her. "I don't know."

"You need to figure it out, or you'll never be happy again either."

"You're not telling me anything I haven't thought about myself. What I need is a solution."

"The answer is the same for you as for the twins. You must be willing to speak of your loss and mourn before you can accept it."

"I talk about Rose a lot."

"You talk about her death, but you seldom say anything about her life. Since I got here, I've learned about how Leah was gone from Paradise Springs for ten years before she returned with her niece. I found out Rebekah's first husband was best friends with your brother Joshua before his death. I know from personal experience your *mamm* makes the best *snitz* pie in the county."

"Everyone knows that."

"The point is, Isaiah, I know a lot about your family because they talk about each other in loving ways, but nobody talks about Rose. Or if they do, they stop when you come near."

"I didn't realize that."

"They love you. They don't want to add to your grief." She put a consoling hand on his arm. "I would be willing to listen if you need an ear."

"Danki." What else could he say? *Holding you will help me more than you listening to me? That when I look into your eyes, I can believe—if only for a second—I'm not a lousy human being who failed the person who trusted me most?*

When she started to say something else, he didn't give her time. He walked toward the ball game where he could submerge his guilt and sorrow behind a practiced smile once more.

Chapter Eleven

For the first time, the evening seemed to drag for Clara. It shouldn't have, because the *kinder* had had an exciting day. The boys shared every detail of visiting the school with Isaiah. When they paused to take a breath, the girls jumped in with their impressions of the school, Neva, the scholars and everything else they'd seen. Each of the *kinder* had a different favorite memory. Andrew liked playing ball. Nettie Mae was delighted with the artwork hanging on the school's walls, and Nancy asked when they could return to play on the swings and have Isaiah swing her high again. Ammon didn't say much until Isaiah asked him, point-blank, what he'd liked best. He considered for a moment and then announced he'd liked the food.

Clara tried not to show her impatience as she prepared a quick supper of ham sandwiches while Isaiah did the barn chores. She was tempted to skip one night of writing a letter with the *kinder*, but they'd insisted. They wanted to tell *Aenti* Debra about their visit to the school.

"Let her know we're big enough to go to school in

the fall," Andrew said at least a dozen times. "Me and Ammon."

"I will," she replied each time, but made the letter shorter than usual. She was glad when the twins didn't seem to notice, and she folded the page and put it in its envelope, sealing it.

After persuading the twins to go to sleep after an extra story was read in the hope of calming them, Clara came downstairs. Isaiah had left the twins' bedroom right after their prayers, and she saw the door to the *dawdi haus* was closed.

She paused long enough to check the letter from Debra was in her pocket before she went to the connecting door. She rapped and called, "Isaiah?" When she didn't get an answer, she knocked again. "Isaiah, may I speak with you about the *kinder*?"

She heard the lock slide on the other side. Was he using it for propriety's sake or to shut the rest of them out? No, that made no sense because she'd seen the faint shadows of loneliness in his eyes when he spoke of the twins going with their family.

"What is it, Clara?" he asked.

At his abrupt tone, she considered waiting until the morning. No, she couldn't. Too much was at stake.

"May I come in and speak to you about a couple of things with the twins?" she asked.

"Ja." He pushed the door open wider, then backed away so she could enter.

As she went in, he vanished into the bedroom. Not knowing what else to do, she pulled out a chair at the table in the center of the main room. She folded her hands on the table and waited.

Isaiah was wiping his hands on a towel as he came out of the bedroom. Without a word, she held out the letter from Debra. He took it and opened the envelope. He read the page before he folded it again and handed it to her.

"She didn't ask anything about the *kinder*," he said as he sat facing Clara. "Nothing about her coming for them."

"I noticed that, too, but the date on the letter is almost three weeks ago. She probably hadn't received a letter from the twins when she wrote this one."

"But you'd have thought she'd ask about future arrangements for them."

"I've been wondering if she's waiting to hear from their grandparents first."

He gave her a dim smile. "You may be right, Clara. The two sides of the family have to agree. I'm sure more letters are on their way."

"I hope so." She gripped the edge of the table as she went on to the real reason she'd intruded on his privacy. "We need to talk about Ammon. I think there's something wrong."

"Is he sick?"

"No. *Ja.*"

"Which is it?"

"I don't know." She began to relate what had happened that afternoon.

His face became grim as he listened, and, though she could see questions in his eyes, he waited until she was finished before he asked, "And you think he's having trouble hearing?"

"*Ja.* Do you know if he's had a lot of ear infections or allergies? Some kids when I was growing up had one or the other, and sometimes they had trouble hearing when their ears were stopped up."

"With four young kids, it seems like one or another is sick all winter. I can't remember anything specific."

"Do you know if Esta kept any medical records for them?"

"I know she had their immunization records, but I don't know about anything else. If she did keep a record, it would be in the top drawer of the dresser in their bedroom."

"Oh." She had closed the bedroom door the morning after her arrival, and it hadn't been opened since... as far as she knew. Maybe Isaiah had gone inside, but she hadn't, and none of the *kinder* had either. "I'll go and check."

"No, I will." He squared his shoulders. "Wait here. It won't take long."

She watched him leave. It would be heart-wrenching for him to enter the room that had been the private retreat of his best friend and his wife. She folded her hands in front of her and bent her head until her forehead was against her clasped thumbs. Her wordless request was for God to be with Isaiah during his search. She didn't raise her head or stop repeating the request until she heard his footsteps in the kitchen.

Making sure that her *kapp* was in place and she revealed no sign of her despair, she gave him a slight smile when he returned to the *dawdi haus*. She didn't say anything about the lines of tension cutting into his face as if he'd aged years while he was gone.

"This was all I could find." As he sat at the table again, he held out four small bright orange booklets that were folded in the center. "Their shot records. You look at these two." He tossed them in front of her. "I'll go through the other two, and we'll see which one is Ammon's. Maybe Esta wrote something in there to help us understand why he seems to be having trouble hearing."

The first booklet she opened was Nettie Mae's, and Clara's hopes rose when she saw a note about the little girl needing to have her eyes checked. Closing it, she opened the other. It belonged to Andrew and contained only the dates of his immunizations.

Looking at Isaiah, she said, "You must have Ammon's."

"I do, but there's nothing in it to help." He handed it to her, and she saw it was identical to Andrew's. A shot record. Nothing else.

Showing him the words in Nettie Mae's, she asked, "Do you think Esta hadn't realized Ammon might be having trouble hearing?"

"*I* hadn't noticed until you said something."

She hesitated, then said, "I'd like him to see a *doktor*. If there's a problem, it's something we need to know before he starts school in the fall."

"I agree."

She breathed a silent sigh of relief. *"Gut."*

His brows lowered. "Did you think I would say no to taking Ammon to have his hearing tested?"

"No."

"At least you sound certain."

"I am." She looked at the orange booklets. "I wish I could be sure we're doing the right thing."

"How can it be the wrong thing? If his hearing is okay, we'll work with Dr. Montgomery to discover what might be the problem."

"Let's take it one step at a time."

He stroked her fingers as he said, "A *gut* idea."

As she smiled, she wondered if he was talking about the boy or if the subject had shifted to the two of them.

* * *

Once Ammon had seen Dr. Montgomery at the medical clinic in Paradise Springs, an appointment with an audiologist was set up for three days later. It was in Lititz, too far away to go by buggy. Clara called Gerry, the *Englisch* van driver Wanda suggested.

The twins enjoyed the short ride in the van to the Stoltzfus farm. Andrew was fascinated by the elderly driver who was as much a baseball fan as the boy was. Soon Gerry and Andrew were chatting like old friends about the Philadelphia team and Andrew's favorite, the Pittsburgh Pirates.

At the familiar white farmhouse, Wanda and Leah along with Mandy were waiting for the twins. Ammon looked uncertain when the other *kinder* got out and then Isaiah climbed in the van, closing the door.

Clara had explained to the boy, as Dr. Montgomery had, why he was going for the testing and that there wouldn't be any needles or bad-tasting medicine involved. Even so, the little boy sat stiffly during the half-hour drive northwest to Lititz.

Beyond the center of the pretty village, Gerry flipped on his turn signal and pulled into a long, low shopping plaza. For a moment, Isaiah thought the *Englischer* had made a wrong turn; then he saw the name of the audiology company on one of the storefronts. When Isaiah noted a nearby pizza parlor, he asked Ammon if he wanted to get pizza and take it home for his siblings. The little boy nodded so hard Isaiah had to struggle not to laugh.

When they got out of the van, Ammon gripped Isaiah's hand as hard as he could. Clara opened the door to a space that resembled the medical clinic in Paradise

Springs. She went to the desk to sign Ammon in and collected a clipboard with several pages on it.

Isaiah filled in what information he knew about the boy's health history as well as his parents'. Carrying it to the desk and paying for the office visit, he rejoined Clara and Ammon by a water dispenser that fascinated the little boy each time a bubble rose to the top.

An inner door opened, and a young woman in a pale yellow broadcloth shirt and jeans stepped out. She was almost as tall as Clara, but her hair, pulled back in a ponytail, was matte black. Walking to them, she said, "I am Trudy Littleton, one of the audiologists here." She spoke slowly and enunciated each word with care. "Are you Ammon?"

The little boy stared, then nodded.

She smiled and motioned for them to follow. Dr. Montgomery must have explained Ammon had lost his parents, because Trudy addressed Isaiah as "Uncle Isaiah." He'd have to thank the *doktorfraa* the next time he saw her.

First, Trudy led them to an examination room. She listened to Ammon's heart before peering into his ears and his throat.

"Everything looks normal," she said. "No signs of scarring or other injury in his ears. Let's see what else we can learn."

Again Ammon clutched his hand as Isaiah followed Clara and Trudy along a hallway. When Trudy opened a door at the far end of the hall, he saw the room beyond had a huge square cube to one side. The walls were covered with carpet. The single door had a tiny window, and another large window was at the far end by a simple table and chair.

"This is our testing facility," Trudy said. "It's sound-

proof so we can measure what Ammon is hearing."
She picked up a set of headphones and asked slightly
more loudly and distinctly, "Do you know what these
are, Ammon?"

He shook his head.

Trudy's smile returned. "A silly question for a plain
boy, isn't it?" She set the headphones on her head, ad-
justing the earphones over her ears. "You wear them
like this." Taking them off, she said, "When you go inside and wear these, I'll play music for you. When you
hear it, I want you to raise your hand like this." She
put up her right hand. "Then we'll play other games.
Okay?"

Ammon glanced at Isaiah, abrupt fear in his eyes.

"Can I go in with him?" Isaiah asked.

"You may, but please don't give him any cues. We
must determine what *he* can hear." She opened the door
and motioned them to go in.

He heard her ask Clara to take a seat to one side before the door closed and sound cut off. The cube was
lined inside with odd protrusions and more carpet. A
pair of chairs was placed so the occupants could look
out the window.

Trudy moved into sight, and a click resonated in the
room. "If you want to sit and put on the headphones,
Ammon, we'll get started."

Isaiah guided the little boy to a chair. Sitting him
there, he put the smaller set of headphones hanging
from hooks on the wall on Ammon. He took the chair
next to the boy as Trudy explained over the loudspeaker
that they'd start with tones.

Isaiah was amazed how tense he was as he watched
the little boy raise and lower his hand. He saw Trudy's
encouraging smile while Ammon didn't move; then the

kind began saying words he must be hearing through the headphones. The words were random. Some came in quick succession while others seemed to have long breaks between them. He wondered what Ammon was hearing.

The speaker's click sounded again, and Trudy asked them to come out. She left Ammon with an aide in a nearby room filled with toys before, holding a manila folder, she led Isaiah and Clara to another door partway along the hall. Clara glanced at him, and Isaiah had to shrug. He had no idea what the tests had revealed.

The room had a desk and several chairs. The mini blinds at its single window were closed. The audiologist gestured for them to sit in two chairs by the desk. She went around to the desk and sat facing them. Opening the top drawer, she drew out a piece of paper. Graph blocks created a small rectangle on one side of the page. No marks had been made on it.

"This is the tool we use. It's called an audiogram," Trudy said, pointing to the graph. "When a patient is tested, the audiologist makes an X for the level of hearing in the left ear. We make a small circle for the level of hearing in the right ear. The numbers along the left side are for the horizontal lines and represent loudness. Quiet at the top and louder as the lines go down. We make the mark at the softest sound the patient hears at each note. The numbers along the top are for the nine vertical lines and have to do with the pitch of the sound. Each line from left to right goes higher in pitch. Think of it as a piano keyboard. The low notes are on the left, and the notes go higher as we go along the keyboard."

"What are the important numbers for Ammon to be able to hear?" Clara asked.

Trudy drew a box near the top of the audiogram and

colored it in. "This is what's called the critical speech area. Pitches between 500 and 4000. For children, we like to see the loudness marks between 0 and 15. Anything in that box is considered good hearing. Do you have any other questions?"

Isaiah shook his head, not wanting his voice to crack with anxiety.

Beside him, Clara said, "I don't have any more questions."

"Good." Trudy opened the file folder and drew out a single sheet. She put it on the table between him and Clara. "Here are the results of Ammon's test. As you can see, your concerns about his hearing are justified."

He stared at the graph. A single X was drawn in the critical speech area. The circles ran across the bottom of the audiogram, and the other Xs were scattered between, though most were closer to the bottom than the top.

"Does this mean," Clara asked in a strained voice, "he can't hear much in his right ear?"

"If he can hear anything with his right ear," Trudy replied, "I'd be surprised. His hearing in his left ear is diminished. That he speaks so well is a blessing, but his speech will regress if his hearing isn't augmented. My suggestion is you have Ammon fitted for a hearing aid in his left ear as soon as possible. It'll allow the sounds he can hear to be amplified, especially in the critical speech area."

"What about his right ear?" Isaiah asked.

She sighed. "From the physical examination and the audio test, it's clear the nerves in his right ear are damaged. He can't hear vibrations in it. A hearing aid won't help. In fact, it might be detrimental because earwax can build up behind a hearing aid, and that could lead to ear infections."

"Do you think that's what caused the hearing loss?" He couldn't stop staring at the graph and the row of circles at the bottom.

"It's possible, though, as I said, I saw no signs of scars from multiple ear infections or any other damage caused by an injury. He may have been born with the nerves already defective." She gave them a sad smile. "There's no way to know without being able to talk to his parents. We need to work with what is and forget about what might have been."

"What do we need to do?" Clara asked.

"The first thing is to have him measured for a mold to make the hearing aid's insert for his ear. With your permission, I'll have my assistant do that."

The audiologist rose and left the room after Isaiah nodded, again not trusting his voice. Thank the *gut* Lord for Clara! She hadn't failed the boy.

Trudy returned and held out typed pages to him. "Here's basic information on the care and maintenance of a hearing aid. However, with a child Ammon's age, the most important thing is to get him accustomed to wearing it whenever he's awake. Be prepared. Some children resist because they hate having something in their ear or being teased. Others are bothered by the abrupt increase in what they can hear."

"His little sister has started wearing glasses." Clara chuckled. "She wasn't too happy, but Isaiah convinced her they were the very thing she needed. He can do that for Ammon, too, ain't so?"

He forced a smile as grief surged from his heart. He had no idea how to convince a five-year-old that wearing a hearing aid was no big deal. Glancing at

Clara, who was asking more questions—ones he hadn't thought of—he knew he could depend on her to help him. Again he thanked God for sending her.

It's more than I deserve, he added, *but keep the twins in Your hands. They need You more because of my failures.*

He lowered his head, missing the closeness he'd once had with God. It was as if his prayers were having to rise to a very distant heaven instead of being heard by a loving parent who was never far away. He wished he could find his way to the relationship he'd had with God before Rose's death.

Trudy's voice intruded into his thoughts, and he looked up to see her holding out more papers, these folded into three parts. "These pamphlets will help you with making arrangements for him in the classroom as well as in other public places. The bottom one explains our payment plan for hearing aids. If you have any questions after you read them, please contact the office."

Isaiah took the pages numbly and was glad when Clara thanked the audiologist after Trudy asked them to return to the waiting room while they made the mold for Ammon's left ear. That way, she assured them, the hearing aid would fit when it arrived in a few weeks.

A few weeks? What if Melvin's parents or Esta's sister got to Paradise Springs before the hearing aid arrived? Would they be able to stay long enough for Ammon to get it, or would it have to be forwarded to where they lived?

Enough! He was worrying about inconsequential things. The family would want to help the *kinder*.

"Are you all right?" Clara asked as they sat on the chairs they'd used before.

"No."

"Me neither." She gave him a fleeting smile before lapsing into silence.

And there was nothing more to say other than how glad he was she was there with him. Those words he must keep to himself.

Chapter Twelve

Clara heard the rattle of buggy wheels on the stones in the lane and looked out the window. Isaiah! What was he doing at the house in the middle of the day? She wiped her hands on the dish towel and left the rest of the dishes soaking in the sink.

The twins were already swarming over Isaiah by the time she stepped outside. They greeted him with the same enthusiasm whenever he returned to the house, but they seemed a bit more excited than usual.

During the past two weeks, the days had flowed one into the other without much of note other than taking Ammon to Lititz to have his hearing aid fitted. The concerns he wouldn't want to wear it were for naught because he was delighted to be able to hear his siblings. It was the first thing he reached for in the morning and the last thing he took off at night. And Nettie Mae became less resistant to wearing glasses now that he had the hearing aid. Clara had warned them more than once that just because they had special tools to help them didn't mean they were any different from any other *kind* in the district. Each plain youngster had to learn being part of the community was more important than standing out.

As she neared, Isaiah went around to the back of his buggy and opened it. He pulled out bright blue pieces of plastic and black rods and netting. As he tossed each item on the grass, the twins became more excited.

"What's that?" Clara asked as he grabbed several of the larger pieces. She jumped aside when he dragged them past her.

"It's a trampoline. Or at least it's supposed to be once it's assembled." He dropped the pieces onto the ground not far from the sandbox and went to get more. When the twins picked up a few smaller parts near the buggy, he pointed to the spot where he wanted them put. "Daniel got it at the house where he's working. He's renovating a big farmhouse for an *Englischer* and his wife."

She glanced at the piles of parts on the grass. "They didn't want the trampoline?"

"No. From what Daniel told me, it was in the barn when his clients bought the house. Their *kinder* are grown, so they don't have any use for it. Daniel talked to them about the twins, and they decided to give him the trampoline for them."

"How generous!" She smiled. "It looks as if you've got your work cut out for you. There are a lot of pieces."

"Daniel is coming over later to help me put it together. He put one up for Joshua's youngsters last summer. He says he remembers most of the steps." He gave her a half smile. "Which is *gut* because we don't have any assembly instructions."

"I'll keep the kids away from it."

"You?" His smile broadened. "I'll watch them this afternoon."

"You aren't going to the forge?"

He shook his head. "I haven't taken as much time with the twins as I'd like. I want to while I can."

Clara blinked abrupt moisture from her eyes at the resignation in his voice. The *kinder*'s family could come at any time and take them, but they avoided speaking of it. Like the twins, they'd learned to pretend everything was fine.

"All right," she said. "I'll get supper ready."

"Or you could stay out here and work with us."

"I don't want to barge in on your time with them."

"How could you? You're part of their lives, too. Don't you want to help us? It'll be fun, Clara, and we could use fun in our lives."

The dampness in her eyes threatened to coalesce into tears. She blinked them aside as she nodded. He was right. She was taking everything too seriously.

"That sounds *wunderbaar*," she said, and took the hand he held out to her.

"C'mon!" he called to the twins. "Let's get this sorted out so we can put it together." As they began to try to figure out the pieces of the trampoline, she realized she'd forgotten how to have fun.

She didn't want to forget again.

By the time Daniel had arrived and they'd set to work assembling the trampoline, Isaiah was grateful for his younger brother's assistance. Clara excused herself to let them work and insisted the *kinder* go in the house with her so one of the heavier pieces didn't tumble on them.

It took them almost two hours to set up the trampoline and make sure it was safe. Isaiah was pleased when Clara and the twins reappeared as he and Daniel were putting away the last of the tools. She carried a pitcher of lemonade that was sweating as much as they were.

The afternoon was humid, and thunderheads threatened over the western hills.

Taking a glass filled with ice and lemonade, he said, "Exactly what I was thinking about."

"I guessed." She smiled at the youngsters staring with delight at the trampoline. "The twins were eager to do something while they waited for you to finish, so we squeezed lemons." Looking at his brother, she added, "Daniel, would you like to join us for dinner?"

"*Danki*, Clara," his brother said after draining his glass and holding it out for a refill, "but I need to get home and help with Shelby's physical therapy. She won't let anyone else help her with practicing going up and down stairs."

"She's got *you* well-trained." Isaiah couldn't help envying his younger brother, who had fallen in love with a girl who came with a ready-made family.

"I'm wrapped around her little finger. Hers and Hannah's." Daniel finished his second glass of lemonade and handed it to Clara. He waved to them before heading to where his light brown buggy horse waited.

The *kinder* were clamoring to test the trampoline even before the buggy left. Cautioning them to put a big space between them so they wouldn't bump into each other, Isaiah lifted them, one after another, through the opening in the netting. As the trampoline shifted beneath them, they grabbed on to the netting and looked scared.

"Just bounce," he said.

Ammon did, jumping high and coming down hard. He fell to his knees and then flat on his face. He pushed himself up. The side of his face was reddened, but he was grinning.

"Bounce gently," Clara urged. "A little motion will

make you go a lot." She grinned when the girls began to move with more confidence.

Soon all four *kinder* were leaping around the trampoline like mad rabbits. Their squeals of excitement were sweet music. Not quite laughter, but closer than he'd heard from them since that tragic night.

When the twins took a break to drink more lemonade, Isaiah asked, "Shall we try it, Clara?"

"You go ahead." She took a step away. "I should get dinner on the table."

"Not until you have your turn." He grasped her hands and tugged her forward.

"Clara's turn! Clara's turn!" shouted the twins, jumping with excitement as if still on the trampoline.

"You hear them." He yanked off his work boots and tossed them and his socks to one side. "They think it's a *gut* idea for you to take a turn." He grabbed her by the waist and lifted her onto the surface.

She gasped and clung to the netting to keep herself on her feet. "Give me a warning next time."

"I gave you one this time."

"Not much of one."

"But it was a warning." He swung up and began moving along the unsteady surface.

It was more fun than it looked, though it wasn't easy keeping his balance. Every downward motion seemed to create a stronger upward one. Starting slowly, he increased the pressure he put on the trampoline, jumping a bit higher each time. The twins cheered when he flapped his arms like a bird taking flight.

Spinning through the strengthening wind, which blew in heated gusts, he faced Clara. "You aren't jumping."

"I'm trying to stay on my feet. It's easier to give the twins advice than to do this myself."

"It's easier if you jump."

She laced the fingers of one hand through another section of the netting and held her *kapp* in place with the other as the wind swirled its strings across her cheeks. "I'll have to take your word for it."

He bounced hard, and she released the netting to throw out her arms to try to keep her balance. Grasping her hands, he pulled her to face him. "No, you don't."

"Isaiah! I'm going to break my neck!"

He halted his bouncing and steadied her as she was about to tumble off her feet. "Take it slow, Clara. You'll see how much fun it is."

"That's your opinion," she retorted, but gave him a saucy grin.

Again he began the slow, steady bouncing. He didn't release her hands as they went up and down together. Her grin became a gleeful smile when they bounced higher and higher.

"It's fun!" she shouted.

Thrilled he'd convinced her to toss aside her overwhelming sense of duty and enjoy herself, he looked into her pretty eyes that sparkled like ice in the pitcher. He was lost in their earth-brown depths. Hearing something like a heartfelt sigh, he wasn't sure if it came from his throat or hers. There was nothing in the world but the two of them and the slick surface of the trampoline beneath their bare feet.

As he thought that, he slipped when a gust of wind pushed him sideways. He fell forward but twisted to avoid hitting Clara. As he struck the trampoline, his breath bursting out of him, he realized she'd tumbled backward at the same time and had rolled out of his way. Before he could get to his feet, she'd crawled out of the trampoline and was standing on the grass, panting from exertion.

Isaiah climbed down, too, and she halted him from saying anything by pointing to the trampoline and shaking her head.

"I've learned my lesson," she said, leaning on the netting. "I'll leave this to you and the twins. This isn't something I can do by myself."

Ammon looked at her, as serious as a deacon scolding a member of the *Leit*. "In the Bible, it says, 'I can do all things through Christ which strengtheneth me.'"

She smiled. "It does, but I'm not sure if Paul had trampolines in mind when he wrote to the Phillipians."

"It means *all* things," the little boy insisted.

"He's right." Isaiah wasn't sure how much longer he could hold in his laughter at the little boy's attempt to reassure her. "It does say *all* things. We don't get to pick or choose."

Ammon nodded. "That's what *Mamm* says." Sudden tears flooded his blue eyes. "I miss *Mamm*. I miss her and *Daed*."

Gasps came from his siblings, and they frowned, wanting him to stop talking about their parents. Isaiah was too shocked to move, but Clara didn't hesitate. She went to her knees to wrap her arms around the *kind*. He threw himself against her and sobbed.

The other twins stared at Ammon, and Isaiah could see them struggling to contain their grief. It was impossible. One after another, their faces fell.

When Clara reached out and gathered Nettie Mae to her, the little girl dissolved into sobs. Isaiah wrapped his arms around Nancy and Andrew. They cried, not like young *kinder*, but with the bone-deep weeping of someone far older who had suffered the worst blows life could bring their way.

An abrupt detonation of thunder followed a flash of lightning. He scooped up the little girl and boy and ran toward the house. Clara followed with Ammon and Nettie Mae. As soon as they entered the kitchen, all four *kinder* ran into the living room and crouched by the sofa, their heart-rending cries filling the silence between the rumbles of thunder.

"Go to them," Clara urged. "They need you."

"I don't know what to say to them." Something released inside him as he admitted he was at a loss for what to do.

"Say to them what you'd say to anyone else." She grasped his arms and looked at him. "Say to them what you wish someone had said to you when Rose died."

He stared, riveted by her advice. Why hadn't he thought of that himself? Many times, he'd wanted someone to sit and listen to him talk—or not talk—about Rose without telling him he was brave or he was strong enough to bear the burden of his loss.

He took one stiff step, then another toward where the *kinder* huddled together, looking for comfort from one another. Realization flashed like lightning through his mind. They believed they could find solace only from each other in their shared loss.

Sitting on the floor beside them, he didn't touch them. Instead he spread his arms in both directions along the sofa cushions, offering them an open invitation when they were ready. He wasn't sure if they were aware he'd come over to them because they hid their faces behind their hands or each other's shoulder.

"You know your *daed* and *mamm* would have come home to you if they could have, don't you?" he asked.

None of the youngsters replied, but they froze, and he knew they were listening to what he said. *God, please send me the right words. Let me be Your conduit to their hearts.*

"It's true," he went on aloud. "There's nothing your *mamm* and *daed* would have wanted more than to return to you."

"But they didn't!" The pain in Andrew's voice sliced through Isaiah, because he empathized with the boy. Being left behind by someone you love, especially when that person wouldn't have chosen to go, was agony.

"I know, and it hurts when I think about things I want to say to them."

"You too?" Nancy raised her head.

"All the time. Your *daed* was excited to see the gates when they were finished, and I couldn't wait to show him, but I couldn't. Not like I used to, but in my heart, I know he's near and celebrating with me."

"But," Nettie Mae said around a sob, "I talk. *Mamm* no talk. *Daed* no talk. Want to hear them!"

"Don't listen here." He pointed to his left ear before tapping the center of her narrow chest. "Listen here. In your heart."

"Where God is?" asked Andrew in awe.

"Ja." Envy struck him again, but this time for the boy's simple faith that hadn't wavered in the wake of his parents' deaths. He wished his had been as strong. Could it be again? All he needed to do was walk the path God had given him. Now wasn't the time to be thinking of his troubles. He needed to help the twins, who were looking to him for help.

Clara stepped forward and sat on the other side of the *kinder.* She held out her arms, not saying a word. The girls launched themselves into her embrace. She held them close and comforted them. The boys inched nearer. She motioned for them to join in the group hug. Andrew and Ammon threw their arms around their siblings.

From the center of the hug, Clara began to sing *Jesus Loves Me*, and the youngsters joined one after another. When they stumbled on the *Englisch* words and looked ready to cry again, she switched to *Deitsch*. She began a different hymn when they finished, and the *kinder* sang until their tears stopped. She kept singing as the youngsters' eyelids grew heavy. While the twins fell asleep around her like a litter of puppies, she continued singing, making the hymns sound like both a prayer and a lullaby.

She extracted herself from among the *kinder* as the last one nodded off, worn out by the day's events and the release of the emotions they'd kept bottled up. Walking into the kitchen, she leaned her hands on the table and sighed. "I know I shouldn't pray for them to be able to set their grief aside because that would mean forgetting their parents. But for a few moments…" She glanced at him as he rose to follow her. "I'm sorry. I shouldn't have said that."

"It's fine. I know what you mean. It's not easy to walk between the *gut* memories and the grief. But it's a beginning for their healing."

"How about your healing, Isaiah? When is that going to start?"

Words failed him as he saw the sympathy on her face. There must be something he could say, but he had no idea what. As thunder crashed around them and wind-driven rain lashed the windows, the storm within him was louder. A calm would settle around the hills once the clouds passed, but it wouldn't be easy to quiet the turbulence inside him.

She raised a hand toward him, but he pushed himself away from the table and strode into the *dawdi haus*, shutting the door. He was as brittle as improperly tempered cast iron. If she touched him, he'd shatter as the metal would when struck by his hammer. He had no idea how he'd ever put himself together again.

Chapter Thirteen

Isaiah gave the long, flat piece of metal a final hit before putting it to one side rather than into the coals again. Stepping away, he wiped his forehead with the back of his hand. It was impossible to concentrate on work. He hadn't been prepared yesterday for the twins opening up about their grief over their parents' deaths. He was grateful for Clara's help as well as her pushing him to do what he needed to as the *kinder*'s guardian. But he kept hearing Clara's questions in his mind.

How about your healing, Isaiah? When is that going to start?

He should have answered her instead of walking away. He would have answered her if he'd known what to say. He'd wanted to say his healing was well underway, but he wouldn't lie. The more he thought about her penetrating questions that had stripped away the defenses he'd kept in place, the more annoyed he got. She didn't understand. Nobody did.

God does. The taunting, truthful voice in his mind burst out.

He ignored it as he tried to ignore Clara's questions. It was impossible.

The sound of a horse and buggy outside his smithy was a welcome respite from his thoughts. Or it was until he saw Curtis Mast step out of the buggy.

Isaiah silenced his groan as his father-in-law strode toward him. Forcing a smile, he called a greeting to Curtis.

"Busy?" the older man asked.

"Always, but being busy is better than not being busy, ain't so?"

Curtis nodded, then said, "I know it's not our way for a *daed* to interfere, but Ida Mae and I were wondering if we should plant extra celery in the garden this year."

The Amish tradition of serving celery at weddings demanded extra rows be sowed in the gardens of families expecting to host a wedding after the harvest. Any family who put in extra spent most of the summer warding off curious questions about which son or daughter was marrying and to whom. Only when the couple's intentions were published during announcements at a church Sunday service were suspicions confirmed or dashed.

But why was Curtis asking him?

"I don't have an answer for you," Isaiah said as he lifted off his leather apron and hung it on a hook beyond his forge.

"You haven't made your mind up yet?"

"Yet?"

"We're two grown men, Isaiah. You married one of my daughters. Don't you think, as part of the family already, you should let me know what your plans are since you're walking out with one of my other daughters?"

Isaiah opened his mouth, then shut it. He was too astonished and wasn't sure what to say. He tried again. "Did Orpha say…?"

"She hasn't said anything, but I've seen how she looks when she comes home late after walking out with you."

"I'm not walking out with Orpha."

"What?" Curtis's eyes grew as round as a coal on the forge.

"I don't know what she's said—"

"She hasn't said anything, which is why I assumed you two had reached a serious understanding." He tugged off his straw hat and rolled the uneven brim between his fingers. "So you're not walking out with her?"

"No. My time's spent here or with the Beachy *kinder*. Orpha must be walking out with someone else."

His father-in-law stared at him in disbelief, then sighed. "I'd hoped you would decide to marry her because I know you're a *gut* man who would provide a *gut* home for her. But apparently she's decided on someone else."

"It would seem so." His calm voice hid his exultation that Orpha wouldn't be pressuring him any longer to marry her. "It sounds as if congratulations will soon be in order, Curtis."

"Time will tell, but at least I know whoever she's with is plain because he drives a buggy. It's not like the bishop's Katie Kay who has jumped the fence to the *Englischers*."

"Is that for sure?" He couldn't ask Reuben, who must be torn up to have his daughter turn her back on her people.

And Micah… Isaiah wondered how his younger brother was dealing with these rumors. Micah had been busy on several construction projects, and Isaiah hadn't had much time to talk with him. He needed to make time.

Curtis shrugged, his mind on his daughters rather than the bishop's. "She's gone to live with an *Englisch* girl, so who knows whether she'll come back or not?" Putting his hat on again, he turned to leave. "If you hear who Orpha is spending time with, let me know."

The older man was gone before Isaiah could reply, which was just as well. No matter how bothersome Orpha had been, he wasn't going to carry any tales he heard to her *daed*. She was Rose's sister, and he owed her that much loyalty.

Clara had been delighted when Isaiah offered to bring pizza home for supper that night. It'd been such a treat when they'd had it after Ammon's hearing test, and the *kinder* would enjoy having it again. They'd been subdued, but brightened when she mentioned having pizza.

She wished the promise of pizza topped with pepperoni and mushrooms was enough to get herself on an even keel. Throughout the day, it was as if a shadow draped over her, something she hadn't experienced since her arrival in Paradise Springs. She wasn't sure if the shadow was from the storm of tears yesterday or if caused by the thunderstorms rolling through one after another during the afternoon. She was on edge.

But why? She should be rejoicing that the twins had realized it was okay to show their grief. It might be the first step toward convincing them to laugh again. But how could she revel in their breakthrough when Isaiah clung to his grief? She wished she could understand how he was able to offer the *kinder* what they needed when he refused to accept the same from her. Although she didn't want to believe what she could see, it seemed to her that he acted as if he deserved to be miserable. It made no sense.

Or did it? She'd been unhappy since she received Lonnie's letter. Only because she'd come to Paradise Springs and met Isaiah and the twins had she relearned how to smile and tease and enjoy simple, *wunderbaar* things.

Or maybe her uneasiness had nothing to do with him and the twins. Maybe it was from the two letters delivered that morning from the *kinder*'s grandparents. Like the one from their *aenti*, the letters were filled with news about where the couple was working in Africa. These had been written with the twins in mind, so she didn't have to edit as she read to them, but neither letter mentioned if or when their grandparents were coming to Paradise Springs.

How much longer would it be before they arrived? Clara had been at the Beachys' house for more than a month. She wasn't in a hurry to leave because she loved spending time with the twins. Having an hour in the evening to talk with Isaiah was a blessing, too, though she must make sure they didn't end up holding hands as they had on the trampoline. Had he guessed she'd stumbled because her knees had gone weak at his touch?

"You're wasting time better spent on doing something other than fretting," she chided herself.

While the boys played with their trucks and the girls with plastic horses they made gallop across the floor, Clara cut out clothes for the twins from the fabric she'd found in the other storage room upstairs. They were growing fast, especially the boys. They needed play clothes and nicer clothing to wear to services on a church Sunday. Today was a *gut* day to spend with the task because she could sit near the *kinder*, ready to offer a hug whenever it was needed, and not seem to be hovering.

The twins noticed what she was doing and asked which garment was for which *kind*. The girls were delighted with the light green and dark blue fabric she had for their dresses. As they wore the same size, they discussed which of them would wear which color first. The boys were less interested in color and more concerned that their new trousers didn't have hems halfway to their knees as youngsters their age often did, so new pants didn't need to be made every time they grew another inch. She assured them the hems wouldn't be any deeper than Isaiah's, but didn't mention why. With the *kinder* due to join their Mennonite relatives, their clothing could be quite different. She had no idea how conservative their *aenti* and grandparents were.

As the sky clouded for another round of thunder, lightning and rain, Clara put aside her sewing. The twins were getting antsy being stuck in the house, so she asked, "I've got my scissors out. Would you like me to cut your hair, boys?" She smiled at Andrew and Ammon. "Did your *mamm* cut your hair in the kitchen or bathroom?"

"Kitchen," Andrew replied, then lowered his eyes as he spoke about his *mamm*.

She guessed he didn't want anyone else to see tears in his eyes. Giving his shoulders a gentle squeeze, she wasn't surprised when he leaned into her instead of pulling away as he might have before yesterday. Perhaps now that they'd started to release their grief, they'd heal. It would take a very long time before the mention of their parents' names didn't cause pain. She hoped time would help reminiscences of the happy times eclipse their sorrow.

"*Mamm*'s shears here," Nancy said, opening the drawer near the stove where Clara kept the matches and the other odds and ends needed in the kitchen.

"*Gut.*" She reached in the drawer and pulled out the scissors. She also used a book of matches to light the propane lamp over the table as the clouds continued to thicken. Tossing the matches in the drawer, she closed it and said, "Please get me two bath towels, Nancy. You know how many two are?"

The little girl held up three fingers.

With a smile, Clara lowered one. "Put one towel on each of those fingers, and you'll have two towels. Nettie Mae, will you get a clothespin from the laundry basket?"

"One?" She held up a single finger.

"Perfect."

"What about me?" Ammon asked.

"You can help by getting one of the booster seats the girls use while Andrew pulls out the chair we'll use."

The *kinder* scurried in four different directions and did as she asked. Oh, how she was going to miss their eagerness to help! And their sweet smiles and their many questions. Tears welled up in her eyes, but she dashed them aside as she took the towels from Nancy. She put one on the floor and set on top of it the chair Andrew had moved away from the table. Ammon placed the booster seat on the chair.

When she motioned for him to climb up, Ammon scrambled like a squirrel climbing a tree. She wrapped the second towel around his neck and held it in place with the clothespin beneath his chin. After she had him hand her his hearing aid, because she didn't want to risk snipping its thin wire, she put it in her pocket for safekeeping. She took a small mirror Melvin probably had used for shaving off the wall by the sink and handed it to the little boy.

"Be careful," she said.

"I will." His shoulders stiffened with his resolve.

The other *kinder* watched and chattered with each other and her as she cut Ammon's almost white hair. It was as fine as corn silk and clung to her fingers. She shook them to send the strands drifting to the towel on the floor.

The kitchen door opened, and Isaiah came in as Clara was finishing the last section of Andrew's hair.

"No pizza?" she asked.

"I thought we'd go to the pizza parlor and eat it there," he replied.

The twins cheered, and she had to put a hand on Andrew's shoulder to keep him from jumping like the others. She made the final snips before unhooking the towel from around his neck. "There." She shook the towel over the wastebasket, making sure the hair fell into it. "All done. As soon as I clean up, we can go for pizza."

"But what about *Onkel* Isaiah?" asked Ammon, who was talking more and more each day.

At that thought, she handed the device to him, and he slipped it into place with ease. It hid behind his ear and was almost invisible beneath his hair. More than once, she'd had to peer at him to make sure it hadn't fallen off.

"Aren't you going to cut his hair?" Ammon continued. "It's too long, too."

"Ja," interjected Nancy from where she was dancing around Isaiah with her twin sister. "Cut his hair, too! *Mamm* cut Andrew's and Ammon's and *Daed*'s."

The little girl halted as she mentioned her parents. Her face didn't crumble, but she was on the verge of tears. As she had with Andrew earlier, Clara put her arm around the youngster's thin shoulders and gave her a gentle hug. The little girl grabbed two handfuls of Clara's apron and pressed her face into it.

Knowing she needed to do something to lighten the mood in the kitchen, Clara asked, "Well, Isaiah, do you want me to cut your hair?"

Isaiah gave the slightest shrug, which meant the decision was in her hands. Hoping a quick trim of his hair would bring back the *kinder*'s *gut* spirits, she motioned toward the chair.

Andrew had already pulled the booster seat off it by the time Isaiah crossed the kitchen and sat. The twins gathered around the table to watch her cut his hair.

"Ready when you are," he said with a smile and a wink for the youngsters.

She hoped they'd giggle at him, but they only grinned. She had to be content with that.

Moving behind Isaiah, she listened to the twins tease him while she wrapped the towel around his shoulders and closed it with the clothespin. Where the towel had draped over the boys to their waists, it barely covered his broad shoulders.

She averted her eyes and picked up her scissors. "Your hair is longer than the boys' was," she said as she clipped and combed and cut more as he watched in the mirror to make sure his hair was the proper style and length set by the district's *Ordnung*.

"Getting my hair cut wasn't at the top of my list of priorities in the past few weeks."

"I know, but you don't want the deacon coming around to chide you for letting it grow to your shoulders."

He smiled. "You know if Marlin comes here, it won't be to chide me about my hair."

"True." His hair was almost as soft as the boys', but its color was much richer. "And it's true you'd do anything to avoid his matchmaking. Even let me cut your hair."

"You did a *gut* job with Ammon's and Andrew's, so why not?" He continued to tease her and the twins as she made sure his hair was even.

When she stepped around him to do the front, his gaze rose and locked with hers. Her fingers froze as she held a section of his hair between them. Had she believed cutting his hair would be no different from doing the boys'?

His almost gray eyes were unlike the bright blue of the *kinder*'s, but revealed so much more. The emotions within them were not the least bit childish. Nor was the tingling response his steady gaze created within her.

She dropped the hank of hair and started to move away. Gently he caught her wrist, keeping her where she stood.

"Don't," he whispered.

Don't what? Don't move away? Leave his hair half-cut? Look at him as if her heart was about to dance right out of her?

"Clara, it's okay." His quiet words wouldn't reach the twins, who'd gotten bored and gone to color in the living room. "We know where we stand." One corner of his mouth quirked, and she couldn't tell if he was trying to grin or trying not to. "Okay. Where you stand and where I sit."

She didn't smile as she finished trimming his hair. What would he say if she said her brain had lost complete control of her heart? She *knew* it would be foolish to fall in love with a man who had told her right from the beginning he didn't want to marry her. Hadn't she learned anything from her relationship with Lonnie?

But this was different.

With Lonnie, she had fallen hard and fast, but, in retrospect, she realized it hadn't been more than a crush and the opportunity to have a life with a man who appreciated her instead of believing she made a mess of everything, as her *daed* did.

But this love—and she couldn't pretend it was anything else—for Isaiah was real.

Utterly real.

Real and unrequited, and she was a fool to heed her heart when it was leading her to a grief greater than she'd ever known.

Chapter Fourteen

The news of an Amish family in a neighboring district needing money to pay for the hospital bills after the *daed* severed his finger while repairing a piece of equipment spread rapidly through Paradise Springs. His two sons had been in the field with him and had swiftly brought help, so there was hope the reattached finger could be saved. Isaiah heard about the accident the next morning when one of his regular customers came in to get his horses reshod. By the time he returned home that evening, Clara had learned about the tragic events from his *mamm*. Reuben had told her. The family of the injured man was in their bishop's other district.

By the next morning, someone had come to his brother's store with a stack of flyers announcing a chicken barbecue to raise money for the family. Amos put the flyers next to the cash register where everyone could see them, and he slipped copies into each bag of groceries when people checked out. The barbecue was going to be held at the school not far from where the man's family lived, about two miles from the Beachys' house.

Clara offered to bring her special potato salad along

with other favorite dishes, and Isaiah packed a dozen horseshoes for the men to enjoy tossing. The twins were excited to wear the new clothing she'd made for them, and Clara agreed, though the garments would come home with green splotches from playing in the grass. Vinegar would loosen the stains, and she'd made the blue dresses, dark pants and light green shirts as play clothes.

Isaiah hitched up Chip to the family buggy while Clara made sure the older twins were sitting as still as possible while they held covered dishes on their laps. The girls perched on the front seat between Clara and him. Nettie Mae held a package of napkins, and Nancy cuddled a plastic bag filled with paper cups. The youngsters looked serious about their obligations to get what they held to the school without letting it fall.

"All set?" he asked when Clara climbed in, tying her black bonnet over her *kapp*.

"*Ja*."

"Checked the stove and the faucets?"

"*Ja*. I know the Bible doesn't say we're better safe than sorry, but it's something my *mamm* taught."

"Mine, too." He smiled as he slapped the reins on Chip, and they began driving toward the road.

As they approached the school, the road became crowded with buggies and cars and pickup trucks. It was like a mud sale but in the summer when nobody had to worry about ruining their shoes in the mire.

The aroma of chickens sizzling over a charcoal fire reached Isaiah before he drew the buggy to a halt. In spite of himself, his mouth watered. He hoped his stomach wouldn't grumble and embarrass him. Parking the buggy where a boy directed, he got out and helped Clara with the *kinder* before he went to unhitch Chip. The boy who was handling the parking wrote the number thirty-two on the side of the buggy with a piece of chalk, then marked Chip's halter with the same number before turning him out in a nearby field with the other horses.

By the time he was finished, Clara and the twins had vanished into the crowd. He hoped it wouldn't take too long to find them after he delivered the horseshoes to the near side of the school where they could set up a game. The *kinder*'s ball field was on the other side of the building, far enough away to keep everyone safe.

Isaiah drew in another deep breath of the delicious scent of cooking chicken and the unmistakable aromas of lemonade and chocolate. As soon as he found Clara and the *kinder*, they'd enjoy a *gut* meal.

He edged through the crowd, greeting those he knew and nodding to the people he didn't. His steps slowed when he saw Orpha standing by one table and putting out bowls of baked beans. She glanced at him, smiled and turned away to talk to Larry Nissley. Isaiah saw Larry was grinning like a fool. Larry must be the man walking out with Rose's sister. Orpha was quick-witted, and Larry was quick to speak before he thought. Theirs would be an interesting match, but he wished them well because they looked happy together.

"Having second thoughts?" Daniel and his twin brother Micah joined him. The two dark-haired brothers looked almost identical except Daniel had a cleft in his chin and Micah didn't.

Isaiah accepted the glass of lemonade Micah held out to him. "Second thoughts about what?"

"Orpha Mast. Word was going around you two would be making an announcement this fall."

"You know better," Isaiah said after he took a sip of the fragrant lemonade, "than to listen to rumors."

"I told you." Micah nudged his twin with his elbow. "Isaiah planning to marry Orpha was a rumor."

"But what about the other rumor?" asked Daniel, and his eyes began to twinkle.

"Which rumor would that be?" Isaiah enjoyed his brothers' teasing. Often when he saw Andrew and Ammon jesting with each other, he thought of how the Stoltzfus siblings always found ways to make each other laugh.

Laugh? How were they going to convince the Beachy *kinder* it was okay to laugh? He'd tried everything he could think of, and Clara had done the same, but the twins still refused to laugh. When asked why, their answer was the same. They'd been told not to laugh. Who could have done such a thing to young boys and girls?

"I'll give you a hint," Micah said. "Starts with *C* and sounds a lot like Clara Ebersol and you walking out together."

"Oh, no, not you too." He gave an emoted groan.

The twins exchanged a glance before Daniel asked, "Us too what?"

"Matchmaking."

Micah held up his hands. "Whoa there, big brother. All I did was ask if you'd heard the rumor about you two. A simple question."

Isaiah had to admit his brother was right. He apologized and added, "It seems anywhere I go with Clara and the *kinder*, someone is trying to make sure we spend time together."

"I thought you liked her." Daniel's dark brows lowered. "Is there some problem with her?"

"No. She's very nice, but nice isn't enough to base a marriage on."

"No?" Daniel began counting off on his fingers.

"Ruth's husband, Elmer, is a nice guy. Joshua's Rebekah is nice. Ezra's Leah is nice. Amos's—"

Isaiah chuckled and held up his hands in surrender. "You don't have to go through the whole list of our siblings and their spouses to make your point."

"Gut."

"But in addition to being nice people, our siblings' spouses are in love with our brothers and sisters."

"And Clara is in love with you." Jeremiah, the brother who was a year younger than Isaiah, said from behind him.

Looking over his shoulder, Isaiah hid his shock. Jeremiah was the quiet one in their family. He spoke only when he believed he had something to add to the conversation. He was the least likely to try to get a rise out of someone or to tease them. If anyone in the family could be described as serious, it was Jeremiah. And Jeremiah was saying Clara was in love with Isaiah, as if it were the least unexpected news in the world.

"She loves the *kinder*, not me." Something sliced into his heart at his own words. "Once the twins' family comes for them, she'll head home. End of story."

"Stories often end with happily-ever-after." Daniel's smile broadened. Draping an arm over Jeremiah's shoulders, he said, "I saw ice cream being brought out. You know you'll want a sample."

Isaiah was relieved when the two walked away, but was surprised when Micah remained. He liked ice cream as much as Jeremiah did, and they'd often vied to see who could get the last spoonful out of the container.

He waited for his brother to say something, but when Micah remained silent, he asked, "How are you doing, Micah?"

"You know how you're annoyed about matchmaking?"

"*Ja.*"

"That's how irked I get when someone asks me how I am. And there have been a lot asking since Katie Kay Lapp left the community."

"That's very irked."

Micah nodded. "Very, very irked."

"But how are you?" Isaiah asked, serious. "And I'm not asking because of Katie Kay."

"I'm fine, and that hasn't changed because she's gone. Katie Kay and I were something I thought might work out some day, but it's not going to happen."

"Sorry that—"

"Don't be sorry, Isaiah. I'm not." He winked and chuckled. "To prove that, I'll tell you that I've noticed Tillie Mast giving me the eye lately. Maybe I'll see if she needs a ride home tonight."

"Be careful with a Mast girl. Curtis and Ida Mae are ready to marry them off to anyone who looks at them twice."

Micah laughed and slapped him on the shoulder. "Look who's talking. The man everyone is talking about. They're interested in whether you'll marry Orpha or Clara by year's end. I've been asked about that close to a thousand times."

"You're exaggerating."

"*Ja*, but not by much. Hey, it's my turn to toss horseshoes. See you later, bro."

Isaiah smiled as his brother crossed the schoolyard to where the horseshoe games were underway. Micah had picked up a lot of *Englisch* slang while working on various construction projects with *Englischers*.

Where were Clara and the twins? The crowd seemed

to be growing by the minute, and he wanted to make sure those hungry youngsters got fed before the food was gone.

When he found them, the boys were already discussing if they wanted their chicken with the barbecue sauce or without. The girls were more interested in the pretty cakes set in a row on a pair of tables. They smiled, along with Clara, when he suggested they join the line waiting to select what they wanted.

It took him and Clara as well as Neva Fry to get their six plates from the serving line to one of the blankets spread on the grass. He thanked the schoolteacher, who waved and hurried to help other parents with more *kinder* than hands to load and carry plates.

They enjoyed the delicious meal, and he smiled when the boys asked about getting seconds. Nobody left hungry from an Amish fund-raising meal. He went with the boys to get more chicken and sides. Though he wondered how they'd eat everything, their plates were soon clean again.

"Why don't we walk around a bit before dessert?" Clara asked when the twins began to discuss which sweets they wanted. "Let what we've eaten settle a bit."

"The best idea I've heard in a long time." Isaiah pushed himself to his feet and smiled as he offered his hand to help her up. When she smiled and let him take her hand, his heart felt lighter than it had in longer than he could recall. Though she withdrew her fingers from his as she turned to help the *kinder* pick up their plates and forks so they could carry them to one of the long plastic washtubs, she wasn't scurrying away as she had before.

He was too aware of her fingers close to his as they walked side by side among the crowd. He itched to grasp hold of her slender hand, but he couldn't be unaware of the eyes following them and the twins. Giving the rumors substance would be the worst thing he could do for her, the twins and himself. Clara would be leaving once the *kinder* were settled. He couldn't forget that, but he also knew he'd never forget her.

"Isaiah, can I talk to you for a moment?" came an all-too-familiar voice from behind him.

He turned to see Orpha. "Certainly."

"If you'll excuse us," Clara began, reaching to herd the twins away.

Orpha put out her hand. "No, please stay, Clara. You should hear this, too."

When Clara bent and whispered something to the twins, they nodded and scampered away toward where his *mamm* was putting plates of cookies and sliced pieces of pie on a folding table. Isaiah smiled, realizing Ammon had been able to hear Clara's soft voice as the others did. What a blessing she'd been in the *kinder*'s lives as well as in his!

"I don't want to keep you, but I do want to say I'm sorry." Orpha rubbed her hands together as she looked from him to Clara. "I shouldn't have taken out my frustration with my parents on the two of you. Neither of you have been anything but kind to me." She turned to Clara. "What you said at Hersheypark about spreading vitriol made me realize how I was making you into scapegoats. *Danki* for the reminder that our Lord taught us to treat each other as we'd want to be treated. And I wasn't, but I'm going to try harder to do that."

"*Danki*, Orpha," she said. "I know it isn't easy for you to say this."

"It isn't, but it's easier than it would have been if I hadn't discovered what love is. Real love." She glanced toward where Larry was pretending not to be watching them. Averting her eyes, she said, "I'm not sure where discovering love will take me. Or when, but I know I'd be foolish to settle for anything less than true love." A sad smile edged along her lips. "Rose told me that. I hope you'll forgive me."

"You know we already have," Isaiah replied as Clara nodded beside him. *Now if I could forgive myself.* He was glad those words were only in his mind. They sounded pitiful and complaining...and they were. Why wouldn't his thoughts heed him? Forgiveness was necessary if one wanted to be closer to God.

Did he want to keep a space between him and God? Like Orpha's anger being spewed at him and Clara, it was the easy way out. But not God's way for him.

His eye was caught by Reuben coming to stand beside *Mamm.* She laid a gentle hand on his sleeve. She left it there for the length of time it took Isaiah to blink, but he couldn't miss the way the bishop slanted toward her. The two motions were as loud as a shout.

Reuben and *Mamm* were falling in love. No, he corrected himself. They *were* in love. Their second chance at a once-in-a-lifetime love, a true gift from God. He looked to where his oldest brother Joshua sat with his family and his second wife. Joshua had been granted that *wunderbaar* gift also.

He heard his brothers' voices echoing from his memory. They'd believed Clara was in love with him. Was it possible for him to receive the same blessing?

Ja, came the soft voice of his conscience. *It's possible because you've already been blessed with the second chance.*

He watched Clara assisting the twins to carry their desserts. Dear, sweet Clara who had set aside her life to come to help him and the *kinder*. She loved the twins without reserve, but, as he'd sensed almost from the beginning, she held back a part of herself from everyone else, including him.

Had God brought her into his life to help him see he could trust the path set out for him? Or was Isaiah supposed to help *her* heal? It was an unexpected thought and a startling one he needed to consider and pray about, because he'd never guessed that helping her might be the way to help himself.

Clara swung Nancy's and Nettie Mae's hands as they stood in line to wait for ice cream. The little girls bounced from one foot to the other and chattered like squirrels as they discussed which flavor to pick. With the choice of chocolate, chocolate peanut butter, strawberry and vanilla, it wasn't an easy decision. In addition, they could select chocolate sauce or crushed pineapple to go on top of their scoops.

"What you want, *Aenti* Clara?" asked Nancy.

"I'm trying to decide between strawberry and vanilla."

"Want chocolate," Nettie Mae announced, and people around them grinned.

"Me, too." Nancy paused, then added, "But peanut butter, too."

That set off another round of discussion between the little girls. Clara listened with a smile. The conversation would keep them busy while the line inched forward.

Scanning the crowd that had grown larger, she knew the injured man's family would be grateful for the generosity of those who had donated food and come to share it and time with each other. Clara recognized many people, but more she didn't. She wondered if the unfamiliar plain folks were from Reuben's other district. A lot of *Englischers* had come to the chicken barbecue, as well. She'd met a few of them at Amos's store or around Paradise Springs, but most were strangers.

A gasp caught in her throat as she stared at a man striding through the crowd as if he were the host of the gathering. It wasn't possible, was it? She found him again among the crowd. Her eyes weren't fooling her. Nobody walked through a crowd as Floyd Ebersol did. His head was high, and his eyes scanned those around him as if looking for someone. But she knew the truth. He was keeping track of those who watched him.

Pride was an abomination to the Amish, but not her *daed*. He wanted to be the center of attention wherever he went. More than once, he'd said he hoped the lot would fall on him, so he could serve as an ordained minister or deacon. He'd admitted to aspiring to be a bishop, though she doubted he could be as humble as their bishop or Reuben Lapp was.

She looked around, but didn't see her *mamm*. It wasn't a big surprise, because *Mamm* had seldom left the house since she'd broken her hip. She now walked with a painful limp. Many times Clara had wanted to ask her *mamm* if she stayed in the house, except for chores, because *Daed* didn't want to share any attention with her. Clara prayed it wasn't because her *daed* deemed *Mamm* unworthy of being seen with him because she hobbled.

Reaching the front of the line, she focused on helping the girls order their ice cream. She shook her head when asked if she wanted some, too. She couldn't imagine putting anything in her roiling stomach. As she turned to lead Nancy and Nettie Mae to a spot where they could eat their ice cream before it melted on their clothes, she saw her *daed* walking in her direction with a determined expression.

"Go and sit with the boys," she said to the twins. "I'll be there in a minute."

With grins already colored pink and brown from their ice cream, the two girls obeyed. She watched, and they'd reached the boys just as her *daed* stopped in front of her.

"Clara," he said as a greeting.

"How are you doing, *Daed*? Is *Mamm* here? I didn't realize you were coming. You should have…" Her voice faded when his brows lowered in his customary frown. This time she deserved his silent censure. She'd been babbling.

"I hear you're being courted by a minister." He didn't let her reply before he said, "Of course, you must not make a mess of this as you did with Lonnie Wickey."

Reminding her *daed* that nothing she'd done had led to Lonnie marrying another woman would be a waste of breath. "No," she said in the calmest tone she could muster, "I'm not being courted by a minister. Isaiah Stoltzfus, who is the guardian of the *kinder* I'm taking care of, is a minister, it's true, but we aren't walking out together."

"You should encourage him. A minister would be a *gut* match for you, and as a widower, he must be eager to wed and would likely overlook what happened with your previous betrothal."

Clara was shocked speechless. In spite of his chiding about her shortcomings, she hadn't expected her *daed* to think her unworthy of being loved for herself.

"Floyd Ebersol?" asked Isaiah from behind her.

She closed her eyes. How much of her *daed*'s comments had he overheard? She wished the ground would open right where she stood and swallow her.

"Ja?" Daed squinted at Isaiah. Did he need glasses as Nettie Mae did? If he thought they made him look old or less dignified, he'd eschew them as the little girl had tried to. "You are?"

"Isaiah Stoltzfus." He smiled as if no tension hung in the air. "I want to tell you, Floyd, that your daughter has been a blessing. She has been a great help with the twins. *Danki* for allowing her to come and help us. Her kindness toward us speaks well of her upbringing."

Clara was astonished as Isaiah continued, saying what *Daed* would want to hear. Each time Isaiah praised her, he made it sound as if her *daed* was the reason she'd done well. In a way, it was true, because she'd treated the twins as she'd prayed he would treat her. With love and understanding instead of impatience and unreasonable expectations.

Her *daed* preened, accepting Isaiah's words as his due, and he smiled when Isaiah said, "I'm sorry to take Clara away from you, but we need to check on the twins."

"Of course." He waved them away.

Clara kept her feet from sending her running away at top speed. Instead, she walked beside Isaiah. When he glanced over his shoulder, she did the same and saw her *daed* talking with another man.

Isaiah grabbed her arm and pulled her behind the school. Sitting her on the back steps, he sat beside her. She started to rise, saying she had to check on the twins, but he halted her.

"Leah and Mandy are watching them. They'll be fine." He brushed a strand of hair from her face. "But what about you? How are you?"

"I'm okay, too."

"You looked pretty upset, so I decided to butt in. I figured I owed you for when you saved me from Orpha's machinations, but I was surprised when someone said the man you were talking to was your *daed*."

"Danki." She looked at her folded hands. If she said more, the jagged tears in her throat might burst out in sobs.

"Be honest with me, Clara."

"I am."

He shook his head. "Not about why seeing your *daed* upsets you."

Raising her head, she asked, "How much did you hear of what he said?"

"Not much. With everyone around, it's hard enough to hear myself, let alone anyone else." He put one hand over her clasped hands. "What are you afraid I heard?"

"Not afraid. Ashamed."

"Ashamed? You? Clara Ebersol, you're the most loving, generous person I've ever met. You've put your life on hold to help strangers with bereaved *kinder*, and you've helped those *kinder* begin to heal. What could a person like you be ashamed of?"

She should put a halt to the conversation, but her heart demanded to unburden itself to someone she could trust. "My *daed* expects me to be perfect."

"Nobody is perfect."

"Floyd Ebersol's daughter must be. He won't let me forget what he sees as my greatest failure because he believes it reflects on him, too."

"What failure?"

Clara plunged into the story of how she'd been courted by Lonnie Wickey, the promises made and the promises broken. It took less time to tell than she'd guessed.

"But where did *you* fail?" Isaiah asked when she was done.

"I failed in my *daed*'s eyes by humiliating my family. I wish I could make him see I never want to do anything to hurt him and *Mamm*."

He lifted her hands between his and sighed. "There are some battles you'll never win."

"So I should give up?"

He shook his head. "No, but you should accept what's impossible to change. And it appears your *daed* is one of those unchangeable parts of your life."

"*Danki*, Isaiah. I guess I've got a lot of lessons to learn."

"All of us do." His gaze searched her face, and she wondered what he was looking for and if it was there. "We need to keep learning until we take our last breath because life is challenging."

"How did you get so wise?"

"Hard lessons." He released her hands and framed her face with his large hands.

His mouth found hers, silencing any protests before they could form, though she didn't want to be anywhere but with him. His kiss was gentle, and she curved her arms around his shoulders as he deepened the kiss until quivers rippled through her. How could she have thought his kiss would be like anyone else's? It was beyond *wunderbaar*.

When he raised his head, she remained where she was. She traced one of his pale brows with a single fingertip. He smiled before pressing his lips to her palm. That was sweet, but not what she yearned for. She drew his mouth to hers. He held her close until she couldn't guess if the frantic heartbeat was hers or his.

He lifted his mouth away again. This time abruptly. The softness vanished from his face as dismay filled his eyes. Standing, he didn't look at her. "I'm sorry, Clara. I shouldn't have done that."

She didn't rise as she wrapped her arms around herself, fearing she'd fall to pieces in front of him. Sorry? Did he mean kissing her was a mistake?

Fool! That's what you are. A second man is saying he made a mistake after he kissed you!

"Don't worry, Isaiah," she said, staring at the ground. "It won't change anything." Her words were the truth. She'd felt like an idiot when she came to Paradise Springs because she'd fallen for a handsome man who acted as if he loved her. When she left Paradise Springs, she'd feel the same way...for a different handsome man.

No, this pain was far deeper because her love for Isaiah was far stronger than anything she'd experienced with Lonnie.

The shadow of his hand moved toward her, then jerked away. She closed her eyes, but the sound of his steps disappearing around the side of the school were like blows against her heart. She hung her head and wept.

Chapter Fifteen

Before the week had passed, Clara knew her plan to avoid Isaiah until the twins' family came for them was doomed to failure. They had to share meals and taking care of the *kinder*. When he closed the door connecting the main house to the *dawdi haus*, she remained as aware of him as if the walls had become transparent. And the twins talked about him. Their affection for him had not changed.

Nor had hers, and that was the problem. Too often, the remembered sensations of his lips on hers played through her mind. Those memories urged her to toss aside caution and risk her heart again.

Isaiah had been very clear—right from the beginning—he wasn't ready to marry again. He'd been honest when he told her that his focus had to remain on his obligations. Even their *wunderbaar* kisses could not deter him from doing as he must. He couldn't let his work at the forge slide, because too many local people depended on him to shoe their horses. He never would shirk his duties as a minister. Nor would he do less than everything he could to take care of the *kinder*.

Despite knowing that, she'd followed her heart to

him. She'd been foolish with him as she'd been with Lonnie. More foolish, because she should have learned from her earlier mistakes. She could forgive her *daed* for his pride, but would *Daed* forgive her if he believed she'd destroyed another opportunity to marry well?

Hochmut. Her *daed* had too much of it; yet she would never change him. Isaiah was right.

She needed to concentrate on changing her heart, which refused to heed anything but its yearning for Isaiah. She needed to follow Isaiah's lead and concentrate on something other than being in love with him. Looking around the house, she sighed. The floors were swept. The dishes were done. Dinner was ready to be cooked. The *kinder* were playing quietly upstairs. She'd weeded the garden that morning. She could start the laundry, but it was too late in the day for it to dry before night fell. Maybe reading would help. She hadn't had time since she'd arrived, and she'd packed a book, planning to finish it while in Paradise Springs.

Going to her room, she edged around her bed. She picked up the book from the table where she'd stacked the few things she'd brought with her. She gasped when something fell out. An envelope. She recognized it, though she couldn't recall putting the letter in the book.

Opening the envelope, she drew out the single page as she sat on the edge of her bed. She read the words she'd read dozens of time already. The letter was from Lonnie, the last one he'd written her to let her know he was sorry about how things had turned out. He confessed he'd believed he loved her, but he'd discovered what love was when he met the woman who became his wife. He'd never wanted to hurt Clara, but he had to follow his heart. Giving up the love he'd found and honoring his offer of marriage to Clara would have led to them being miserable the rest of their days.

She looked at the final paragraph. Her eyes filled with tears that blurred the words that she hadn't truly understood until now:

> Clara, I treasure the time we shared, and I hope some day we can view that time with smiles and know what we shared was part of our journey to true and lasting love. I wish for you what I've found. You deserve someone who will make you happy instead of just content.

Lowering the page to her lap, she whispered, "I'm sorry, Lonnie. I've been blaming you for what happened exactly as my *daed* blamed me. What happened was nobody's fault. You fell in love with someone else. You couldn't help what your heart wanted, and, if I'd cared about you as much as I should have, I would have been happy for you. And for me, because you're right. I didn't love you, and you didn't love me enough."

She closed her eyes. She could finally look beyond her wounded pride to the truth. But had she learned to listen to *gut* sense? No! If her rational side had its way, she wouldn't be listening to her heart, which drew her to Isaiah.

Sounds came from the twins' room, and she folded the letter and put it in its envelope. "Goodbye, Lonnie," she whispered. "I hope you're always as happy as you deserve to be."

Clara didn't have any more time to think about the letter and her realizations about herself because the *kinder* seemed more wound up than usual. They ate their afternoon snack so quickly she wondered if they even tasted the chocolate chip cookies. She was glad to shoo them outside to play while she cleaned up from their snack. But first she wanted to check on the mail and any messages on the answering machine. She'd been sure that they would have heard from the twins' family by now.

No light blinked by the phone in the shack by the road, and the only mail was a blacksmithing supply catalog for Isaiah. She carried it to the house and put it on the kitchen table. Picking up the dishes left by the twins, she filled the sink with soapy water.

She used to put his mail beside where he sat in the living room in the evening, but now he rushed to the *dawdi haus* before the twins went to bed. She half expected him to take his plate and eat in the other part of the house one of these nights. The *kinder* had begun to ask why he wasn't spending more time with them.

Everything they'd built for the twins was falling apart. The sooner the *kinder*'s family returned and could start the youngsters on their new life, the better it would be for everyone.

Oh, how she wished she could believe that! The thought of not seeing them every day cramped her heart. She couldn't think about never spending time with Isaiah again. If she did, she wasn't sure she could continue with their tacit agreement to pretend nothing had changed.

A motion caught her eye, and she looked out the window. A half scream burst from her throat when she saw smoke was curling out of the stable window. Fire!

She threw the dishcloth in the sink and raced out the

back door. Where were the *kinder*? They'd been in the yard moments ago.

Screaming their names, she grabbed the garden hose. It was too short. It'd never reach the stable. She needed to call for help. But she couldn't when she didn't know where the twins were. She shrieked their names again, scraping her throat raw.

Andrew burst out of the gray cloud. He yelled for help. She grasped his shoulders and shook him to reach past his terror.

"Where are the others?" she asked.

He pointed at the stable.

"Go and call the fire department," she ordered as she gave him a shove toward the phone shack. "Call 911! Tell the firemen to come right away. Can you do that?"

"Ja." His voice trembled on the single word.

"Go!"

She ran to the stable. A single glance over her shoulder told her Andrew was speeding toward the end of the farm lane as fast as his legs could pump. She hoped he could do what she'd asked. If he couldn't, she'd have to make the call herself.

After she made sure the *kinder* and her horse were out of the burning building.

The smoke met her at the door. Hot and smothering and as solid as a wall, it tried to drive her back from the fire's domain. She pushed forward. Holding her hands over her nose and mouth, she scanned the stable. Thick smoke hid the ceiling and reached almost to the floor. She heard her horse moving in panic.

Clara lowered her hands enough to cry out, "Ammon!" *Oh, dear Lord, let him be able to hear me!* "Nancy! Nettie Mae! Where are you?"

She heard muffled sobs. The stall in front of her

on her right side. Holding her apron over her nose and mouth, she ran in. She almost tripped over two small forms huddled in one corner beside a bale of hay.

"Clara!" they called together, jumping to their feet. Nancy and Nettie Mae!

"Is Ammon with you?"

The girls looked at each other but didn't answer.

She knelt and grasped each one by the shoulder. Closer to the floor, the air wasn't as thick with smoke. She sent up a grateful prayer as she repeated her question. When the girls hesitated, she hurried to say, "We need to get out of here."

Rising, she pushed them ahead of her to the door. She shoved them out and gasped a deep breath of the fresher air. Again she asked them where Ammon was.

Both girls shrugged, their eyes wide with terror.

Telling them to go to the front porch and wait there, she turned to head back in. Where should she look? Flames were licking along the eaves. She wouldn't have much time to find the little boy.

A small hand tugged her skirt before she could move. Nettie Mae!

"Ammon hiding, too," the little girl said.

"Where?"

"He not mean to—"

"I know he's sorry." She didn't have time for the *kind* to explain. "But where is he? Do you know?"

"He love Bella."

Clara hoped she was translating the little girl's cryptic statement. Ammon had gone to rescue her horse. If she was wrong, she wouldn't have another chance. Even if she was right...

She told Nettie Mae to join her sister on the front porch. Hoping the *kind* obeyed, she ran into the smoky stable. It was the hardest thing she'd ever done, but getting out alive with Ammon was going to be more difficult.

Isaiah heard a fire alarm rise to an ear-piercing pitch. It was the one belonging to the Paradise Springs Volunteer Fire Department in the center of the village. He dropped his hammer and yanked off his leather apron. He banked the embers on the forge, then raced around the building between him and the parking lot. He didn't slow until he reached the road.

As he got there, the main fire engine zipped past, followed by trucks and cars driven by volunteer firefighters. A red pickup slowed long enough for him to hold out his hands to the three men in the back. Two plain and one *Englischer*, he saw as he swung up beside them. The truck took off after the fire engine before his feet touched the truck bed.

Dropping beside the men amid the piles of gear labeled PSVFD, he asked, "Where's the fire? Is it a building?"

As one, they shrugged. The *Englischer* explained they'd been working nearby and reached the fire station in time to see the fire engine race out. They'd grabbed the rest of the turnout gear and jumped into the red pickup without asking questions.

Awkwardly each man found gear and pulled it over his clothes. Isaiah didn't bother with boots, because he wore protective ones in the blacksmith shop, but he helped others find ones that fit.

A shrill screech came from behind the vehicle. A police car was catching up with them. Following it was an ambulance. His stomach clenched. His hopes that it was nothing but a grass fire were dashed. Was it a car accident?

Please don't let it be that, God. The twins were too fragile to deal with more funerals.

He heard a curse and a prayer. He looked at the other men, not sure which had said which. Then he noticed where the truck was turning and looked along the familiar road to see a plume of smoke rising in malevolent blackness less than a half mile away.

He started to stand to see better. He was grabbed and pulled down.

"It's the Beachys'!" someone shouted.

He shook off the hands but didn't stand. He couldn't risk his life. Not when Clara and the twins could be in danger. Groaning, he hid his face in his hands.

Don't let me to be too late again! Let me be there in time this time!

The prayer played over and over in his mind as he raised his head to see the fire engine race past the house. He sent up a quick prayer of thanksgiving. He saw motion on the front porch. One…two…three… Where was Ammon? And where was Clara?

He knew the answer when he saw flames stretching out a stable window. Clara was wherever Ammon was. If the boy was in the stable, she'd be there, too.

Help us, Lord! Don't let me be too late. Not this time. Not for them.

The pickup squealed to a halt, and Isaiah jumped out. He heard buggy wheels clattering behind him as help arrived from neighboring farms. Orders were being shouted in every direction as the firemen hooked a hose to the pumper and ran another line toward the pond beyond the big barn.

Isaiah ran toward the stable. He heard shouts behind

him, but he didn't stop. If Clara and the boy were inside, they didn't have time to wait for the firemen to finish getting their hoses ready. Suddenly the oft-heard jest that the Paradise Springs Volunteer Fire Department had never failed to save a foundation was no longer funny. Things could be replaced but not people.

That was a lesson he'd learned over and over, and he didn't want to be taught it again today.

"Clara! Ammon!" he shouted as he pushed through the smoke trying to force him back.

The flames roared like a tormented beast from the far end of the building. If a spark flew to the main barn, that could be destroyed, too. He hoped the cows had the sense to move away. The chickens would be hiding closer to the house.

But Clara wouldn't go to safety until the *kinder* did.

He shouted their names to his right.

No response.

He drew in a deep breath to shout them again, then began coughing as the smoke choked him with its gray, cloudy fingers.

A hand grasped his.

Clara!

He didn't know if he said it aloud or not, but he pulled her toward him. His arm went around her slender waist. He could feel her straining to breathe.

"Ammon?" he shouted over the ear-shattering crackle. This blistering beast was nothing like the fire he controlled on his forge.

"Out."

"I didn't see him."

"He's out."

"Then let's get out, too!"

"Bella!" she choked, pulling away from him.

Or at least he thought she said that. The swirling smoke swallowed her before she'd gone more than a couple of steps. He followed, glad he could turn away from the most vicious heat.

He heard her horse before he could see Clara and Bella through the smoke. The horse was pushing against the stall, seeking any way out—though, he knew, if the door was open, Bella might not flee. Thick smoke mixed with fear scorched a horse's brain, making it impossible for one to escape.

Grabbing a smoking blanket off a stall door, he dunked it in the watering trough. He heaved it over Bella and grabbed her mane. She tried to pull away, but he shouted for her to come with him. Pulling her out, he looked for Clara.

He couldn't see. Anything. The smoke was growing blacker by the second, and his eyes burned as if twin pyres had been lit in them. He groped for the other stall. The crackling of the fire had become a roar that swallowed his shout.

He bumped into something soft. Clara! Coughing and gagging, she leaned against the stall door.

He seized Clara by the waist and tugged on Bella. Bending his head as if he strode through a storm wind, he gulped in the cooler air toward the floor while he rushed toward the door. He herded her before him. Bella followed, shying on every step.

Overhead something creaked. Were the rafters failing? If the roof collapsed, they'd be crushed.

Then fresh air filled his lungs. He started to cough, but kept moving forward. Water sprayed over them. It was aimed at the stable, but the mist was icy cold after the inferno inside. Shouts came from every direction, but he couldn't sort them out. Bella pulled away and galloped around the house and out of sight.

Small forms ran toward him and Clara, who leaned more heavily on him with each step. Arms reached out to catch the youngsters before they could get too close to the fire. He hurried Clara toward the twins.

They threw their arms around him and Clara. As he released her to hug them, she collapsed to the ground and didn't move. The twins shrieked in terror.

He wanted to as well, fearing, once again, he'd been too late. He dropped to his knees beside her and moaned, "Don't leave me, Clara. Lord, don't take her, too. Please."

Chapter Sixteen

Isaiah watched the other firemen putting out the last of the hot spots around the stable as he paced between the house and the fire engine. The captain had refused to let him fight, telling him he was too emotionally involved. He'd proved it by rushing into the stable. That everyone, including Bella, had been saved was no justification for what he'd done. Isaiah knew the captain would have more to say once the cleanup was done, and he would accept whatever punishment the captain handed out. He'd let his fears overcome his training, and he could have endangered his fellow firefighters if they'd had to come to his rescue.

The stable was a scorched skeleton of timbers. The building had been too involved by the time the firefighters arrived. However, other than smoke stains, the larger barn was undamaged and the animals, except a few chickens, were safe. The missing chickens would likely reappear when they were hungry.

Isaiah had no idea how the fire started. He was careful. He didn't leave a lamp in the stable, not wanting one of the horses to bump into it and tip it over. Maybe the *kinder* had seen something. He gave them a quick hug before *Mamm* appeared and took them into the house. At the same time, the EMTs had rushed Clara into the ambulance to work on her. They'd told him to wait outside, out of the way.

Glancing at where the ambulance stood in the yard, he had to believe the fact it hadn't rushed off to the hospital meant she was going to be okay. She had to be okay. He couldn't bear the thought of another woman he loved dying.

Ja, he loved her. With his defenses seared away, he couldn't ignore the truth any longer. He loved Clara Ebersol. He loved her magnificent red hair and her snapping eyes that mirrored her emotions, whether she wished them to or not. He loved her sense of humor and her sense of duty with the *kinder*. He loved her faith that was as much a part of her as her scintillating smile. He loved her courage and her weaknesses, including the one she never spoke of: her fear she wasn't *gut* enough to meet anyone's standards, including her own.

He loved *her*.

And he wanted to tell her how wrong her fear was. She was the most *wunderbaar* woman he'd ever known.

Isaiah paused in his pacing when Finn Markham approached him. The EMT was also a member of the Paradise Springs Volunteer Fire Department, and Isaiah had worked with him on several occasions. He'd never thought he'd need the tall *Englischer* in his official capacity.

Finn clapped a hand on his shoulder. "Good news, Isaiah. Clara is breathing well on her own."

"Will she have to go to the hospital?"

"Her blood oxygen levels are low, but that's to be expected. We'll check again in a half hour. If they've stabilized, she won't have to go."

"Can I see her?"

"I don't think I could stop you." Finn gave him a bolstering smile. "She's been asking about you and the children. We've tried to reassure her that you're all okay, but I don't think she'll believe that until she sees you with her own eyes."

"I'll get the *kinder*."

Putting a hand on Isaiah's arm, the EMT said, "It'd be better right now if it's just you. She's pretty weak. She breathed in a lot of smoke, and it'll be a few days before she's 100 percent again. The kids may get her too excited, and that's going to have an impact on her oxygen levels."

"All right." He took one step, then stopped. "*Danki*, Finn. I owe you a debt I'll never be able to repay."

"Have your mother make me one of her *snitz* pies, and we'll call it even."

"If I know *Mamm*, she'll make you a dozen."

Finn grinned. "And I'll eat every bite." To Isaiah's back, he added, "Just don't take Clara's breath away with your manly charms."

Isaiah laughed as he hadn't been sure he'd ever be able to again. But the sound was short-lived. His steps slowed as he approached the ambulance. How was he going to find the right words to apologize to Clara for letting her down? If he'd been at the farm, she wouldn't have had to go into the stable to rescue the twins and the horse.

Sending Finn pie was an easy way to repay his debt to his friend, but how was he going to repay his debt to Clara for failing her?

Clara's heart danced in her aching chest when Isaiah heaved himself into the ambulance. The sight of his face, blackened by smoke, was the best medicine she could have. But raising her head was too much, and she began to cough.

"Whoa there," Jasmine, the other EMT, said as she put her fingers on Clara's wrist to check her pulse. "Take it easy. I can tell he makes your heart go pitter-patter, but we want your heart rate slower, not faster."

Leaning her head back on the thin pillow on the gurney, Clara nodded.

"If you promise to be good," Jasmine continued, "I'll give you time alone while I start filling out my report."

"I promise." Isaiah's hoarse voice didn't sound like his own. "And I'll make sure she's *gut*, too."

"I'm sure you will." The vehicle bounced when the EMT jumped out.

When Isaiah sat on the low stool Jasmine had been using, Clara smiled past the oxygen tubes connecting her nose and lungs to a nearby tank. He was careful not to jostle any of the IV tubes running into her left arm.

Shock made her heart skip a beat when he grabbed her left hand. She fought not to cough so she could hear what he said.

"I should have been here. I'm sorry." He pressed his forehead to her hand. "I'm so, so sorry, Clara. Please forgive me."

Her other fingers rose to brush aside the hair that fell forward onto her skin. The clatter of the IV startled her, but she ignored it. "Forgive you for what?"

"For not being here."

"But you *were* here. You saved Bella and me. We're alive because of you."

"If I'd been here, you wouldn't have had to go into the stable, and you wouldn't be lying here with these machines hooked up to you."

"Do you think you could have kept me out when the

twins were inside?" She raised a single eyebrow, though the slight motion sent a pain across her head.

Her attempt at humor did not bring him a smile and fell flat because he was too caught up in his despair to hear what she said. Why? She was alive. The *kinder* were alive. The stable was gone, but not the other outbuildings or the house. Why was he insisting on punishing himself for what *hadn't* happened instead of being grateful for what had?

Then she realized what was in his head and his heart. Before she could halt herself from saying the words she didn't want to believe were true, she asked, "You think if you'd been at your house that day Rose wouldn't have died?"

"*Ja*. No. I mean—" He clamped his lips closed, but the potent emotions in his eyes burned her almost as fiercely as the fire's embers had.

"Tell me what you mean." Instinct warned her that he needed to keep talking until he broke open the half-healed scars within his heart and let out the pain infecting him.

For a long moment, he said nothing. He shifted as if he planned to get up and leave. She feared he wanted to run away again from the grief and guilt he'd carried with him for too long.

"I tried hard to keep her safe," he whispered. "I never came into the house smelling of smoke from the forge."

"I've wondered why you change clothes in the barn and wash up out there."

"Rose should never have married a blacksmith when the faintest wisp of smoke could bring on an asthma attack."

"That's easy to say, but when the heart gets involved, *gut* sense goes out the window." She closed her eyes and drew in the deepest breath she could. When she began to cough, she groped for the cup of water Jasmine had left on a nearby shelf.

Isaiah pressed it into her hand. He watched as she took a drink, and she realized he would have helped her swallow past her raw throat if he could. "Are you okay?" he asked.

"I'll be if I take it easy. That's what Finn and Jasmine said."

"You should listen to them. They're skilled EMTs."

"And you should listen to me, Isaiah. How many times have you praised my common sense?"

"A lot."

"But you wouldn't have thought I had a lick of sense if you'd seen my reaction to the news my fiancé had married someone else."

A faint smile tipped the corners of his mouth. "Nobody would have faulted you for that."

"My *daed* did, but you've helped me see that he can't be other than he is. We can't change the past."

"I agree."

"Why are you trying to convince yourself Rose didn't love you when you got married?"

"Orpha said—"

"That she lied to hurt you." She pushed herself up to sit on the gurney, and the machines around her reacted to her motion. Waiting for them to calm down, she said, "It's not Orpha. It's you. *You* don't believe Rose loved you. No, you believe it, but you don't want to. You'd rather wallow in your self-loathing."

"Don't be silly. That's not what I feel."

She put her hand over his on the side of the gurney. "If I had to guess, I'd say guilt is your protection against the heavy weight of your loss. The *kinder* have hidden their pain, and you have, too. Now they're facing it. Are you less courageous than a five-year-old or a three-year-old who is coming to accept the invitation from God to walk the path He's given them? Can't you believe as a grown man what each of those *kinder* accepts with innocent faith? God will never give us more than we can handle when we depend on Him to see us through."

When he wrapped his arms around her and leaned against her shoulder, tears running down his face, she held him close. She guessed it was the first time he'd allowed himself to cry since Rose had died over a year ago. In that time, the pain had feasted on him like a parasite. But he'd released the dam he'd built to hold in the pain, and the floodtide surging over him would help wash it away forever.

Later that evening, Clara leaned one shoulder against the frame of the door between the kitchen and the living room. She was much better, able to draw a breath without coughing. The EMTs had given her instructions to call 911 if her symptoms returned, and the paper sat in the middle of the kitchen table.

Isaiah motioned for the *kinder* to join him in the living room. His eyes were lined in red, but his shoulders seemed to have risen at least an inch as he began to set aside the burden of guilt he'd been carrying. He had many months of healing ahead of him, but, like Andrew, Ammon, Nancy and Nettie Mae, he'd begun to move in that direction.

She watched as Isaiah sat on the floor with the twins. They eyed him uneasily, and, for once, he didn't smile to ease their concerns.

Or hers.

If the fire chief's suspicions were true, what the youngsters had done this afternoon had been far worse than forgetting to pick up their crayons or spilling a glass of milk. The twins squirmed, a sure sign of guilt. She hoped Isaiah would be gentle when he knew how virulent guilt could be. It'd nearly stolen his happiness for the rest of his life. However, she was sure of one thing: Isaiah wouldn't be like her *daed* who'd lambasted her for embarrassing him and the family with her broken betrothal. His friends had trusted him with the *kinder*, and she did, too.

"Do you want to tell me about what happened this afternoon?" he asked with the calm tone they'd learned worked best with the *kinder*.

All four exchanged uneasy glances.

Andrew spoke first. "It was an accident."

"It?" asked Isaiah.

"Fire, ain't so?" asked Nettie Mae.

"Ja." Isaiah's lips tightened, and Clara guessed he was trying not to smile at the little girl's ingenuousness. "I'm sure the fire was an accident, but who will tell me what happened?"

"I will." At Ammon's answer, Clara had to keep her smile hidden. She was grateful the little boy was taking an active part in their conversations. She wondered how much longer Andrew would be the youngsters' unchallenged leader.

"Go ahead," prompted Isaiah.

The little boy's tale was short and to the point. He and Andrew wanted to prove to their sisters that they knew how to light a lantern and decided to prove it in the stable. "We wanted to show them we could take care of a pony, so we could get one like *Daed* promised."

She held her breath, waiting for Isaiah's response.

He asked, "And?"

"We took the matches out of the drawer when Clara

wasn't looking." Ammon blinked back tears as he turned to her. "We're sorry, Clara, for touching things we shouldn't have."

"I know." She didn't want to interrupt the conversation.

"We tried to stomp the fire out," Nancy said.

Clara bit her lip to keep her gasp of dismay from erupting. If one of the *kinder*'s clothing had caught fire, the fire would have become a true tragedy. She murmured a soft prayer of gratitude to God for watching over the twins and saving them from their folly.

"Pieces of hay and fire went everywhere," Andrew added. "That's when we got scared."

"So you ran, Andrew?" Isaiah asked.

The boy nodded.

"And you hid?" Isaiah focused on the girls.

They nodded.

"And I went to get Bella," Ammon said, "but couldn't find her in the smoke."

"We're thankful we found you *and* Bella in the smoke." He leaned toward them. "What you did was very dangerous. Any of you—and Clara—could have died. You must never touch matches without permission again until you're big enough."

"No more," Nancy said.

Her twin nodded and reached for her braid to chew on. Clara had meant to help her break that habit, but she was glad Nettie Mae had its comfort. Next week, if she was still there next week, she'd start working with the little girl to convince her to stop putting her hair in her mouth.

"And we keep our promises," Andrew said, sticking out his chest in a pose he must have thought made him look grown up.

"Gut," Isaiah said. "This is one you *must* keep."

"We will." Ammon rose to his knees. "We'll keep

it like we've kept our promise to *Mamm* when she said no more laughing."

Clara heard a choked sound from Isaiah and knew he was as astounded as she was. Not once had she imagined the twins' *mamm* had been the one to order them not to laugh. She squatted so her eyes were level with the *kinder*'s. "When did she say that?"

"Before she and *Daed* left and didn't come home," Ammon said. Thick tears welled up in his eyes.

As Clara held him close, trying to offer him what solace she could, she wondered if the misunderstanding had arisen because Esta was worried about being late and had tried to keep the youngsters quiet so she could finish whatever she needed to do before she and Melvin left for the auction. How many words had she herself said in haste and come to rue afterward? But, at least, what had been done could be undone.

She looked over Ammon's head to where Isaiah was comforting the other three. "Your *mamm* and *daed* want you to laugh whenever you want to for the rest of your lives. The sound of laughter is very light, and it reaches all the way up to them in heaven."

"They hear us laughing?" asked Nettie Mae.

"*Ja*, so laugh when you want to, because your parents will be happy to hear you."

"I gonna." The little girl raised her chin. "Lots and lots."

Isaiah's gaze caught hers, and she saw his sorrow matched her own. But she also saw in his eyes hope for better times ahead and knew they were on their way to healing their hearts.

"Whew!" Isaiah said as he came down the stairs along with Clara after putting the *kinder* to bed. "I wasn't sure if we'd get them to sleep."

"It's been a tough day for them."

"For everyone." He gave her a half smile as he curled an arm around her shoulders as they went toward the kitchen. "One of the worst days of my life, but also one of the best because this house will ring with childish laughter soon." He opened the door to the *dawdi haus*. As he started to bid her to have a *gut* night's rest, he paused and said, "Oh, I forgot about this."

She watched while he went to the table and picked up an envelope. Handing it to her, he said nothing. Her eyes widened when she saw the international stamps on it.

"From the *kinder*'s grandparents?" she asked.

"*Ja.* We can read it tonight and share it with them in the morning, if you'd like."

"That's a *gut* idea." She opened it, pulled out the pages inside and began to read aloud:

"'Dear Andrew, Ammon, Nancy, Nettie Mae, Isaiah and Clara,

'First, we want to thank you for the *wunder-baar* pictures and stories about the *kinder*. We've received each letter with joy. It's such a blessing to get to know our *kins-kinder* better. We wish we had more time with you.

'And that brings us to something we want to address to you, Isaiah. As you may or may not know, we haven't had the amount of time we would have liked to spend with our *kins-kinder*. Our call to serve has taken us to many places, and our visits to our son and his family have been few and far between. Melvin was concerned about his *kinder* not knowing us. He mentioned that when he spoke with us before he asked you, Isaiah, to serve as guardian for the twins if anything happened to him. We know he asked you to assist Esta in his place. Hearing you agreed to both without hesitation has told us much about the man you are. A *gut* man and a God-fearing one who has served his Lord to the best of his abilities, and a man who wouldn't shirk his duties to his friend's family.

'Clara, we have come to know you through your kind letters, which have filled our hearts with joy. The twins' lives have been made better by you being in them, we're sure. But we know you're there only temporarily.

'A long-term solution must be found for the *kinder*. We cannot bring them here to live with us, and from what we've heard from Debra Wittmer, she's in a similar situation. Our love for our *kinskinder* will never change, but, Isaiah, would you consider taking them permanently? They need a *gut* home and a *gut daed*. We believe you can provide that home and be their *daed*.'"

Clara lowered the letter and whispered, "Did I read that right? They want you to adopt the twins?"

"That's what it sounded like to me." He started to grin. "I'm glad it sounded that way to you, too."

"Do you think it's possible?" she asked, wondering what the *kinder* would say when they heard of this. She prayed they wouldn't feel unwanted by their grandparents and *aenti* as she'd felt unwanted by her *daed* for too many years.

"*Ja*, it's possible for the Amish to adopt. My sister, Esther, and her husband have."

She shook her head. "I wasn't talking about the legalities. I meant is this something *you* want to do? Do you want to change from a temporary *daed* to a permanent one? It's such a responsibility, Isaiah."

"I can do it, but I'll need help."

"Your family—"

"Your help, Clara." He grasped her hands, lacing his fingers through hers. "Nothing has changed."

"I can stay as long as you need me."

"But you didn't let me ask first."

"Ask what? You said you needed my help, and I'm glad to give it."

He shook his head. "Stop being scared of disappointing me as your *daed* has made you believe you've disappointed him, Clara. Listen to your heart. If you won't, then listen to mine."

Her breath caught as she realized what he was saying. She'd been caught up in wondering how the *kinder* would react to the news and hadn't thought of anything else. Certainly nothing as *wunderbaar* as what she believed he was asking of her.

His smile widened. "Clara, are you willing to go from temporary nanny to permanent *mamm* and wife? My wife?"

"Are you sure?"

"More sure than I've been of anything in my life. I have been praying for the right time to propose, and I think this is it. I'm not asking because of the *kinder*. I'm asking because I love you. Do you love me?"

"With all my heart…except for the part that belongs to four mischievous twins."

"I can offer you almost all my heart…everything except for what belongs to four imps. But you haven't given me your answer, Clara. Will you marry me?"

"*Ja*, I'll marry you."

He let out a whoop, then glanced toward the ceiling.

"I hope I didn't wake them before I can…" He caressed her cheek, and she slanted her face into his warm palm.

When his mouth found hers, she knew she'd never understood the breadth of happiness until this moment. They still had a lot of grief to deal with, but they'd be doing it together.

Laughter sounded around them, and Isaiah pulled away. In shock, she saw the twins giggling with the ease she'd prayed for.

"What's funny?" Isaiah asked in a feigned gruff voice.

"Kissing is funny," shouted Andrew before dissolving into laughter again. The other twins joined in.

"You've got it almost right." Isaiah drew her into his arms once more. "Kissing isn't funny. It's fun." And to prove his point, he kissed her again and again until they were laughing as hard as the youngsters.

Epilogue

Clara brought another tray with two pitchers of freshly squeezed lemonade. She set them on the tables in the middle of the yard before admiring how much of the new stable had been already rebuilt. There were fewer volunteers than for a full barn raising, but the new stable would be finished before dark tonight except for a coat of paint to match the barn. The smoke stains there were covered by the new white paint.

Esther and Ruth walked over to the table. They were the only two of Isaiah's siblings she hadn't met before, because they lived too far away for easy visits when Ruth had a young baby and Esther was very pregnant.

"Perfect timing," Esther said. "The men were talking about taking a break and hoped you were making something *gut* to drink."

"Tell them to *komm* and get it!" she replied with a laugh.

Esther cupped her hands over her mouth and shouted, "Lemonade!" At Clara's shock, she laughed. "I used to be a schoolteacher. I know how to be heard."

Cheers met the announcement, and the men put aside their tools before hurrying to the table to quench the thirsts they'd been working up on the hot, humid day.

Clara smiled when Isaiah moved close to her and smiled. "I heard some interesting news."

"Not more rumors, I hope."

He gave an emoted shudder, then chuckled. "I got this news right from the horse's mouth."

"That's no way to talk about your *mamm*." Wanda wagged a finger at him, and everyone laughed.

"What's the news, Isaiah?" asked Esther. "You can't leave us hanging like clothes on a line."

"Do you want to tell them, *Mamm*, Reuben?" asked Isaiah.

Reuben grinned and said, "Wanda and I will be publishing our intentions to marry in October."

More cheers erupted, and everyone was hugging everyone else.

Isaiah took Clara's hand and drew her away from the crowd. Out of earshot, he said, "I hope you're not disappointed that we won't be the next one to get married."

"As long as we get married."

"Let's get married two weeks after Reuben and *Mamm*. It'll give everyone time to prepare for a second wedding, and we should be able to get in a few visits to family before the adoption proceedings begin."

"Those can't be started until the relinquishment of parental rights paperwork is signed by Melvin's parents and Debra."

"It'll be soon, and then you'll be a wife and a *mamm*."

She put her arms around his neck, not caring if anyone saw them. "And you'll be my forever husband and their forever *daed*."

"There's nothing I want to be more." He confirmed that with a kiss.

* * * * *

Dear Reader,

The fear of letting go can keep us from enjoying the moment we're living right now. Both Clara and Isaiah take on the task of caring for four orphaned children, knowing that soon they will need to hand those children over to members of their extended family. Learning to live every minute and trusting that God is leading them in the direction they must go is a lesson they—and all of us—must learn. I would like to think I would be as willing to love deeply and then let go as Clara and Isaiah are, but anyone who has lost someone dear to them knows that can be the most difficult part of life.

Stop in and visit me at *www.joannbrownbooks.com* Look for my next story in the *Amish Hearts* series coming soon.

Wishing you many blessings,
Jo Ann Brown

AMISH REFUGE

Debby Giusti

This story is dedicated
to my cousins—
David, Eric, Sandy and Bill—
for the wonderful memories
of going home to Ohio.

O Lord, You have been our refuge
through all generations.
—*Psalms* 90:1

Chapter One

Serpent would find her and kill her. Tonight.

Miriam Miller woke with a start, chilled to the bone. She rubbed her hands over her arms and blinked against the night air seeping through the broken car window. Tugging her crocheted scarf and threadbare jacket across her chest, she straightened in the driver's seat and gazed through the windshield.

A police car with lights flashing braked to a stop on the edge of the narrow, two-lane road not more than twenty feet from where she'd parked, hidden by trees and underbrush.

Fear clutched her throat.

The cop—a bull of a man with a heart as dark as the night—stepped to the pavement and played his flashlight over the tall pines. Her pulse pounded and a roar filled her ears. She could envision the serpent tattoo that wrapped around his neck, the snake as heinous as the man.

She had been a fool to think she could elude him by hiding in the woods. Even more of a fool to succumb to the fatigue brought on by the drugs he had used to subdue her.

Fisting her hands, she swallowed the bile that filled her mouth and steeled her spine with resolve. He'd caught her once. He would never capture her again.

She reached for the key in the ignition and held her breath as he pushed aside a tree branch and peered deeper into the woods. With the flick of his wrist, a flash of light caught her in its glare. Just that fast, he was running straight for her.

Before she could start the engine, he opened the driver's door and yanked her from the car. Screaming, she fell at his feet, crawled away on all fours and struggled to right herself.

He kicked her ribs. Air wheezed from her lungs. He grabbed her hair, turned her to face him and pulled her upright.

She thrashed her arms, kicked her feet then jabbed her fingers deep into his eyes.

He cursed, covered his face with his hands and stumbled backward. "Why you—!"

She lunged for her car.

A bag of craft supplies lay on the floor mat. Frantically she dug for the shears, relieved when her hand gripped the sharp steel.

He struck her shoulder, knocking her off balance. She cried in pain. Another blow, this one to her head.

She tightened her hold on the scissors, raised her hand and stabbed his neck. He groaned, momentarily stunned. She scrambled into her car, slammed and locked the door, and turned the key in the ignition. He grabbed the door handle and banged on the window, his hateful face pushed flat against the cracked glass.

The motor purred to life.

"Thank You," she silently prayed to a God in whom she'd only started to believe.

Serpent railed in rage.

She jammed the accelerator to the floorboard. Her head flew back as the sudden momentum jerked the car forward, throwing her attacker to the ground.

Her heart pounded nearly out of her chest and her hands shook so hard she could barely steer the car along the narrow path that led back to the pavement. She glanced at her rearview mirror.

Bathed in the red glow of her taillights, Serpent raised his fist, his curse faintly audible even over the hum of her engine.

Her stomach roiled.

She accelerated. The car fishtailed. Blood seeped from the gash to her forehead. She wiped her hand across her brow and blinked back the swell of panic that clamped down on her chest. Her breath caught as she glanced at her speedometer, knowing she was driving much too fast.

Her cell phone, with its dead battery, sat on the console. If she had a car charger, she would call for help. Not the authorities. She couldn't trust law enforcement, but her older sister, Hannah, would know what to do.

Headlights flashed in her rearview mirror. Her heart stopped. He was following her.

She increased her speed, all too aware of her threadbare tires and the threat of ice on the mountain road. The engine whined as she rounded a turn. Gripping the wheel, white-knuckled, she worked to hold the road.

Pop! The right rear tire deflated.

The blowout caused the car to shimmy across the pavement and career down a steep embankment. In the path of her headlights, she saw the river, edged with ice.

She screamed, anticipating the frigid water. Unable to swim, she'd drown. At the last second the car came to an abrupt halt, mired in mud. Her head hit the steering wheel. She moaned and blinked back the darkness that swirled around her.

A warning welled up from deep within her.

Run!

Dazed, she grabbed her phone, crawled from the car and staggered into the woods. Pushing through brambles, she ignored the sharp thorns that scraped her arms and tugged at her jacket. A clearing lay ahead.

In the distance she saw a farmhouse. A warm glow beckoned from the downstairs window. She turned to see the police cruiser racing down the hill, seemingly oblivious to where her car had gone off the road.

Could Serpent see her, even in the dark?

The memory of what had happened four nights ago washed over her—Miriam, her sister, Sarah, and their mother lost in the North Georgia mountains. Wrongly, they'd thought the cops would provide help.

Her heart broke. Tears filled her eyes and her body ached, but she willed her legs forward. The farmhouse was her only hope.

She crossed the clearing and reached the house. Clutching the wood banister, she pulled herself up the stairs to the porch. Relief overcame her, along with exhaustion. Too spent to lift her hand to knock, she gasped when the door opened.

Warmth from inside washed over her. A tall, muscular man stood backlit in the threshold. "Help me," she pleaded, her head whirling. She grabbed his hand. "He…he wants to kill me."

Abram Zook reached for the frightened woman who fell into his arms. Her plaintive cry for help touched a broken place deep within him. Instinctively he pulled her close and cradled her to him.

His sister, Emma, limped down the stairs, wrapping a shawl around her bedclothes.

"Abram, why are you standing in the doorway at this time of night?"

Coming toward him, she gasped, seeing the woman in his arms. "*Gott* help us."

"*Gott* help this woman," Abram countered.

He carried her to the rocker near the wood-burning stove and gently placed her on the chair.

Emma retrieved the lantern from the table but stopped short when the screech of tires pulled her gaze to the still open doorway. "Abram, look."

He glanced to where his sister pointed, seeing headlights approaching much too fast along the icy road.

"Stay with the woman."

Emma reached for his arm. "You cannot save the *Englisch* from their foolish ways. Do not get involved."

He shrugged off her warning. "The bridge is out. I must alert the driver."

Abram stepped onto the porch. His eyes adjusted quickly to the dark night.

"Take the lantern," Emma insisted from the doorway.

Ignoring the request, he ran toward the road, flailing his arms to flag down the oncoming vehicle.

The car screeched to a stop. The driver lowered the window. Abram raised his hand to his eyes, unable to see the driver's face in the glare of the headlights.

"Did a car pass by here?" the man demanded, his voice as brittle as the ice on the roadway.

"The bridge is out. You must take the other fork in the road." Abram pointed to where the narrow country path split.

The man glanced back. "Did she go that way?"

Abram would not betray the woman he had cradled against him. "Your car is the first I have seen tonight."

Cursing, the man turned his vehicle around and screeched away from Abram. The back wheels spun on the slick pavement. He took the fork and accelerated.

Abram hurried back to the house.

Emma locked the door behind him. "Who was that man?" she asked.

"I do not know."

"He was looking for the woman." She stated what they both knew was true.

"Perhaps, but he will not find her tonight."

"I tell you, Abram, she will bring trouble to this house."

"She is in need, Emma. We will take her upstairs."

He lifted the woman into his arms and felt her startle. "I have you. You are safe."

She was thin, too thin.

His sister held the lantern aloft and climbed the stairs ahead of him. On the second floor she pushed open the door to the extra bedroom.

As Abram stepped past her, light from the lantern spilled over the woman's pale face. His sister inhaled sharply.

He glanced down, taking in the blood that spattered her clothing, the gash to her forehead and the scrapes to her hands and wrists.

His heart lurched.

What had happened to this woman on the run?

"You are awake?"

Miriam blinked her eyes open to daylight filtering through the window then turned her gaze to the man standing in the doorway of the small bedroom where she lay. He had a ruddy, wind-burned complexion with a dark beard and shaggy black hair that fell below his ears. His white shirt hugged his broad chest and puckered against the suspenders attached to his trousers.

Her mind slowly put the pieces together as she glanced from his clothing to the stark bedroom furnishings and back again to her larger-than-life rescuer. Was she dreaming or had she somehow, in the dead of night, found refuge in an Amish house?

Memories flashed through her mind. Struggling to put her thoughts in order, she tugged the quilt closer to her chin.

His brow knit. "You are afraid?"

Of him? Should she be?

She glanced behind the man to where a woman stood. Petite, with wide eyes and rosy cheeks, she wore a pale blue dress and white apron. Her hair was pulled into a bun under a starched cap. Miriam strained to remember, recalling only snippets of how the woman had tended her cut and dressed her in a flannel nightgown. At least that much she could recall.

The Amish man turned to the woman next to him. "Emma, she needs to eat."

Miriam shook her head. Food wasn't important. Being free of Serpent was all that mattered. Then, just that fast, her stomach rumbled, reminding her she hadn't had more than a few crackers in four days.

Gathering her courage, she swallowed hard and gave voice to the question that pinged through her head. "Who...who are you?"

"My name is Abram. We will talk soon."

He stepped into the hallway and pulled the door closed behind him.

"Wait," she called.

The door opened again. He stared at her, his face drawn, eyes pensive.

Was he friend or foe? She couldn't tell.

"My cell," she explained. "I need to make a phone call."

"I do not have your cell," he stated.

"But it was in my hand, then I dropped it into my pocket." She raised her voice for emphasis. "You have my clothes."

He glanced at the woman. He'd called her Emma. Was she his wife?

"You have found a phone?" he asked.

"No, Brother." The woman shook her head. "A phone was not among her clothing."

"That can't be right," Miriam objected. Why couldn't they both understand? "Do you know what a cell phone looks like?"

The man pursed his lips. His face clouded, either with anger or frustration. "My sister did not find a cell phone among your things."

"Do you have a phone? A landline? Or a computer with internet access?"

He raised his hand as if to silence her. "You must eat. Then we will talk." The door closed.

Miriam groaned with frustration. She threw off the covers, dropped her feet to the floor and sat upright. Her head throbbed and her mouth was thick as cotton. Gingerly, she touched her side, remembering the blow to her ribs.

Her muscles ached and the room swirled when she stood. Holding on to the wooden bedframe, she pulled back the sheer material that covered the window and glanced outside. In the distance she could see hills and a winding road, no doubt, the one she had raced along last night. She shivered, remembering her car careering over the embankment and heading for the icy water.

The muffled sound of a door slamming on the first floor forced her gaze to the yard below. The man left the house and walked with purposeful strides across the dormant winter grass. He had donned a black coat and felt hat with a wide brim and turned his head, left to right, as if to survey his land as he walked.

A crow cawed overhead. She strained to hear the sounds that usually filled her ears, of cars and sirens and train whistles. Here the quiet was as pristine as the landscape.

Glancing again at the man, she touched her hand to the windowpane, the cold glass taking her back four days.

A jumble of images flashed through her mind. The middle-of-the-night traffic stop on the mountain road. Two cops, one with the serpent tattoo insisting she leave her car. Her mother's confused outrage, escalating the situation until the second man stepped to the pavement and brandished his gun. The shots rang in her memory.

She closed her eyes, unwilling to go deeper into the tragedy. Instead she thought of her time at the cabin when she and her sister had been held captive.

Sarah!

Grief weighed upon her heart. Hot tears stung her eyes. Her sister, just barely twenty-one, had been carted away last night by a tall, skinny, red-haired man. His threat to silence Sarah if she didn't stop crying played through Miriam's mind and made her gasp with fear.

She choked back a sob of despair and wiped her hand over her cheeks, intent on regaining control of her emotions. She had escaped from the cabin. Now she had to find Sarah and learn the truth about her mother.

With a series of determined sniffs, she turned her focus back to the Amish man as he neared the barn and pulled the door open. He glanced over his shoulder. Then looked up. His gaze locked on hers.

Her cheeks burned. She dropped the curtain in place and stepped away from the window. She didn't want him to see her watching.

She had to get away, away from the mountains and back to civilization where she would find trustworthy officers who would enforce the law. Once they learned how she and her family had been attacked, they would hunt down the corrupt cops and help her find her sister.

She had to find Sarah. She had to find her alive.

Chapter Two

"What do you want from me, Lord?" Abram had finished feeding the horses and now stared at the gray sky, wishing *Gott* would part the clouds and speak to his heart.

Bear trotted from the corner where he slept to rub against Abram's leg as if even the farm dog understood his confusion. Bending to rub Bear's neck, Abram took comfort in the animal's doleful gaze and desire to please.

"You are a smart dog, but you do not understand the human heart." Neither did Abram.

As Bear ambled back to his favorite corner, Abram straightened and stared again at the sky, questioning his own sensibilities. No woman had made him feel so much emotion since Rebecca. His first and only love had been taken too soon, which, as his faith told him, was *Gott*'s will. Although if that were true, then why in the dark moments of the night did he question *Gott*'s wisdom?

He turned his gaze to the second-story window where the woman had stood earlier. Abram had not learned her name, yet he yearned to know more about her. She had fallen into his arms, seeking help, not knowing of his failings in the past.

What had come over him, thinking thoughts about another woman? Especially an *Englisch* woman?

A righteous man lusted not with his eyes nor his heart. The admonition sprang from deep within him, darkening his already somber outlook.

He left the barn and headed for the house, turning as a car pulled into his drive. The sheriff braked to a stop and crawled from his squad car. He was mid-fifties with graying hair and tired eyes that had lost their sparkle years earlier.

Abram approached the car and extended his hand. "Samuel."

The sheriff—Abram's uncle—smiled ruefully as the two men shook hands. "You're the only one in the family who acknowledges me, for which I'm grateful."

"*Yah*, but if you returned home to Ethridge, you might find some who would offer welcome."

"Your mother, perhaps. She is a good woman who knows how to forgive. I don't think your father would be as charitable."

Abram knew too well his father's unwillingness to forgive. "My father does not understand a man who leaves his faith."

"The Amish way was not my way. We have talked of this before." Samuel sniffed. "You're a good man to allow me into your life, Abram."

"I welcome you as the sheriff of Willkommen. You keep the peace so I can live in peace, as well."

He studied his uncle, seeing the shadows under his eyes and the flash of regret that could not be hidden. "Yet you still question your decision."

Samuel's brow furrowed. "What makes you think I'm not at peace?"

"I see it in the set of your jaw and the bent of your shoulders. You carry a heavy load."

"No heavier than you, my nephew. You still grieve for Rebecca."

"*Yah*, and for the mistake I made out of my own pride. Not going to the *Englisch* hospital when her labor pains started cost Rebecca her life, as well as the life of our child. That is the burden I carry."

"And the bishop?"

"He says I am forgiven."

"Yet, what about you, Abram? Can you forgive yourself?"

The sheriff's eyes pierced the wall Abram had placed around his heart. Three years had passed but the wound was still so raw. A wound he feared would never heal.

Just like Emma's limp and his good friend Trevor's tragic death, some mistakes lasted forever.

"God doesn't exact payment for our wrongdoings, Abram. Remember that."

"My father would say you are wrong, Samuel."

"Does your father not have his own burdens?"

Abram smiled weakly. "I was his burden."

"Perhaps in your youth when you were struggling to find your way, but you remained Amish. That should have brought him comfort."

Longing to shift the conversation away from the past, Abram said, "You did not come here to talk about my transgressions."

"You're right." Samuel pointed to the mountain road. "Old Man Jacobs said two cars raced down the hill last night. Curtis Idler and my new deputy, Ned Quigley, are talking to him now and trying to get more information."

Abram turned his gaze to the road. "I am surprised Ezra Jacobs could see anything at night and even more surprised that he would contact the sheriff's office. As far as I know, he is one of the few *Englischers* who never installed a phone line."

"True, but his son, Walt, has been checking in on Ezra and left a cell for him to use in case he needed help."

"Did he need help last night?" Abram asked.

"Not help, but he was concerned." Samuel raised his brow. "What about you, Abram? Did you see cars racing down the mountain?"

"Something has happened?"

"One of the cops in the next county found an abandoned car that ran off the road and nearly landed in the river. I'm headed there now. My deputies will join me when they finish talking to Jacobs."

"The mountain road can be slick and dangerous, yet you question me?"

"I thought you might have seen something. The car was found just over the county line and not far from your property."

How could Abram forget the man last night who was driving too fast?

"Besides, I had time to kill," the sheriff confessed. "Bruce Tucker, the chief of the Petersville Police Department, guards his turf like a bulldog. He'll insist his own officers search the scene before he invites me or any of my deputies on site."

Abram had heard talk about Tucker being less than cordial. "Chief Tucker does not welcome your help?"

"He does not want anyone's help. Some folks call him a *bensel*. Others say he is *schmaert* like a *hund*."

"A silly child or smart like a dog. You have not forgotten the language of your childhood, Samuel."

"I have not forgotten anything, Abram." Samuel frowned. "But you didn't answer my question. Did you see a car on the road last night?"

"*Yah*. The driver was going fast. I flagged him down and warned him about the bridge."

"Was anyone else in the car?"

"I saw only one person."

"Can you describe the driver?"

"The glare of headlights was in my eyes. He leaned out the window, but I could not see his features. He turned the car around and took the fork in the road, heading west."

"What about the make of car and the license plate?" Samuel pressed.

"A black sedan. I did not think it was important to notice the license plate."

"Did you check the time?"

"Soon after midnight."

"Yet you were awake and saw his lights in time to warn him?" Samuel asked.

"Sleep is sometimes not my friend, as you must know."

His uncle glanced at the house. "What about Emma? Did she see anything?"

"Emma does not have trouble sleeping."

"Fortunate for her." The sheriff slapped Abram's shoulder in farewell before he returned to his car.

As he pulled onto the roadway, Abram climbed the steps of his porch and sighed deeply. He had to find out more about the woman upstairs.

He wanted to know who was after her and why.

Miriam stared at the tray of food Emma had brought to the guest bedroom. She had tried to eat, but her stomach was queasy and her mind kept flashing back to the smattering of details she could remember about the traffic stop.

In addition to the food, Emma had also provided a clean change of clothes—an Amish dress that she'd pulled from the blanket chest sitting in the corner of the room, along with an apron. Miriam considered herself a jeans-and-sweater type of gal, but the dress fit and she appreciated having something other than a flannel nightgown to wear.

Emma, probably mid-to-late twenties, was a foot shorter than Miriam with a pretty complexion and a sweet smile. She also exuded an abundance of patience as she showed Miriam how to straight-pin the dress at the bodice and waist. Working together, they had subdued Miriam's somewhat unruly hair and twisted it into a bun.

Spying a number of skeins of yarn along with crochet hooks and knitting needles in the blanket chest and, knowing she needed some outlet for the nervous energy that swelled within her, Miriam had asked if she could use the yarn to make a scarf for her newfound friend.

Emma seemed to appreciate the offer and her eyes sparkled as she lumbered to the door. Miriam couldn't help but notice the deformed angle of her left foot that caused her to limp.

The Amish woman's handicap was obvious. Miriam clasped her hands to her heart, wondering about her own wounds, growing up within a dysfunctional family.

Maybe here in the quiet of this Amish home, she would quell the turmoil that had been the norm in her life for far too long. Then she thought of all that had happened and realized she was asking too much. Some scars cut too deep.

Sighing, she wrapped her arms around her waist and jerked when her finger snagged against the sharp tip of one of the straight pins. A bead of blood surfaced almost instantly. She glanced around the room, looking for a box of tissues. Seeing none, she neared the porcelain pitcher and washbowl on the oak dresser. After pouring water over her finger, she dried her hands on the thick towel and repositioned the pin to prevent another prick.

Footsteps sounded, coming up the stairs. Her heart pounded, expecting Abram to open the door. Confusion had rocked her the last time he had done so. As much as she appreciated him giving her shelter for the night, she didn't want to face his penetrating eyes and stern gaze.

Miriam had seen the sheriff's car in the drive. Had Abram mentioned the woman hiding in his house?

The steps drew nearer. A knock at the door. "May I enter?"

His voice was deep, stilted. Did she detect an edge of impatience?

She wrung her hands to calm the trembling that came unbidden. What was wrong with her? She had done nothing wrong.

Again flashes of memories washed over her. Hot tears burned her eyes. She wiped at her cheeks, needing to be clear-headed and alert when she faced this giant of a man. No doubt he would question who she was and why she had stumbled into his life.

Another knock.

She stepped to the door and ever so slowly pulled it open. He stood on the other side, too close. Much too close.

Her breath hitched. She took a step back, needing to distance herself from his bulk and the smell of him that filled her nostrils with a mix of fresh soap and mountain air.

His hair, now neatly brushed back from his forehead, fell to where his beard hugged his square jaw, framing his face and accentuating the crystal blue of his eyes.

He dropped his gaze, taking in the simple dress she wore. Pain swept his face. He swallowed hard. "I will be downstairs. We need to talk." Without further explanation, he closed the door, his footsteps heavy as he descended the stairs.

She didn't want to talk to him. Not now. Not when so much had happened. If only she could find her cell phone. She needed to call Hannah. Her older sister had always known what she wanted, and it hadn't been to remain in Tennessee with a mother who showed the classic signs of early onset Alzheimer's.

Miriam needed help and someone to lean on for support.

Abram's broad shoulders came to mind.

She shook her head. She couldn't trust him. She couldn't trust any man, not even the Amish man who had saved her life.

Chapter Three

Standing at the kitchen counter, Abram gulped down the last swig of coffee and wondered again about what had brought the mysterious woman to his door.

Should he have told Samuel? Her fear the night before had made Abram hesitant about revealing her presence. Thankfully his uncle had not asked him point-blank about the woman. Abram would not lie, but he need not divulge information that could terrorize her even more.

He placed the mug in the sink and rubbed his temple to still the pressure that had built up over the long hours he had tried to sleep. Seeing the woman wearing Rebecca's clothing had been a new stab to his heart. Of course, Emma had not realized the effect it would have on him.

The woman needed clothes to wear while her own things were being washed. His sister was shorter than their visitor, so offering Rebecca's dress had been a practical solution, except for what it had done to his equilibrium.

"You wanted to talk to me?"

He startled at the sound of the woman's voice and

turned to face his guest. "I did not hear you come down the stairs."

His heart lurched again, seeing her in Rebecca's dress. He gripped the kitchen counter to steady himself and to make certain he was in the present and not dreaming of his wife yet with another face.

In an attempt to slow his racing heart, he searched for common ground. "The coffee is hot."

She shook her head. A strand of hair fell over her pale cheek. "I'm full from breakfast."

"Then you had enough to eat?"

"More than enough. I'm grateful for your hospitality."

"I do not know your name."

"Miriam," she quickly replied.

He waited, expecting more. Then, when she failed to respond, he raised his brow. "Should you not have a family name, as well?"

"Of course." Her face flushed. "It's Miller."

"Your father's name?"

"Actually, it was my mother's surname." She paused before adding, "My mother lived in Willkommen as a child. I was headed there to find her sister, but I got lost on the mountain roads. Is the town far?"

"Ten miles at most."

She took a step closer, her gaze expectant. "Then you might know Annie Miller."

"I know Eli Miller. His wife's name is Hattie. Perhaps your aunt has married?"

"I… I…" She faltered. "I don't know. My mother had only recently mentioned that she had a sister."

"You should ask more from your mother."

She wrung her hands. "I could call my sister if I had my phone."

"Could your phone have dropped from your pocket?" he offered, hoping to soothe her unease.

"Maybe. I'm not sure. What about a computer? I mentioned it upstairs, but you didn't answer me. Don't some Amish people use computers for business?"

"I do not have electricity to run a computer, nor a computer. That is not the way I live."

She held up her hand. "I didn't mean to offend you."

"I did not take your comment as an offense."

Her oval face was tight with worry. She rubbed her arms.

"You are cold?" he asked, concerned for her well-being.

"I'm fine, except I need my phone."

"There are phones in Willkommen. You can call from there."

She raised her hand to her forehand and carefully played her fingertips over the blackened bruise. "The problem is that I can't remember my sister's number. We haven't talked in…"

She shook her head and bit her lip as if she couldn't finish the thought that played heavy on her heart. "My sister's number is programmed in the contacts on my cell, that's why I need to find my phone."

"Perhaps you cannot remember her number because you are tired. You did not sleep well?"

She dropped her hand and bristled ever so slightly. "My problem is not lack of sleep."

He had pushed too far. Abram pointed to her forehead. "Someone hit you?"

"I fell," she corrected. "Your sister was kind enough to clean the wound last night."

A man had chased after her. A man who, according to her own words, wanted to kill her. A husband perhaps. Abram glanced at her left hand where he had not seen a ring as the *Englisch* were accustomed to wear. He did, however, see the bruise marks around her wrists.

Nervously she wiped her hands along the fabric of her dress. "Thank you for the clothing. It belongs to someone in your family? Your wife? She…" A furtive glance. "She is away?"

"My sister did not tell you?"

Innocent eyes. How could someone seemingly so open with her gaze be chased by a crazed man? He hesitated, weighing the thoughts that tangled through his mind.

"Tell me what, Abram?"

His chest tightened at the inflection of her voice when she said his given name.

"I'm sorry," she quickly added.

Had she noticed his surprise?

"Is it impolite to use your first name?" she asked. "I don't know Amish customs nor your last name."

"Zook. My name is Abram Zook. My wife, Rebecca, and my unborn child died three years ago."

Miriam's face clouded as if feeling his pain. "I'm sorry, Mr. Zook, and I apologize for any impropriety on my part." She touched the bodice of the dress Rebecca had so carefully stitched.

The front panel had challenged his wife when the fabric refused to lay straight. The memory of her bright smile when she had mastered the problem brought heaviness to his heart. The dress had been the last she had made before learning she was with child.

He turned, unable to face the woman in his wife's clothing. Instead he stared through the kitchen window. His gaze took in the hillside and the winding road that had brought the *Englisch* woman to his door.

"I've upset you after you were nice enough to take me in." She sighed. "As soon as I have my phone, I'll be on my way."

Slowly he turned to face her, needing to gauge her reaction to his next statement. "The sheriff said a car ran off the road, not far from here, but in the next county."

Fear clouded her eyes. She rubbed her neck and glanced down. "Did...did you tell the sheriff about me?"

"He did not ask if I had visitors so I did not tell him."

She glanced up, her gaze a swirl of unrest. "I haven't done anything wrong."

"I did not think you had." He hesitated a long moment before adding, "Yet a man followed you last night. He is your husband?"

Shock—no, horror—washed over her pale face. "I would never have anything to do with an animal like him."

"Yet he was looking for you."

She raised her chin. "I ask that you trust me. I'm innocent of any wrongdoing, but the man is evil. I don't want you or your sister to get involved. That's why I have to leave. Now. Can you take me to Willkommen? From there, I can catch a bus to Atlanta."

"I will take you to Willkommen, but not today." Not while law enforcement in two counties was investigating an abandoned car. For her own safety, the woman needed to stay put.

"But I have to contact my older sister in Atlanta."

He nodded. "You can do so when we go to town tomorrow."

She took a step back. Frustration clouded her gaze. "What will I do until then?"

The back door opened and Emma stepped inside,

carrying a basket of apples. She glanced questioningly at Miriam and then at her brother.

He lifted his hat off the wall peg and stepped toward the open door. "Our guest wishes to help you."

His sister's face darkened. "Where are you going, Abram?"

"The fence needs repair. Lock the door after I am gone."

Emma caught his arm. "You are worried that the sheriff will return?"

"I am not worried." He stepped onto the porch.

"You did not eat this morning, Abram," his sister called after him. "You will be hungry."

"I will survive."

"*Yah*. You are a strong man."

Before the door closed he heard Emma's final comment. "Perhaps too strong."

His sister knew his weakness almost as well as he knew it himself.

"*Gott*," he mumbled, looking up at the sky and shaking his head with regret. "Forgive me for my prideful heart."

"Wait!" Miriam hurried past a startled Emma and grabbed a black cape off the hook by the door. Throwing it around her shoulders, she raced from the house.

"Abram," she called.

Surprise registered on his square face as he turned. Or was it impatience? With his pensive gaze and stoic expression, the man was hard to read.

"I need your help," she said, running toward him.

He hesitated a moment, probably thinking of the fence that demanded his attention.

"You're right about my phone." Miriam stopped

short of where he stood. "It must have fallen from my pocket."

She looked at the winding mountain road in the distance and the grassy pasture that led toward a thick wood. "But, I'm confused. Do you know the direction I would have walked last night? I remember coming through the woods, then a clearing."

"The sheriff mentioned a car bogged in mud at the river's edge." Abram pointed to the stand of trees at the far side of the pasture. "The county line is just beyond those pines that mark the end of my property. The river curves close to the road there. I believe it is where you left your car."

Overwhelmed by the vast area she would have to cover, Miriam pulled in a deep breath and nodded with resolve. "I'll start by looking around the house first."

"You have heard the saying, 'a needle in a haystack'?"

The seriousness of his tone made her smile. "Does that mean I should give up before I start?"

His full lips twitched and a spark of levity brightened his gaze. "We will search together. I will help you, Miriam."

She liked the way he said her name as well as his offer of assistance. Returning his almost smile with one of her own, she felt a huge weight lift off her shoulders. "Thank you, Abram."

"We will begin here." He pointed to the stepping stones upon which they stood. "And we will take the path through the pasture. Perhaps you followed it last night."

Without further delay he dropped his gaze and walked slowly toward the drive. Miriam followed close behind him, searching the winter grass cut short enough that a cell phone would be visible.

On the far side of the dirt drive she paused and breathed in the serenity of the setting, then smiled as a big dog with long, golden hair ambled out of the barn. She patted her hand against her thigh, calling him closer. "What's the pup's name?"

Abram stopped to watch the dog sidle next to Miriam. "His name is Bear."

She rubbed behind the dog's ear. "You're big as a bear, but sweet." She cooed to the dog before looking up at Abram. "He's part golden retriever?"

"With a mix of Lab."

Again she lowered her gaze to the dog. "How come I haven't seen you before this?" Bear wagged his tail and nuzzled closer as if enjoying the attention.

"He sleeps in the barn. You did not see him last night because I had closed the doors to keep the horses warm."

"I'm glad I got to meet you today, Bear." With a final pat to the dog's head, Miriam straightened and took in the pristine acreage around Abram's house. In the distance, a number of horses grazed on the hillside. "The animals are yours?"

"*Yah.* The others are in the barn." A look of pride and accomplishment wrapped around his handsome face. "Horses are necessary for the Amish way of life. They provide transportation. They pull our plows and haul produce and products to market."

"They're beautiful, but a car and tractor would make your life easier."

"Easier does not mean better." He returned to his search, leaving her to ponder his statement.

So many people yearned for modern conveniences to enhance their quality of life. But did possessions bring contentment?

Her mother had traveled the country, looking for happiness. Instead she had found unrest and confusion.

In her youth Miriam had longed for a father to love her and the security of a stable home. She had found neither.

Like the elusive memories of her past, the wind tugged at the hem of her dress and wrapped the fabric around her legs. For a fleeting moment she felt a new appreciation for the Amish way and almost a kinship with this man who embraced the simple life.

Hurrying to catch up to Abram, she asked, "What can you tell me about the sheriff? He's from Willkommen?"

"Originally he came from Tennessee. His name is Samuel Kurtz. He is my mother's brother."

Not what she had expected to hear. "The sheriff is your uncle?"

Abram studied the surprise she was hard-pressed to control. "Does that seem strange to you?" he asked.

"A bit." Actually it surprised her a lot. "How can an Amish man work in law enforcement?"

"Before baptism, young men and women decide how they will live their lives, whether they will remain in the community or move elsewhere. My uncle did not wish to remain Amish. Our family is from Ethridge, Tennessee. Samuel came to Georgia to make a new life for himself. He is respected here. A year ago, he was elected sheriff."

"You moved here to be near your uncle?"

"The land brought me. The price was good. I wanted to make a new home for myself and my wife."

"Did you ever consider leaving the Amish way, like your uncle?"

"Once, but I was young and foolish. Thankfully, I

changed my mind and realized what I would be leaving." His eyes softened. "The Amish walk a narrow path, Miriam, but we know where it leads. My uncle wanted something else for his life."

"And he's happy?" she quizzed.

"You will have to ask him." Abram motioned her toward a path that cut across the pasture. "This is the way you walked last night."

She glanced back at the house. "How can you be so certain?"

"Your footprint is there in the dirt."

Glancing at where he pointed, she recognized the faint outline of her shoe.

"Which means we don't have to search the entire pasture to find my cell." Feeling a swell of relief, Miriam hurried forward, hoping her phone would be as easy to find as her footprint.

Abram led the way, seemingly intent on the quest, until the sound of a motor vehicle turned his gaze to the road.

"A car is coming," he warned. "You must go back to the house."

She wasn't ready to give up the search. "I haven't found my cell."

He took her arm, his grasp firm, and turned her around. "Hurry. Someone comes."

The intensity of his tone drove home the danger of being seen. Fear overcame her and she ran toward the house. Was she running for protection or running into a trap?

Everything inside Abram screamed that he had to protect Miriam. From what or from whom, he was not sure.

He ran to the road and stepped onto the pavement

just as the Willkommen sheriff's car rounded the bend. Abram glanced back at the pasture. Miriam was still running, the black cape billowing out behind her.

His heart thumped a warning for her and one for himself, as well. His actions since Miriam had stumbled onto his porch were so outside the norm that it seemed as if someone else had taken control of his body and his mind.

Seeing his uncle at the wheel of the squad car, Abram raised his hand in greeting. Samuel slowed the vehicle to a stop and rolled down the window. Abram leaned into the car.

His uncle's face was drawn, his eyes filled with sadness.

"Go home, Abram, and lock your doors." Samuel flicked his gaze to the fleeing figure in the distance. "Keep Emma inside."

Thankfully, his uncle had not questioned Miriam's even gait and, instead, had mistaken the *Englischer* for his sister.

Knowing something serious was underfoot, Abram pressed for more information. "What is it you are trying to tell me, Samuel?"

"I mentioned that the Petersville police found a car at the river's edge. When I got there, they were searching the back seat and taking prints. They found a woman's purse."

"The handbag belongs to the person who owns the car?"

The sheriff nodded but the pull of his jaw told Abram more than a purse was at stake.

"The trunk of the car was locked. They were preparing to break it open when I left."

A nerve twitched in Abram's jaw. A roar filled his ears. He strained to hear the sheriff's words.

"The car is registered to a woman, age twenty-four. The police are trying to track her down."

Emma's warning about Miriam floated again through Abram's mind. *She will bring trouble to this house.*

What had become of the peace and surety of his life? Overnight he had gone from calm to chaos.

"The woman who owns the car is from a small town outside Knoxville," Samuel continued. "One of Chief Tucker's officers contacted the authorities there. Seems she lived with her mother and younger sister. All three women have been missing for a number of days. No one knows where they went. The daughter told the neighbors her mother had Alzheimer's, yet the neighbors claimed the mother seemed normal."

Miriam had not mentioned her mother's dementia.

"The younger sister's twenty-one." The sheriff tugged on his jaw. "She's missing, as well."

"What are you saying, Samuel?"

"I'm saying you need to be on guard, Abram. Deputy Idler will stop by once they learn what's in the trunk. I wanted him to alert you and the other Amish families who live out here if anything points to foul play. The circumstances are different, but I keep thinking about Rosie Glick, that Amish girl who went missing some months ago."

"Supposedly, Rose ran off with an *Englisch* boy."

"That's what we thought at the time. Now I'm not so sure."

Abram could no longer keep silent. "There is something I need to tell you, Samuel, that might tie—"

Glancing at his watch, the sheriff held up his hand to

cut Abram off. "It'll have to wait. I've got to get back to town. Art Garner, one of my deputies, was involved in a vehicular accident on the road leading up Pine Lodge Mountain. He's being air-evacuated to Atlanta. I told his wife I'd drive her to the hospital."

"You will return tomorrow?"

The sheriff shook his head. "I need to handle some business while I'm in the city and won't be back for at least three days. The Petersville police will be in charge of the investigation. Idler will be the point of contact on our end. He'll keep you updated if new information surfaces."

The sheriff narrowed his gaze. "Be careful, Abram. Watch your back until the women are found."

"But, Samuel—" Before Abram could mention his houseguest, the sheriff pulled his sedan onto the roadway and sped down the hill, taking the fork in the road that headed to Willkommen.

Tension tightened Abram's spine as he gazed at his house in the distance. Miriam had come back out of the house and was standing on the porch, tugging at her hair. Was she fearful of what the sheriff had found?

Slowly he walked toward her. In his mind, he laid out the many questions he needed to ask. Before he reached the drive, the sound of another car cut through the stillness.

"Go inside, Miriam," he called. "Now."

Her eyes widened, but thankfully she complied and closed the door behind her just as one of the Willkommen deputy's cars pulled into the drive.

Curtis Idler, midforties with a muscular build and receding hairline, climbed from the passenger side and nodded to Abram. He pointed to a second deputy behind the wheel. "You know Ned Quigley?"

"We have never met, but Samuel has mentioned his name." Abram bent and peered into the squad car. Ned was probably ten years younger than Idler, but a big man with full cheeks and curly hair. The deputy raised his hand in greeting. Abram nodded before turning his focus to Idler.

A scowl covered the older deputy's drawn face and angled jaw. "I came to warn you, Abram. A woman, probably midfifties, was shot twice. Her body was locked in the trunk of the car that was abandoned by the river. Looks like she's been dead a few days. Thankfully she was zipped up tight in a plastic mattress bag or you would have smelled her even here."

Abram's stomach soured at the thought of the dead woman jammed into the trunk of a car.

Idler pulled a smartphone from his pocket. He tapped on the cell a number of times and then angled the screen so Abram could see the picture that came into view.

"I know you Amish are against photography, but you need to see this."

As much as Abram did not want to look at the phone, his eyes were drawn there.

"The murdered woman's name is Leah Miller. She's from Tennessee. This is the suspect we're looking for," the deputy continued. "A killer who's considered armed and dangerous."

Abram's heart lurched as he stared at the photo.

A killer? Armed and dangerous?

Something was terribly wrong.

Abram fought to control his emotions as Idler

climbed into the passenger seat and Quigley backed the car out of the drive.

All Abram could see was the photo on Idler's phone.

The photo was of Miriam.

Miriam was not a killer. Or was she?

Chapter Four

Miriam stood next to the woodstove, but even with the warmth from the burning logs she felt chilled to the core. Her hands shook as she shoved hair back from her face and braced herself for Abram's reproach.

Emma washed apples in the kitchen sink, her back to Miriam, for which she was grateful. The woman's silence was indication enough of the tension that filled the house.

Abram's heavy footfalls on the porch signaled his approach before the door opened and he stepped across the threshold. He glanced at Miriam with hooded blue eyes then he spoke to his sister in what must have been Pennsylvania Dutch from the harsh guttural sounds Miriam couldn't understand.

Emma nodded curtly and scurried out of the kitchen and up the stairs, leaving Miriam to wrap her arms tightly around her midriff and pull in a deep breath. She was determined to stand her ground against the tall and muscular man whose presence sucked the air from her lungs.

Serpent had warned her about other police officers

working with him. He'd insisted that alerting law enforcement would cause Miriam more harm than good.

"I do not know what the sheriff told you," she said, taking the offensive before Abram could accuse her. She spread her hands. "As I mentioned to you earlier, I have done nothing wrong."

"You are quick to rationalize behavior about which I have not spoken."

Gathering courage from deep within, she refused to lower her gaze. "I will leave as soon as possible," she said through tight lips. "But I need my clothing and my phone. I also need transportation to Willkommen. As I mentioned earlier, I presume there is a bus that will take me to Atlanta."

"Yah." He nodded. "The bus runs at the end of the week."

"Do you know the schedule?"

He shook his head. "But you can check when we are in town."

"If you drop me at the bus station, I can—"

What would she do without money? Somewhere along the way, she'd lost her purse, although she kept an emergency stash of fifty-dollar bills in the glove compartment of her car. Hopefully the police wouldn't flip through the pages of the vehicle maintenance book where she had hid the money.

Abram was staring at her.

"I'll be safe with my sister, Hannah, in Atlanta," she said, trying to pick up her train of thought.

"The person you hoped to call with your phone?"

Miriam nodded. "That's right."

"Still you do not remember her phone number?"

"The number is programmed in the contacts on my phone," Miriam explained. "I told you all this earlier."

He raised a brow. "Yet you told me nothing about your mother."

She took a step back. "My mother?"

Miriam's cheeks burned. She didn't need a mirror to realize how hot and flushed she must look.

Abram pointed to the kitchen table. "It is time we talk freely."

He indicated the bench where he wanted her to sit. She lowered herself onto the long wooden seat and remained silent as he sat across from her.

The table was smooth as silk and gleamed with shellac or polish or a mix of both. She glanced at his large hands, noting the scrapes and calluses, realizing he had probably made the table.

Serpent's hands were soft with short, pudgy fingers. What he lacked in size, he made up for with brute force.

She cringed, remembering the strike to her forehead and the jab to her ribs. Without thinking, she touched the tender spot at the side of her brow.

Abram's eyes followed her hand. "Who hurt you?"

She could no longer hide the truth. "A policeman who has a serpent tattooed on his neck."

"You stayed with him?"

"Not willingly."

Abram flattened his palms on the table. "Why do you hesitate telling me your story?"

"My story?" Did he think this was make-believe?

"What happened, Miriam? Why were you with him? Why do you have bruises on your wrists?"

Unwilling to relive the experience, she started to rise. Abram caught her hand. His touch was firm, yet gentle, and his gaze was filled with understanding.

She stared at him for a long moment, searching for

any sign of aggression. All she saw was compassion and a concern for her well-being.

Pulling in a ragged breath, she lowered herself onto the bench. She had nowhere else to turn and no one, other than this Amish man, to help her. She would have to trust him with her *story*, as he called it. He had taken her in and he deserved to know the truth about what had happened on the mountain.

Her mouth was dry, her throat tight. She pulled her hand free from his hold and toyed with her fingers, weighing how to begin.

"I... I lived in Tennessee with my mother and younger sister, Sarah. My older sister moved to Atlanta a few years ago."

"Hannah?" he asked.

"That's right. She's two years older than I am." Miriam paused, struggling for a way to explain the reality of her life. "Our mother was a free spirit of sorts."

She glanced at Abram. "Do you understand that term?"

The faintest hint of a smile curled his full lips. "Although the Amish end their formal education at the eighth grade, there is much that can be learned outside the schoolhouse."

"I didn't mean to imply that you weren't educated. I just wasn't sure if you had heard of the expression."

"You said your mother was a free spirit." He brought her back to the subject at hand.

Miriam wiped her fingers over the tabletop, wishing her life had been as smooth. "Mother carted us across the United States. We rarely stayed for more than a few months in any one place."

Thinking back to her youth, Miriam shook her head. "We were pulled out of so many schools. We longed for a normal life. We had anything but stability, living with our mother."

"How did you get to Tennessee?"

"Friends invited Mother to visit. They had a small home for rent outside of Knoxville, and we moved in. Not long after that she started showing signs of dementia. I took her to a local doctor who diagnosed her with early onset Alzheimer's. You're aware of the condition?"

Abram nodded. "I am."

"Her mind slowly deteriorated."

"Yet you brought her to Georgia?" he asked.

"Which is what she wanted, although in hindsight we never should have left Knoxville."

"But you always did what your mother wanted."

"Which now sounds foolish and immature." She hung her head, thinking of the real reason she had agreed to travel to Georgia. Abram didn't need to know her motives. She'd made a horrific mistake, one that would haunt her for the rest of her life.

"A few months ago," Miriam continued, "Mother started talking about an estranged sister with whom she hoped to reconnect."

"This is the aunt who lives in Willkommen?"

Nodding, Miriam added, "Annie Miller is her name, although I'm not sure where she lives or if she even exists. Mother became insistent that she needed to see her sister. Prior to that, she had never talked about her family or siblings, and we never brought up the subject."

A sigh escaped Miriam's lips. "Knowing it was a subject she didn't want to talk about kept us from asking questions. We knew her parents had died and that she'd rejected their faith."

Abram's eyes widened ever so slightly. "Your mother did not believe in *Gott*?"

"She believed there was a God, she just didn't believe she needed Him in her life. Or that we needed Him. We lived near San Antonio for a period of time and visited a few of the missions. I saw something there that I wanted in my own life. A love of God. An ability to turn to Him in times of need. A belief in His goodness and mercy."

"Did you tell your mother how you felt?" Abram asked.

"I tried. She became agitated and insisted I was being foolish. We moved not long after that."

"Which made you even more hesitant to discuss faith."

Miriam's heart warmed. "That's it exactly. To maintain peace and some semblance of family stability, we skirted any mention of the Lord."

"And now?" He raised his brow.

She was puzzled by his question. "I don't understand."

"How do you feel about *Gott* now?"

"I…" She tried to identify her feelings. "I'm not sure. I started attending a church in Tennessee when Mother's condition grew worse. I was searching, maybe reaching out for help. The people were welcoming, but I struggled to accept the fullness of their faith in God. Perhaps I had pushed Him aside too many times."

Turning her gaze to the window, she could see the horses grazing on the hillside. "I doubt the Lord would have interest in a woman who grew up fearing to mention His name."

"You were young, Miriam. You had no one to teach you or lead you to faith. Besides, *Gott* would not hold you accountable for the actions of your mother."

"I don't know if that's true, Abram. I worked in a

local craft shop and tried to earn enough money to pay the rent and put food on the table. I didn't need to compound my struggle with issues of faith."

She offered him a weak smile. "We've gotten off topic. You wanted to know about Serpent."

Painful though it was to give voice to the flashes of clarity that circled through her mind, she slowly and methodically explained, as best she could, the middle-of-the-night traffic stop that turned tragic.

"I was driving. It was late and the mountain roads confused me. Seeing the police lights in my rearview mirror brought relief, until I saw the serpent tattoo on the neck of the so-called officer. He made me leave the car. My mother became agitated. She lunged from the back seat, screaming, and rushed at him with raised fists. A second guy remained inside the police vehicle. I had the feeling he was in charge and that Serpent was doing his bidding."

"Can you describe him?"

"I wish I could. The flashing light on the roof of the car blinded me. When my mother went after Serpent, the other guy stepped to the pavement and turned his weapon on her. He fired once, twice. I didn't see his face. All I saw was my mother's blood."

Hot tears burned her eyes. "I… I don't know what happened after that. Sarah was still in the car. I struggled to get to her. Serpent struck me and knocked me out. I never saw my mother again."

The tight expression that washed over Abram's face chilled her. "What have you learned?" she demanded, anticipating the answer before he spoke.

He took her hand. "The police found an older woman's body in the trunk of your car."

Miriam dropped her head and moaned. She had

feared her mother was dead, but hearing the words spoken was like a knife piercing her heart.

Abram circled the table and slid next to her on the bench. His muscular arms wrapped around her and pulled her into his embrace.

For so many years she had longed for strong shoulders to support her. Never had she suspected comfort would come from an Amish man whose upbringing and background were so totally different from hers.

She buried her head against his chest and cried heart-wrenching sobs for all that had happened. For the trip to Georgia that had ended in tragedy. For Sarah, who had been taken and might never be found again. And for the horrific murder of the mother Miriam had loved so much, who had never loved her in return.

"I will not let this man hurt you again," Abram whispered as he gathered Miriam deeper into his embrace.

As much as he wanted her to remain there, she eventually pulled back. Her face was blotched with tears, but even then he saw her determination to muster on.

She sniffed and wiped her hands over her cheeks. "There's more to tell, Abram."

He relaxed his hold on her, knowing she needed space.

She dabbed at her eyes and bit her lip. Then, playing her fingers over the smooth finish of the table, she drew in series of jagged breaths and straightened her spine as if gathering courage and finding the wherewithal to continue.

"Serpent—" Her voice was raspy and little more than a whisper when she finally spoke. "Serpent took my sister and me to a cabin. I heard water. We could have been near the river. He tied each of us up in different rooms. I was worried about Sarah, but no matter how hard I struggled, I couldn't get free."

She swallowed hard. "I... I pretended to be asleep when he checked on me. When light filtered through the window the next morning, he forced me to swallow a pill. I spit it out, but he struck me and said he would kill Sarah if I didn't take the drug. I pretended to do so and then coughed it up when he left the room. The next time, I wasn't as lucky. He clamped my jaw closed until the pill dissolved in my mouth."

Abram could only imagine the terror both Miriam and her sister had experienced. A rage against the two men grew within him.

"Days passed in a blur," she said, her voice growing stronger. "I heard snippets of conversations. Some on the phone... One night a guy with a deep voice stopped by. I overheard just a portion of what they said. They kept mentioning *trafficking* and *women*. The night I escaped, another man came to the cabin. I saw him through the window. He was tall and skinny with red hair. He hauled Sarah away and Serpent said he was going to dispose of her."

Abram took her hand and was relieved when she squeezed his fingers.

"When Serpent came to give me more drugs, I didn't respond. He probably thought I was still sedated. Later, after what seemed like hours, I broke free from the rope that had held me. He had become complacent and had forgotten to attach the cord to the bedposts. I slipped outside and found the key to my car on the floorboards. He must have heard the engine start because he ran from the cabin before I pulled onto the main road."

"But you escaped, Miriam."

She nodded. "I was crazy with fear and so tired. I hid in the woods, but he found me and chased me. One of my tires had a blowout and my car almost ended up in the river. Somehow I got out and started running. Then I saw the light in your window."

"*Gott* led you here."

"I… I was worried when I saw you talking to the sheriff. Serpent said he would pin my mother's death on me. He said all the cops in this area were working together with him. He said they would believe his story."

"What he claimed has proven true, Miriam. Curtis Idler, the Willkommen deputy, said the police are searching for you. They suspect you killed your mother. Yet I do not understand how they could believe such an evil man with the serpent on his neck. He cannot be an officer of the law."

"But his car had a flashing light and a sign that read Petersville Police Department."

"The chief of police in Petersville is not to be trusted, so perhaps this Serpent, as you call him, is working with law enforcement, after all. I know my uncle will help you."

"Then I must tell him what happened."

Abram shook his head. "Samuel is traveling to Atlanta and will be gone for three days."

"I can't wait that long." Miriam's voice was insistent. "Serpent needs to be stopped now, before he hurts anyone else."

Emma hurried into the kitchen and stared at both of them. "Forgive me. I thought you had finished talking."

"You are right, my sister. We have finished our conversation." Abram released hold of Miriam's hand and stood. "Tomorrow we will go to Willkommen."

"But—"

"Tomorrow, Miriam. Until then, you will stay with Emma and me."

Chapter Five

Miriam shook her head with frustration as she thought about what terrible things could have befallen her sister. She needed to find Sarah as quickly as possible.

"You are upset with my brother," Emma said, drawing close. She placed a comforting hand on Miriam's shoulder. "He is worried about your well-being."

"Did you hear that the Petersville police suspect me of killing my own mother?"

Emma nodded and pointed to the small holes drilled through the ceiling. "The heat from the stove rises to warm the bedrooms. Abram's voice travels, as well. I tried not to listen, but I could not help but overhear what he said to you."

Miriam gazed into Emma's blue eyes, not nearly as crystal clear as her brother's but bright and filled with understanding. "How could they think I would do that? There is no evidence."

"Except this man who held you captive. You do not know the lies he has told."

Pulling in a ragged breath, Miriam fought the tears that welled up. She wiped her hand over her face and struggled to control her upset. "I'm usually not this fragile."

Emma raised her chin and smiled. "I see strength when I look at you, Miriam. Not weakness. That is why you and Abram butt together. He is not used to a woman who speaks her mind."

"Am I that demanding?" she asked.

"Demanding is not the word I would use. You see things one way. Abram sees them another way. Soon, you will learn to work together."

"We could work together if he would take me to Willkommen."

"But what good would it do if the Petersville police arrest you?"

Emma patted Miriam's shoulder.

"Those who want to do you harm and those who suspect you of a crime would not think to find you here," the Amish woman continued. "You must remain hidden from view. Abram is a man of his word. Tomorrow, he will take you to Willkommen."

The *clip-clop* of a horse's hooves sent both women to peer out the window. Emma grabbed Miriam's hand when Abram appeared, guiding the horse and buggy to the back porch. "It seems my brother has changed his mind."

Miriam squeezed Emma's hand and then opened the door before Abram climbed the stairs to the back porch.

"We're going to town?" she asked, her heart overflowing with gratitude.

"*Yah.* Nellie is hitched and waiting. We will talk to Samuel's deputy, Curtis Idler. If my uncle left him in charge, then we can trust him."

"You both must be careful," Emma cautioned. "What if this Serpent is prowling about?"

"Hopefully he won't look for a woman in Amish clothing," Miriam said.

"Wear my bonnet." Emma pulled the wide-brimmed hat from the wall peg. The shape reminded Miriam of what pioneer women wore to the keep the sun off their faces.

"We must hurry." Abram removed the black cape from a second peg and wrapped the heavy wool around Miriam's shoulders. Emma helped tie the bonnet under her chin.

"There is a blanket in the buggy if you are cold." He opened the door wider. "We will leave now."

Miriam's heart raced, knowing she could be in danger. At least Abram would be with her.

He helped her into the buggy. "Sit in the rear," he suggested. "You will be out of sight there."

She crawled onto the second seat and nodded to Emma as the horse started on the journey to town.

Abram sat in the front, the reins in his hands and his focus on the road.

Was Miriam making a good decision? Or would she regret leaving the refuge of Abram's home?

Abram's neck felt like a porcupine with his nerve endings on alert. With each breath, his muscles tensed even more as he sensed a looming danger, although he did not know from where the danger would come.

Maybe he was being foolish to leave the security of his home and travel to town. Out in the open, anything could happen.

He flicked his gaze over his shoulder to Miriam. Her eyes were wide, her face drawn. She clasped her hands as if in prayer and looked like a typical Amish woman with her black cape and bonnet. Then her gaze turned to him and a bolt of current coursed through him, as palpable as the lightning that looked ready to cut through the darkening sky.

Why did this woman—this *Englisch* woman—affect him so?

He turned his focus back to the road and lifted the reins ever so slightly. Nellie always responded to the slightest movement of his wrists and today was no exception. The mare increased her pace, the sound of her hooves on the pavement as rhythmic as a heartbeat.

Abram eyed the darkening sky. If only they could outrun the rain that seemed imminent. A harbinger of what would come?

"The day is turning dark," Miriam said from the rear. "What happens if it storms?"

"Sometimes we find shelter. Today we will continue on." Although, he knew Nellie could be skittish if lightning hit too close and thunder exploded around them. He would not share his concern with Miriam. From the tension he heard in her voice, she was worried enough.

Approaching a bend in the road, Abram pulled back on the reins and slowed Nellie's pace. He wanted to ensure nothing suspicious appeared ahead of them as they rounded the curve. His gut tightened when he spied police cars in the distance swarmed around a buggy. His pulse thumped a warning and his throat went dry.

"What is it, Abram?" Miriam leaned forward. Her hand touched his shoulder.

"A roadblock. There are a number of Petersville police cars and a deputy's car from Willkommen. It appears they are searching a buggy."

"What can we do?" she asked, her voice faltering.

He yanked on the reins. Nellie made a U-turn in the roadway and began retracing the route they had taken.

"The Petersville police suspect you murdered your mother. We must return home."

Moments later a car engine sounded behind them. Abram glanced around the side of the buggy. A black sedan with a flashing light on the roof was racing toward them.

"We are being followed. The car looks like the one I saw the night you escaped."

"It's Serpent."

Once they rounded the bend, Abram steered the buggy to the edge of the road and pulled back on the reins.

"You must hide." He pointed to a thicket. "There, in the woods."

Miriam crawled to the front of the buggy and held Abram's outstretched hand as she climbed to the pavement.

"Hurry," he warned. "Go deep into the woods. Find cover there."

Abram's heart pounded as he watched her flee, knowing he had made a terrible mistake. They never should have left the security of his house.

The black sedan raced around the bend and pulled to a stop. A man dressed in a navy shirt and khaki pants stepped to the pavement. He slapped Nellie's flank as he approached Abram.

"What is it you want?" Abram asked.

The man wore a scarf around his neck. Although muscular, he had small eyes with drooping upper lids, flattened cheeks and a short, upturned nose. His mousebrown hair was thin on top but long on the sides.

"Why'd you turn your buggy around?" he demanded.

Abram pointed to the sky. "The clouds are dark.

Rain is in the air. I do not wish to drench my buggy, my horse or my clothing."

The man stepped closer and peered past Abram into the rear of the carriage. "Someone was with you?"

"As you can see," Abram tried to assure him, "I am alone."

The man turned his gaze to the forest. He took a step forward. "There. I see movement." Just that fast, he ran toward the thicket exactly where Miriam had gone moments earlier.

Abram hopped from the buggy and started to follow.

A second car, this one from the Willkommen sheriff's office, pulled up behind the black sedan.

"Abram, stop."

He turned, spotting Ned Quigley, the newly hired sheriff's deputy.

"Did you see the guy driving the black sedan?" the deputy asked.

Abram beckoned him forward. "He ran into the woods."

"Stay with your buggy," Quigley said. "I'll find Pearson."

Pearson. Evidently Serpent had a name.

Abram ignored Quigley. He would never stay put when Miriam was in danger.

He pushed through the bramble. The deputy followed close behind.

Pulling in a ragged breath, Abram searched the forest. He had to find Miriam. He had to find her before Serpent did.

Miriam's heart nearly exploded in her chest, seeing Serpent follow her into the woods.

She couldn't outrun him, but where could she hide?

Her breath hitched and a roar filled her ears, nearly drowning out his footfalls as he trampled through the underbrush.

Overhead thunder rolled and the forest darkened with the encroaching storm.

A lump filled her throat and she struggled to keep the tears at bay. She couldn't cry. Not now, not when she needed to outsmart the snake that was so heinous.

More footsteps sounded. How many men were searching for her?

Abram had been right. She should have stayed undercover at his farmhouse instead of throwing herself into harm's way. More thunder rumbled as ominous as the situation she was in.

A cluster of rocks was visible through the pines. Would they provide a hiding spot?

Carefully she picked her way through the bramble, averting the twigs and branches that would snap if she stepped on them. Any sound would alert Serpent.

She gulped for air, her lungs constricting with the tension that made her hands shake and her heart lurch.

Careful though she tried to be, her foot snagged on a root. She toppled forward and caught herself just before she landed in a pile of dried leaves. Thankfully, at that very instant, a bolt of lightning crashed overhead and a blast of thunder covered the sound of her fall.

Regaining her footing, she scurried behind the rocks, willing herself to meld into the outcrop of granite. The skies opened and rain fell in fat drops that pinged against the rocks, the trees and the floor of the forest.

A deep guttural roar sounded, like a wild beast's bellow. Serpent was standing only a few feet away on the other side of the rock, venting his anger. If only he would be deterred from coming closer.

More footsteps. Her heart nearly ricocheted out of her chest. She flattened her hands and cheek against the granite trying to disappear into the stone.

"I know you're here." Serpent's voice, laced with fury.

Could he hear her heart beating uncontrollably in her chest?

"Pearson?" another voice called, deep and demanding.

Serpent grumbled.

"There he is." Abram's voice.

Relief swept over Miriam.

"You're on a wild-goose chase," the first man said as he drew closer.

"I saw something," Serpent replied.

The deep-voiced man snickered. "You saw that skunk standing at your backside."

"What!" Serpent groaned.

The putrid and unmistakable stench of a skunk's spray filled the air.

Leaves rustled wildly, followed by the sound of footsteps racing back to the roadway.

"Looks like Pearson learned his lesson about chasing varmints in the woods." The deeper voice chuckled.

"He has other lessons to learn," Abram said, his tone sharp and without the joviality of the other man's. "Tell him to leave me alone."

"I'll tell him," the man answered. "Although I doubt it'll do any good."

The voices became fainter, but even though the danger subsided, Miriam continued to tremble. Serpent had been too close.

Abram would come to get her, she felt sure, when the men had left the area. She and Abram would return to the farmhouse where she would remain until the road-block was lifted.

But would Serpent continue to search for her? And if he found her, what would happen then?

Chapter Six

The next morning Miriam stood at the kitchen window and peered at the mountain road, searching for any sign of a dark sedan. Yesterday Abram had returned to the woods and found her as soon as the two lawmen had left the area. Grateful though she was, Miriam was still concerned about her safety.

She had risen early to help Abram's sister. Apples needed to be peeled and pies baked for market, but the nervous churning in her stomach made her want to hide upstairs, away from the peering eyes of anyone who might pass by the farm.

Emma seemed oblivious to Miriam's anxiety and chatted amicably as she worked. Stepping away from the window, Miriam wrapped her arms around her waist, debating how to still her unease.

"As I mentioned last night, I have many pies to bake," Emma said as she placed a bowlful of apples on the table. "You will help me?"

Longing to allay the tension that tightened her shoulders, Miriam reached for the apple peeler. Using her hands would be therapeutic and might take her mind off the man who wanted to do her harm. Plus, Emma and Abram had provided her safe lodging. The least she could do was to help with the baking.

After peeling more than a dozen apples, Miriam heard Abram outside and, stepping to the sink for a drink of water, she peered from the window. "Does your brother ever stop working?"

Emma scooped flour into her cupped hand and then dropped it into the mixing bowl. "A farm requires work. He has a shop in addition. Livestock to care for, crops to grow."

"And you make pies to sell at market," Miriam said as she placed the now empty water glass next to the sink.

"Our apples are plentiful and the *Englisch* enjoy my baked goods. It lets me help Abram with the expenses."

"You help him with many things, Emma."

She smiled meekly. "We work together. He needs someone to cook his meals and wash his clothes. To put up the vegetables from the garden."

"The jobs his wife did."

"That is right. Without a wife, he could not handle the farm in addition to the house. Plus, it brings comfort knowing that I am helping offset some of the expenses by selling my pies at market. Work is not a bad thing."

"No. Of course not. And you're a good sister to care for him, yet surely you want a husband and a home of your own."

"*Gott* will provide when the time is right."

"You mean when Abram has found a wife."

Emma nodded sheepishly. "The problem is that he does not seem interested."

"Are you perhaps too accommodating?"

Emma glanced at Miriam. "What are you saying?"

"Abram doesn't look for another wife because you take care of him."

The Amish woman blushed. "I do not think that is the case. He would take a wife for more reasons than to share the work."

Miriam had to smile. "Is there no Amish man who strikes your fancy?"

"Most of those who are looking for a wife are younger."

"I can't believe Abram is the only widower in your community."

"Actually, Isaac Beiler lives nearby. He owns a dairy. You can see his farm from the front windows. He has one son. A sweet boy named Daniel."

Miriam returned to the table and continued peeling apples. Emma made the piecrust and rolled it into perfect circles that fit the disposable pie pans.

The women sliced the apples and added sugar, cinnamon, nutmeg and a pinch of salt before they filled the shells and covered the tart fruit with a latticed top crust.

"You baked at home?" Emma asked, watching as Miriam fluted the edges of the shells.

"My mother never baked, but I always enjoyed working in the kitchen."

Emma nodded with approval. "You seem to know what you are doing."

Later, when Emma pulled the last of the pies from the oven, Miriam inhaled the savory aroma that permeated the kitchen with a welcoming warmth of home and hearth, what Miriam had always longed for in her own house. Regrettably her mother's sharp rhetoric, especially as the dementia changed her personality, had dispelled any feelings of welcome or warmth.

Once she and Emma had cleaned the kitchen, the

Amish woman pulled a bowl from the cupboard. "I will start cooking for the evening meal."

Miriam glanced at the cupboard, surprised by what she saw laying on top. "Is that a rifle?"

"*Yah*. Abram hunts. Sometimes I go with him."

"I wouldn't think—"

Emma tilted her head. "We hunt for food, Miriam. Deer, rabbits, wild turkeys."

"Is the gun loaded?" Miriam asked.

"What good would it be if it were not? Foxes and coyotes come after the livestock. We must keep them safe."

Miriam nodded. "From what I've seen, Emma, you work as hard as your brother."

Emma winked. "Some say the women work harder. We are up early to light the stove in the morning and the last to hug the children at night."

A knock at the door startled both of them.

"Check first to see who's there," Miriam warned. Her pulse pounded with dread. What if Serpent had returned?

Emma peered from the window and then rose on tiptoe to look down upon the person, evidently a very little person, standing on the back porch.

Emma laughed. "It is Daniel." She opened the door wide. "Let me help you with the milk."

An adorable boy, not more than five or six, stepped into the kitchen. He carried two large glass jugs that he placed on the floor just inside the door.

"Daniel is our milk delivery man. He lives on the farm just across the way."

The dairy run by the widower. Miriam stepped closer, totally taken with the boy's sparkling blue eyes and bowl-cut blond hair. His rosy cheeks and cautious smile instantly stole her heart.

"Daniel brings us milk from his father's dairy," Emma explained.

"You must be very strong," Miriam enthused, "to carry such heavy jugs so far."

The boy's chest puffed out and he nodded as if knowing the delivery job demanded not only brawn but also expertise and skill.

"Daniel, you have come at the perfect time." Emma pointed to the pies cooling on the sideboard. "Perhaps you would like a slice before you return home."

"*Yah*, I would like that. *Danki*."

The boy took a seat at the table and eagerly attacked the pie Emma placed in front of him. Miriam poured a glass of milk for the young lad and, before he lifted the glass to his lips, the door opened. Abram stepped inside, bringing with him the smell of fresh straw and lumber and the outdoors.

He smiled seeing their guest. "Daniel, did you save some pie for me?"

"*Yah*. Miriam will pour you a glass of milk, too."

She quickly cut a slice for Abram while he washed his hands and face. He returned to the kitchen with his hair neatly combed and his angular face scrubbed clean and ruddy from labor, and sat across from the boy. "I saw you helping your *datt* in the field. You did a fine job with the horses."

The boy beamed as he shoved another forkful of pie into his mouth. "I am a hard worker."

"I know you are. Your father relies on your help."

"He says we need a woman to help, too."

Miriam couldn't help but notice Emma's reaction. The color rose in her cheeks as she returned the cut pie to the sideboard.

"Your father would make some woman a good husband," Abram added, seemingly oblivious to his sister's reaction.

"He says I need a mother," the boy added without hesitation.

"And what do you say, Daniel?" Abram pressed.

"I say *Gott* will provide."

Abram chuckled. "You have a good head on your shoulders. Perhaps you need a bit more pie."

"*Datt* waits for me. I must go." He cleared his plate and fork from the table and handed them to Emma. *"Danki."*

She quickly wrapped a whole pie in a strip of cheesecloth and tied it with a knot. "Here, Daniel. Take this home for you and your father."

The boy's eyes widened.

"Carry it with two hands," she instructed, pointing him toward the door. "I will watch you from the porch."

The boy's expression clouded. "But you never watch me."

She glanced at Abram. "Today I will."

No doubt, Emma sensed Abram's unease. Once Daniel said goodbye and he and Emma left the house, Miriam rinsed the dishes in the sink.

"You have done a good job with the baking," Abram said, eyeing the rows of pies cooling on the sideboard.

She was surprised by his statement. "How do you know I was involved?"

He rose and carried his plate and fork to the sink.

"Because your face is streaked with flour." He wiped his hands on a nearby towel and dropped the cloth onto the counter.

Turning, he gently flicked white powder from her cheek. His touch was light and brief, and her skin drank in his nearness as if she were desperate for some sign of acceptance. She leaned closer, inhaling the clean scent on a man who enjoyed nature and the outdoors.

Emma's voice could be heard calling goodbye to Daniel, but all Miriam thought about was Abram's touch and the beat of his heart when she had rested her head on his chest yesterday.

His fingers dropped to her lips. "It looks like a bit of sugary apple caught at the side of your mouth. That's how I could tell you were hard at work. The pie I tasted was delicious, so I thank you for preparing it for me."

"I… I…"

She could hardly think of anything to say. Her mind kept remembering when she had been wrapped in his arms and wished to be there once again. Then she wouldn't have to worry about what had happened on the mountain road and that a man with a vile tattoo was prowling the countryside looking for her.

Emma pushed open the kitchen door.

Abram stepped away, leaving Miriam overcome with a sense of loss.

He smiled at his sister and pointed to Miriam. "Rebecca's pies—" he started to say.

Miriam's breath caught. *Rebecca*? Abram had confused her for his wife. A pain stabbed her heart.

Why was she drawn to this man who was so totally different from her? A man who still loved a woman who had died some years earlier, a woman whose clothing Miriam was wearing?

Any interest Abram might have showed to her was really directed to his wife. He was confused by the dress. He wasn't touching Miriam's lips, he was yearning to touch his wife's.

"Excuse me." Miriam wiped her hands on the nearby towel. "I need to go to my room."

Seems Miriam had followed in her mother's footsteps. Her mother had trusted no one and wandered from town to town looking for acceptance that she'd never seemed to find. Her negative outlook on life had caused Miriam to keep a tight hold on her own heart, as well. She hadn't allowed anyone to come close, especially not a man who put her world into a spin.

"Are you all right?" Emma asked as she followed her up the stairs. "You appeared upset when Abram mentioned Rebecca's name. Her pies were never as golden brown as ours today, which was the point he was trying to make."

Miriam knew the truth. Abram had confused her for his wife.

"I'm tired, Emma. If you don't mind, I'd like to lie down for a bit."

"Yes, of course. You have been through so much."

After Abram's slip of the tongue, Miriam needed to make plans to leave Willkommen and head to Atlanta. But how would she contact Hannah? If they couldn't connect by phone, Miriam might be able to contact her via email. To do that, she would need a computer.

"You told me that the *Englisch* buy your baked goods," she said before Emma left the room.

The Amish woman nodded. "I have some regular customers who I count on weekly."

"Do any of them live nearby?"

"The Rogerses' house is about four miles from here. They have a standing order of two loaves of bread, a pie and two dozen cookies each Saturday."

"Their house is situated along the road to Willkommen?"

"Actually, it sits back from the road. I used to take the route that crosses over the river. The bridge is not strong enough for an automobile, but a carriage can pass there. Although sometimes a horse can get spooked."

"That's the road that passes in front of your house?"

Emma nodded. "But Abram is worried about our safety, and he does not like the water."

"What do you mean?"

Emma shrugged. "I should not bring it up."

"But you mentioned it."

"I did, although I should not talk about Abram." She bit her lip and sighed. "His best friend when he was fourteen was an *Englischer.* Trevor was older and drove his father's car too fast. Abram was with him. There was a sharp curve and the car skidded off the road and into the lake."

Miriam could see the pain wash over Emma's face. "What happened to the *Englisch* boy?"

"Abram saved himself but—" Emma pulled in a stiff breath. "He could not save Trevor."

"I'm sorry, Emma."

"*Yah*, it was hard on all of us. Abram especially."

Miriam could only imagine how tragic the drowning had been.

"The accident happened in Tennessee, but the memory returns whenever Abram is around any body of water. For that reason, he stays away from the river and the bridge and, although a longer journey, we take the other fork in the road. While it causes us to backtrack, Abram does not have to worry about the bridge." Emma's face brightened. "I have an idea. You can go with me to the Rogerses' house on Saturday. They are good people. You will like them."

"Do they have a computer?"

"I do not know about a computer, but I am sure they have a phone so you can call your sister."

By Saturday, Miriam hoped to be in Atlanta. She looked down at the blue dress she wore and brushed a smudge of white flour from the skirt. "I must wash my clothes, Emma. You need to show me where you placed them."

"I will wash next week. It is no trouble. Your things are in the barn, soaking since they were spotted with blood."

"You don't need to do my wash. Just tell me where you keep the soap or laundry detergent."

"You will see them near the wash barrel."

In addition to clean clothes, Miriam also needed money for her bus ticket. "I'll rest now and maybe go to the barn later," she said as a plan took hold.

"You will take the evening meal with us?"

"Yes, of course. I'll come downstairs later to help you prepare the food."

"Only if you feel strong enough. Perhaps I tired you too much with baking the pies."

"Absolutely not. I enjoyed the work."

"And I enjoyed the company."

Glancing out the window, Emma smiled. "I see Isaac is coming to visit."

Miriam stared over the Amish woman's shoulder and nudged Emma playfully. "He probably wants to thank you for the pie."

"Perhaps. Although I suspect he wants to talk to Abram. They are alike, those two, although in different ways."

Miriam raised her brow. "Meaning?"

"Isaac knows he must work within the Amish way, but he uses some other resources in his business." No doubt seeing Miriam's confusion, she added, "A dairy needs refrigeration if he is to sell to the *Englisch*."

"You mean Isaac uses electricity?"

"*Yah,* it is allowed, but the power runs only to the dairy barn. It is *verboten*—not allowed—in the house."

"The bishop sets the rules?" Miriam asked.

"We live by the *Ordnung,* but each bishop leads his own community. Some communities and some bishops are less strict in adhering to the old ways."

"Does Abram have electricity in his woodshop?"

Emma shook her head. "Abram would not, but he does use diesel fuel to run some of his woodworking machines. Diesel is allowed."

"I don't understand."

"Some members of our community came from Ethridge, Tennessee, years ago. You have heard of that town?"

Miriam nodded. "Abram mentioned it."

"Ethridge is made up mainly of Old Order Amish. They live as the Amish have since first coming to America. They do not have running water in their homes as we do here. Nor does anyone, even those doing business with the *Englisch,* use propane. Diesel motors are allowed, but that is all."

"Abram said part of the community left Ethridge and moved here."

Emma nodded. "A new community usually develops when a group of families have like ideas about the way they will live. Sometimes they move to find farmland, as Abram did."

"So your community is less conservative compared to Ethridge, where you grew up?"

"Except Abram. He remains very conservative."

"And his wife?" Miriam asked. "How did she feel?"

Emma smiled sweetly. "She loved Abram. What could she say?"

A knock sounded at the door below.

"It is Isaac." Emma tugged a strand of hair back from her face and hurried into the hallway. "I need to welcome him."

Emma's feelings for Isaac were obvious. Although Miriam had never loved a man, she had hoped to find someone someday. Someone who would walk through life at her side. Both of them in step and working together.

But love would have to wait. As much as she admired Abram and found his home and way of life peaceful, Miriam would never fit into the Amish community. Or could she?

Abram studied the wood he had stacked against the wall of his workshop. In times past, he had been considered a master craftsman. The work had brought joy and a steady income from the items he had sold in town. But that was before Rebecca had died.

He touched the arm of the hickory bentwood rocker he had only begun to make. For the last three years, it had remained a visible reminder of his deceased wife.

Deep in his heart, Abram knew Rebecca would have wanted him to find someone else. Emma had hinted at the fact several times. But he did not deserve happiness after what had happened. He had never verbalized his thoughts to his sister nor did he give voice to the question that troubled him now.

Why would he search for someone to replace Rebecca when his own stubbornness had claimed her life?

Yet ever since Miriam had appeared on his doorstep, he wondered if there could be something—or someone—else that would fill the void Rebecca's passing had left.

Abram shook his head with regret. He didn't need joy. He needed redemption. His father was right. He had been too easily taken off task as a youth. He would not let himself be thrown off course now.

The door to his shop opened and Isaac Beiler entered. Tall and stocky, the dairyman dipped his head in greeting. "Emma said I would find you here."

Abram left the rocker and stepped closer to his neighbor. "I thought you came for another pie." He was hard-pressed to stop the smile that tugged at his lips and he was glad when Isaac's eyes responded with twinkling good humor.

"Emma is always generous with her baked goods," Isaac said. "She is generous with her heart, as well. She invited Daniel and me to join you for supper this evening."

Isaac's wife had died thirteen months earlier. "Emma sees you losing weight, my friend. You and Daniel both need a good meal to fill your bellies. I do not know how you manage the dairy and the household. I would waste away if Emma were not living with me."

"She is a good woman." The neighbor rubbed his beard. "With Daniel, my thought was always to find a mother for my son."

"Yet in all these months, you have not found anyone?" Abram questioned what they both knew to be true.

Isaac sighed. "There is a woman, although I am not sure how she feels about me. With the dairy and raising my son, I have little time to court."

"Ah, but Isaac, you must make the time."

"By adding more hours to the day?" the neighbor smiled ruefully.

"There is always time for love."

"You are not one to follow your own advice, Abram."

The two men chuckled, but their joviality turned serious with Isaac's next comment.

"Daniel told me about the lady who has come into your home. I questioned Emma. She hesitated to tell me about the visitor until I mentioned seeing the sheriff's car on the road. She said the woman—Miriam—was injured and you gave her refuge. Your sister is worried about you, Abram."

"Worried? In what way?"

"That you do not realize what could come of this. Did you tell your uncle about the visitor?"

"I tried, but he needed to get back to town and did not have time to hear me out."

"What about the bishop? He has time to listen."

Abram did not want the bishop or any of the elders involved. The fewer people who knew about Miriam, the better. At least until Samuel returned to Willkommen.

"The bishop provides wise guidance," Abram explained. "But I do not need his counsel at this time."

He hoped Isaac would be satisfied with his answer, but the neighbor pushed on.

"Deputy Idler stopped by the dairy yesterday and told me about the abandoned car and the older woman's body found in the trunk. The timing makes me think your houseguest is somehow involved. Have you questioned her?"

Although Abram would rather not discuss the newcomer, he knew Isaac could be trusted.

"A man held her captive. He is on the loose. When Samuel returns to Willkommen Miriam will tell him what happened. Until then, she must remain hidden, and the best place to do that is here with me."

"She wears Amish clothing."

"Because she has nothing else to wear. The bishop would not want her going without clothing."

Isaac shrugged. "He would not."

"Once Samuel returns, the problem will be resolved. You understand I am acting out of concern for the woman. She was hurt and injured. I had to take her in. Is Emma unsettled by her presence?"

"She likes Miriam, but as I mentioned, she is worried about you."

"Emma worries too much. I am fine, Isaac."

"And what happens if the man who held her captive comes after you or after Emma? I do not need to remind you, Abram. The Amish way is one of peace, not conflict."

"If a fox is killing chickens in your coup, Isaac, do you stand by and watch? Or do you go after the fox?"

Isaac lowered his gaze and kicked at a mound of sawdust on the floor. "Be careful, my friend."

"We will be fine."

Glancing up, Isaac nodded. "Then I will return home now. Daniel and I will see you this evening."

After his neighbor left, Abram continued to think about Isaac's comments.

Was Abram making good choices concerning Miriam? He wanted to keep her safe. Hiding her on his farm was the right decision, but Emma was worried. Was she worried about their safety or Abram's heart?

Chapter Seven

Peering from her bedroom window, Miriam spied the Amish neighbor leaving Abram's workshop. He joined Emma at the front of the house where she was talking to Daniel. The young boy played with a stick that he threw in the air and then ran to catch. Bear sauntered around the corner of the house as if wanting to join the fun.

Even from her lofty vantage point, Miriam noticed the warmth in Emma's expression as she laughed with the child. Hopefully, the dairy farmer and his son would continue to occupy Emma's attention for some time.

Miriam turned her gaze to the workshop. From what she knew of Abram's routine, he would hopefully stay put for at least an hour or two.

With no time to lose, Miriam hurried down the stairway and out the kitchen door. She wrapped the black cape around her shoulders and raced along the path she and Abram had walked her first morning on the farm.

Miriam's car had bogged down near the river just past the edge of Abram's property. Surely the police had finished their search and, unless they had hauled the vehicle off to Petersville, she expected to find her car exactly where she had left it.

Thoughts of her mother's body found in the trunk made her sick with grief. She fisted her hands and forced the thoughts to flee. She couldn't mourn her mother now. She had to think of finding her sister, Sarah, and getting to Atlanta.

Still hoping to find her cell, Miriam kept her gaze on the edges of the path she walked and only occasionally glanced over her shoulder to make certain no one was following her. She didn't want Abram to stop her.

She needed to leave the area and that required a bus ticket, which meant she had to retrieve the emergency stash of money from her car. The police would have searched her vehicle but, how thoroughly, she wasn't sure. Even if they had looked at the maintenance manual in her glove compartment, hopefully they hadn't riffled through the pages.

A stiff wind blew across the pasture. She pulled the cape more tightly around her shoulders and increased her pace. She didn't have time to dawdle. Miriam had to retrieve the money from her car and return to the farmhouse before Abram or Emma noticed her absence.

All the while she walked, she listened for the sound of a car engine, knowing she would have to hide if she saw Serpent's dark sedan driving along the mountain road. To her relief, all she heard was the caw of crows flying overhead.

Nearing the fence that edged Abram's property, Miriam hurried forward to the open gate through which she must have passed the night of her escape. Leaving the pasture, she looked back at the farmhouse still visible in the distance. Once again she thought of the light shining in the window that had been her beacon of hope when she was trying to elude Serpent.

Turning her back on the peaceful scene, Miriam

scurried deeper into the underbrush where the thick growth of pine trees mixed with hardwoods blocked the sunlight. The temperature dropped and the sharp bramble forced her to slow her pace.

Carefully she picked her way around the prickly bushes that caught at her dress. Two nights earlier, she hadn't worried about thorns or sharp branches. She'd only thought of staying alive.

Skirting a particularly large bush, she inadvertently stepped on a twig that broke underfoot with a loud *crack*. The sound seemed amplified in the dense forest. She stopped behind a gathering of bushes to catch her breath and listen. Surely no one was close by, but she had to be careful.

As much as she wanted to keep moving forward, an internal, niggling voice cautioned her to bide her time. The forest stilled but another sound filled her ears. Rushing water.

Peering through the underbrush, she spied the river. The moving water was what she had heard while being held in the cabin and brought back memories of the hateful man who had held her captive.

She blinked her eyes, trying to clear the vision that sickened her. Serpent.

Was he real or imagined?

She blinked again but the vision remained.

Her heart stopped. The man who had held her captive stood staring in her direction.

Miriam's pulse raced. He must have heard the twig break. Although the thicket behind which she hid offered protection, she knew any additional movement would have him running to investigate.

He pursed his lips, took a step forward and stopped. *Please, God, don't let him see me.*

Serpent stood still for a long moment and then turned toward her vehicle.

Sending up a prayer of thanks, Miriam watched him wrap a handkerchief around his hand, open the driver's door and peer inside. Bending down, he felt under the seat before he rounded the car, opened the passenger door and rummaged through the glove compartment.

Leaves rustled behind her. Startled, she glanced over her shoulder. A squirrel scurried through the underbrush. Letting out a tiny sigh of relief, she turned her gaze back to the river's edge.

Serpent had disappeared.

Her heart crashed against her chest. A lump of fear lodged in her throat. Frantically she flicked her gaze around the clearing and then back to the car. Where had he gone?

Another swish of movement sounded behind her.

She started to turn.

A hand clamped over her mouth.

Powerful arms grabbed her and held her tightly against a rock-hard chest.

She gasped, fearing her fate. Serpent had captured her again.

Abram's heart beat out of his chest from fear so strong it had taken his breath away. He had seen Serpent. The man who had hurt Miriam. She had come so close to stepping into the open and startling the horrific man from his search.

A few minutes ago Abram had peered through the window of his woodshop and had seen her scurrying through the pasture after Isaac had left him. Following after her, Abram had spotted the man with the tattoo and feared Miriam was unaware of the hated man's presence. Thankfully, Abram had gotten to Miriam before Serpent had spotted her.

"Serpent is prowling in the bushes," he whispered in her ear as he held her close to his heart. "If you move, he will hear you."

She must have recognized his voice because she stopped struggling and relaxed against his chest. Turning her head ever so slightly placed her lips close to Abram's. Too close.

His heart jerked from her nearness.

"Where did he go?" she asked, her voice shaky with fear.

"I do not know."

"But you saw him, Abram. Right?"

He nodded. "*Yah,* I did."

"You saw the scarf around his neck. He's trying to hide the serpent tattoo, but it's there. He's the same man who chased after me in the woods."

"And the one who held you captive." Anger welled up within Abram directed toward the man who had accosted Miriam.

"Stay here," he cautioned. "I will circle the clearing and try to determine whether Serpent is still in the area."

Miriam grabbed his hand tightly. "Be careful. He's evil."

"Do not fear for my safety." Abram had to warn her. "But if he finds you, scream. I will hear you."

She nodded, her face void of color and her eyes wide with fear.

Abram stepped away from her. His whole being wanted to keep her close, but he needed to determine where Serpent had gone.

His hunting skills proved useful as he made his way

stealthily through the underbrush. Nearing a break in the tree line, he had a clear view of the mountain road.

A dark sedan sat parked on the side of the pavement. Serpent stood nearby, staring at smoke rising from a chimney visible through the trees.

Old Man Jacobs's cabin.

From that location Ezra Jacobs had a view of the road as it curved around the mountain. As Samuel had mentioned, Ezra had seen the cars racing along the roadway two nights ago and had called the sheriff. What else had he seen?

As Abram watched, Serpent opened the driver's door and slipped in behind the wheel. Making a sharp U-turn he gunned the engine and drove up the mountain on the road that led to Petersville. Was he going back to town or back to the cabin where he had held Miriam? If only Abram could follow him to find the hiding spot.

But Miriam was waiting for him. He needed to take her home and lock the doors behind them. Then Abram would pay a visit to Old Man Jacobs. He wanted to find out what the man had seen. Two cars driving much too fast down the mountain, or had he seen even more than that?

When Abram stepped back to the clearing, he saw Miriam in her car rummaging through the glove compartment.

"I told you to remain hidden," he said as he neared.

"I saw Serpent drive away. I needed my cell phone charger." She held it up along with a wad of bills. "And some money I kept in the glove compartment. I'm glad the police didn't find the bills or haul my car away."

"The Petersville police department has had problems

in the past. This time their oversight worked to your advantage. What about your cell phone?"

"It's not here, but with the charger, I'll be able to use the phone when I do find it."

"I have money, Miriam. You could have asked me if you needed anything."

"You've already done too much."

Abram pointed to the smoke visible through the tree line in the distance. "An old man lives in a cabin there where the smoke is rising. I want to talk to him. He may have seen something."

"I'll go with you."

"It would not be wise."

"I'm concerned about my own safety, but I'm even more worried about Sarah. The man might know something about my sister. Or he may know about the cabin where we both were held. Let's go now," Miriam suggested.

"The distance is farther than it looks. I will take the buggy."

Miriam was silent as they walked back to the house. Hopefully she realized she would be safer remaining at the farm. But from what he knew about Miriam, once she got an idea in her head, there was no changing her mind.

Abram was not used to headstrong women or *Englisch* women who spoke their mind. He almost chuckled. In a way, he found it refreshing, which is something he would not share with the bishop or even Isaac Beiler.

Some things were better left unsaid.

Chapter Eight

"I'm going with you," Miriam said as Abram hitched Nellie to the buggy.

"You are staying here with Emma."

She shook her head. "I'm accompanying you."

"Serpent may be in the area," Abram said, no doubt trying to convince her of the folly of riding with him.

She looked down at the blue dress and apron. "He won't recognize me in Amish clothing, Abram. You needn't fear."

He dipped his head in agreement. "As you said, he should not recognize you wearing the *plain* clothing, unless he catches sight of your pretty face. I do not want to chance putting you in danger."

Bear trotted forward and nuzzled her leg. Miriam patted the dog's head then, gripping the side of the buggy, she hefted herself into the rig.

"You don't understand, Abram." She settled onto the rear seat. "I can't stay here at the house while you talk to a man who might know something about my sister. I'm going with you. You don't have a choice."

Abram muttered something that sounded like German under his breath, followed by, "Amish women are not so brazen."

She had to fight to keep from smiling. "You find me brazen?"

He shrugged. "Would 'determined' be a better choice of word?"

"Brazen or determined. Either one suits me just fine. I don't want to stay at the farm and wonder what you've found out from Mr. Jacobs. I need to see the area where he lives. I've forgotten much of what happened when I was held captive. No telling what might trigger my memory."

She nodded her head decidedly. "I heard running water, like the sound of the river scurrying past the cabin where I was held. If we find the cabin, I may remember who shot my mother. It wasn't Serpent. From the little I recall, the other man seemed in charge, as if Serpent could have been working for him. I need to find that man and also the redheaded guy who hauled Sarah away."

"It is my desire to find those men as well, but I still want you to stay here." Abram shrugged his shoulders as if wondering how he could convince her otherwise. "My uncle will bring everyone involved to justice, you can be sure of that."

"Your uncle's out of town, Abram, and I refuse to wait. We'll go together to Old Man Jacobs. We'll explore the back mountain roads. Something might come to light."

Once Nellie was hitched, he climbed into the buggy and sat on the first seat directly in front of Miriam.

Emma stepped onto the back porch. "I am worried about both of you."

"You are too much filled with concern, my sister."

But she had every right to be upset. A stranger had burst into their peaceful lives and thrown them into havoc.

"We won't be gone long." Miriam tried to sound optimistic as she waved goodbye.

Abram jostled the reins and Nellie started forward, the buggy swaying side to side in a comfortable rhythm Miriam found soothing.

With another flick of the reins, the mare increased her pace just after they turned onto the mountain road. The wind buffered Miriam's face, the morning air brisk and fresh. She settled back in the seat.

"There are blankets in the rear if you are cold," Abram shared. "You can reach them, *yah*?"

She turned, grabbed the woolen throws and wrapped one around her legs. She placed the second one over Abram's legs.

He smiled but kept his eyes on the road. "The morning is cool but not cold. I am fine, Miriam Miller."

Yet he didn't remove the throw.

The ride up the mountain took less time than Miriam had imagined. Abram pulled up on the reins and encouraged Nellie onto a narrow dirt path that angled more sharply up the mountain. The path was pitted with holes that caused the buggy to sway wildly back and forth.

Abram groaned. "We will stop here," he said when they came to a small clearing. "And walk the rest of the way."

He helped her out of the buggy, his hands strong around her waist. Once on the ground, she looked up, realizing how tall he really was.

Standing so close to Abram made her breath catch. He stared down at her with questioning eyes that made her heart pound. Was it his wife he saw when he looked at her? The thought made Miriam step back, but the buggy prevented her from going far.

Abram swallowed hard and dropped his hold on her. "Ezra Jacobs's cabin is nearby."

She glanced at the underbrush, the steep incline and the dirt path pocked with holes. "He could use a bit of home improvement."

"A recluse does not wish for company."

They started up the hill together. Abram reached for her arm and guided her along the path.

Her first inclination was to refuse his help, but the sincerity of his gaze made her realize she didn't need to prove her independence with Abram.

Having a man at her side was a pleasant change. She enjoyed the strength of his hand and the gentleness of his hold.

Once at the top of the steep incline they stepped into a larger clearing. A cabin sat nestled in the trees, overrun with vines. The porch listed and the stairs looked far too rickety for Abram's large frame, but he climbed the steps and knocked forcefully on the door.

When no one answered, he reached for the knob and pushed the door open. Miriam peered around him into the dark interior.

Although small, the cabin was neat and tidy. The floor was swept and the narrow bed pushed against the far wall was covered with a colorful blanket. An old beagle with graying hair lay curled on a small rug at the foot of the bed.

The dog raised his head, wagged his tail and hobbled toward them. Miriam bent to pat him then, seeing the blanket move, she grabbed Abram's arm and pointed to the cot.

Together they entered the cabin and approached the bed. Her heart stopped as she leaned closer to Abram. "Is he all right?"

Abram touched the man's arm. "Ezra, it is Abram Zook. You need to awake."

The old man's eyes fluttered open. He stared up at Abram then furrowed his brow. His voice was crusty with sleep when he spoke. "You're trespassing."

Abram smiled. "Perhaps, but I thought you were dead."

Just that fast, the man pushed aside the blanket, rolled to his side and sat up, wiping his eyes. "Tarnation, Abram. I'm breathing, ain't I? Don't know why you came barging into my cabin unannounced. A simple knock at the door would have raised me from my sleep."

The beagle stood next to the bed and waited expectantly until the old man scratched behind the dog's ears.

Relieved that Ezra appeared fit, Miriam stepped closer. "Sir, I'm Miriam Miller. Can we get you something? Maybe a glass of water?"

"Coffee. Strong and hot. The pot's on the counter ready to go. Just hit the button. Pull three cups from the cabinet and you can join me."

His gaze narrowed. "You said you're a Miller. Any kin to Harold Miller in Petersville?"

"I'm not sure. Does he have daughters named Leah or Annie?"

"Harold's got six sons. No daughters. His wife died when the last one was born."

"I'm sorry."

"We all were." He pointed to the kitchen area. "Turn that switch on the coffeepot, hear? A man could die of thirst, waiting for a cup of coffee, as slow as you're moving."

Miriam chuckled under her breath and hurried to do the man's bidding.

Abram patted the older man's shoulder. "Ezra, I talked to Sheriff Kurtz yesterday. He said you saw two cars racing down the mountain road the other night."

The old man nodded. "One had flashing lights."

"Did you think it was a sheriff's car?" Abram asked.

"Could have been, or one of those cop cars from Petersville. They patrol the road up to Pine Lodge Mountain."

"It runs by your cabin?"

"That's right. On a quiet night, I can hear cars driving to the lodge."

"Sheriff Kurtz wondered if you could provide more information about what you saw."

"You mean the ruckus in the woods?"

Abram leaned closer. "Tell me what happened."

Jacobs shrugged and rubbed his brow. "Wish I could, but my mind plays tricks on me. I remember some things and forget others. Couldn't remember much yesterday when I talked to the deputies. 'Spect I won't be able to remember any more today."

"Let's go back to what you do remember," Miriam said as she returned to his bedside. "Have you seen me before?"

Ezra stared up at her and then shook his head. "Seems I'd remember you."

"Why's that?"

"You look like someone I used to know."

"Leah Miller was my mother? Did you know her?"

"Can't recall. Names don't stay. Only thing that seems to stick are faces. I've seen you or seen someone who looked like you, but I can't tell you where."

"Is there another cabin nearby?" she asked. "Or did

you see me with a man who had a snake tattooed on his neck?"

Ezra shook his head. "Can't recall."

"What about a pretty blond girl?"

He rubbed his jaw. "I haven't seen anyone with blond hair for a while."

"Does that mean you haven't seen a blond-haired woman in the area?"

He nodded. "'Spect that's what it means."

Miriam sighed and turned to stare at the light coming through the still open doorway. Her gaze shifted to the cell phone on a nearby side table. The phone was a basic model without text or internet capability.

"Is that your cell, Mr. Jacobs?" she asked.

"Sure 'nough. You need to make a call?"

"If you wouldn't mind? I'd like to contact my sister in Atlanta."

"Won't be a problem. Long distance don't cost any extra, but go outside. You can't pick up anything in here."

Ezra's lips quivered into a half smile. "'Course, most times I can't get the right number plugged in with those small buttons." He pointed to a pair of reading glasses. "Helps if I use the spectacles. You need them?"

She shook her head. "Not the glasses, but I appreciate you letting me use the phone."

"What about the coffee?" he asked as she headed for the door.

"It's brewing."

Miriam hurried onto the porch and called directory assistance in Atlanta. Once connected to the automated operator, she requested the phone number for Hannah Miller and then repeated the name twice for clarity. Making herself understood was a challenge, but she responded to the prompts as best she could and was crestfallen when the search failed.

Miriam disconnected, feeling a heaviness to her heart. If only she could talk to Hannah.

She stepped back into the cabin, laid the phone on the counter and inhaled the rich aroma of fresh-brewed coffee.

"Did you contact your sister?" Abram asked.

Miriam shook her head. "Evidently, Hannah doesn't have a landline."

She moved into the makeshift kitchen. "What do you take in your coffee, Mr. Jacobs?"

"You're making me feel old. My name's Ezra and I take my coffee black."

She quickly fixed his coffee and placed it on his bedside table, then poured a cup for Abram and one for herself.

The hearty roast was hot and good. Even Ezra seemed to rally after his first sip. "I always drink my coffee at the table," he said as if she should have realized his cup needed to be placed there.

He gripped the metal-frame headboard and pulled himself to his feet. The beagle stood next to him, and Abram hovered close by, ready to offer a hand. Ezra walked slowly, but without problem, to the table. With a huff, he pulled out a chair and sat with a sigh of relief. The dog dropped to the floor at his side.

Miriam selected a chair across the table and Abram slipped into a seat on the opposite end. Once they were situated, he looked at the old man and smiled. "Tell us what you *do* remember, Ezra."

"Just the two cars racing along the roadway. I had fallen asleep sitting in the rocker by the fireplace."

He looked down at the faithful mutt who wagged his tail as if begging for a treat.

"Gus woke me." Ezra scratched the dog's ears. "He needed to do his business. When I opened the door to let him out, I heard the squeal of tires and the sound of an engine. Peered through the trees. Didn't see much except the flashing light."

"Have you noticed anyone walking through your property recently?"

The old man's eyes widened. "I told you about the sheriff's deputy."

Abram smiled. "You did tell us. Have you seen anyone else?"

Ezra closed his eyes for a long moment. Miriam wasn't sure if he was thinking or if he had fallen back to sleep.

"I've got a face." He blinked his lids open, a look of pride in his rheumy eyes.

"Someone you've seen recently?" Miriam pressed.

"That's right."

"Is it someone from around here?"

"Can't say where he's from. All I've got is his face. He's skinny as a beanpole with sunken cheeks that make his eyes kind of bug out."

Miriam's heart fluttered. She leaned across the table and stared at Ezra. "You saw a thin man nearby?"

"Tall and thin, although I can't remember exactly where I saw him."

Her pulse raced. "Was there anything else about the man that stands out in your mind?"

Ezra nodded and pointed to the top of his head. "His hair."

Miriam glanced at Abram, who was staring at her, his face tense.

"What was it about his hair?" she asked, knowing before Ezra said anything else.

"His hair was kind of wiry and puffed out around his pale face. But it was the color that I remember." Ezra dropped his hand back to Gus's neck. "The guy had bright red hair."

A red-haired man, tall and skinny. The man she had seen at Serpent's cabin. The man who had taken Sarah.

"Was a woman with him?"

Again the old man closed his eyes. Miriam counted off the seconds, but when he opened his eyes, he shook his head. "I don't remember any other faces."

"A young woman, blond hair, blue eyes," she prompted, hoping to prod his recall.

Again he shook his head.

Miriam's heart shattered. The red-haired man had been spotted, but Ezra hadn't seen her sister. If only he could remember something more.

She glanced at Abram, hoping he could help, but all she saw was sorrow in his expression, as if he knew the questions that tugged at her heart.

What had happened to her sister?

And was Sarah alive...or dead?

Seeing the pain on Miriam's face, Abram wanted to reach out and take her hand. The expectation in her eyes when the old man had mentioned the redhead had been dashed when Ezra failed to remember her sister.

Abram would never share his concern with Miriam, but he feared for Sarah's safety—if she was still alive.

Had there been other women taken on the mountain? Travelers driving over the narrow roads, unsure of the terrain? Women were vulnerable and especially so at night.

Abram's stomach soured, thinking of how women would be used. *Gott* have mercy on Sarah and on any other women caught in such a wicked net of perversion.

He and Miriam needed information about Serpent. They also needed to find the ring leader who had killed Miriam's mother as well as the red-haired man who had Sarah.

"Ezra, keep thinking back over the last few days and try to remember what you may have seen. Miriam and I will visit you again."

The old man reached down to pat his dog. "'Spect Gus and I will be here when you return."

"Is there anything you need?" Miriam stood and glanced into the small kitchen. "Food or household items?"

"Don't need a thing. My boy lives in Chattanooga. He comes down to visit at times and keeps me well stocked. You don't need to worry about me."

But Abram was worried. Something sinister was happening on the mountain.

Concerned for Miriam's safety, Abram checked outside before he hurried her back to the buggy. Once she was settled in the rear seat, he flicked the reins for Nellie to begin the journey home.

Leaving Ezra's property, they bumped their way down the potholed path and turned left onto the mountain road. Nellie picked up her speed once she turned onto the pavement, as if knowing they were headed home.

Nearing the next bend in the road the sound of a car alerted them to oncoming traffic. Abram eased up on the reins as a car zipped around the turn.

A black sedan with a stocky man at the wheel. He

barely glanced at Abram before he accelerated and the car sped up the hill.

Miriam gasped. Abram glanced back, seeing the color drain from her face.

"It was him." She groaned. "Serpent."

Abram peered around the corner of the buggy, but the car had disappeared around the bend.

She grasped Abram's arm. "Did he see me?"

Abram shook his head, wanting to reassure her. "He was looking at the mountain, Miriam. He did not notice either of us."

At least, that was Abram's hope.

Chapter Nine

Abram was on edge the rest of the afternoon after seeing Serpent. Even while grooming the horses and handling the afternoon chores, he kept watch over the house in case the kidnapper came searching for Miriam.

He had cautioned her to remain indoors, away from the windows, and to hurry upstairs if anyone knocked at the door. The house would provide protection. At least, that was his hope.

By evening some of his anxiety had eased and he looked forward to seeing Isaac again, and especially Daniel. The young boy brought joy to his heart with his innocence and wonder.

For too long, caring for his farm had sapped the life from Abram. When had he changed? he wondered, thinking back to when life was good. Easy enough to realize. The joy had left the night Rebecca died.

The weight of his grief had been too much to bear at first. Each night he had reached for Rebecca in his bed, only to find nothing; even the sweet smell of her had disappeared all too soon. Some days he couldn't remember her face, which caused him pain.

After finishing his work, Abram washed his hands

at the pump outside. He shook off the water and dried them on a towel that hung nearby.

Daniel stepped onto the porch and waved a greeting. "Emma said to tell you that the food will be ready to eat in half an hour's time."

"That is good. I am hungry." He smiled at the boy. "I am sure you are, too."

"*Datt* says I am always hungry." His blue eyes were wide with innocence.

Abram's heart tugged, thinking of the son he and Rebecca had been expecting. A child who had died in delivery due to Abram's stubbornness and failure to listen to his wife.

Suddenly, Abram was no longer hungry.

"Tell Emma I must go to the barn first."

"I will tell her." The boy scurried into the kitchen.

A chill blew off the mountain and pulled at Abram's shirt. He hurried to the barn, needing time to collect himself before he sat at the table.

Bear greeted him but he ignored the dog, passed the horses' stalls and headed to a storage room. Opening the door, he pulled back a tarp and stood staring at the cradle he had made for his child. The hardwood gleamed with oil he had painstakingly rubbed into the cherry wood. Each spindle had been sanded with love for the child he never knew.

He let out a deep sigh, wishing he could in some way go back and start his life again. Then he realized the foolishness of his thoughts. Mistakes once made could never be unmade; a truth he had learned the hard way as a youth. Emma still bore the marks of his mistake. Trevor's death was all too poignant of a reminder, as well.

"It's beautiful."

He turned to find Miriam staring through the doorway. Bear sat at her feet.

"Did you make the cradle?" she asked.

"Yah." Turning from her tender gaze, he replaced the tarp, stepped from the small storage room and closed the door behind him.

"Your workmanship is lovely, Abram. Do you sell your cradles at the market?"

"I have only made one cradle."

She nodded as if filling in the portion he did not wish to tell her. "I'm sorry about your baby."

"It was *Gott*'s will." Brought on by Abram's stubborn pride to live the Rule as he felt his ancestors had done with no deviation. If only he had listened to his wife. Rebecca had said he was unbending because of the mistakes he had made in his youth and his desire to prove himself to his father. Perhaps she had been right.

"Emma sent you to find me?" he asked.

Miriam shook her head. "She and Isaac are talking. Supper won't be ready for a while. I'm looking for my clothes. Emma said they're soaking in a bucket."

He pointed to the opening at the rear of the barn. "You will find the wash bucket through there."

When she started for the doorway, he touched her arm.

"You do not need to be concerned about your clothing. Emma washes at the first of the week."

"The last thing Emma needs is more work. I'm perfectly capable of doing laundry."

"By hand?"

She nodded. "Of course. Do you think I'm some type of prima donna who shies away from work?"

He shook his head. "No, you are industrious and determined."

She stopped and looked up. He could see the flecks of gold in her brown eyes.

His heart raced and a tightness pulled at his gut. How could he react so strongly to her nearness when seconds earlier he had been grieving for his wife? He did not understand his response to this woman who had made his life seem inside out and upside down.

"You surprise me, Miriam Miller."

She raised a brow. "Because?"

"Because I do not understand the *Englisch* ways. What is it you need?" he asked, recognizing the deeper meaning of his question. What did this *Englisch* woman need or want with an Amish man who lived a *plain* life?

"I need to go to Willkommen."

"Quigley told me the roadblock will not be lifted until tomorrow night. The following is market day. We will go to Willkommen then."

"I'd like to go sooner than that so I can contact Hannah."

"You have remembered your sister's cell phone number?"

Miriam shook her head. "No, but I can email her."

Even if the roadblock ended, going to Willkommen would be dangerous. Did she not remember Serpent passing them on the mountain road?

"Day after tomorrow will be soon enough," he stated.

"Emma mentioned *Englisch* neighbors that might have a computer."

Abram raised his hand as if to cut her off.

She sighed with frustration then turned and hurried out the door at the back of the barn. Bear scurried after her.

Abram wanted to grab her hand and tell her he would take her to town this instant if that was what she wanted, but making such a dangerous trip would mean he was losing his mind as well as his heart.

Miriam had trouble eating her supper. The food was delicious, but the man sitting across the table from her was the problem. At least Emma and Isaac were having a nice time. From the flow of chatter, they didn't seem to notice Miriam's silence. Daniel sat next to her, equally quiet, although he kept glancing at her plate.

"You do not like the food?" he whispered, sounding much more grown up than his years.

She smiled, grateful for his thoughtfulness and relieved to have someone other than Abram on whom to focus.

"I nibbled on pie earlier and spoiled my appetite," she explained, hoping to deflect his concern.

"I had a big slice of pie, but I am still hungry."

"Growing boys need food."

He nodded in agreement and then turned back to his plate.

"Do you want more potatoes, Daniel?" Emma asked.

"*Yah*, please. And a biscuit."

"Son, you must wait until Emma asks," his father quickly reproved.

"But she asked if I wanted potatoes." The boy didn't see the problem, which brought a smile to Miriam's lips.

Forgetting herself, she glanced at Abram. Often pensive and solemn, tonight his eyes were bright. A smile curved his lips and caused her heart to skitter in her chest.

"My sister is happy to have a boy at the table who likes her cooking," he told Daniel. "You can have seconds on anything you like."

"You'll spoil him," Isaac cautioned.

"Not spoiled, but loved." Emma placed a large spoonful of mashed potatoes on his plate and a biscuit topped with a pat of butter that melted over the side of the golden roll.

"Save room for pie," she added.

"*Datt* says you make the best pies in the whole world."

Emma's cheeks pinked. She glanced shyly at Isaac. "Does he now?"

Daniel nodded. "And he's right."

Everyone at the table laughed, even Miriam. Again she glanced at Abram and felt more than a tug at her heart. Her earlier annoyance melted like the butter on the boy's biscuit. Abram's laugh was deep and warm and engaging, making her want to stretch out her hand to touch him as if even the distance across the table kept them too far apart.

For a moment she forgot about everything except sitting across from him, enjoying the delicious meal Emma had prepared and shared with neighbors. The moment offered a reprieve of hope and warmth. If only life could remain like this forever.

Not long after that she realized her mistake when Abram hurried from the table after dinner to feed his animals and tend to his livestock. Was he fleeing from her?

Miriam washed the dishes while Emma and Isaac talked on the front porch and Daniel played nearby with Bear. She could hear his laughter as he and the dog frolicked in the front yard.

With the falling twilight, the house grew shadowed. Miriam wasn't sure when Emma wanted the gas lamps lit so she continued to wash and dry and put away the dishes by the natural light coming through the window.

A car's headlights appeared on the road, which caused her to shudder. Was Serpent coming back for her? At least Isaac was still on the property and Abram nearby. No reason for Miriam to be unsettled. But she was.

She placed the last plate on the shelf then glanced up and spied the rifle lying on top of the cupboard. Knowing it was there brought comfort.

Working quickly, she poured out the wash and rinse water and wiped her hands on the towel, ready to scurry upstairs if the car turned into the drive.

She let out a deep breath when it continued on at the fork, probably headed to Willkommen.

Emma had said the Rogerses' house was four miles away along the road that led over the river. She could easily walk that distance. If the Rogers had a computer and were connected to the internet, and if they didn't mind her using their system, she could send an email to Hannah.

Although she knew Abram wouldn't want her traipsing around the countryside, she needed to contact her sister, and if she left early enough, he might not notice she was gone.

Abram had ignored her mention of the neighbors earlier. She wouldn't bring them up again. Nor would she ask Abram to accompany her. She didn't want him exposed to danger. Instead, she could leave a note for Emma, if she could find paper and pencil.

Searching in a nearby basket of stationery, she happened upon a tablet and pencils. Ripping off a blank sheet, she took it and one of the pencils to her room.

She would need a good night's sleep so she could get up before dawn. Abram rose early. She would have to be careful so he didn't hear her.

Miriam didn't want to disturb his life any more than she already had done. Serpent was ruthless and he didn't care who he hurt. She could never forgive herself if something happened to Abram or his sister.

Her plan was to leave as early as possible in the morning. If she heard a car, she would hide in the woods.

Miriam wouldn't let Serpent find her. Not tomorrow. Not ever.

Abram couldn't sleep and it was not his wife he was thinking of as he tossed from side to side. His thoughts were on the beautiful woman who had sat across from him at dinner and kept her gaze lowered. Then Daniel had made her laugh.

The look she had shared with Abram stirred a cold place deep within him. Without stopping to think, he had laughed deeply, feeling the grief of the past slip away and a warmth and joy return that was restorative, like a spring shower or warm sunshine after a cold winter.

As much as he enjoyed the feeling, he was concerned by the ever-stronger feelings he was having for the *Englisch* woman.

What would the bishop say about Abram's actions? The bishop would probably counsel Abram to guard himself from the *fancy* woman who would move on without looking back. He would also remind Abram that the Amish remained within their faith when they married. The only way his relationship with Miriam could develop was if she joined the Amish church.

Frustrated by the dead end he seemed to be facing, Abram rose from bed, slipped on his trousers and went to the window to study the night sky. The stars twinkled, causing him a moment of melancholy. Rebecca always said the stars were a sign from those who had gone before as well as a visible sign of *Gott*'s love.

Rebecca had said many things that were not what the Amish believed, but Abram had not countered her thoughts. Tonight he wished she would tell him what to do.

A dog barked in the distance. Abram stared into the night. Something caught his gaze.

Movement?

His neck tensed. A fox stalking one of his chickens? Or something more sinister? Hopefully not the man with a serpent tattoo on his neck.

Abram left his bedroom and quietly walked downstairs and into the kitchen. There he stared out the window at where he had earlier seen movement.

Opening the back door, he slipped onto the porch and breathed in the cold night air. His gaze darted to the chicken coop and the shop, then the barn and woodshed as if daring Serpent to make a move.

Standing deathly still, Abram strained to make out the various sounds of the night. An owl hooted. A rodent scurried through the underbrush. Again, a dog barked in the distance. Abram stared into the night for a long time until the prickling in his neck eased. He saw no other movement and only heard familiar sounds he recognized.

Turning, he stepped back into the kitchen.

"He was out there?"

Miriam stood in the middle of the kitchen with a lap blanket around her shoulders, her hair hanging free.

He closed and locked the door behind him.

"I wanted fresh air," he said, hoping the excuse sounded plausible.

"I don't believe you, Abram. You heard something."

He shrugged. "I saw movement, but that does not mean I did not need fresh air as well."

"Was it Serpent?"

"I saw nothing more than a movement that could have been a fox or coyote. Even a raccoon. I doubt Serpent could remain quiet for as long as I stood on the porch. You need not worry tonight. You are safe."

"Thank you."

"For listening to the night?" he asked.

"For protecting me. I've never had anyone care about my well-being."

"Perhaps not your mother, but what of your father?"

"I never knew my father, and my mother thought more about herself than her children."

Abram heard the hurt in her voice that could not be feigned.

"I am sorry, Miriam. A father provides love and support for his children. You missed that growing up."

"I missed a lot of things that you have here."

Abram stepped closer. "You mean the farm and the picturesque landscape?"

"I mean working with your hands and turning off the world. You're not bombarded with messages and phone calls."

"Yet I have few of the things you are used to in your life."

She nodded and then stepped closer. "But do they matter?"

He touched her hair, feeling its silky softness.

Moonlight drifted through the window, spotlighting her in its glow. Her eyelids fluttered closed and her lips, full and soft, parted ever so slightly. She tipped her head.

More than anything, he longed to lower his lips to hers and drink in the softness of her skin and the heady smell of her. For one long moment Abram's stable life tilted off-kilter and all he could think of was how much he wanted to kiss her.

Suddenly her eyes flew open and she drew back with a gasp. "I'm sorry."

Without offering an explanation, she turned and ran up the stairs, leaving him alone in the dark kitchen.

What was wrong with him? He never should have drawn so close to her or allowed himself such thoughts. A more righteous man would have told her to return to her room and not to worry about Serpent. Instead he had thought only of himself and his own wishes.

What did Miriam need?

She didn't need an Amish man who could only offer her hard work and little worldly recompense. He had withstood the pain of Rebecca's passing, but he could not endure seeing Miriam hurt.

Her needs came first.

Not his.

Abram's almost kiss rocked Miriam's world. All she could think of was how his lips would have felt brushed against hers as he pulled her into his arms and held her tight.

Then she'd opened her eyes, not knowing where she was or what she was supposed to do next. So she'd done the only thing that came to mind, the very thing her mother had always done when people started to get too close. Miriam fled upstairs to the protection of the guest room.

Standing with her back to the closed door, she dropped

her head into her hands, expecting her heart to explode in her chest.

The near kiss had changed everything. Or had it?

The realization hit hard.

Abram hadn't been thinking of her. He had been thinking of kissing his wife.

Miriam had acted like a fickle schoolgirl. He wasn't interested in her. Why couldn't she remember that she was wearing Rebecca's clothing? The kitchen had been dark, which was even more reason for him to think of her as someone else.

She crawled into bed then jammed her fist into the pillow as she turned onto her side. Hot tears burned her eyes. Rebecca had been a lucky woman to have a strong and determined man like Abram love her so completely that even three years after her death he was still longing for his wife. Miriam felt like a fool. She would never make that mistake again.

Eventually she fell asleep only to dream about a tall Amish man who kept running from her. Why wouldn't he stop so she could talk to him? Then she saw why he kept moving forward. He was running toward a woman in the distance.

The woman glanced over her shoulder at him and smiled.

He called her name but she wouldn't stop. He called to her again and again.

The name he called out was Rebecca.

Even in her dreams, Abram was running after his deceased wife.

Chapter Ten

Miriam woke with a start. She glanced at the window and groaned, seeing the gray morning sky through the window. Why had she slept so late today of all days? She had planned to rise before sunup and leave the house at the first light of dawn. Abram was probably already up and he was the last person she wanted to run into today.

After rising from bed she quickly straightened the covers and arranged the quilt before she dressed, again in Amish garb. She was getting the hang of using straight pins to fasten the fabric and felt comfortable in the calf-length cotton just as she felt comfortable in this Amish home. Drawing in a deep breath, she opened the bedroom door and tiptoed down the stairs.

On the last step she hesitated, hearing sounds from the kitchen—the scrape of a cast-iron skillet on the stove followed by the clink of glasses and the clatter of plates.

Emma was preparing breakfast and the smell of fresh-baked biscuits wafted through the house and made Miriam's mouth water. As much as she would have enjoyed the hearty meal, Miriam needed to leave without being noticed lest Emma convince her to stay.

And Abram? Would he be relieved to have her gone?

She couldn't think about Abram with his crystal-blue eyes and full lips. She had to think about Hannah. Her sister would come to her rescue and take her to Atlanta. Surely law enforcement in the city would begin an investigation into her mother's death and Sarah's disappearance.

Miriam crossed the main room and carefully opened the front door. The hinge creaked. Her breath caught. She stopped and listened, then let out a shallow sigh as the oven banged open and a metal baking pan dropped onto the top of the stove.

Grateful her departure hadn't been noticed, Miriam slipped outside and pulled the black cape around her shoulders. She glanced at the mountain, relieved that no cars were in sight, and then scurried down the steps and across the front yard to the road that passed in front of Abram's house, the road that would take her to the Rogerses' farm.

Glancing back, she looked for some sign of Abram. All she saw was the cluster of trees that blocked her view of the barn where he was probably tending to the horses. With a heavy heart, she started to run, not knowing what she would find on the road ahead. Emma had mentioned a broken bridge that was still accessible. Miriam didn't like heights and her family had never stayed anywhere long enough for her to learn to swim. If only the bridge would be sturdy enough to allow her to cross safely.

She couldn't dwell on the danger. Instead she needed to focus on accessing the internet so she could email Hannah.

A lump thickened her throat as she ran. She wouldn't see Abram again. He would go on with his farm while she made a new life for herself in Atlanta.

After the peace of the countryside, she wasn't sure city life would be to her liking. At least she would be free of Serpent and safe in Atlanta.

Yet she had felt safe with Abram, as well.

Safe from Serpent but not safe to guard her heart. Her heart was in danger with Abram, which was a different kind of problem.

If only Abram had seen who Miriam truly was instead of seeing only the dress and apron that reminded him of his wife.

Abram sensed that something was amiss.

Leaving Nellie's stall, he stared through the open breezeway, his gaze flicking across the pasture as he listened for the squawk of chickens or the neigh of one of the horses grazing in the distant pasture.

What had caused his unrest?

The kitchen door opened and Emma motioned him to the house. The thought of biscuits, sliced ham, eggs and corn mush whet his always eager appetite. An even more alluring thought was sitting across from Miriam.

He waved to Emma in response to her call then returned to the barn to add more water to the horses' troughs.

Bear rose from his bed of straw, stretched and padded forward to stand by his empty bowl.

"I haven't forgotten you." Abram poured kibble into the dog's dish and then sighed seeing the gray that tangled through Bear's once golden coat. "What happened to my watchdog? The years have passed too quickly.

You are a faithful companion, but you have become fat and lazy in your old age."

Bear titled his head as if hearing the concern in his master's voice.

"We have a serpent on the loose and both of us must be on guard." Abram patted the dog's head then returned the bag of food to the storage room and hurried to the water pump.

After washing his hands, Abram entered the house, inhaling the savory aroma of biscuits and fried eggs and bacon. He glanced at the empty table.

"Our guest has not risen?" he asked his sister.

"She was tired last night, although I thought the smell of breakfast would wake her."

The rumble of a car engine sent Abram to the front of the house. He peered out the window.

Serpent's black sedan headed up the hill. Not who Abram wanted to see, not this early, not ever. The man should stay in Petersville and never set foot in Willkommen or the surrounding area, if Abram had his way.

"Who is it?" his sister called from the kitchen.

"The man with the tattoo who searches for Miriam."

Emma entered the living area and moved toward the window. "That one is an evil man."

"Perhaps. But we will let *Gott* read his heart."

"Now you are not worried about him?"

"I did not say that. But we cannot judge."

"I can voice my opinion."

Abram had to smile. Although petite and slender, Emma sometimes spoke her mind and if something troubled her, she would not be still.

"I must check on Miriam." Emma started up the stairs. "She needs to be warned that the Serpent is in the area."

Abram returned his gaze to the window. Serpent's car had disappeared around the bend in the road. Where was he going and when would he return?

Stepping onto the porch, Abram listened to the silence, hoping it would last. Emma's cry cut through the quiet and sent Abram's heart racing. He ran inside and met her at the foot of the stairway.

His sister's eyes were lined with worry. "Miriam is not in her room."

"She washed her clothes last night. Perhaps she is gathering them off the line." Abram hurried to the kitchen. "I will find her."

"I'm afraid she's gone." Emma's words followed Abram out the door. He raced to the barn.

"Miriam?" he called as he passed Bear and the horse stalls and headed to the rear doorway.

Her clothes hung on a line behind the barn, protected from the wandering eye of any person who traveled along the roadway. Emma had been particular about where she hung clothing to dry. With Serpent on the prowl, Abram was grateful for the secluded clothesline.

But at the moment, he was more interested in finding Miriam than where she had hung her clothing. He flicked his gaze left and right. His stomach roiled, realizing Emma's statement was true. Miriam was gone.

Quickly he hitched Nellie to the buggy. Emma met him outside the barn.

"Miriam asked me about any *Englisch* neighbors who might have a computer she could use to contact her sister. I told her about the Rogers."

"She mentioned them to me, as well." Worry tangled Abram's heart. "If she took the fork in the road, Serpent would have seen her. He could have captured her by now."

Emma shook her head. "I told her the road to the bridge is the fastest route."

"But the bridge is out."

"Only partially. A person on foot could traverse the crossing without problem."

"Unless the rotten wood gives way. I'm going there."

"She wants to contact her sister, Abram."

He nodded. "Perhaps that is so, but she is in danger with Serpent nearby."

The sound of a car downshifting turned Abram's gaze to the mountain. His eyes narrowed as he caught sight of lights on the roof of a black sedan.

Although he could not see the driver from this distance, he knew who was at the wheel. The realization made his blood boil.

The man with the serpent tattoo.

He was coming for Miriam.

Chapter Eleven

Miriam didn't like heights and she didn't like rushing water, both of which she had to face if she were to pass over the river and continue on to the Rogers's farm.

Gazing over the side of the bridge's broken guardrail made her stomach woozy as she peered at the rain-swollen water below. Sharp gusts of wind rushed across the surface of the river, forming froth and white caps.

She shivered from the cold that seeped through her cape and also from fear as she gazed into the turbulence below. Emma had said the bridge was navigable. Miriam wasn't so sure.

Two sections of the bridge platform were still standing, but the guardrails had collapsed and the entire structure appeared rickety at best.

The sound of water rushing over the rocks was as ominous as the gray skies overhead and the gathering storm clouds. The morning had started out clear and had given her hope. Now, peering at the dark clouds above and the even darker water below, her hopes were dashed. She had been foolish to leave the security of Abram's home. Walking four miles wasn't the problem, but crossing over the water on a dilapidated bridge was. The wood creaked as an even more forceful gust of wind swirled from the west.

Miriam glanced over her shoulder, longing to see Abram's farmhouse in the far distance, but the thick woods and rolling hills obscured it from sight. Fisting her hands, she fought for resolve. She couldn't rely on the protective Amish man. She had to forge on, quite literally.

Pulling in a determined breath, she mustered her courage and took a step forward. Through the broken slats, she saw the churning water. The downward drop-off caused her head to swim. She reached for a still-attached portion of the handrail and gasped when it broke under her hold. The rotten wood crashed onto the rocks below.

Her heart pounded and fear gripped her throat.

Arching her back, she raised her arms in a frantic attempt to maintain her balance.

You'll fall to your death. The warning came from within. The internal threat sent another chill to tangle along her spine and manifest in outward shivering that sucked the air from her lungs and left her gasping.

Above the roar of the water she heard a rhythmic cadence. Not a car but the *clip-clop* of a horse's hooves.

"Miriam?"

Recognizing Abram's voice, she steeled her resolve to keep moving forward. Cautiously, she took another step and then another.

Abram had come to stop her, yet he wasn't thinking of her own good. He was thinking of the other woman who had worn this dress. The woman he longed for Miriam to be.

"Kommst du hier." The guttural inflection of his

voice sounded as ominous as the raging river. He was angry with her for leaving without saying goodbye.

He raised his voice. "Come here, Miriam. The bridge is weak. Crossing is too dangerous."

She waved a hand in the air, hoping he wouldn't follow her. She needed to be free of Abram. Free to find the Rogers' farm and use their computer. Technology she needed, even if Abram rejected the modern conveniences of the world.

"Turn around. Get in the buggy."

More demands that didn't take into consideration her plight.

"Go home, Abram. Tend to your farm. Live in the past with your memories."

"I live each day in the present, Miriam. But I live wisely, putting my faith in *Gott*."

"Your *Gott*, as you say, did not save your wife. He won't save me. I have to take care of myself."

Abram's silence tore through Miriam's heart. She'd hit a nerve that was too sensitive and too painful. Instantly she regretted her caustic tongue.

She had no reason to bring more pain to Abram's life. He carried enough of his own.

"I'm sorry." She turned, hoping he would see the depth of her contrition and her desire to make amends.

Another burst of wind tore along the riverbank, caught her full skirt and caused it to billow out around her legs. The strength of the blast of air threw her completely off balance. Suddenly the trees, the broken bridge and the water below swirled around her.

"Abram!" she screamed as she started to topple off the bridge.

Her fall was aborted by Abram's strong hands that

gripped her tightly and pulled her into the safety of his embrace.

She gasped, thinking they both would tumble into the water. He pulled her even closer and lifted her into his arms.

"No," she moaned. "Let me go."

"Do as I say." He swept her off the bridge and carried her to his buggy.

She fought against his hold. He had saved her from the river, but she couldn't return to his farm.

"Shh," he soothed. "You must be quiet."

"I will not be silent." She struggled to free herself from his hold.

"It is for your own good," he warned.

"You cannot control me."

"This I know to be true, Miriam. But you must listen and comply. Do you not hear the car? He is coming to find you."

Miriam stilled and turned her face toward the sound, somewhat muffled and hard to distinguish over the tumbling water and the wind rustling through the trees.

The sky overhead darkened even more. Her stomach tightened. She knew what the sound of the engine meant. Serpent was coming after her.

If he found her, he wouldn't let her live to escape again.

Relieved that he had successfully tucked Miriam into the rear of the buggy moments earlier, Abram now stood next to Nellie and watched Serpent's car screech to a halt at the edge of the road. The swollen river pounded over the rocks and rushed under the bridge. Overhead the sky darkened with an approaching storm that appeared to be as volatile as the man climbing from his car.

"Stop where you are." Serpent's voice was laced with anger.

"What do you want?" Abram demanded.

"I want the woman in the buggy with you. I saw her foot as she climbed in. You've been hiding Miriam Miller somewhere near your farm."

"I am not sure the woman you speak of has done anything wrong."

"She's a suspected murderer and you're a fool to believe anything she says otherwise."

Serpent pulled a weapon from his waistband. "Tell her to step down from the buggy or I'll start shooting."

"Then you will be a killer."

"I'll kill you if you stop me from apprehending her."

He cocked his gun and aimed it at the buggy.

Abram started walking toward Serpent.

"Wait, my brother."

He turned at the sound of Emma's voice and, although concerned for her well-being, he was grateful his sister had insisted on coming with him. She climbed from the buggy.

"I do not understand why you needed to see me, sir." Emma's voice was calm and engaging as she stared at Serpent. "Surely, I have done nothing to cause you upset."

The man's face twisted. He glanced from Abram to Emma.

"Put down your gun," Abram demanded.

Serpent shook his head. "I don't know what kind of tricks you and your sister are playing, Zook, but I'm convinced you know where the woman is hiding. She's a criminal, and if you help her escape, you'll be prosecuted and sent to jail, along with your sister."

His gaze flickered to the surrounding countryside. "I searched your farm last night."

Abram's instincts had been right after all.

"She might not be holed up on your property," Serpent continued, "but I'm convinced she's hiding someplace not far from here. I'll keep watching, and if you make a misstep, it will be your last."

"You do not frighten me."

"That's because of your false Amish pride. But pride can't stop a bullet and pride can't make a woman come back to life. Tell the woman you're protecting that I'm coming after her. And tell your Amish friends that if they're hiding her, I'll send them to jail. The bottom line is that I'll find her, Zook." He started to get into his car and then added, "Next time she won't get away."

"I can't stay with you any longer," Miriam insisted from the rear of the buggy once Serpent's car had disappeared from sight.

Abram helped Emma into the front seat and climbed in beside her.

"Serpent was ready to kill both of you when he thought I was hiding in the buggy," Miriam continued. "As gracious as you were, Emma, to confront him, you were putting yourself in danger. What would have happened if he had stepped closer and found me hiding in the rear?"

Tears welled up in Miriam's eyes. She couldn't let any harm come to Abram and Emma. "Take me to the Rogerses' house. I'll email my sister and wait for her there."

"Mr. Rogers and his wife are visiting their daughter in Nashville." Abram grabbed the reins. "They will not be home until next week."

Emma glanced back at Miriam. "I'm sorry, I did not know about their trip." Her voice was filled with regret. "I never thought you would try to find their farm alone. You should have told us what you needed."

But she had told them she needed to contact her sister. Neither Abram nor Emma realized what was at stake. If Serpent was part of a trafficking ring, the whole county would be impacted negatively by his criminal activity.

"We should all leave here and go someplace safe," Miriam suggested. "Come with me to Atlanta."

Abram grunted and flipped the reins, causing the horse to increase her speed. "A farm must be maintained. I cannot leave my animals."

"Just until I can tell my story to honest lawmen who will come after Serpent."

"Samuel will return to Willkommen tomorrow, Miriam. We will go to town for the market. You can talk to him then."

But would he believe her story?

Miriam rubbed her forehead, hoping to ease the pounding headache that had started while she was on the bridge.

Jammed into the rear of the buggy, she felt lost. Would she ever get to Atlanta? Yet leaving meant saying goodbye to Abram, which was the last thing she wanted to do.

Chapter Twelve

On the way back to the house Abram kept a sharp eye on the road and listened for Serpent's car. He needed to keep Miriam out of sight and out of the vile man's grasp until his uncle returned to Willkommen.

Pulling into the drive, Abram hopped out of the buggy and closed the gate behind them. Usually it stood open to welcome all. Under the circumstances, Abram needed to use any means to keep Serpent at bay. A gate was not much of a barrier, but it would stop unwanted visitors from driving directly to the house.

"I do not want to raise my hand against another man, but Serpent must be stopped," Abram mumbled to himself after the women had hurried into the house. "I will not let him harm Miriam or Emma."

Hopefully, *Gott* would provide the protection they needed so Abram could maintain his desire for good and still hide Miriam's whereabouts. From what Serpent had said, it sounded as if he thought Miriam was holed up someplace away from the farm, for which Abram was grateful.

The storm clouds that had grown darker over the morning at the river's edge now turned the day into night. His trusty dog trotted to greet him as he un-hitched Nellie in the barn and quickly groomed her.

"Remember the serpent, Bear. We must be vigilant and ensure he does no harm." Once Nellie was settled in her stall, Abram hurried to the house, but he could not outrun the downpour. The sky opened and the rain fell with fury.

The walkway turned to mud and caught at Abram's footsteps. Lightning cut across the menacing sky fol-lowed by a deafening roar of thunder.

He stomped his feet on the porch to loosen the mud from his boots before he stepped into the warmth and comfort of his kitchen.

Miriam stood at the dry sink with her back to him, her skirts full around her legs. She appeared to be beat-ing batter in a bowl.

For a moment his heart stopped, thinking it was Re-becca. Then she turned and he was struck again by the reality of who had changed his life.

The woman at the dry sink was not his wife. She was Miriam with her troubled gaze and eyes that studied him far too deeply as if always questioning his reaction.

He could not let her know the way his heart lurched and his lungs constricted, making each breath difficult when he was around her.

He was not thinking of his wife or the past, which is what Miriam had mentioned in her anger at the river's edge. He was thinking of this newcomer to his life who had shattered his *plain* world and caused him to think thoughts of a new beginning and hope for the future. But she was not interested in an Amish man who dis-avowed all the technology and electrical devices she was used to having in her *Englisch* world. Nor was she interested in embracing his Amish faith, which meant there could be no future for them. Abram was a fool to allow his heart to have dominance over his reasoning.

He steeled his gaze and pulled in a deep breath, struggling to maintain a firm control of his voice and his actions. He had to be strong and assertive to guard his heart and his life.

He didn't need Miriam to disrupt the status quo and cause him to think of what could be. What could be was not reality, and Abram lived in the real world. A world of hard work and faith in *Gott*. A world where family came first and the *Englisch* ways were kept from polluting the serenity of the Amish life.

Miriam would never understand him or his ways, which meant there was no hope for them. Ever.

End of subject.

"You're wet, Abram. I will make coffee. Sit by the fire to get warm."

Her sincere concern caused another knife to jab at his heart. Her voice was smooth as honey and equally as sweet, and the firm resolve that he had convinced himself was necessary suddenly crumbled. All he wanted was to pull her into his arms, as he had done at the bridge when he had feared she would fall into the water.

Had she felt the erratic pounding of his heart? Did she know how much he longed to have her in his arms again?

Silly, foolish feelings that were not to be allowed.

Without so much as a word, he walked past her and hurried up the stairs to his bedroom. The room where he and his wife had shared the joys of wedded life, but also the room where her life had ended along with the baby's. *The Lord giveth life and the Lord taketh life away.*

And now?

Was the Lord giving Abram a new life? Or was he

ripping out his heart and sucking the very breath from him so that nothing in the future would ever compare with Miriam?

Abram slammed the bedroom door behind him and reached for his Bible. The scriptures had comforted him after Rebecca's death.

Would he find comfort from the readings now? Or would even the Word of *Gott* bring added confusion?

Why had Miriam sought refuge in Abram's arms when she was running from Serpent?

Abram knew the reason.

Gott had known his loneliness and had longed to bring comfort, but instead of comfort, Miriam's presence had brought chaos and tumult.

"Forgive me." Abram shook his head as he prayed. "I know not what to do."

The kitchen grew dark, making Miriam long for electricity and lights. Emma stood at the stove, stirring red sauce, seemingly unaware of the dark skies and pounding rain that thrummed against the tin roof. The downpour grew in intensity. Thunder roared and lightning flashed through the darkness with bursts of brightness.

Miriam shivered, chilled by the fury of the storm.

"We are safe here in the house," Emma assured her, no doubt seeing Miriam grimace as each roll of thunder rumbled overhead.

"I don't like storms," she stated emphatically.

"Rain is good for the land. Abram will till the fields soon. The rain will help to soften the soil."

"Rain doesn't bother me, but lightning and thunder do."

Emma glanced out the window. Miriam followed her

gaze. Visibility was worse than poor, making the barn and pastures beyond blurred by the downpour.

"You would still be walking to the Rogerses' home if Abram had not taken the buggy to find you."

Miriam looked at the Amish woman. "I appreciate his thoughtfulness."

Emma added salt to the sauce. "You do not understand Amish men."

Miriam raised her brow. "I don't know what you mean."

"An Amish man is proud. He works hard. He takes care of his family, his wife, his children. He is the leader of the family. He embraces the Word of *Gott* and lives by the teachings of Christ."

"*Englisch* men do the same. At least, some of them."

"Perhaps, but Amish men commit totally to the women they love."

"Good men exist outside the Amish community," Miriam insisted. Yet the one man who had broken through her guarded heart *was* Amish.

Miriam swallowed the lump that formed in her throat. "You don't have to spell out what you're trying to tell me."

The Amish woman raised a brow. "You understand then?"

"I understand Abram still loves his wife."

Emma shook her head. "Then you don't understand."

Miriam sighed with exasperation. "What are you trying to say, Emma?"

"Do you see the way he looks at you?"

"Of course, and I know why. I'm wearing his wife's clothing. He looks at me with longing because he longs for Rebecca."

Emma harrumphed. "Is that what you think? I noticed that you washed your clothing, but they were hanging outside and got wet in the rain. I moved them into the barn to dry."

"Thank you. I wasn't thinking."

"Just like you aren't thinking correctly about Abram. Wear your *fancy* clothes and see how he looks at you then."

"I wouldn't call my jeans and sweater fancy."

"*Fancy* is a term we Amish use for anything other than our *plain* clothing. You understand? It is an expression, *yah*? But you talk around my comment."

"You mean Abram won't look at me at all if I wear regular clothes?"

Emma shook her head and sighed. "It is not something we need to discuss further. Our midday meal must be cooked."

Miriam didn't understand the sharpness of Emma's tone. She sounded as if she was accusing Miriam of being the one at fault.

How could that be? Miriam had done nothing to provoke Abram or his sister. All too quickly she realized her mistake. Miriam had brought tumult and danger to their peaceful lives.

Chapter Thirteen

The sound of a car engine forced Abram to gaze from his bedroom window. The deputy sheriff's squad car pulled into the drive. Curtis Idler braked to a stop, left the dryness of his car and opened the gate. Rain drenched him in seconds. His face seemed twisted with frustration as he climbed back into his car and drove into the yard. He parked near the back porch and eyed the sky through the window. The rain eased and he took the opportunity to leave the protection of his car and run to the porch.

He banged on the door.

"Abram?" Emma called from the first floor.

Racing downstairs, Abram passed his sister and hurried into the kitchen. Miriam had backed into the pantry, her eyes wide with worry.

"It is the deputy from town. My uncle trusts him. Perhaps you should too."

"No, Abram. I can't."

"You have nothing to fear, Miriam."

"Not today. I'll wait until your uncle returns."

He did not understand her hesitancy when she had been so eager to go to town.

"Please, Abram." Her eyes pleaded with him. "I can't explain my feelings, but don't make me talk to anyone now."

She glanced at the kitchen door as once again the deputy knocked, demanding entrance.

"Hurry upstairs," Abram said, seeing the worry that tightened her face. "I will call you when he is gone."

Gathering her skirts in her hands, she ran from the room. Her footfalls sounded as she climbed the stairs. The click of the bedroom door closing gave a sense of finality to her departure.

"Get coffee," Abram told Emma. "The deputy is wet from the rain."

Opening the door, he motioned the man inside. Idler wiped his feet on the braided rug Rebecca had made and stepped toward the table.

"Coffee sounds perfect," Curtis said after Abram had made the offer. "The rain's coming down so hard I couldn't see."

"You are far from town." Abram stated the obvious.

Emma poured a cup of coffee and placed it on the table in front of the lawman.

"There is fresh cream and sugar." She pointed to the cream pitcher and bowl of sugar on the table.

He shook his head. "Black is fine. I didn't come for refreshment."

Abram accepted a cup from his sister, took a long pull of the hot brew and eyed the deputy, waiting for him to divulge the reason for this second visit within two days.

"Sheriff Kurtz isn't sure he'll get back to town tomorrow. He put me in charge until he returns."

"What about the roadblock?" Abram asked. "Has it not been successful?"

"That was Chief Tucker's idea."

"The chief of police from Petersville?"

Curtis nodded. "He's convinced the killer is still in the area and wants to do a house-by-house search."

Abram bristled. He placed his cup on the table and pulled in a breath before he spoke. "Even I know that a warrant would be required prior to a house search. Does the sheriff think of himself as above the law? From what I have heard, it sounds as if the man has a high opinion of himself."

"You don't understand, Abram."

"I understand enough to know he will not find welcome here."

"He's going to search all the Amish homes," Curtis said.

"Doors will not open to the chief or his men."

"Here's the thing, Abram. A killer's on the loose. You folks are in danger. I'm trying to tell as many of the Amish as I can."

"This supposed killer is the woman whose photograph was on your phone? You think she killed her mother?"

"That's right. But without transportation, she would be hard-pressed to leave the area."

"Have you forgotten the bus that comes to Willkommen? She could have gone north to Knoxville or south to Atlanta."

"Except the clerk at the bus station hasn't seen anyone matching her description. He knows most folks in town."

"But he does not know all the Amish."

Curtis nodded. "You're right, although I don't think the killer is Amish."

"Someone could have driven her," Abram suggested,

hoping the search would shift to some other portion of the state.

"That's a possibility, if she knew someone in the area."

"Has anyone seen her?"

"Not a soul." The deputy took a long swig of coffee and then wiped his lips and sniffed. "I'm sure you've kept your eyes open."

"I have seen a surly man with a scarf around his neck."

Idler smirked. "You're talking about Pete Pearson. He can be pushy to say the least."

"I do not want him prowling around my property. If you see him, tell him to leave the Amish alone. We do not need his protection or his accusations, and we do not want to face a roadblock the days we go to market."

Curtis held up his hand. "The roadblock ends tonight. The Petersville mayor refuses to pay any more overtime to his police officers. However, squad cars will be patrolling the roadways and officers will be on the lookout for the woman on the run."

"Are you searching for the right person?" Abram asked.

"We've got one lead, Abram, and it seems sound. Keep your eyes open and let me know if you see anything suspect."

The deputy rose and handed Emma his empty cup. "Appreciate the coffee."

A floorboard creaked overhead. The deputy glanced up. "Someone visiting?"

Emma smiled sweetly. "The mice have been bad this year. We brought one of our cats inside. She is a good mouser who is growing fat and causing the floors to creak when she leaps from the bed."

"Only rodent I like," the deputy snarled, "is a dead one."

He nodded to Abram. "See you in town."

Emma frowned at Abram when the deputy was not looking.

Abram raised his brow at her. "I'm sure Deputy Idler would enjoy an Amish dessert with his supper this evening. Especially after he was so considerate to warn us, Emma. Didn't you mention having an extra apple pie?"

Thankfully her face melted into a smile. "The pie is in the pantry. I'll wrap it in cheesecloth for protection from the rain."

The deputy slapped Abram's shoulder. "Thanks for your thoughtfulness."

Emma hurried to the pantry and returned with the pie.

"You folks stay safe." The deputy held the pie close to his chest and scurried to his car.

Abram closed and locked the kitchen door.

"Can we trust him, Abram?" Emma asked, her face pensive, her arms wrapped protectively around her waist.

"We can trust him as much as we can trust anyone at this point. The pie will keep his mind off the creaking floorboards and the cat we never allow in the house."

As the car pulled out of the drive and turned onto the main road, heading back to town, Bear started to bark.

Abram shook his head at his lazy watchdog's poor timing before he called up the stairs to Miriam. "The deputy is gone."

She came to the top of the landing. "I can't stay here, Abram. I have to leave. I'm a danger to you and Emma."

"The roadblock ends tonight. We will go to Willkommen in the morning. There we will find more information. Perhaps we will find your aunt."

"I need a computer to email my sister."

Abram nodded. "We will find that, as well. But tonight you must remain here. You are safe with me."

At least, he hoped she was.

The day seemed to last forever or perhaps it was Miriam's unease that made time tick by so slowly.

She'd started the morning nearly falling into a raging river. Moments later she'd eluded Serpent, thanks to Abram's quick reaction. The Willkommen deputy's visit some hours later, along with the stormy sky and intermittent rain, had fueled her anxiety even more. Now with the lunch meal over and the dishes washed and put away in the cupboard, she wondered how to endure the rest of the afternoon.

Emma seemed as flustered as Miriam felt.

"I'm worried about Daniel," the Amish woman said as she headed once again to the front window and peered in the direction of the Beiler dairy. "He usually brings milk soon after our *middaagesse*."

Miriam came up behind her and patted her arm.

Emma smiled weakly. "I should have said our noon meal. Why has he not yet brought the day's milk?"

"Perhaps his delay is due to the storm," Miriam offered.

"Suppose the boy is sick? He does not have a *Mamm*, and Isaac must tend to his dairy cows. The child would be alone, perhaps feverish—"

"You're jumping far ahead of things, Emma. I'm sure there's an explanation for why he's late that has nothing to do with illness."

Emma nodded and slowly turned away from the window. "Still I worry. The child is always punctual. He will start school in the next session. I will miss seeing him each day."

"Isaac will deliver the milk instead," Miriam added with a wink.

"You have been with us a short time, Miriam Miller, yet you see into the heart of things."

Miriam smiled. "I see your heart that is filled with love for Isaac."

Emma shook her head as if wanting no such talk in spite of the twinkle in her eyes. "I will bake cookies. That is one way to attract Daniel. Even with this distance between the two farms, he is drawn to the sweet smell of my baking."

As Emma hurried into the kitchen, Miriam returned to the window. She wouldn't tell Emma, but she, too, worried about the young boy on the road with Serpent making his presence known so frequently. As much as she wanted to believe the hateful man would not bother a child, there was nothing she would put past Serpent.

A chill settled over her and she shivered. Rubbing her arms, she stared into the distance wondering where the snake was hiding. He was out there somewhere, watching and waiting.

Reluctantly she joined Emma in the kitchen, but her heart wasn't in the baking. She peered through the kitchen window to where Abram mended the fence that cordoned off a distant pasture. A cold wind blew from the north and caused his shirt to billow in the gusty air. He worked without his coat and with only his wide-brimmed hat to shield his face from the buffeting rain.

Before the first batch of cookies went into the oven,

Emma glanced at the kitchen clock and headed once again to the front room. Gazing through the window, she groaned.

"The rain has eased, which is good, and I see Daniel, but he is carrying three bottles of milk instead of the regular two. The load is much too heavy." She tsked and shook her head. "The boy thinks he is older than his years."

Miriam peered around Emma. "He means to please and works hard like his father."

"*Yah*, but his father does not carry more than he can haul. I fear Daniel will drop one of the bottles, if not all three."

Turning her gaze to the mountain road, Miriam's heart thumped a warning. "Emma, look, it's the black sedan."

Serpent was heading down the hill.

Emma's hand drew to her throat. "I must help Daniel and bring him inside."

She pushed past Miriam, but with the rain-slick roadway and her labored gait, Emma would never get to the boy in time.

"Stay in the house," Miriam insisted. "I'll go instead."

"But Serpent—"

"Daniel and I will be safely inside before he could see us."

Without waiting for Emma to express any more of her concerns, Miriam pushed open the front door. She unlatched the gate and ran to where the young boy stood, trying to readjust his heavy load.

"Daniel, let me help you."

"I can do it," he insisted, clutching two of the bottles close to his chest. The third bottle teetered in his outstretched hand and seemed ready to slip through his fingers.

"Of course you can, but we must hurry. Emma is baking cookies. They are almost done."

She glanced at the sedan. Her pulse raced, seeing the car accelerate even faster down the hill. "Hurry, Daniel."

Taking two of the milk bottles in her right hand, she grabbed the boy's free hand with her left and hurried him along.

Looking over her shoulder, her heart stopped. The car was close. So very close.

Dropping the bottles, she lifted Daniel into her arms.

"Die millich—!" he cried.

"We must hurry, Daniel." She tucked his head into the crook of her neck to protect the child and ran for the house.

Tires screeched. A car door slammed. "Stop."

She wouldn't stop. She had to get the child to safety. Racing up the steps of the porch, she gasped with relief as the door opened. Miriam clutched the boy even closer to her heart and sprinted into the house.

Emma slammed and locked the door behind them. Taking Daniel into her arms, she kissed his cheek and pulled him into her embrace. "Oh, Daniel, we were so worried about you."

"Die millich…the bottles broke." Tears welled up in the boy's eyes.

"Yes, but you are safe."

Serpent climbed the porch steps and pounded on the door.

Emma scooted the boy into the kitchen. "Hide, Daniel, in the pantry."

"He frightens me." Daniel's voice was tight with fear.

"I know, but you must be very brave." Emma hurried him into the hiding place. "We will not let the man hurt you."

Miriam reached on top of the cupboard and grabbed Abram's rifle. Returning to the living area, she stood behind the door next to Emma and nodded.

Gripping the knob, Emma opened the door ever so slightly. "Why are you here?"

"I saw a woman with a boy."

"I was that woman," Emma insisted, her voice calm but firm. "My brother told you to leave us alone."

Miriam's heart thumped. She nudged Emma and shoved the rifle into her hand.

"I don't care what Zook said." Serpent gloated.

Emma raised the rifle. "You *should* listen to Abram."

A dog barked.

Miriam glanced through the narrow crack on the hinged side of the door. Bear ran to the front of the house and scurried up the porch to snap at Serpent's feet.

"Get that hound away from me."

"Pearson!" Abram appeared, his face twisted in anger. "Why do you trespass on my land?"

"You can't scare me, Zook."

Bear bared his teeth and lunged. Serpent tried to kick the dog, but Bear eluded the blow.

"Leave my property and don't come back," Abram's voice was deep and menacing.

"You'll pay for this, Zook." Serpent stumbled down the steps and raced to his car.

Emma closed the door and grabbed Miriam's hand. Tears pooled in Emma's eyes. "When will it end?"

Miriam knew. It would end when she was out of Emma and Abram's home. Only then would the peace of their Amish life return.

Chapter Fourteen

The rain intensified through the night. The *ping* of the fat droplets against the tin roof kept Miriam from sleeping. She walked to the window and stared into the darkness and shivered, knowing who could be out there waiting and watching.

Closing the curtains, she lit the gas lamp and opened the trunk. The dress she had worn today was spattered with mud. Tomorrow she would wear something fresh to town. The smell of cedar from the inlaid wood brought comfort.

She peered at the inscription, handwritten in black ink, on the inside. *To Rebecca. With my love. From your husband, Abram.*

Miriam's heart constricted. Not with jealousy or envy, but because of her own desire to have someone love her as completely as Abram had loved his wife.

Tears burned her eyes, knowing the pain of loss he must have felt when Rebecca and their child had died. He continued to carry that pain, Miriam felt sure. The look of longing in his eyes revealed the depth of his grief, even now.

Wiping her hand across her cheek, she inhaled

deeply to quell the onslaught of sadness that clung to her as surely as the scent of cedar.

Miriam pulled a dress from the trunk. This one in a deep royal blue that almost seemed too rich for an Amish woman. She shook out the fabric and held the bodice against her, then looked down at the skirt that billowed around her legs in a graceful flow that made her feel totally feminine.

She twirled once. Yards of fabric swirled around her legs and, in spite of her heavy heart, she smiled, feeling as graceful as a fairy princess with the skirt swishing back and forth. She almost laughed, until the light flickered, drawing her back to the moment. She wasn't Abram's wife. She was a stranger who had barged into his life. A stranger who had dreamed thoughts of what could have been—of love and marriage, a home and family—all of which Miriam would never know.

A man's love and affection were not in her future. She was her mother's daughter, as much as she wanted to break the generational ties. Yet she would not walk the same path as her mother, who had needed a man to validate her life.

Miriam didn't need a man.

But you want one, her mind taunted. *An Amish man who is bigger than life.*

A door opened into the hallway. Footsteps sounded then stopped outside her door. Miriam's heart lunged. She clasped the dress to her heart, wanting to hide it from sight as if Abram could see through the closed bedroom door and know her thoughts.

She held her breath and looked at the gas lamp. Abram would see the light spilling into the dark hallway from under the bedroom door, and he would know she was awake.

Her right hand raised to cover her mouth as she slowly exhaled the air that burned her lungs, half expecting him to open the door and demand to know why she was holding his wife's dress.

Again she was overcome with regret. She never should have infringed on Abram's life.

Another footfall and another. Abram passed her door and descended the stairs to the first floor.

Daring not move for fear a floorboard would squeak, she listened to the trail of his footsteps through the house. The back door creaked open and then closed.

She extinguished the light, moved to the window and pulled back the curtain. The rain continued to fall. Overhead the moon peered between billowing clouds to illuminate the yard ever so slightly.

Miriam could see Abram walk to the woodshop. He held something in his hand. A chill settled over her. He held the rifle.

Stamping his feet, he entered the shop and then pulled the door closed behind him.

Without his presence in the house, she felt an instant dread. Again her eyes searched the land around the house and outbuildings.

A shadow moved near the woodshed.

Her heart lurched.

Had she imagined the movement or was someone hiding in the darkness?

Sleep had eluded Abram. He had been restless and unable to calm his mind or his heart. Needing to busy himself, he had come to the workshop, planning to sand a table he was making for Emma.

That he had brought the rifle surprised him somewhat, yet his sister had used it this afternoon when Serpent had chased after Miriam and Daniel. Abram had been almost too late returning to the house. Thankfully, Serpent had driven away. Next time, he might not be so easily deterred.

For a long moment Abram stared into the dark recesses of the woodshop and sensed the intruder's presence before he heard the crack of a broken twig outside. Peering through the window, he saw the shadowy figure slink around the side of the woodshed.

A stocky man. Maybe six feet tall. He could not see his face, but he knew it was Serpent.

The man continued along the edge of the building then stopped and peered up at the bedroom windows. Abram angled his gaze toward the house, relieved that the light in Miriam's room had been extinguished. Just so she would remain inside.

Abram reached for the rifle. Holding it in one hand, he slowly opened the door to his shop and stepped into the cool night air. The rain had slackened to a light drizzle. He peered through the mist and angled his head, listening for a footfall to identify Serpent's whereabouts.

A twig snapped.

Abram turned to see the man dart into the clearing.

The back door opened.

Someone stepped onto the porch.

Miriam.

Abram's gut tightened.

Serpent pulled something from his waistband. The moonlight reflected off the object.

Abram's heart stopped at the sight of the handgun.

"No!" he screamed.

Serpent turned toward Abram, standing in the darkness.

"Where's the woman hiding, Zook?"

"I told you to stay away from me, my sister, my farm and—"

Before Abram could complete the warning, the intruder took aim and fired. A muffled rapport. The man was using a silencer.

The bullet pinged off the nearby water pump.

"I'll kill you, Zook, but I'll kill your sister first." He fired again, this time at the shadowed figure standing on the porch.

Abram's breath caught in his throat. He raised the rifle and fired. Bear raced from the barn, growling with teeth bared. He lunged at Serpent. The man turned, nearly tripping over his feet as he ran, cursing, into the night.

"Abram?" Miriam's voice, laced with fright. She fled back into the house.

He ran forward, his heart thumping at what he might find. After entering the kitchen, he closed and locked the door and propped the rifle against the wall, all the while searching the darkness with his gaze.

"Miriam," he called, fearing the worst and praying he was wrong.

He raced into the main room where he found her slumped over the stairs. In three long strides he was at her side, pulling her into his arms. His hands touched her neck, her cheeks, her waist, searching for a gaping hole or blood that would confirm she was hurt.

"You are injured?" he asked, fearing her answer.

She gasped for air. Tears fell from her eyes.

"You were hurt?" Abram restated his question. Why did she not answer him?

His hands wove into her hair, not the bun that she usually wore, but long, flowing locks that fell around her shoulders.

Moonlight filtered through the nearby window and bathed them in its glow.

"Tell me you are all right," he demanded, his voice insistent.

"I'm…" She tried to speak. "I'm not hurt. The bullet whizzed past me. I could feel the force of its momentum, but the round did not strike me. At first I couldn't understand what had happened. The sound was muffled. I thought gunfire was louder?"

"He used a silencer." Unable to think of what he would have done if she had been injured, Abram pulled her close and silently gave thanks.

He did not deserve *Gott*'s blessings, but Miriam did not deserve *Gott*'s condemnation.

"You might not have recognized him," she said, her voice low and filled with emotion. "The moon peered from the clouds as he approached the house. I saw his face. It was Serpent."

"He mentioned my sister." Abram tried to reassure her. "Serpent thought Emma was on the porch. He wanted to kill her to get back at me."

"But I was the target, Abram."

"What happened?" As if hearing her name, Emma came to the top of the stairs, holding an oil lamp. Her face was puffy with sleep yet pulled tight with concern as she stared down at them.

"Serpent came back," Miriam said, staring into Abram's eyes. "He nearly killed me once. He tried to kill me again."

Chapter Fifteen

Morning came too early for Miriam. Emma rapped at her bedroom door before the first light of dawn. "Breakfast is almost ready."

Miriam rubbed her eyes and tried to wipe away the grogginess that hung on after her restless night. Sleep had eluded her. She had heard Abram pace through the house, no doubt, standing guard lest Serpent return. Abram's vigilance had put her even more on edge, knowing that Serpent could still be nearby. More than anything, she longed to erase everything that had happened and fall into a deep sleep.

Then she remembered today was market day. That meant a trip to Willkommen where she could find an internet connection and contact Hannah. She also hoped to find information about her aunt. If Sheriff Kurtz was back in town, she would tell him what had happened so he could arrest Serpent and throw the wicked man in jail.

Slipping from bed, she donned the fresh blue dress she had found in the trunk. After pulling her hair into a bun, she put on the white *kapp* Emma had showed her how to wear and an apron.

The rich aroma of fresh-baked biscuits assailed her as she entered the kitchen. Coffee perked on the stove.

Emma smiled in greeting. "The dress fits you well."

"I found it in the trunk." Miriam ran her hand over the full skirt. "Will it upset Abram to see me wearing this dress?"

"His thoughts are on the present, Miriam. He will not notice the dress but rather the woman wearing the dress."

The comment took Miriam aback. Her heart fluttered as she hurried to the kitchen door. "I'll get the milk from outside."

She stopped short before she grabbed the doorknob, thinking of what had happened last night and the bullet that had been too close.

"Stay here," Emma cautioned. "Abram will bring the milk when he returns from the barn. I'm sure he wants you to remain inside for your own safety."

Miriam appreciated Abram's concern for her well-being and thought again of his embrace last night. He had held her tight, his heart beating rapidly in his chest. Foolish though it was, Miriam hadn't wanted to leave his arms.

A knock sounded at the kitchen door. Miriam eyed Emma.

"It's Abram," his sister assured her. "Will you open the door? His hands are probably full with the milk and butter."

Miriam pulled back the curtain that covered the window and peered out just to be sure. Her heart thumped in response to Abram's handsome face that stared at her through the glass. Just as Emma had said, he carried a jug of milk in one hand and a glass container of butter in the other.

"Sorry," she said as she threw open the door. "I wanted to be certain it was you."

He stepped inside, bringing in fresh morning air and the scent of the outdoors. "That was wise after last night."

She closed and locked the door behind him.

Emma, her hand poised over a skillet of scrambled eggs, stared at both of them. "This man is even worse than we first believed. He must be stopped."

Abram nodded in agreement. "That is why Miriam will talk to Samuel. He will track down Serpent and arrest him."

"If only he can find any other men who are involved." Emma spoke the words that troubled Miriam.

So much depended on today and how the sheriff would respond to the information she planned to provide.

Emma's brow lifted as she raised the skillet off the stove. "You are sure Samuel will be back in Willkommen today?"

Abram poured himself a cup of coffee and one for Miriam, which she gladly accepted.

"Samuel planned to be gone three days, but Curtis mentioned that the sheriff could be delayed longer. We will find out when we get to town."

"Daniel asked yesterday if he could ride to market with us." Emma plated the food. "I told him we could not give him a ride. I am concerned about the boy's safety in case anything happens."

"Because of me." Miriam gave voice to what Emma had failed to mention. "My presence here puts all of you in danger."

"It is not because of you," Emma quickly explained. "You are an innocent victim, Miriam. Serpent is the one at fault."

"Emma is right," Abram insisted. "The serpent is the problem. He could make more trouble. If so, we do not want Daniel to be caught in the conflict."

"That's what I told Isaac," Emma said with a nod. "He is worried about our safety, but he is especially concerned for his son."

"*Yah*, I do not blame Isaac." Abram refilled his cup. "The boy is precocious and smart as a whip."

"He's stolen my heart," Miriam said.

Emma placed the plates on the table. "Mine, as well."

"We will see him later today when Isaac comes to town. Daniel is never far from his father's side," Abram stated.

"Isaac seems like a nice man," Miriam mused, watching Emma's expression soften with the mention of the neighbor's name.

"Yet—" Abram took a long pull from his coffee "—Isaac does not keep the Old Order."

Emma put her hands on her hips. "We are not still in Ethridge."

"The old ways were good ways," he insisted.

"Then perhaps you should have stayed in Tennessee."

Miriam had never seen Emma so determined to make a point or so vocal. Her frustration with her brother was evident as she threw the biscuits in a basket and set them on the table.

As if trying to ignore Emma's outburst, Abram pointed Miriam to the table. "We must eat now."

They each took their seats and bowed their heads as he offered a prayer. "*Gott*, we give thanks for the food You provide and for our ability to farm the land and prepare this meal. May the work of our hands give honor to You. Amen."

The tension remained taut as they ate in silence.

Once finished, Abram rose from the table. "It is time to pack the buggy. The road is long and we must get to market in time to unload and set up our stall."

Miriam hadn't finished her breakfast, but thinking about what they might face later today had taken away her appetite. Emma's eyes were downcast and she toyed with her food. Was she upset with Miriam for disrupting their lives?

"I'll wash the dishes, Emma. I'm sure you need to help Abram load the buggy." After grabbing her plate and silverware, Miriam hurried to the sink.

Abram left the table and headed for the door. "I will hitch Nellie and bring the buggy to the side of the house."

The door slammed behind him, causing Miriam's heart to lunge in her chest. "I'm sorry, Emma."

"He is not angry with you, Miriam, he is angry with himself. He fights an inner battle. My brother holds on to the past, yet we know when things are gripped too tightly, they sometimes break. Abram feels his life shattering around him."

"I did it. Coming here was a mistake."

Emma placed her plate on the counter and gently touched Miriam's arm. "Abram struggled to follow the Amish way in his youth. He made mistakes, as we often do."

Miriam thought of her own mistake in driving her mother and sister to Georgia.

"Our father is not one to easily forgive," Emma continued. "Abram embraces the old ways in hopes of redeeming himself in our father's eyes. Yet nothing can remain as it once was. Life is a process. No one stays an infant. Growth and change are a part of life just as life and death are part of the cycle."

Looking down at the dress she wore, Miriam regretted the role she played in Abram's struggle. "I have opened old wounds and caused his grief to return anew."

"It is not you," Emma assured her. "Abram needs to forgive himself. Right now he thinks only of his pain. That is self-seeking. He is a better man than that. You have allowed him to dream of what could be. That frightens him. He is not ready to leave the world of grief and guilt he has created."

Emma's words were as confusing as the Amish way. Abram's life never would have changed if Miriam hadn't collapsed on his front porch.

She had questioned why she hadn't gone somewhere else. The neighbor's perhaps. Although other than Isaac's dairy, there were no other homes for miles. What if she hadn't found Abram? She would have wandered through the dark and never come upon a safe refuge.

But Abram's house had been lit; she'd seen the light in the window that had beckoned her. The middle of the night, yet an Amish house had light? She reached for Emma's plate. Had that light been a sign from the Lord so she would find her way?

She shivered, thinking of Serpent following close behind her. She had been exhausted, hungry, weak from lack of food and unable to think rationally or make good decisions.

The truth was Serpent would have found her.

Miriam rung out the dishcloth and watched the water drop back into the sink. The thought of what would have happened made her feel as limp as the dishrag.

Thankfully, Abram had given her shelter and refuge. He had saved her life and kept her safe.

Emma returned from outside and shook her head. "My brother is far too impatient today. He stayed awake keeping watch through the night. He is tired and worried for our safety as we go to town." She scurried to retrieve more baked goods from the pantry as Miriam bowed her head.

"Thank You, Lord. You brought me to Abram. I'm sorry for the upset I've caused in his life, but I'm grateful he saved me. Keep all of us safe, Lord, especially today."

The kitchen door opened and Abram stepped inside and wiped his feet on the rug. His gaze went to Miriam with question. "You are all right?"

"I was saying a prayer for our safety today and giving thanks that you saved my life."

"I did not save you, Miriam. You saved yourself."

Abram was grateful for the clear sky and cool morning air as they rode to Willkommen. Emma was next to him, Miriam sat far in the rear, hidden from sight. She wore a white *kapp* covered with a black bonnet that pulled around her oval face and a cape that she held tightly around her neck. Thanks to the Amish clothing, even Serpent would be hard-pressed to recognize her if they came face-to-face.

The ride took longer than usual. Or perhaps it seemed long because of his anxiety about being out in the open, with no protection, when a man sought to do Miriam harm.

The tension he was feeling eased a bit when the town appeared in the distance. He flicked the reins and Nellie picked up speed, enjoying the exercise.

"A good horse provides for a man, just like a good wife," his father had said, but his father had embraced the old ways and never bent, even ever so slightly. After the accident had injured Emma's leg, he had not allowed the *Englisch* doctor to set her foot, leaving Emma with a decided limp and a constant reminder to Abram of his own carelessness.

The accident had happened when he was fourteen years old and he had carried the burden of guilt ever since. If only he had learned from his mistakes, yet he had remained stubborn when Rebecca's time of confinement had come to completion. Why had he not taken her to the *Englisch* hospital with her first labor pains?

"Is something wrong?" Miriam asked as if she could sense his internal struggle. The woman was amazingly astute and attuned to the way Abram responded to the world. His world. The Amish world.

"Nothing is wrong," he assured her. Except Miriam was in danger and Abram feared for her safety. "We will be at the market soon."

Blocks of small shops and diners welcomed them to Willkommen. People hurried along the sidewalks and cars zipped past them on the road. Abram pulled on the reins for Nellie to halt at the first intersection. As soon as the light turned green, he flicked his gaze right then left, checking for traffic, before he nudged Nellie forward. The mare entered the intersection.

From out of nowhere a car, approaching from the intersecting roadway on the left, ran the red light and headed straight toward them. Abram's heart slammed into his chest. Emma screamed. He pulled back sharply on the reins as the car sped past.

"We could have been killed," Emma gasped as she stared after the fast-moving vehicle.

"The driver—" Miriam's voice was tight with emotion. "Did you see him?"

Abram shook his head. "I saw only the flash as the car passed too close to Nellie."

"He had crazed eyes and a sneer on his face," Emma said. "It seemed as if he sped up as he entered the intersection. His eyes were on the road as he raced through the light. I do not believe he even saw the buggy."

"*Gott* kept us safe," Abram said to calm the fear he heard in his sister's voice. But Emma was right. The driver had increased his speed.

"I saw his face." Miriam's voice was cold as ice.

A chill tingled Abram's neck and tangled down his spine.

Her next statement came as a whisper filled with warning. "The man driving the car was Serpent."

Chapter Sixteen

Miriam couldn't calm her racing heart even as she helped Emma and Abram unload the baked goods and crafts. They quickly set up a table at the side of the large hall, near a partitioned alcove where Miriam could hide if Serpent or anyone else involved with the Petersville police stepped inside. Abram and Emma seemed as aware of the danger as Miriam did. They hovered close and kept their eyes on the main door where shoppers, mainly *Englisch* ladies, started to appear.

Once the baked goods were arranged, Miriam turned to Abram. "I need to use a computer to contact my sister," she reminded him.

"After I find out if Samuel has returned to town."

Abram headed to the back door that led to the street where the buggy was parked. Through the open doorway, she watched him unload the handcrafted items he had made in his shop and carry them to the stall. Abram's fine craftsmanship and attention to detail easily made his woodworking stand out from other similar items Miriam noticed for sale.

"You could open your own store," she said as she placed his woodcrafts next to Emma's pies.

He grumbled.

"You should take pride in your ability, Abram."

"Pride is not from *Gott*. He gives gifts. It has nothing to do with me."

"But you use those gifts to give Him glory. Your woodworking ability is amazing."

"Your words puff me up too much, Miriam."

"Humility is knowing from where your giftedness comes," she countered.

Seemingly ignoring her words, Abram glanced around the marketplace then touched her arm. "Stay here with Emma. I will see if the sheriff has returned. His office is two blocks away, at the end of the alleyway in the rear of the market."

"Find out if anyone has seen a young blond woman with a thin, red-haired man. Also don't forget my aunt. Inquire about Annie Miller."

"I will ask at the sheriff's office and at some of the other stores around the square."

She grabbed his hand. "Thank you."

His gaze narrowed. "Serpent's focus was on the road when he passed us at the intersection. He did not notice who was in the buggy, but you need to be careful. The road he was on eventually leads to Petersville. Perhaps he has left Willkommen, but we cannot know for sure. You must be vigilant. The Amish clothing provides some cover but—"

"I'll stay out of sight," she quickly assured him.

With a nod Abram turned and strode out the back door of the market. Staring through the open doorway, she watched him for a long moment, expecting Abram to glance back and raise his hand in a wave or to at least offer her a smile of reassurance.

Instead he turned the corner and disappeared from

sight. She wrung her hands and stepped into the shadowed alcove, knowing all too well that Abram was immersed in a world that didn't include her.

Breathing out a deep sigh of regret, she peered from her hiding spot to see a full-figured Amish woman approach Emma.

"What is it with your *bruder*?" the woman asked. "I had hoped my daughter, Abagail, would catch his eye, but he does not seem interested in finding a wife."

"Eva Keim." Emma straightened her shoulders. "You know I cannot speak for Abram."

"No, but perhaps you could invite Abagail to visit."

"I will think on this," Emma said diplomatically.

"She would make a good wife for your *bruder*."

"I'm sure she would."

When the woman returned to her own stall, Emma slipped behind the alcove. "I am worried about Isaac. Usually he has arrived at the market by this time of day."

"Perhaps Daniel has delayed him," Miriam offered.

Through the open rear doorway and, as if on cue, Miriam saw a buggy pull to a stop. Daniel jumped to the sidewalk and ran inside. He quickly found Emma, who had moved out of the shadows.

"Why are you running so fast, Daniel?" she asked. "You look upset."

"*Yah*, a car passed us too quickly on the road. It nearly ran us into a ditch. I was frightened."

Emma laid her hand reassuringly on the boy's shoulder. "Who was it that caused you such fright?"

"I think it was the man who ran after me yesterday." The boy pointed to his neck. "He wore a scarf and he screamed at us as he passed by."

Emma hugged the boy and turned her gaze to Miriam.

Her stomach roiled. She had no right holding back information that allowed the killer to roam free. She had to tell the sheriff as soon as possible about everything that had happened. Serpent had to be stopped before he hurt someone else.

Not Daniel. *Dear God, don't let anything happen to the sweet child or to his father or to Emma.*

Or Abram.

Her mother had been killed and her younger sister taken. How would she find the strength to go on if something happened to Abram?

"Keep him safe, Lord," she prayed aloud. "Keep them all safe."

Chapter Seventeen

Upon entering the market, Isaac had confirmed the scare with the black sedan and his own concern for his son's safety. Now he and Emma were talking in hushed whispers so as not to let Daniel hear what they were saying. They were probably worried for the safety of both the Beiler and Zook households since Miriam had brought a killer into their midst.

She regretted her hesitation in notifying the authorities. Surely, Samuel Kurtz was back in town by now. Abram trusted him. She needed to, as well.

Needing to rectify her mistake, Miriam pulled the bonnet even closer to her face and the cape around her shoulders, and slipped out the back door, following the route Abram had taken to the end of the block. There she turned left and continued along the alleyway that led toward the center of town. Approaching the end of the second block, she spied the sheriff's office directly across the street.

Gathering her courage, Miriam headed to the corner crosswalk, but what she saw stopped her in midstep.

Her heart ricocheted in her chest. The sheriff had exited his office and was deep in conversation with another man in law enforcement. Miriam didn't need to see the man's face to know who he was. She recognized the scarf around his neck.

The sheriff was talking to Serpent.

She turned, needing to distance herself from both men. Seeing the sheriff so actively engaged with her hateful captor meant Samuel might be corrupt, as well. Did the sheriff know about the cabin and the way Serpent and his accomplice hunted women on the mountain road?

Memory of that fateful hijacking flooded over her again. Tears filled her eyes. She wiped her hands across her cheeks and tripped over her skirt as she turned to flee.

A man stood in the alleyway, blocking her escape. She flicked her gaze down the street. Where could she go?

"Hey, lady. Is something wrong?" the man said as she ran past him.

He raised his voice. "Do you need help?"

She shook her head and lifted her hand, hoping he would understand her need to hurry away.

"Sheriff," the man called out. Was he an overzealous Good Samaritan or part of Serpent's ring of corruption?

Fear grabbed her throat and wouldn't let go. All she could do was run. Except she couldn't run fast enough. The sound of footfalls followed her. Was it the man in the alleyway or Serpent?

She turned left at the next corner then made a fast right down another alley. At the intersection of a side road, she turned left and then right again.

Although unable to catch her breath, she was afraid to stop, knowing at least one man, if not more, was chasing after her. As much as she wanted to collapse in fear, she had to keep moving forward.

I can do all things through Christ who strengthens me.

Miriam had learned the scripture when she'd attended church and Bible study in Tennessee. Too soon, she had turned away from the good people who had wanted to help her. Was it due to fear of their admonition after she told them about her nomadic life and her unstable mother?

Or was she still ashamed of her mother as she had been growing up? Ashamed of her inability to keep a job or to create a loving home or face life's adversities? Her mother always ran away, which was exactly what Miriam was doing now. She was running from Serpent and the man in the alley and from the sheriff who might be involved in the corruption.

She needed to run away from Abram, too, and head to Atlanta. But what if Hannah wouldn't accept her into her home? Her sister had left three years ago and she'd never looked back or called to inquire about their health or their well-being.

The terrible truth was that Hannah wasn't interested in Miriam or her life. She was focused on other things that didn't involve her younger sisters and a dysfunctional mother.

Tears streamed from Miriam's eyes. She turned another corner and screamed.

Standing in front of her was Serpent.

His beady eyes widened. "It was you all along dressed in those stupid Amish clothes." He lunged for her.

Pulse racing, she turned to flee. Her foot slipped on

one of the uneven pavers. She lurched forward, catching herself in time.

He grabbed her bonnet and ripped it from her head.

"No!" She ran, forcing her legs to move faster.

He chased after her, all the while cursing and calling her vile names.

Nearing the street corner, she heard the *clip-clop* of a horse's hooves and hesitated for half a second.

Serpent caught up to her. He grabbed her cape. She shrugged free and ran into the street, directly into the path of an oncoming rig.

The Amish driver screamed a warning, but she couldn't stop. Serpent was on her heels and she would rather be run over than be captured again.

Abram hurried back to the market, expecting to find Miriam. He peered into the alcove and around the various stalls, searching for the *Englisch* woman who looked Amish with her tresses pulled into a bun and the *kapp* tucked securely on her head.

She was slender and tall and moved with a grace he found fetching. As he peered at the various *plain* women arranging their wares and selling to the customers who happened through the large common area, he saw no one that came close to Miriam's poise or beauty.

Emma was chatting with Isaac. He touched Emma's arm and smiled, causing a tug at Abram's heart. Why had he not noticed before now how Isaac leaned close to his sister as they talked, his attention totally focused on her?

She seemed equally smitten by the Amish man who placed his arm on the support beam against which she leaned. If Abram did not know better, he would expect Isaac to pull Emma into his arms and kiss her on the spot.

As much as Abram wanted to walk away and give them time together, he needed to find Miriam. Clearing his throat to get their attention, he stepped closer.

Emma looked up, startled. She pushed away from the support beam and tugged at her apron. Isaac dropped his arm and took a step back.

"I'm sorry to interrupt," Abram said.

Emma shook her head. "There is nothing to interrupt." But her flushed cheeks and dropped gaze said otherwise.

"Where is Miriam?"

Emma glanced around the warehouse as if she only now realized Miriam was gone. "She went to the buggy to get more supplies." Emma turned to Isaac, her gaze beseeching him to share what he knew about their houseguest.

He peered into the vacant alcove. "It has been some time since I have seen her. At least fifteen or twenty minutes."

Abram was already heading to the back door. Various scenarios played through his mind and none of them was good.

Once outside, he raced to the buggy but found it empty except for a carton of homemade pies. Hurrying past the Amish men who were enjoying a bit of socialization while the womenfolk sold their wares, he peered into the next buggy and the one after. Fear grabbed his throat. He wanted to scream Miriam's name and raise his fist in frustration, neither of which would bring her back to him.

Abram started down the street, but seeing no one in the distance, he turned into the alleyway he had taken earlier. If Miriam was hoping to talk to the sheriff, she would have gone this way.

Please, Gott, let my concern be for naught. Surely she was close by. Perhaps she had grown tired and was curled in the rear of a buggy. He turned and glanced over his shoulder to make sure he had not skipped over one of the carriages, then, realizing he had checked each of them, he continued along the narrow alley. At the intersection he peered right and left. Shoppers ambled along the thoroughfare. Some carried bags of baked goods from the Amish market. Others held baskets filled with items they had purchased.

The faces became a blur. The one face he searched for eluded him. Where was Miriam? Had Serpent found her?

Abram's heart tripped in his chest. Sweat dampened his brow and the back of his shirt, even though the day was cool.

At the next intersection he spied the sheriff's office. Earlier, Abram had stopped to inquire about his uncle. Ned Quigley had told him that Samuel had returned to town but was out of the office. Art Garner, the deputy injured in the vehicular accident on the road leading up Pine Lodge Mountain, remained on a respirator, unresponsive, with his wife at his bedside. The accident had occurred the morning after Miriam had appeared on Abram's porch and before he had realized the extent of the danger that surrounded her.

He hurried on to the next corner and studied the street. His gut knotted, his hands fisted and the thoughts that raced through his mind would have him confessing before the bishop if he acted them out.

Why had Miriam left the market? The woman was headstrong and determined to contact Hannah. Finding her aunt was another need. Abram had tried, but no one knew of an Annie Miller who had ever lived in Willkommen.

Hearing someone call his name, Abram turned to see Daniel running toward him. His blond hair blew in the wind. He clutched his wide-brimmed felt hat in his right hand and in the other hand he held something close to his chest.

"What do you have, Daniel? You're running faster than the wind."

"A bonnet and cape. I found them." The boy held them up for Abram to see. "Why would an Amish lady leave them on the street?"

"Where were they, Daniel?"

The boy placed the items in Abram's outstretched hand then pointed to the end of the next intersection. "At the corner by the traffic light."

Abram's stomach tightened. "You must go back to the market before your father starts to worry."

"But he said I could go into the alleyway and check on the horses," the boy insisted.

"Did he now?" Abram pointed him to the market. "You are farther than the horses. Hurry back, Daniel, and do not stop to talk to anyone. Stay with Emma and your father. I will return to the market soon."

The boy nodded and hurried along the alleyway. Abram watched until he turned a corner and disappeared.

Gripping the two clothing items, Abram hurried to the intersection Daniel had mentioned. He had to find Miriam. But looking up and down the street at the various shops, he wondered where she could have gone. Then an even darker thought filled his mind.

Had Serpent captured her again?

Chapter Eighteen

Miriam huddled in the corner of a tiny church where she had found shelter. "Thank You, Lord, for the buggy that knocked Serpent to the pavement and allowed me to escape. Thank You, too, for this open church that provided a place to hide."

Looking up, she stared at the small cross hanging at the side of the altar. "Oh, Lord, I was wrong—so wrong—in coming to Georgia. Forgive me and protect my baby sister."

She dropped her head into her hands and cried.

"Miriam?"

Raising her head, she wiped her hands across her cheeks and turned to see Abram standing at the rear of the church. A ray of sunlight broke through one of the windows and washed him in light.

"I didn't know where you were." He hurried toward her and touched her shoulder. "Daniel found your bonnet and cape."

He placed both items next to her on the pew.

"Serpent chased after me. I barely got away. Then I saw the church." Miriam smiled weakly. "God provided a refuge."

Like the refuge of Abram's house.

He raised his thumb and dabbed at the tear still on her cheek. "We will talk to the sheriff."

She shook her head, adamant to stay clear of law enforcement and eager to tell Abram what she had learned about his uncle. "Serpent was talking to someone in front of the sheriff's office. An older man, receding hairline, thick glasses."

"That sounds like Samuel."

"That's what I feared. I refuse to talk to him, Abram."

"The two men aren't working together, Miriam. You can trust my uncle."

Could she?

She stared into Abram's eyes, willing him to understand her concern. Perhaps he wanted everything to end and felt the easiest way to be rid of her was to turn her over to his uncle.

"Did you find any information about my sister or my aunt?" she asked.

His eyes clouded. "No one knew of either woman."

"And my mother's family?"

He shrugged. "Miller is a common name."

Was Abram making excuses?

Miriam glanced again at the cross. *Oh, Lord, help me to see more clearly so I know what to do. Abram trusts his uncle, but I saw him with Serpent. If only Abram would understand my concern.*

"My mother couldn't have made up a town named Willkommen," Miriam said. "She was slipping into dementia, but she could remember things that happened years ago. It was the more recent events that eluded her."

"Perhaps her family lived deep in the mountains," Abram offered as explanation for not finding information about her kin. "Some folks keep to themselves and rarely come to town. Or they could have moved away long ago."

The explanation sounded plausible. Not that she felt any better about the situation. Miriam had come to Willkommen specifically to connect with her mother's family. Now, that seemed impossible.

"Stay here, Miriam. I will bring the buggy to the alley. I do not want you walking along the street where Serpent could see you."

She didn't want Abram to leave her, but he was right. She would be safer in the buggy.

He squeezed her hand. "I will not be long."

Her spirits sank as she watched him leave the church, knowing she would soon be heading to Atlanta, leaving Willkommen and leaving Abram. They were worlds apart, which broke her heart.

Abram parked the buggy in the alley behind the church. He tied the horse to a fence pole and turned his gaze up and down the narrow path, alert to any sign of Serpent. The back of the church was nestled in a cluster of oaks interspersed with magnolias. Their wide, waxy leaves provided thick cover from any passersby. At least, that was Abram's hope.

He hurried toward the church and double-timed it up the side stairway. After easing open the door, he slipped into the darkened interior. His heart stopped. The church was empty.

He glanced at the small cross, his heart hardening in his chest. *Don't take another woman from me, Gott.*

"Abram."

He turned, relief sweeping over him. Miriam sat huddled in a back pew.

"I heard someone open the door to the church. Then

the person turned and walked away. I feared someone had spotted me and was notifying the sheriff."

Abram hurried to reassure her. "I told you Samuel can be trusted."

She shook her head. "I can't trust anyone, Abram."

"You can trust me."

Miriam stared at him as if weighing his words.

Even now she did not believe he would take care of her. Abram knew it to be true.

He pointed to the side door. "We will go out this way. The buggy is directly behind the church."

Together they hurried outside. Abram helped her climb into the rear of the buggy. Once she was settled, he encouraged Nellie forward. Rounding the corner of the church, Abram searched for any hint of danger.

"The market is not far. We will be there soon."

Miriam let out a deep breath. The sound carried with it an increased amount of frustration and fear. No matter how much Abram tried to reassure her, Miriam was in danger. She knew it. So did he.

Chapter Nineteen

Abram turned the buggy onto the market road and pulled to the rear of the complex. "Wait here, until I make certain Serpent is not inside."

He studied the street then stepped into the market complex and again searched the people who milled around the various stalls. Thankfully he saw only local women buying produce and hand-crafted items. A few men chatted with friends. A few more sipped coffee purchased at a shop across the street.

Returning to the buggy, he offered Miriam his hand and helped her down. "This way." He quickly ushered her inside and then pointed her toward an enclosed office. "You can wait in here."

The office had a small leather couch and two straight chairs, in addition to a desk with a computer. Miriam sat on one of the straight chairs.

"Do I have to stay here for the rest of the day?"

"You will not have long to wait. Plus, you can use the computer. The office manager has a meeting across town, but I am sure he would not mind."

"What about the password?"

"Type in 'amishmarket.' All lowercase and no space."

She looked surprised. "You're sure?"

He nodded. "Remember, the Amish can use computers for business purposes."

"But you don't."

"That is right. Still, I know the password." He smiled. "You can trust me, Miriam, even if you do not trust all men."

She sat straighter in the chair and looked somewhat indignant. "What do you mean by that?"

"Your mother's actions made you wary of others, especially men. Did your mother make poor choices about those she invited into her heart? Or did she give the various men in her life more attention than she gave to you and your sisters?"

Miriam's expression told him he was right. He took a step closer and lowered his voice, hoping she heard the sincerity in his tone. "I am not like the men your mother attracted or the other *Englisch* men who caused you pain. You think I am uneducated or a fool or someone who does not understand the ways of your world. You look at the surface and do not look deeper. That is too bad."

"Abram, I'm—"

"You are sorry?" he volunteered. "Are you sorry because you cannot see me clearly? I hope you will heal from the scars you carry from your youth, and I do not mean visible scars. I mean the scars that bind your heart."

He turned and reached for the door. "I will return soon."

Abram found Isaac talking to Emma. "Miriam is in the office. Keep watch. I do not want Serpent to find her."

"You are leaving?" Isaac asked.

"For a short while."

Emma stepped closer. "I told you, you should not get involved."

"I already am. Keep Miriam safe."

"What will happen if she leaves you, my brother?"

He shrugged, unable to verbalize his feelings. "You have mourned long enough for Rebecca," Emma reminded him. "If Miriam leaves, you will mourn her, as well. I do not think she will open her heart to our faith and our Amish ways unless you ask her to do so. But I know you, Abram. You are a proud man. Too proud to ask her to stay."

"Then we will say goodbye," he said, holding his emotions in check. "And she will leave me."

His heart would break, he failed to add.

Miriam couldn't stop thinking of Abram's accusations. Had her mother and the string of self-absorbed men to whom she had been attracted turned her daughters against all men?

Miriam dropped her head in her hands, realizing how her own heart had hardened over time. Abram was right. Her opinion of men was a product of her nomadic youth and the stream of men her mother had allowed into her life.

Miriam didn't trust men. She didn't trust herself, either. She was her mother's child. Surely she was prone to make mistakes just as her mother had done so many times.

And Abram? Could she trust him with her heart? That was the question she kept asking.

Needing to contact Hannah, she scooted her chair to the desk, used the password Abram had provided and accessed her email. Quickly she composed a message to her sister.

Hannah, email back and let me know your phone number. We need to talk. So much has happened.

She briefly explained the hijacking, their mother's death and Sarah's disappearance, and that she had been holed up on the Zook farm in Willkommen.

I'm planning to take a bus to Atlanta and need you to pick me up at the bus station.

Miriam hit Send just as a knock sounded at the door. Emma peered into the room. She smiled at Miriam and stepped inside.

"Abram was worried. I'm glad he found you."

Miriam explained what had happened. "I hid in a church, never thinking anyone would look for me there."

"But Abram did."

"Thanks to Daniel finding the bonnet and cape. He's a good boy, and his father is a good man. You deserve a life of your own, Emma. You don't need to care for Abram."

"I was worried about him after Rebecca died. Things have changed and so has my brother. You have made him think beyond his grief and have given him hope for the future."

"You're wrong," Miriam insisted. "I've brought only problems to his life. No matter what you say, I have to leave. Abram said the bus to Atlanta runs later in the week."

"The bus runs at 10:00 a.m. tomorrow and the next."

"You took the bus to Ethridge when you went home to visit your parents?"

"*Yah?*"

"Did Abram drive you to the bus station?"

"I took the Amish Taxi. Frank Evans makes his living transporting the Amish." Emma glanced at the business cards taped to one corner of the small desk. "See, here is his information. People often use the office computer to contact him."

"The taxi is allowed?"

"We cannot drive, but we can ride in vehicles. It is confusing to one who is not Amish." Emma scowled. "But you cannot leave now. When it is time, Abram will take you to the station."

Miriam sighed, knowing she had already stayed too long. "I just emailed my sister. Once I hear back from her, I'll head to Atlanta."

Emma wrinkled her brow. "But your sister left you, *yah*?"

Miriam nodded. "I can't blame Hannah. There were times when I wanted to leave, as well."

"Yet you did not leave. You are like me, Miriam. You are the one who cares for others. You stayed to care for your mother."

Emma took a step closer. "You told me to think of my own needs. You must do the same. You were a dutiful daughter, but now you must make your own way in life."

"I can't think of anything until Serpent is captured and my sister Sarah is found."

"And after that?" Emma's gaze was filled with question. "What will you do then?"

"I will try to heal my heart."

Emma touched Miriam's shoulder. "You must unchain your heart, Miriam. As I said, we are alike. We can see what we want but we hesitate to accept happiness into our lives. A woman should be with a man. It is the way of life. You are rejecting who you truly are and what is best for you."

"I'm not sure you understand who I am, Emma."

"Take time to think things through, Miriam. I need to return to the stall, but you must not be hasty in your decisions to leave Willkommen. Promise me, you will weigh your options."

Miriam appreciated the Amish woman's concern. "I promise."

When Emma left, Miriam tapped in the URL for the web site for the Amish Taxi and scheduled a pick up at 9:00 a.m. the following morning. Then she checked her email inbox to see if Hannah had responded to her message. She found nothing from her sister, but she did receive confirmation from the Amish Taxi.

Just as she logged off, a noise sounded outside the door and Abram entered the cramped office.

Miriam's heart pounded when a second person stepped through the door. The man she had seen talking to Serpent. Sheriff Kurtz.

Abram had brought the sheriff to the Amish market without talking to her first. What Abram didn't realize was that he had exposed her whereabouts to a man who more than likely was part of the corruption. The sheriff had to be involved after the way he had been focused on Serpent.

Abram hadn't listened to her earlier concerns about his uncle. Instead, he had exposed her to someone working with Serpent.

What was Abram thinking?

Abram stepped to Miriam's side. "Samuel has come to help. He needs to hear your story."

The sheriff pulled up the other straight-backed chair and stuck out his hand to shake hers. He introduced himself and added, "I'm the Willkommen sheriff. Why don't you start by telling me what happened?"

Shrinking back in the chair, Miriam shook her head. "I saw you talking to a man outside your office. He has a serpent tattoo on his neck, only he covers it with a scarf."

"Pete Pearson." The sheriff nodded. "He stopped by to inquire about my deputy who was air-evacuated to Atlanta earlier this week. Pearson helps the Petersville police, but only in an auxiliary role. He aids with traffic and crowd control. He's not a bona fide law-enforcement officer. Abram said another man was with him the night you were stopped."

Miriam nodded but she failed to speak.

The sheriff hesitated a moment before adding, "You need to start at the beginning and tell me the whole story."

"Abram said I am wanted for the death of my mother." She glared at the sheriff. "Do you consider me a suspect?"

Samuel shook his head. "That came from the Petersville Police Department. From what Abram told me about the night you appeared on his doorstep, I in no way think you had any role in your mother's death. Tell me what happened, Miriam, so I can bring the guilty to justice."

She stared at him for a long moment and then haltingly began to recount the night of the hijacking.

Abram's heart went out to her as she shared the horrific details. Samuel had confirmed that the hijackers were not officers of the law. At least, Pearson wasn't. One man kidnapped and held women hostage, the other was a cold-blooded murderer. Both men were felons who needed to be brought to justice.

"My mother didn't understand what was happening," Miriam explained as she got deeper into the story. "Serpent told her to be quiet. She wouldn't calm down. When he grabbed my arm, she lunged at him, screaming."

Miriam dropped her head. Tears fell from her eyes. Abram rubbed her shoulder, hoping to convey his concern and understanding.

A box of tissues sat on a desk in the corner. The sheriff handed them to her. Miriam nodded her appreciation, grabbed a tissue and wiped her eyes. "I'm sorry. I still can't believe my mother's dead."

"What happened next?" the sheriff asked.

"When my mother grabbed my arm to pull me away from Serpent, the other man stepped from the police car. He drew a weapon from his belt and shot her. I… I screamed. Sarah sprang from the car. The other man grabbed her."

"Can you describe him?"

"I wish I could. Serpent struck me and I must have passed out. The next thing I remember was being held in the cabin. I could hear water running nearby."

Miriam's eyes widened. "Serpent put us in two different rooms so we couldn't talk to each other. He tied me to the bed." She glanced at Abram. "I… I presume he did the same to my sister. I heard portions of phone conversations and someone with a deep voice must have stopped by the cabin at some point. He and Serpent talked about other women. The deep voice mentioned Rosie Glick. I heard them both mention 'trafficking.'"

"Rosie Glick was an Amish girl who disappeared about seven months ago. Are you sure that's the name he mentioned?"

"I'm sure."

The sheriff made a note in a booklet he pulled from his pocket and then nodded for her to continue.

"The night I escaped, a red-haired man came to the cabin. I saw him through the window. He hauled Sarah away. He said he'd take care of her."

Miriam put her hand over her mouth. "I think he planned to kill my sister."

Abram continued to rub her shoulder, wishing he could do more to offer support.

"Have you seen your sister since then?" the sheriff asked.

"No, but this is the first time I've been in town. Sarah's five-five with blond hair and big blue eyes. She's twenty-one, slender, pretty and…"

Looking up with tear-laden eyes, she added, "You have to find her. Serpent came after me today. You have to find him and the other man—the ringleader—and send them both to jail for murdering my mother. Find the red-haired man, too, but even more important, you have to find my sister."

The sheriff leaned closer. "Miriam, why didn't you come to me at the beginning?"

"Serpent said he would make it seem that I had killed my mother if I tried to get away, which is exactly what he did."

"Go on," Samuel prompted.

"After Sarah was taken, I knew I had to escape." Miriam continued to retell how she had managed to elude her captor.

When she finished, the sheriff closed his booklet and returned it to his pocket. "Abram told me you found his house."

She nodded.

He looked at his nephew with tired eyes. "But you

didn't tell me about Miriam when I stopped at your farm the next day."

"I didn't know what had happened," Abram confessed. "Only later, after you were headed to the hospital in Atlanta, Miriam told me about the hijacking."

"I trust my men," the sheriff said, "But I can't blame you for not sharing the information with my deputies, especially when Miriam was a possible suspect in her mother's death."

Samuel offered Miriam a sympathetic smile. "I'm glad we finally were able to talk. Be assured I will do everything in my power to track Pete Pearson down and bring him to justice."

"He was in town earlier," Abram reminded his uncle.

"I'll let my deputies know. He should be fairly easy to find."

"Miriam should stay in town," Abram suggested.

She narrowed her gaze. "What?"

"You'll be safer here if Pearson is on the loose."

"But—"

The sheriff pulled his cell from his pocket and tapped in a number. He pushed the phone to his ear. "Curtis, this is Samuel. We need to find Pete Pearson." The sheriff smiled. "That's good news. Have Ned bring him in to the station so I can interrogate him."

Samuel shoved his phone into his pocket. "One of my deputies is with Pearson now. He'll arrest him and haul him in for questioning."

He turned to Abram. "Take Miriam home with you and Emma. She'll be more comfortable there. Pearson will remain in jail. I can't see how a judge would set bail after what Miriam has told me."

Samuel stood and took Miriam's hand. "You go back

to the farm with Abram. I'll need to get a written statement from you, but we'll do that later."

"We'll leave now," Abram said to Miriam as soon
as the sheriff had left. "I'll see if Emma can ride home
with Isaac."

After the arrangements were made, Abram helped
Miriam to the buggy. Once she was comfortably tucked
into the rear seat, he encouraged Nellie into a sprightly
trot. He needed to get Miriam to his farm as quickly
as possible.

As they rode through town, Miriam remained quiet.
Too quiet.

"It will be over soon," Abram assured her.

"I didn't think the sheriff would believe me."

"I told you Samuel is to be trusted."

"I didn't ask him about my aunt."

"But I did. He does not know anyone by that name."

"Maybe it was all in my mother's mind."

"I am sorry you had to relive her death." He thought
for a moment and then added, "When you talked about
her, it sounded as if she was trying to protect you. She
loved you, Miriam."

Miriam's silence tugged at Abram's heart. Verbalizing what had happened had taken a toll. She had to
be exhausted and upset.

Hopefully after Serpent was captured she would be
able to heal. But then what would happen? Would she
go back to Tennessee or head to Atlanta?

Abram knew one thing for certain. She would not
stay in Willkommen.

Chapter Twenty

Miriam found comfort recalling how her mother had tried to protect her during the hijacking. In the confusion of the attack, she had focused on her mother's outrage that night instead of the protective nature of her attempt to stop Serpent. Maybe, as Abram had said, her mother had loved her, after all. The realization took her by surprise. For as long as she could remember, she had believed her mother had thought of her as a complication.

Now Miriam wondered if she had been too hard on her mother. A single mom with no consistent employment. She couldn't remember her mother taking food stamps or welfare, yet they'd had food and clothing. Thrift-shop purchases and beans and rice more days than she'd like to remember, but food and clothing nonetheless.

"Did you ever believe something and then find out you were totally wrong?" she asked Abram.

He remained silent for a long moment. A muscle in his neck twitched. She longed to see his face to read his expression. The back of his head with his hat pulled low provided no clue as to what he was thinking.

Once again she had been too forward and wished she could retract her question. Better to remain silent than to cause more problems. If only she could have boarded a bus today. But how could she find Hannah if she couldn't contact her by phone or email?

A sadness overwhelmed her and she hung her head.

Abram turned his head slightly. "You are crying again?"

His words sounded like an accusation.

She bit her lip and shook her head. "I'm tired, that's all."

"You are worried about what will happen."

He was right but she refused to answer him. She had already said too much.

"And, yes," he continued, "I have believed wrongly and regretted my actions."

Was he talking about taking her into his house? She should have kept running that night and never stopped. But that would have been even more foolish when she'd needed a place of refuge.

"I'm sorry for disrupting your life, Abram." Especially since he had wanted to find lodging for her in Willkommen. Abram didn't want her underfoot. Not now. Not ever.

He shook his head. "You have brought new life to my house, Miriam. You are not a problem. I am the problem. I have held on too tightly to the past. You may have heard Emma say this. She is right. The old ways must sometimes change. The Amish who came to Willkommen did so with the intention of making new rules in which to grow as a community. I could not accept the changes so I have never fit in. It was not their outreach, but my stubborn pride."

"You have the right to follow the ways of the past."

"My wife died because of my unbending pride. I lost a child, as well. This is not easy to carry. Some would say it was *Gott*'s will, but I say it was my stubborn heart that had to be right about everything. That is the burden I carry."

"The church I attended in Tennessee talked about God's forgiveness. We have to be contrite and realize we have done wrong. We also have to desire to change our ways, but if we long to be a better person, the Lord is a forgiving Father."

"*Ach*! But, Miriam, *Gott* is not the problem. My earthly father is. He would never forgive me."

She didn't understand. "Why would your father be upset that you remained close to the way he raised you?"

"In my youth, I erred."

"When you were a boy? Could he not forgive a child for making a mistake?"

"I was headstrong and struggled against the rules he established. I did not want to plow the field and wanted instead to go into town to see my friends, *Englisch* boys, who pulled me into worldly ways. Because I was angry, I hurried the horses and plowed the field too fast. At the corner when I was making a turn, I did not hear Emma's voice. In her kindness, she was bringing me water since the day was hot. I had borrowed a small battery-operated radio from Trevor, my *Englisch* friend, and had the music playing, so I did not hear her call my name."

Abram swallowed hard. "The plow caught her leg. I never heard her screams. My father ran to gather her in his arms. He raised his fist in anger at me and said I was not worthy to be his son."

"Oh, Abram, he spoke in haste and he was worried about Emma."

"He never looked me in the eye again. He acted as if I did not exist."

"Did you ask his forgiveness?"

"I was confused and did more things to upset him. Trevor was older. He had a car. We rode to the lake, but the road was windy and we were going much too fast."

Emma had told her about the drowning, but Miriam knew Abram needed to recount the experience himself.

"At a sharp turn, the car skidded across the road and crashed into the water. I managed to get out."

"And your friend?"

"He was trapped. I tried to save him."

Miriam touched Abram's shoulder. "I'm sorry."

"That is why I left Ethridge after Rebecca and I were married. I needed to prove myself."

"And you proved yourself by adhering to the Old Order."

"That is right. I am the reason Emma limps, yet she came to live with me after Rebecca died, knowing I needed help. Emma's heart does not harbor resentment. She has forgiven me, but I cannot forgive myself."

"Have you asked your father's forgiveness?"

Abram shook his head. "It would not change the way he feels or acts toward me."

"And what of God? Have you asked His forgiveness?"

"He knows my heart."

"But acknowledging our wrongdoings and verbalizing our contrition aloud can be cathartic, Abram."

"Now you are sounding like the bishop." Abram shook his head. "*Gott* took Rebecca from me because of my willfulness as a young man. I did not deserve happiness after what I did to Emma and what happened at the lake."

"You're wrong, Abram. God didn't take Rebecca or your child because of the mistakes you made in your youth. Death is part of life. Sometimes we don't understand why it comes when it does, especially when the person is young and has their life ahead of them."

"What of you, Miriam? You spoke of your own actions and feelings that you have done wrong. Have you asked God's forgiveness?"

Abram was right. She hadn't sought forgiveness. She hadn't put the pieces together to see clearly the part she played in her own mother's wayward life.

"I never thought my mother loved me. Now I realize I might have been wrong."

"Can a mother ignore her child?"

"It seemed that mine had, but I was seeing life through my own childish eyes instead of taking into consideration her own struggle. I'm beginning to look at my youth in a new way."

For so long she had buried the pain of her past in the depths of her heart. Once free from Serpent, then and only then, would she work on forgiveness. By that time, she would have forgotten Abram.

Inwardly she scoffed at herself. Staring at the tall expanse of man as he held the reins lightly in his strong hands, she knew she'd never forget him. She would carry the memory of Abram in her heart for the rest of her life.

The Amish way of life and especially this righteous man who didn't see the good in who he was would remain forever a part of her. She would remember this special time, not because of Serpent and his wicked ways, but because of Abram.

Hopefully, his decision to notify the sheriff wouldn't cause her more duress. Too much had already happened.

She didn't need any more trauma in her life. She needed peace and security, like what she had felt in Abram's arms. But that was in the past. And now Miriam needed to focus on the future.

Tires squealed and an engine whined as a vehicle left Willkommen and raced toward the buggy at breakneck speed. Abram clutched the reins more tightly and silently prayed for Nellie to remain calm, knowing anything could spook the horse when the car passed by.

Miriam leaned forward and grabbed Abram's arm. "What's happening?"

He peered around the corner of the buggy. His stomach soured, seeing the auxiliary police car with the portable flashing lights.

The car increased its speed even more and headed straight toward them.

"What is it, Abram?" she asked again.

The buggy jostled from side to side.

"Sit back and hold on," he warned.

"It's Serpent, isn't it?"

"I… I cannot be sure. He will soon pass us by."

Nellie fought against the bit. "Whoa there, girl," he soothed, trying to guide the mare to the side of the road.

The horse's ears twitched. Abram saw her flared nostrils and the whites of her eyes. "Quiet down, Nellie girl. Everything is okay."

Except everything was wrong. The Serpent was gaining on them. Yet he was supposed to have been taken into custody.

The engine of his car whined. The black sedan passed in a swirl of dust then screeched to a stop in the middle of the road.

Abram tugged on the reins, working to control the mare.

"I thought Ned Quigley was going to apprehend Serpent." Miriam's voice was tight with emotion.

"He must have gotten away."

"Or your uncle was lying."

"Get behind the seat, Miriam. Hide under the tarp."

"It's too late. He's knows I'm with you."

"He knows no such thing. Do as I say."

"But—"

"Now, before he steps from his car."

She scurried into the rear and dove under the tarp.

Abram climbed out of the buggy. "Nice girl," he soothed, rubbing Nellie's flank then her neck.

The mare was as confused as Abram. What had happened to Deputy Quigley and why was Serpent on the loose?

Abram narrowed his gaze as the driver's door of the black sedan opened. Serpent stepped to the pavement but left the motor running and the lights continuing to flash.

"You're leaving town in a hurry," the man growled.

Abram stood his ground. "Move your vehicle so I can pass."

"No way, Zook." Serpent stepped closer. "You've got something I need in your buggy."

"I know of nothing in my buggy that would interest you." He paused a moment and then pulled his lips into a strained smile. "Unless you want to buy an apple pie."

"Don't make jokes, Amish boy. I know Miriam Miller is with you."

Abram did not like Serpent's comment or his tone, and he certainly did not like being called an Amish boy. But his main concern was Miriam's safety. No matter what Serpent tried, Abram had to keep her safe.

"The sheriff wants to talk to you, Pearson."

"Sheriff Kurtz?" Serpent's eyes widened. "I saw him earlier today."

"He wants to talk to you about something that happened a few nights ago," Abram continued. "Deputy Quigley was supposed to have hauled you in for questioning about a car you stopped on the mountain road."

"You're talking crazy, Zook, as crazy as your Amish ways."

Abram refused to be intimidated. "You pretended to be law enforcement."

Serpent inflated his chest. "I *am* law enforcement, farm boy. I work for the Petersville Police Department."

"You work in a part-time auxiliary capacity. It is not the same."

"Since when does an Amish pacifist know anything about law enforcement?"

"I know legitimate officers of the law when I see them. I do not see such a man in you."

Pearson's face darkened. He fisted his hands. "Move aside, Zook. I don't want you to get hurt."

"You cannot hurt me, Pearson."

"Don't be so sure." Serpent tried to push past Abram and peer into the buggy.

"You do not have the right to encroach on my private property," Abram stated calmly.

"Encroach?" Pearson laughed. "Who taught you that ten-dollar word? Surely not the schoolmarm in your one-room schoolhouse."

The Serpent stretched his hand toward the tarp in the rear of the buggy. Abram grabbed his arm. Pearson turned and landed a punch to Abram's chin.

The blow stung, but Abram refused to respond.

Pearson tried to pull another punch. Abram ducked then grabbed Serpent and locked his arms in a tight hold behind his back. In one swift motion Abram removed the weapon from Pearson's belt.

Serpent struggled but Abram held him all the more tightly. Using his free hand, he removed the magazine from the gun and placed the unloaded weapon on the seat of his buggy.

"You'll pay for this, Zook."

"I have done nothing wrong. You are the one who harbors evil in your heart." Abram tugged on the end of the scarf, which dropped to the ground, exposing the tattoo as well as a cut on Pearson's neck.

"You wear the mark of the evil one. Change your ways, Pearson, or you will regret your actions when you come to the end of your earthly journey."

The wail of a siren sounded in the distance.

Pearson glanced at the road, seeing the approaching car, and strained against Abram's hold even more. "You'll regret this, Zook. Chief Tucker will haul you into the Petersville Police Department and explain the rights you don't have. You *plain* folks think you're above the law."

Abram tightened his grip on Serpent, relieved to see the deputy's car screech to a stop. Ned Quigley threw open the driver's door and hurried to offer assistance.

"Sheriff Kurtz said you've had problems with this guy." Quigley slipped handcuffs over Pearson's wrists. "I'll take him in for questioning. We'll hold him for as long as possible. Kurtz will keep you updated."

"I thought you were with Pearson earlier."

Quigley looked perplexed. "Someone's given you wrong information."

Abram would let his uncle resolve the confusion. Right now, he wanted to leave Willkommen and all that had happened behind and return Miriam to the security of his farm.

He climbed into the buggy, and with a flick of the reins, Nellie started toward home. Once they were clear of the two vehicles, Miriam crawled out from under the tarp.

"Is it over?" she asked.

Abram nodded. "Serpent has been taken in for questioning. Hopefully he will stay in jail for a very long time."

Serpent's apprehension meant Miriam was no longer in danger. Nor did she need Abram's protection. While that should have brought relief, all Abram could think about was having to say goodbye to Miriam.

Chapter Twenty-One

Miriam entered the farmhouse and hung the cape and bonnet Serpent had ripped off her on the peg by the door and shivered at the memory of rounding the corner and finding him on the street. Having him chase after their buggy when they were leaving Willkommen sent another shot of nervous anxiety to tangle down her spine. Thankfully Serpent had been apprehended, but even that did little to calm her troubled spirit.

The house was too quiet and she glanced around the kitchen, feeling totally alone. Emma was in town, and Abram was unhitching Nellie. Still shaking from the run-ins with Pearson, Miriam kept imagining what would have happened if Serpent had pulled back the tarp and found her in the buggy. Would Abram have held fast to his Amish nonviolence or would he have fought to protect her?

What did it matter? Abram was too enmeshed in the past. Not the adherence to the Old Order Amish ways—she understood that—but to his life with Rebecca. He couldn't get over her death and would carry the guilt that was ill-founded for the rest of his life.

Such a shame that he couldn't forgive himself.

He had asked her about her past. Had she forgiven her mother?

Miriam glanced around the large kitchen with the finely crafted table and benches and the sideboard where Emma cooled her pies. A clock and calendar hung on the wall. Two oil lamps sat on shelves with tin plates behind them to expand the arc of light when night fell. Everything about the kitchen warmed her heart with a sense of home, the stable home Miriam had never known.

As much as Miriam wanted to climb the stairs and hole up in her bedroom so she wouldn't have to see Abram again, she couldn't run away. Emma would be late coming home and the burden of preparing the meal always fell on her shoulders. Surely, Miriam could prove herself useful instead of being a burden. That's what she'd heard her mother say once about her daughters—that they were a burden. The word still cut a hole in Miriam's heart. How could any mother say that about her child?

Hot tears burned her eyes but Miriam refused to cry. She wouldn't let her face be splotched and red when Abram came indoors. She didn't need his perusal or questioning gaze. She had already said too much to him and had allowed herself to be too taken in by him. She'd learned her lesson.

Love and a happy home weren't for her, especially not with an Amish man who longed for his dead wife. Miriam could never compete, not that she wanted to. If Abram didn't accept her for who she was, then he wasn't the man for her.

She would find someone else.

Or would she?

In reality she knew she wouldn't. She would go

through life with the wall around her heart, the way she had lived for the past twenty-four years. Abram had broken through that protective barrier for the briefest of times. She had made a mistake letting him in. A very big mistake.

Abram dallied in the barn, biding his time. He wasn't ready to face Miriam again. The run-in with Serpent had unsettled him. The man had held Miriam captive and hurt her and had come so close to finding her again.

Perhaps Abram had been too quick to bring his uncle into the situation. Had the meeting at the Amish market led to Serpent learning Miriam's whereabouts? Abram needed to return to the market tomorrow and would talk to his uncle then. Samuel would be able to clarify some of the confusion as well as provide information about how long Serpent would be held in custody.

Although relieved that Serpent had been apprehended, Abram was still troubled about another issue. His sister's earlier admonition continued to swirl through his mind. Emma was right. Abram was prideful. He was also fearful of what Miriam would say if he asked her to stay, to join the Amish faith and give their future a chance. He had lost a love once. He was not willing to open himself to that pain again.

Eventually, Abram ran out of chores that needed to be done. He was weary, not so much from physical exertion but more from a heaviness of heart that weighed down his shoulders.

Tonight he would talk to Miriam once Emma retired to her room. He would ask forgiveness for surprising her with his uncle's visit to the market. He did not want to do anything to hurt her or to cause her harm. He would never be able to forgive himself if he caused her pain. If she readily accepted his apology, perhaps he would find the wherewithal to broach the subject of their future.

Hoping their differences could be resolved and feeling a swell of optimism, he opened the door to the kitchen. Emma had come home and was standing at the stove stirring a pot of soup.

He stepped inside and wiped his feet on the doormat, inhaling the pungent smell of onions and peppers and tomatoes.

"I did not see you come home," he said to Emma.

"Isaac walked me to the front door so we could talk a few minutes before I entered the house."

Abram glanced into the main room. "I do not see Miriam."

"She was so thoughtful and prepared a vegetable soup with some of my homemade noodles. I was relieved when I came in and smelled the wonderful aroma filling the house."

"Where is she?"

Emma's face grew serious. "She's upstairs, Abram. She said she's tired and wants to get some rest."

He glanced at the stairwell. "Surely she will eat with us."

Emma shook her head. "Not tonight. She's not hungry."

"What else did she tell you, Emma?"

"Only that she plans to take the bus to Atlanta."

"When?"

"I cannot say. All I know is that she emailed her sister today." Emma's face softened. She touched his arm as if offering support. "Abram, there is no reason for her to stay here."

"Serpent has been taken into custody. The sheriff

needs a statement from her. And what of the trial? She will have to testify."

"Then she can return. But trials take time. It might be months from now. She must move on with her life."

Emma pointed to the table. "Come and sit, Abram. I will get your soup."

He shook his head and turned toward the door. "I have work to do in my workshop."

"You must eat."

"I am not hungry." Pulling his hat from the hook, he opened the door and stomped into the cold night.

Halfway to the workshop, he stopped and looked at the window of the room where Miriam was staying, hoping he would see her standing at the window. The room was dark and the only thing he saw in the glass was the reflection of the night sky.

His heart felt equally dark. He had tried to give of himself, but he had not given enough. In his youth, he had injured Emma. Trevor's accident had followed soon after. Three years ago he had lost his wife and child. Now he was losing Miriam.

His shoulders slumped as he entered the workshop. Miriam was already focused on Atlanta and the life she would live there. She would say goodbye to Willkommen. She would say goodbye to Abram, as well.

Chapter Twenty-Two

Miriam's mood the next morning was as overcast as the sky, knowing this would be her last few hours in the North Georgia mountains. At 10:00 a.m. she would board the bus to Atlanta. She would return for Serpent's trial, but she would find a place to stay in Willkommen or perhaps even drive up from Atlanta for the day she gave her testimony. Abram would remain on his farm and never know that she had returned to town.

His bedroom door opened and his footsteps sounded in the hallway. He paused outside her door. If only he would knock and ask her to stay or at least offer her some hope that she might have a place in his faith and in his future.

She bit her lip and hung her head, hearing him hurry down the stairs where Emma was, no doubt, preparing breakfast. They had more wares to sell at market today. Miriam would not interfere with their work and their routine. Plus, saying goodbye to Abram would be too painful. She hadn't even told him she was leaving. Another mistake on her part, but she didn't have the courage or the strength to face him this morning.

She had arranged for the driver to pick her up at nine,

in time for the ten o'clock bus to Atlanta. She would leave a note of thanks for Abram's hospitality and Emma's friendship. She was grateful and so very thankful that she had found them.

Gott had provided, as they would say, and Miriam was beginning to see God working in her own life. The teachings that had started when she'd visited the church in Tennessee were put into action here on this Amish farm. She saw the hand of God in Abram and Emma's love of nature and closeness to the land, in their dependence on God's mercy for all things and in their rejection of the world that had gone too far off course.

For so long Miriam had yearned for a simple life where God was the center of the family and all was done to give Him honor. She'd found that here with Abram.

A door slammed below. She neared the window and peered into the morning stillness. Abram came into view, his shoulders back, head held high and his steps determined as he walked to the barn. She took a step back in case he looked up to catch a glimpse of her.

Today his focus was on the barn and hitching Nellie to the buggy. A knife cut deep into her heart. She had hoped he would change, but he wouldn't. He never would. Abram was...well, he was Abram, a strong man with a stubborn streak that could be a blessing or a curse.

A tap sounded at the bedroom door. Miriam hadn't heard Emma's footsteps on the stairway, but she was grateful the Amish woman had come to see her.

Pulling open the door, Miriam almost cried, knowing this would be the last time she would see the sweet face of the woman who had found a place in her heart.

"We are going to town," Emma said, her voice low

as if to keep Abram from hearing. "Come with us, Miriam."

"Did Abram want you to talk to me?"

She could see the truth in Emma's eyes. The woman would not tell a lie, but she couldn't admit that her brother had not mentioned Miriam. Had he even thought of her?

"I know he wants you to join us," Emma pleaded. Yet Miriam knew that what Emma believed and what Abram wanted were two very different things.

"You go, Emma. I need to finish my crocheting." The scarf she was making for Emma. "And cut the fabric for the dress you showed me how to make. I'll stay busy while you sell the rest of your wonderful items."

"Isaac will be working at the dairy for a few more hours, if you need anything. I could stop by his house before heading to town and ask Daniel to visit you. He's good company."

Miriam smiled at Emma's thoughtfulness. "Daniel is so special, but I'll be fine. Have him stay with Isaac."

"If you are sure."

Miriam nodded. "I am." She hesitated and then broached the subject she had already discussed with Emma too many times. "Isaac cares deeply for you. I see it in his eyes, and Daniel beams when you are near. He needs a mother. Isaac needs a wife."

Emma's cheeks blushed. She lowered her eyes momentarily and, when she raised her gaze again, Miriam could see the internal struggle that tore at the sweet Amish woman. "What am I to do about Abram? He, too, needs a wife."

"Your brother will not change until the situation becomes too dire. Right now you are enabling him to go on and not think about the future. He still longs for Rebecca."

"*Ach*, that was so true, but when you came into his life, Miriam, you made him think of what could be."

"He never showed signs of his change of heart to me. Do not lose your own happiness because of trying to help your brother. Isaac will not wait forever. Abram will understand. He talks about what a good woman you are, Emma, and he's right. But you must think of a little boy who needs you and a man who God has placed in your path. You will help Abram if you force him to be on his own. Only then will he realize what he really needs."

"I shall talk to him today. When we return home this evening, I will let you know how he takes the news. You are right, Miriam. Abram is locked in the past. I must encourage him to think of tomorrow."

Tomorrow. The word saddened Miriam. Hannah would meet her at the bus station this afternoon, and by tomorrow, Miriam would be trying to start a new life for herself. After the peace of the Amish life, she wasn't ready to face the hectic pace of the city.

Miriam grabbed Emma's hand. "Pray for me. I, too, need clarity about the future."

Emma nodded. "I will pray for you and Abram. You both struggle with the past."

"What do you mean?"

"Your mother. You cannot see the truth about her heart. She loved you even if she could not express that love."

"I believe it with my head, Emma, but my heart still questions her love."

"My mother wanted Abram and Rebecca to remain in Ethridge, close to her. She wanted what every woman wants, grandchildren around her in her old age. I saw her heart break when Abram left. He was the favorite child, and after Rebecca's death, my mother encouraged me to move to Willkommen to help Abram. As concerned as she was about Abram's well-being, I knew she loved me, as well."

"But what about your father. He never forgave Abram."

"That is how Abram sees the past. In reality, Abram could never forgive our father for his words spoken in haste. Both men are cut from the same cloth. Abram waits for my father to show some sign of forgiveness and our father waits for Abram to ask the same. They will never reconcile until one of them swallows the pride that fills each of them too full."

Emma squeezed Miriam's hand one last time. "Pray for Abram. He needs your prayers and your love."

With a sad smile, Emma hurried down the stairs.

The sound of Nellie pulling the buggy to the edge of the porch drew Miriam back to the window. Her hand touched the cool glass as if she were reaching out to Abram one last time.

He took the basket Emma carried and placed it on the floor of the buggy as she climbed into the front seat. He flicked the reins, signaling for the mare to be on her way. The buggy creaked. Miriam kept her gaze on Abram until he and Emma disappeared from sight.

If only he had glanced back. But Abram didn't need her, he didn't want her. He had his Amish life and everything that entailed. It didn't include an *Englisch* woman who brought strife and danger to his peaceful home.

Miriam would leave today. She would leave the Amish way. She would leave Abram, and that broke her heart.

Chapter Twenty-Three

Miriam quickly dressed in her jeans and sweater, feeling strange in her old clothes that used to be so comfortable to wear. She stuck the wad of fifties she had retrieved from her car in her pocket and then finished crocheting the scarf and left it on the bed with a note for Emma. She had also crocheted a woolen scarf for Abram to wear when the winter came next year. He could wrap it around his neck when the days were cold and he worked outdoors.

She gazed though the window at the horses grazing on the hillside. Would he even remember her or what they had shared by then?

She wrote a second note, this one to Abram, but she kept it breezy and light. No reason to bare her soul at this late date.

With a heavy heart, she hurried downstairs and poured a cup of coffee. After cutting a slice of Emma's homemade bread, she covered it with apple jelly. She would never find breakfast as good in the city. She would never find a life as good as here on the farm.

Once she had eaten, she washed her cup in the sink and then glanced at the wall clock. The car would pick her up in an hour. Not enough time to start a new project. Perhaps she should offer a prayer of thanksgiving for the people who had taken her in. She wasn't used to praying, but it seemed appropriate. She folded her hands and bowed her head.

Lord, You provided a light in the window and a place of refuge in my time of need. Thank You for Abram and Emma and for the love I found in this home. Thank You, too, for their faith that has shown me the importance of placing You at the center of my life. Forgive me the years of abandonment when I didn't have time for You. Forgive me for my unforgiving heart closed to my mother's love. Forgive me for arguing with Hannah before she left home. Lead me to Hannah so we can reconcile. Protect Sarah wherever she might be. If only Serpent would reveal her whereabouts.

She trembled, thinking of sweet Sarah and of what she could be experiencing.

Lord, I can do nothing, but I place her in Your hands, and I trust that You, oh, God, will honor my prayer and keep her safe. Let me not grow despondent about what is to come, but let me know that You walk with me into each of my tomorrows. With Your help, I will not despair, but I will find a new life even if it is without Abram. Send an Amish woman into his life who will love him the way I do.

Love him? The thought startled her.

She shook her head. It was time to admit her feelings. She loved Abram.

If only he could have recognized her love.

She sat for a long moment reflecting on all that had happened. Then realizing there was something more to tell the Lord, she bowed her head again and prayed aloud.

"Lord, You know my heart, but I still need to confess my sinfulness. I made the trip to Georgia to find my mother's estranged sister, hoping she would accept Mother into her home so the burden for my mother's care would be lifted from my shoulders. I thought only of myself. Forgive me, Lord, for my selfishness in my mother's time of need."

She sighed. "And, Lord, I love the Amish way and long to join this community of believers and the faith they follow. If only it were possible."

A faint knock sounded at the door. Miriam checked her watch. The driver was early.

She opened the door to find Daniel standing wide-eyed with his right hand outstretched.

"Did Emma tell you to visit me?" she asked, appreciating the Amish woman's thoughtfulness.

He shook his head. "No, but *Datt* told me this belongs to you. I found it in the pasture."

He opened his hand and revealed Miriam's cell phone.

Hot tears of relief burned her eyes. The Lord had heard her prayer.

"Oh, Daniel, I am so glad you found my phone. Thank you."

"It was protected by a pile of rocks. *Datt* said it should still work even with the recent rain. He said you can use the electricity that runs to the dairy barn to charge your phone."

Some of her heaviness of heart lifted. She would be able to see if Hannah had answered her email. Once she retrieved the contact information, she could call Hannah since her sister's number was programmed into Miriam's phone.

"Let me get the charger." She pulled the apparatus

from the plastic bag that held her few belongings and hurriedly walked with Daniel to his father's farm.

Isaac greeted her warmly and ushered her into the barn where he pointed to the electrical outlet. "I wanted Daniel to give the phone to you before we left for market. We can wait until after you have made your call, if you would like to go to town with us."

"Thank you, Isaac, but I'll stay here. You've been so helpful. I'm very grateful to you and Daniel."

Miriam plugged in the charger and connected it to her phone, feeling another swell of relief as the cell turned on. Hannah had not sent a reply email, but Miriam quickly accessed her contacts and memorized her sister's phone number. She never wanted to be without a way to contact Hannah again.

Sending up a prayer of thanksgiving, she tapped the number into the keypad and pulled the phone to her ear, expecting to hear Hannah's voice. But the call went to voice mail. Miriam's euphoria plummeted so much that she almost failed to speak when she heard the beep.

"Hannah," she finally gasped. "It's Miriam. I've been hiding out in Willkommen. It's in the North Georgia mountains. I found refuge with the Zooks, an Amish family. I'm catching a bus to Atlanta later today. Can you pick me up at the bus station downtown? I sent you an email, but I'm not sure if you got it."

She pushed the phone closer. "I'm sorry about our argument when you left. Oh, Hannah, Mama's dead. She was killed by a man who stopped our car on the mountain road. Sarah was taken and I don't know where she is. The police…they were involved…at least, most of them. I have so much to tell you. I'm begging your forgiveness for the hurtful words I said. And Mama—I'm sure she loved us even if she couldn't show that love."

The voice mail beeped again, indicating the end of the recording. Had Miriam told her sister enough? Tonight she would arrive in Atlanta and she would fill her in on everything else.

Miriam allowed her phone to partially charge before she left the barn, latching the door behind her. Isaac and Daniel were on their way to town and, just as yesterday, Miriam felt very much alone.

She ran back to Abram's house and hurried up the drive, but when she turned the corner of the house, she came to an abrupt stop.

Serpent.

Her heart crashed out of her chest and her pulse raced. She started to run, but he was too fast and too strong. He grabbed her shoulder and threw her to the ground. The cell phone slipped from her fingers. She screamed and raised her hand to protect her face as his fist crashed against her forehead, hitting her in the same place he had hit her before.

She tried to roll away from him, away from the heinous tattoo, away from the man who would take her to his mountain cabin and kill her.

Serpent had found her again. The last thing she thought of before she slipped into darkness was Abram's handsome face that she would never see again.

Chapter Twenty-Four

Abram helped Emma set up their stall at the Amish market and, after the morning rush of customers subsided, he hurried to the sheriff's office.

Curtis Idler sat at his desk and greeted Abram with a warm handshake. "I'm sure you're here to talk to Samuel. He's at city hall with the mayor. I expect him back shortly."

"I wanted to know how the questioning went with Pearson. Did he reveal anything you can share with me?"

Curtis's smile waned. "Ned Quigley questioned Pearson after bringing him in yesterday. We held him overnight, but this morning a police officer from Petersville provided an alibi. They had worked together the night Miriam said her car was hijacked."

"The officer must have mixed up the dates," Abram objected.

"Ned said Pearson's alibi is tight. We couldn't hold him after that."

The reality of what Curtis was saying struck Abram hard. His chest constricted and a roar filled his ears. He leaned over Curtis's desk. "Are you telling me that Pearson, the Serpent, has been released from jail?"

"That's it exactly, Abram. He walked out of here this morning. The sheriff planned to tell you after his meeting."

"Then Miriam is in danger."

Curtis held up his hand. "Pearson is not a killer, Abram. You've got that wrong."

"I am right about the Serpent." As much as Abram wanted to deflect his anger onto Curtis, Abram knew he was at fault for leaving Miriam alone.

He glanced at his uncle's desk. "Tell Samuel to meet me at the farm. I fear for Miriam's life. If anything happens to her—"

Unable to continue, Abram stormed out of the office and hurried to the market to find his sister.

"I'm going back to the house," he told Emma. "Miriam cannot stay alone at the farm with Serpent on the loose."

"Be careful, Abram. Isaac should arrive soon. I will go home with him. But get to Miriam and make sure she is safe. She cares deeply for you, Abram. Open up your eyes and see the truth. Things change, and you have to bend, my brother. Tell Miriam how you feel and start by inviting her to join our faith."

His sister's words hit Abram hard. Miriam cared for him. Was Emma speaking the truth?

He hurried to the buggy and headed out of town. Nellie responded to the flick of the reins and was soon trotting at a rapid clip, but not fast enough to suit Abram.

Pearson knew Miriam was staying at the farm. He could have been watching them this morning. Watching and waiting until Abram and Emma had left the house.

Would Miriam be there when he arrived?

A mile out of town Abram spied Isaac's buggy coming toward him. Little Daniel sat next to his dad.

Abram pulled Nellie to a stop and called across the roadway to Isaac. "Pearson was released from jail, and I am concerned for Miriam's safety. Did you see his car on the roadway?"

"We saw no sign of Serpent. Daniel found Miriam's phone. She was charging her cell in the dairy barn when we left our house. The only car that passed by was the Amish Taxi."

"Frank Evans's service?"

"*Yah*. He said Miriam had requested a ride."

A chill settled over Abram. The bus to Atlanta stopped in Willkommen today. "I must hurry. Emma is at the market. Would you bring her home? And find Samuel. Ask him to drive to the farm. I might need his help."

"*Yah*. Of course. Be careful, Abram."

But he did not respond to Isaac's warning. He was too worried about Miriam and whether he would find her gone.

The ride home never seemed so long. Abram's mind kept playing tricks on him with terrible thoughts of what Serpent would do if he found her.

Please, Gott, keep Miriam safe.

Rounding a bend in the road, Abram spied the Amish Taxi approaching. He flagged the vehicle down and called out to the man at the wheel.

Frank rolled down his window and waved to Abram. "I had a scheduled pickup at your house. Miriam Miller. But she wasn't there when I arrived. I pounded on both the front and back doors of your house and checked the barn and woodshop. No one appeared to be home."

"You saw no one?" Fear gripped Abram's throat.

"The house sat empty. At least, that's how it seemed."

"She wanted a ride to the bus station?"

Frank nodded. "That's right. She scheduled the pickup so she could catch the 10:00 a.m. bus to Atlanta."

Abram said nothing else. He flicked the reins and encouraged Nellie to go even faster. He had to get home, and this was one time he wished for faster transportation. Nellie was a faithful horse that had served the family well, but she was too slow. Everything inside him screamed to be with Miriam. He knew deep down that something was terribly wrong.

He continued to worry when he turned into the drive. He leaped from the buggy, climbed the porch stairs and hurried inside, shouting her name.

"Miriam, where are you?"

Taking the stairs two at a time he climbed to the second floor and pushed open the door to the guest room. A note sat on the dresser.

He reached for it, afraid of what he would find.

"Thank you for opening your home to me, Abram, and for your generous hospitality."

What? He had invited her into his family. It wasn't a matter of hospitality. It was more. Far more.

Note in hand, he raced to Emma's room and on to his own, but failed to find Miriam.

"You made me feel welcome," he continued to read. "I felt such peace and comfort in your home."

He wanted her to feel more than comfort. He wanted her to feel acceptance and, yes, even love.

He ran to the barn, pushed open the door to find Bear whining to get out. "What happened, boy? Did you see Miriam?"

The dog barked and wagged his tail, which provided Abram no clue as to what had happened. He ran to the woodshed and his workshop and the outbuildings. Frank said he had checked them all as well, but Abram needed to make sure Miriam was not in any of the locations.

He turned to stare at Isaac's dairy barn. Perhaps she was making another phone call. A surge of relief swept over Abram. He started to run, eager to find her and tell her how he really felt. He would beg her forgiveness for his lack of understanding, for calling in the sheriff and for all the things he had done to hurt her, especially for believing his uncle when Samuel said Serpent would be held behind bars. He had thought Miriam would be safe at the farm today, but he had been wrong. Dead wrong.

Running along the drive, he stopped short, spying something in the grass. Stooping, he reached for the shiny object. A cell phone.

He tapped the screen. A picture of Miriam with two other women, one a bit older and the other a young blond. Miriam's sisters. Daniel had found the phone and returned it to Miriam, yet she had dropped it.

Abram's ears roared. Miriam would never accidently drop her phone. It had been knocked from her hand in a struggle.

His head swirled. He felt sick and afraid. Anger swelled within him at his own stupidity.

He heard the whine of an engine before the sheriff's car came into view. Samuel pulled into the drive.

Abram opened the passenger door. "Miriam is gone. Serpent must have her. We need to find the cabin where he held her before."

"Get in."

Once Abram had climbed into the squad car, Samuel pulled onto the road, heading up the mountain. "Where's the cabin?"

"I do not know, but she mentioned hearing water."

"There's a cabin not far from the river where she

abandoned her car," Samuel volunteered. "The Petersville police said they would search the place, but we need to check it out ourselves."

Samuel's hands were tight on the steering wheel. "We'll go without lights or siren. I don't want to warn Pearson we're on to him. Surprise is our best weapon."

But would it be enough?

The sheriff pushed his foot down on the accelerator as he grabbed his radio and contacted the dispatcher.

"Miriam Miller has been taken. Alert all deputies and first responders. Roads leading from the Zook farm need roadblocks. Issue a BOLO for Pete Pearson, auxiliary member of the Petersville Police Department. Contact the chief of police there and get him involved."

Trees and boulders flew past the window. All Abram could see was Miriam's face, twisted with fear, and Serpent standing over her, the vile tattoo wrapped around his neck, with a gun to her head.

"Hurry, Samuel," Abram said, uncertain as to the impact of a look-out bulletin with the local law enforcement. "We have to get to Miriam. We have to get to her in time."

Miriam awoke to a déjà vu experience, hearing water and smelling the musty cot on which Pearson had tied her. She pulled against the restraints, needing to free herself.

Over the pounding of her heart, she heard a one-sided conversation that indicated Pearson was on his cell.

"That's right. I've got her at the cabin."

A long pause. "He recognized me today and remembered the woman. He was planning to notify the sheriff. I had to kill him."

A lump formed in Miriam's throat. Was he talking about Abram? Had Pearson killed him?

"You killed her mother," Serpent continued.

Miriam turned her head to hear more clearly.

"Just because she was screaming and saying how much she loved her daughter." Serpent's voice was raised, his anger evident. "You're as guilty as I am."

The reality of what he had revealed washed over her. In the heat of the attack, she had blocked out her mother's words. Now, as she relived again the moment prior to her mother's death, they returned in a flash of recall and, although still unable see the shooter's face, she heard her mother's words of love spoken from the heart.

"I love you, Miriam!"

The open wound that had festered deep within Miriam for so long, the wound of being unwanted, of being unloved, knit together as surely as if the Divine Physician Himself had sutured the gaping hole closed.

She was loved. Tears stung her eyes, but she wouldn't give in to them. She had to free herself so she could know what had happened to Abram. And Emma. Was that dear woman hurt, as well?

Abram couldn't be dead. It couldn't be true. It had to be a lie.

Chapter Twenty-Five

Abram felt like a caged grizzly bear when they found the cabin by the water's edge empty. He climbed back into the sheriff's squad car.

"Where to now?" Samuel asked, his voice as hard as steel and reflecting the way Abram felt.

"Ezra Jacobs's place. Jacobs said he saw a tall red-haired man that matched the description of a person Miriam had seen at the cabin. The old man's memory is not the best, but perhaps he will have remembered more about what happened."

Samuel accelerated. "Hold on," he told Abram as he pulled onto the mountain road, heading for the turnoff to Jacobs's cabin. He made the sharp turn onto the narrow, pitted roadway that led up the steep incline, sending gravel and dirt flying.

They braked to a stop in front of the cabin, leaped from the car and raced to the porch. The sheriff called Ezra's name and announced, "Sheriff's office," before he entered the small abode. What they found took Abram's breath.

The old man lay on the floor in a pool of blood. His faithful dog, Gus, whined at his side.

The sheriff knelt beside Ezra and felt for a pulse. He looked up with heavy eyes and shook his head. "He's gone."

Pulling out his cell, he called Dispatch and requested backup. "We also need the coroner, a crime scene specialist and an ambulance to transport the body to the morgue."

A siren sounded, heading their way.

"Tell everyone to go silent," Samuel said to the dispatcher. Within seconds, the shrill wail died.

As Samuel pocketed his cell, a car charged up the gravel trail and braked in front of the cabin.

Deputy Curtis Idler climbed from behind the wheel and hurried to join Abram and the sheriff.

"What happened?" he asked before he looked down and saw the body. He let out a lungful of air and shook his head. "Looks like we've got a killer on the loose."

Not the story Curtis had given Abram earlier when the deputy had claimed Serpent was innocent of wrongdoing.

"Did you question Ned Quigley about releasing Pearson?" Abram demanded as he tried to control his anger.

Curtis held up a hand defensively. "I told you what Quigley said. Pearson's alibi was airtight."

"I'm beginning to think I hired the wrong guy," the sheriff said. "Do you know where Ned is now?"

Curtis shook his head. "I haven't seen him all day. His girlfriend called and said he had a stomach virus, but I'm not sure if we can trust her."

"Why not?"

"She worked with the Petersville Police Department as a file clerk some years back. If any of those cops are bad, she might be part of the group."

"I'll deal with Ned when we get back to town," the

sheriff assured Curtis. "Right now, we have to find Miriam Miller. Pearson may have her. She was previously held in a cabin situated near running water."

"Water? You mean the river? What about the abandoned cabin on the other side of the roadway?"

Samuel nodded. "We've already checked it out."

Abram stepped onto the porch and rounded the cabin. Jacobs had spotted the red-haired man. Surely the old guy didn't travel far from home, which meant Red had been close by. At the rear of the cabin, Abram spied the continuation of a roadway that angled under an overhang of oaks and disappeared up the mountain into the thick forest.

He came back and told Samuel.

"Let's go." The sheriff and Abram took the lead with Curtis following in the second car. The path was steep and rough, but they soon came upon a waterfall. The running water Miriam had heard.

Getting out of his squad car, Curtis drew his gun and pointed to a thick patch of hardwoods and pines. "I'll check to the right. You two head to the left."

Samuel held up his hand. "Stay behind me, Abram. Or you can wait in the car."

"I am going with you."

Abram wanted to push quickly through the brush, but Samuel insisted they take it slow. "We have to use caution and cover. We don't want Pearson to see us first."

He was right, of course, but Abram kept thinking of Miriam being held against her will.

Let her be alive. Please, Gott. I beg forgiveness for all my transgressions. For my sinful past. Do not let my failings keep You from helping Miriam.

The sharp report of a gunshot sounded behind them. Samuel turned and ran, retracing his steps as he headed in the direction of the gunfire. Abram passed him, fearing the worst. It couldn't be Miriam.

"Get behind me," Samuel warned. But Abram refused to slow down. He needed to find Miriam.

Passing the area where they had parked the cars, they raced into the thick brush, following the path Curtis had taken. Not more than fifty feet into the thicket, they spied the cabin and Pearson's body on the front porch with a bullet in his chest. Just like Jacobs, the Serpent lay in a pool of his own blood.

Curtis knelt over him and touched his neck. "He had a weapon."

"Did you identify yourself as from the sheriff's office?" Samuel asked.

"Of course I did," Curtis insisted. "He wouldn't drop his weapon. I didn't have a choice."

"Miriam?" Frantic to find her, Abram started for the cabin.

Curtis stepped in front of him. "I'll go first. You don't know who's in there."

"I do not care. I need to find her."

The sheriff stared down at where Pearson lay. He pursed his lips and turned to glare at Curtis.

"What?" A muscle twitched under Curtis's eye.

"Pearson's gun is still in his holster."

"He had another weapon. It must have fallen into the bushes."

Samuel took a step toward the deputy. "Give me your gun, Curtis."

"What are you talking about? Pearson was a criminal. He kidnapped a woman. She's tied up inside."

"Have you seen her?" Samuel stepped closer, his voice low and menacing.

Abram inched closer, needing to get into the cabin.

"Stay where you are." Curtis aimed his gun at the sheriff but flicked his gaze to Abram.

"Calm down, Curtis. There will be an investigation," the sheriff said. "If you're telling the truth, you'll be exonerated."

"You always think you know best. I was in line for sheriff until you decided to run for office. I knew I didn't have a chance. People thought you were the honest candidate because of your Amish background. They don't know that you left your community because you couldn't follow the rules."

"Give me the gun, Curtis." The sheriff inched closer. Abram did the same.

"You'll never get away with this," Samuel warned.

"Of course I will," Curtis boasted. "I'll blame it all on Pearson. He was a loser. He wouldn't follow my lead. He made me kill that old woman. I didn't want to, but she started screaming. At least her daughter didn't see my face. Pearson and I had been a team, but he got pushy and shoved his weight around. The mother was protective of her daughter, saying how special she was and how much she loved her. It made me sick."

Curtis shook his head with disgust. "My mother left me in a motel until child services picked me up. I was stuck in that room for two days. How do you think that feels, Sam? Do you have any idea? You were raised in a loving family and you turned your back on them. I didn't have anyone to love me."

"I'm sorry for your childhood, Curtis." Samuel's voice was filled with understanding. He took a step closer then extended his hand as if willing Curtis to give him the weapon. "I'll get you help. Someone to talk to you. You didn't do anything wrong, Curtis. I understand why you're upset at your mother. Did you kill the woman because she reminded you of your mother?"

Curtis's expression revealed the sheriff had hit too close to home. The deputy shook his head. "Shut up, Sam. Don't talk about my childhood."

"You were a good kid. Your mother loved you. Something unforeseen must have happened to her so she couldn't get back to you." Another step. "Now give me the weapon. You can trust me."

Sam lunged. Curtis fired. The sheriff gasped, clutched his side and fell to the ground.

Abram raced toward the deputy. A second shot winged his chest and knocked the air from his lungs. He tumbled to the porch then crawled up the steps. Abram's vision blurred and the cabin swirled around him. Time stood still for one long, painful moment, then…

Footsteps sounded. He looked up, seeing Miriam dragged from the cabin with her arms tied in front of her. Curtis yanked her down the steps and into the brush.

Abram stumbled toward Samuel and felt his neck for a pulse. He was breathing, but his pulse was erratic. Abram grabbed the sheriff's cell and pressed the prompt for the dispatcher.

"The sheriff…needs an ambulance," Abram said when the woman answered. He pulled in a deep breath and continued on. "The cabin…sits up the mountain behind Old Man Jacobs's place. Have the sheriff's office set up a roadblock at the fork in the road to town. Contact the Petersville police. Instruct them to block the mountain road that leads there, as well. Curtis Idler his taken a hostage and will be heading in one of those two directions."

Samuel struggled to speak after Abram disconnected. "Go...now. Take...keys."

"I'm not going to leave you," Abram insisted.

"You drive. You can. Remember... Trevor."

Trevor, the friend who had taught Abram to drive, who had loaned him his radio, who had encouraged him to leave the Amish way of life.

"I...know..." Samuel gasped for air. "You were... behind...the wheel."

The day of the accident. The day Trevor had died.

After Emma's accident, Abram had gone joyriding with his friend. Trevor had let Abram drive. He'd been reckless, moving too fast on a windy lakeside road.

"Go..." Samuel insisted. "Now."

"The ambulance is on the way. Hang on."

Abram grabbed the keys from Samuel's pocket and ran toward the clearing. He climbed behind the wheel of the sheriff's squad car, remembering his youth and the times Trevor had let him drive.

He turned the key in the ignition and stepped on the accelerator. The car lurched forward. The radio squawked as the deputies called in their locations. They were still too far away to help.

Abram gripped the steering wheel, seeing Curtis in the distance. The deputy was driving much too fast along the winding mountain road. Abram was as well, but he could not let him get away with Miriam.

Isaac's dairy came into view. He saw his own farm in the distance. Just so Emma and Isaac and little Daniel were still at the market and not anywhere near Curtis. Sirens sounded in the distance, approaching on the road from town. Their roadblock would stop the deputy. At least that was Abram's hope.

The deputy's car approached the fork. Abram's heart

stopped. Curtis took the road to the right, the road that passed Abram's house. The road that led to the bridge.

"No," Abram bellowed. The bridge looked stable enough, but the wood was rotten and would buckle with any weight. Miriam would be hurled into the water.

Just like Trevor so long ago.

Abram pushed the car faster. His hat flew off, his hands were white-knuckled on the steering wheel. He screeched around the bend. In the distance he saw the deputy's car heading straight for the bridge. Abram laid on the horn, needing to warn him. Curtis had to stop.

Abram's heart jammed in his throat as the deputy's car sailed across the bridge. In a split second the wooden platform groaned then crumbled like a child's toy, toppling the squad car—along with Miriam—into the raging river below.

Accelerating even faster, Abram drove to the edge of the bridge, screeched to a stop and leaped from the car. He threw off his jacket, kicked out of his shoes and dove into the water.

The frigid cold took his breath. He beat the rapid current with strong strokes that took him to the middle of the river. The car was already partially submerged.

Diving down into the murky river, he grabbed the passenger door that hung open and felt inside, searching for Miriam. She was not in the car, neither was Curtis. A cracked windshield big enough for a body to hurl through paralyzed him for one long moment.

Gott help me.

He surfaced for air, grabbed a breath and then dove deep again, beneath the car that was slowly sinking.

Miriam's sweet face, her smile, her eyes…she was all he could think of.

Where was she?

He stretched his arms, thinking of Christ who had died on the cross. *Gott, do not let her die.*

His hand touched something. A piece of fabric. He pulled it close, feeling the softness of her flesh. He wrapped his arms around her waist and kicked to the surface.

Sheriffs' cars clustered at the edge of the road. Police from Petersville had already lowered a boat into the water.

"Here!" Abram shouted, kicking his legs and holding Miriam close with one arm while he raised the other overhead.

"There's Zook," an officer shouted. "He's got the woman."

The boat neared. Hands reached for Miriam and pulled her from the water.

"I am all right. Get her to safety," Abram insisted.

When he started to swim, he realized his folly. He could not move his left arm. An officer in a second boat pulled him to shore. "You're wounded, Abram. It's a wonder you could swim at all."

But he had. He had found Miriam and saved her.

Once on land he raced to where she lay, pale as death, on a stretcher. "How is she?" he asked the medic who was working on her.

The EMT shook his head. "We're taking her to the hospital."

"I must go with her," Abram insisted.

"You can't. We'll bring another ambulance. Looks like you need to be treated, as well."

Abram's heart broke as the EMTs lifted Miriam into the ambulance. Would he ever see her again or had *Gott* taken another woman from him? A woman he loved and wanted to cherish for the rest of his life?

Emma was right. He had lived too long in the past. He wanted a future with Miriam.

But would she survive?

Chapter Twenty-Six

Emma and Isaac met Abram at the hospital. They had brought fresh clothing that Abram changed into, grateful for their thoughtfulness, as well as a plastic bag containing Miriam's belongings and her cell phone.

"How is she?" Emma asked, her face drawn and filled with worry.

He shook his head. "The doctor is with her."

Emma touched his arm. "They said you saved her, Abram."

He nodded.

"But you are wounded yourself, my brother."

"The wound is not deep. It will heal." He glanced at Isaac and then back at his sister. "Where is Daniel?"

"Eva Keim and her daughter are with him," she reassured him. "And Samuel? Is there news?"

"In surgery." Abram's voice tightened. "If he survives, he will have a long recovery."

"Curtis Idler's body was found," Isaac shared, his eyes downcast. "He did not survive."

Abram nodded. "Curtis was working with Serpent and is the one who killed Miriam's mother."

"What of the newly hired deputy?"

"Ned Quigley is a good man and a trusted officer of the law."

The day passed slowly. Abram appreciated Emma and Isaac's support, but his total focus was on Miriam.

The intensive care rules allowed visitors to be with the patients for only short periods. Abram's gut wrenched each time he entered her room, seeing her hooked to machines that monitored her heart rate and blood pressure and other vital signs. An IV bag of medication hung by the side of her bed and dripped life-giving antibiotics into her vein. She had aspirated water and the doctor worried about pneumonia setting in.

Abram placed the bag containing her things on the stand by her bed and wondered how long it would be until she was alert enough to know it was there.

By late afternoon Isaac was growing fidgety and increasingly concerned about his dairy cows and their need to be milked.

"Go home," Abram encouraged. "Take Emma with you. I will use the Amish Taxi and return to the farm later. The horses need to be watered and fed. The other animals, as well."

"I can do the chores," Emma offered.

"I appreciate your help, Emma, but you cannot do all of them." He thought of his sister's difficulty in walking. "You have already done so much for me. Go with Isaac. He needs you."

"But—" She started to object.

Abram took her hand. "It is time for you to have a family of your own, Emma. You saved me after Rebecca's death, for which I will always be grateful. Now it is time for you to embrace your own life."

"Are you sure, Abram?"

"More than anything I want you to be happy. You forgave me, Emma, when I could not forgive myself. Now I must let go of the past." He turned to look through the glass window into Miriam's room. "Now I must focus on the future."

Emma squeezed his hand. "I am praying for you, Abram, and for Miriam." Turning, she wrapped her arm through Isaac's. Together they walked out of the intensive care unit.

Once again Abram entered Miriam's room. He drew a chair next to her bed and took her hand as he sat. Her hair was matted from the river and her slender face was ashen, but Abram had never seen a woman more beautiful or more courageous. She had been through so much.

The doctors said he had saved her in the nick of time. Although infection was a concern, they were more worried about the drugs Serpent had used to subdue her. If only she would open her eyes and respond.

Abram rubbed her hand and leaned closer to the bed.

"Miriam, I do not know if you can hear me. It is Abram. I was wrong about so many things, but I know one thing for certain. I love you with my whole heart. I need you. Come back to me."

The nurse allowed him to remain at Miriam's bedside far longer than the allotted visiting period, but later that evening she ushered him into the hallway. "Go home, Mr. Zook. I know you have a farm to tend. You can do nothing here. We expect her to sleep through the night and most of tomorrow. Come back in the afternoon. We'll know more then."

Abram's heart was heavy as he rode home in Frank Evans's taxi. Thankfully the driver did not chatter as he usually was prone to do. Perhaps he realized Abram needed time to think and pray.

Entering the house, Abram felt numb with confusion and worry. Emma was there to greet him, along with Isaac.

"How is she?" his sister asked as she poured a cup of coffee for Abram and set it on the table.

"The same. The nurse encouraged me to go home. I... I did not want to leave but...the farm."

Isaac stepped forward. "I took care of the animals. You do not need to worry."

But he was worried. He was worried about Miriam.

"As Emma mentioned at the hospital, Eva Keim and her daughter, Abagail, are keeping Daniel tonight," Isaac continued. "I will pick him up tomorrow after the cows are milked. I can take you to the hospital before I get Daniel."

Abram appreciated the offer.

"I have a plate for you to eat, Abram." Emma ushered him toward the table. "You must be hungry."

He could not eat. Not now. "I will eat tomorrow."

Abram dragged himself upstairs. The door to Miriam's room hung open. He looked in, remembering the night he had placed her on the bed with her blood-stained clothes and her bruised and scraped face.

His mind flashed back to the moments they had shared: walking along the pasture path, in the barn and workshop, and on the stairway when he had taken her into his arms.

His arms were empty now. Would he ever hold her again?

Entering his bedroom, he reached for his Bible, but he did not have the strength to open to the words of scripture. He merely clasped the well-read book to his heart.

Forgive me, Gott, for the mistakes I have made. I see more clearly now that I was the one at fault and not my datt. I could not save Trevor so long ago, but You helped me save Miriam. I can no longer look back, yet I know a future with Miriam will never be unless she comes into the Amish faith. Right now, I ask that You allow her to live. Even if she refuses my faith, I will never forget her and will never stop loving her from afar.

Chapter Twenty-Seven

After a sleepless night Abram left his bed early to do the chores and get everything ready for his departure. He planned to stay at the hospital until Miriam was released. He would bring her home to recuperate here with him. With Emma's good cooking and with the threat of Serpent gone, Miriam would heal both physically and emotionally.

True to his word, Isaac picked Abram up at his house and carted him to the county hospital.

"Shall I return this evening?" Isaac asked.

Abram appreciated the offer but he shook his head. "I will stay at the hospital tonight. I do not want to leave Miriam again."

Isaac nodded. "Do not worry about the farm. I talked to Eva Keim's twin sons. They will help."

"You are a good neighbor, Isaac, and a good friend."

"We take care of each other, Abram. It is the Amish way."

The way of life Abram had always lived. Only once, in his turbulent youth, he had yearned for a more worldly life. Emma's accident and Trevor's death had brought him back to his Amish roots.

Gott had brought good from those two very tragic situations. Hopefully good would come from Miriam's ordeal, as well. Abram had found the woman he wanted to walk with through life. If only she felt the same.

But she was an *Englischer* and he was *plain*. The divide stood between them. Hopefully it would not prove too large to reconcile.

Renewed in hope, he hurried into the hospital and headed for Intensive Care. He stopped at the nurses' desk to speak to the kind woman wearing scrubs who had reached out to him yesterday.

"How is Miriam?" he asked.

The nurse's smile was bright, which filled him with relief. "She had an amazing recovery. The effects of whatever drugs her captor had given her wore off last night. We started her on oral antibiotics and were able to release her from Intensive Care this morning."

Abram lifted up a prayer of thanksgiving and then smiled back at the nurse, eager to see Miriam. "Could you tell me to which room you have moved her?"

The nurse's face clouded. "I'm sorry, Mr. Zook. She's gone."

His heart lurched. "What?"

"A reporter stopped by, asking questions."

"A newspaper reporter?"

The nurse nodded. "That's right. I think it worried her. Soon after that she checked herself out of the hospital against doctor's orders. We would have liked her to stay another twelve hours or so, but we couldn't keep her against her will. I thought she would have contacted you."

"Where did she go?"

"I'm not sure. Do you know a man named Frank?"

"*Yah*, he runs the Amish Taxi."

"He picked her up. Hopefully he can help you find her."

"May I use your phone?"

"Of course." She handed a phone to Abram and pointed to a small desk and chair in the corner. "You'll have more privacy over there. Dial 8 to get an outside line."

Abram's hand was shaking as he plugged in the number for the taxi service. Frank answered on the first ring.

"Miriam Miller," Abram said. "Where did you take her today?"

"To the bus station. She caught the bus to Atlanta."

Abram's world shattered. He sat clutching the phone, unwilling to accept what he had just heard.

Miriam had left him.

He had given her safe refuge. He had also given her his heart. But it was too little too late.

Miriam did not want an Amish man. She did not want Abram. No matter how much he wanted her.

Eleven days later...

Miriam walked to the window of the hotel room and looked at the street below where cars hurried, rushing through the city, heading to their destination. She had been in Atlanta for almost two weeks and had not found Hannah nor heard from her in all that time. Her older sister seemed to have disappeared just as surely as Sarah had.

Perhaps Hannah had discarded her old cell for a newer model with a new number and then left the city for places unknown. If so, the two sisters might never reconnect. The realization brought a heavy weight to rest on Miriam's shoulders.

The neon sign for the bus station flashed in the distance and brought memories of the day she had arrived in Atlanta, expecting Hannah to meet her. Instead she had found only strangers in the station. Crestfallen, Miriam had made her way to the cheap hotel nearby where she had spent the night crying from loneliness and a confused heart.

How much she yearned for the life she had found in the North Georgia mountains. In her mind's eye, she saw Abram's handsome face and felt his strong arms surround her as he lifted her into the buggy. She envisioned Emma waving from the porch and heard the *clip-clop* of Nellie's hooves. If only she could be with them again.

Leaving the window, she reached for the blue fabric, recalling how Emma had helped her cut the pattern. Miriam settled onto the bedside chair, threaded her needle and started to sew. The rhythmic in and out of the needle and thread through the cotton cloth brought comfort and soothed her troubled spirit as she labored in the night. With each stitch she remembered the special world she had left behind.

At last, her work completed, she slipped into the Amish dress and gazed at her reflection in the mirror. Staring back at her was a new woman who was ready to leave the *Englisch* world behind. Miriam didn't need or want the things of this life. Instead she yearned for the *plain* way of the Amish. She longed to embrace their faith in God, their love of family and their appreciation for hard work and simple blessings.

Abram may have already moved on with his life, but even without him at her side—as heartbreaking as that would be—Miriam wanted his faith.

She glanced away from the mirror, no longer needing to see her reflection. She knew who she was. She was an Amish woman who was eager to return home.

Chapter Twenty-Eight

Standing on the hillside, Abram looked down at his farm and Isaac's dairy in the distance. Emma and the dairyman would soon marry. Daniel would have a mother, and Abram's sister would find the happiness she deserved.

Abram was happy for her. He turned back to his work and pulled the wire more tightly around the fence post, thankful for physical labor that occupied his hands. If only it could occupy his mind, as well. No matter what he did, his thoughts were always on Miriam and how much he longed to see her again.

Once the wire was attached, Abram stared up at the sky. The sun peered out from between the clouds and the warm hint of spring filled the air.

"A young man's fancy..." He thought of the adage about a man's heart turning to love and shook his head.

He was no longer a young man and he had found his love.

The sound of a car engine caught his attention. He turned, seeing the Amish Taxi driving from town along the fork in the road.

A friend must be coming to visit Emma. Abagail

Keim had stopped by twice since she and her mother had kept Daniel. Perhaps she was visiting again.

Turning back to his work, Abram ignored the sound of the car door slamming. Then, realizing he needed to be considerate of Abagail's feelings, he turned to wave a greeting.

But what he saw made his heart lurch.

He blinked, unwilling to believe his eyes.

An Amish woman wearing a blue dress stepped from the taxi. She was slender, with golden-brown hair, and stared at him from a distance. Then she waved and started running, past the house and up the hill.

"Abram," she called. "I've come home."

His heart burst with joy. He dropped his tools and raced to meet her, his arms wide as she ran into his embrace.

"Oh, Miriam," he sighed, inhaling the sweet smell of her. "I have missed you so."

"I... I had to leave, Abram. I had to try to find Hannah. But she was gone. I thought I would learn to live in the city, yet my heart broke each day there without you."

She pulled back and stared into his eyes as if she, too, couldn't believe they were together again.

"I kept hearing your voice, Abram. You kept saying, 'Come home to me.' I knew you were calling me back to Willkommen."

"Miriam, I love you. I have loved you since the first moment I saw you. We will make this work."

"Yah," she said with a twinkle in her eyes and pointing to the blue frock she wore. "Did you see the dress I made? Emma taught me how to cut the fabric, and I finished it in Atlanta. Stitching it together by hand made me realize where my heart really wanted to be. With

you, Abram, living the Amish life and being a member of the Amish church."

"Oh, Miriam. You are all I have ever wanted."

He lowered his lips to hers and then, scooping her into his arms, he twirled her around and around. They kissed until they were dizzy and giddy with laughter.

Their playfulness turned serious as he drew her even closer and looked deeply into her eyes. "I love you, Miriam Miller, and I always will. You bring joy to my heart and to my home. Plus you were right about voicing my contrition aloud. I talked to the bishop about my past. That weight has been removed from my heart, which is now filled to overflowing with my love for you."

Again, they kissed. She molded into his embrace, their hearts entwined, as Abram wrapped her tightly in his arms, never wanting to let her go.

Epilogue

"I packed cheese and bread and fruit for the journey." Emma handed the basket to Miriam, who placed it on the floor of the buggy.

Miriam smiled with gratitude. "You have done too much."

Emma waved off the comment. "Promise you will write to us when you arrive in Ethridge and let us know about the wedding plans? Isaac and Daniel and I want to be there to celebrate with you and Abram."

"I'll write and let you know, even before the date is published at church."

"It is *gut* that Abram and our *datt* have reconciled. That is your doing, Miriam."

She shook her head. "No, Emma, the credit goes to Abram. He had to forgive himself. Once he did, he was able to ask forgiveness from his father. Their relationship, at least through the mail, seems strong, although I have to admit that I'm worried about meeting him."

"Our *datt* has a gruff exterior but a heart of gold."

Miriam rolled her eyes and laughed. "Now I'm even more concerned."

"I promise, our parents will love you."

"You're sure?" Miriam asked.

"*Yah*. As Daniel says, 'Cross my heart.'"

Both women laughed for a long moment and then the smile on Emma's face waned. "I am glad you will stay in Ethridge until the investigation is over and all those involved in the trafficking ring are brought to justice. Isaac saw more reporters in town, asking questions. He fears the stories they write in their newspapers will draw attention to Willkommen."

"Abram says I will be safer in Tennessee. We wouldn't be able to go if you and Isaac hadn't offered to take care of the farm."

"It is good we live close." Isaac approached the buggy. "Abagail's twin brothers will help, as well."

Daniel left the workshop and skipped toward them, with Abram and Bear following close behind. The boy blew into the wooden train whistle Abram had made. The deep, soulful sound filled the air.

"Daniel, you must not blow the whistle around Nellie," Emma cautioned lovingly. "You will spook her for sure."

The boy hurried to Emma's side, his eyes wide with excitement. "Abram said he will teach me woodworking when he and Miriam return."

Emma touched his cheek lovingly. "That is something to look forward to, *yah*."

The boy nodded then turned to Miriam and smiled slyly as if he had a secret to share. "*Mamm* baked cookies for your basket."

"Your new *mamm* is very thoughtful." Miriam loved the way Daniel had accepted Emma into his life.

"How many of the cookies did you eat, Daniel?" Abram asked as he neared.

"More than *Datt* thought I should."

The adults laughed and watched as Daniel chased Bear around the yard.

Abram's face grew serious. He turned to Isaac. "Be careful, my friend. There is talk that this hijacking operation is large. More could happen. Ned told me."

"I have heard the same. I will take care of Emma and be on guard lest anything else occurs. And do not worry. We will not divulge where you and Miriam have gone. Your secret will be safe with us."

"But we will eagerly await your return." Emma squeezed Miriam's hand. "The talk at the market is that Samuel will have a long recovery, although Ned Quigley is doing a good job as acting sheriff."

"If he can do enough," Abram mused. "At least he is searching for Sarah."

"The Petersville police chief is helping him," Isaac added. "It appears he was not involved in the corruption."

"Ned promised to write me if he learns anything new," Miriam said as she hugged her soon-to-be sister-in-law and then Isaac. "Abram and I continue to pray."

"*Gott* will answer us with good news, I am sure," Abram said before he hugged his sister and helped Miriam into the buggy. "We must go, if we are to catch the bus to Ethridge."

Isaac shook Abram's hand and then slapped his back. "The twins will drive your buggy back this afternoon when they come to work on the farm."

"They will be good farmers by the time we return."

Abram climbed in beside Miriam and lifted the reins.

Daniel ran to stand between Isaac and Emma and raised his hand in farewell as the buggy turned onto the roadway, heading to Willkommen.

"Take care of Bear and Gus," Abram said as he glanced back over his shoulder. Ezra Jacobs's beagle ambled out of the barn, wagging his tail. The well-being of the old dog had tugged at Abram's heart until he had found Gus wandering aimlessly in the woods.

Daniel waved. "*Yah*, we will."

When the farm and Isaac's sweet family were out of sight, Miriam shrugged out of her cape, enjoying the warmth of the day.

"The flowers will be in bloom soon," she said, eyeing the countryside as they passed by.

"The letter from my mother said she is painting the house and watching her celery grow," Abram shared.

Miriam laughed, remembering the celery served at Isaac and Emma's wedding. "There are many customs I must get used to, Abram."

"I will help you learn them all."

"What if your parents don't like the woman you have chosen to marry?"

"Ah, but they will love you. After the wedding, we will move into the house next door that belonged to my *grossdaadi*, my grandfather, and my *mammi*, my grandmother. It will be a time to reconcile with the family I left behind." He gently elbowed her, his eyes twinkling. "And a time to get to know my new wife."

"A honeymoon," she said, smiling. "As the *Englisch* say."

He laughed and took her hand. "Hopefully, *Gott* will bless us soon with children. Lots of children who will help their mother in the kitchen and their father in the fields."

"And in the workshop," she added. "Your business is growing, Abram. So many people at the market love your work. I knew they would."

"You encouraged me, Miriam. For that I am thankful."

He pulled back on the reins and the buggy came to a stop. Turning to face her, he tucked a strand of hair behind her ear. "Most of all, I am thankful for you, Miriam. That you came into my life and set me free from the past."

He kissed her for a very long time. Her heart leaped for joy and was filled with hope for the future. A future with Abram.

She raised her face to the sun, peering through the clouds. Spring, a wedding, children in the future and her Amish protector who had saved her life and saved her heart.

As Nellie started moving again, Abram wrapped his arm around Miriam's waist and pulled her close. "Soon we will be one, Miriam. An Amish man and an *Englisch* woman—"

"An *Englischer* turned Amish," she added with a smile.

"What could be better?" he asked.

"Nothing," she sighed.

Nothing could be better than living the rest of her life with Abram at her side.

"Thank You, God," she whispered. "Thank you, Abram."

He raised his brow and leaned closer. "Did you say something?"

"I said thank you for saving me, for loving me and for asking me to be your wife."

"Our life will be *gut*," he said with a flick of the reins.

"Yah." Miriam smiled. "Our life will be very, very *gut*."

* * * * *

If you enjoyed AMISH REFUGE, look for these other titles by Debby Giusti.

THE AGENT'S SECRET PAST
PLAIN TRUTH
PLAIN DANGER

Dear Reader,

I hope you enjoyed *Amish Refuge*, the first book in my AMISH PROTECTORS series. Amish widower Abram Zook never expected a battered woman to appear on his front porch in the middle of the night. Especially not an *Englisch* woman. But Miriam Miller's car has been hijacked, her mother's been murdered and her younger sister carted off to who knows where. Miriam needs to hole up and stay safe, and what better place than on an Amish farm.

This story is about forgiveness. If you struggle to let go of a painful past, I hope Abram and Miriam's journey will touch your heart and bring you to a place of new beginnings. I'm praying for you!

I love to hear from readers. Email me at debby@ debbygiusti.com or write me c/o Love Inspired, 195 Broadway, 24th Floor, New York, NY 10007. Visit me at www.DebbyGiusti.com and at www.Facebook.com/ debby.giusti.9.

As always, I thank God for bringing us together through this story.

Wishing you abundant blessings,
Debby

Get 4 FREE REWARDS!

We'll send you 2 FREE Books plus 2 FREE Mystery Gifts.

Counting on the Cowboy
Shannon Taylor Vannatter

Reunited by a Secret Child
Leigh Bale

Love Inspired® books feature contemporary inspirational romances with Christian characters facing the challenges of life and love.

FREE Value Over $20

SPECIAL EXCERPT FROM

Love Inspired®

With his orphaned nephew depending on him, Amish carpenter Eli Troyer moves to Harmony Creek Hollow to start over. And when schoolteacher Miriam Hartz offers to teach hearing-impaired Eli how to read lips, he can't refuse. Given both of their pasts, dare they hope to fit together as a family…forever?

Read on for a sneak preview of
THE AMISH SUITOR *by* **Jo Ann Brown**,
available in June 2018 from Love Inspired!

"If you want, I can teach you to read lips."

"What?"

Miriam touched her lips and then raised and lowered her fingers against her thumb as if they were a duck's bill. "Talk. I can help you understand what people are saying by watching them talk."

When he realized what Miriam was doing, Eli was stunned. A nurse at the hospital where he'd woken after the wall's collapse had suggested that, once he was healed, he should learn to read lips. He'd pushed that advice aside, because he didn't have time with the obligations of his brother's farm and his brother's son.

During the past four years he and his nephew had created a unique language together. Mostly Kyle had taught it to him, helping him decipher the meaning and context of the few words he could capture.

"How do you know about lipreading?" Eli asked.

"My *grossmammi*." She tapped one ear, then the other. "...hearing...as she grew older. We...together. We practiced together. I can help." She put her hands on Kyle's shoulders. "Kyle...grows up. Who will...you then?"

Who would help him when Kyle wasn't nearby? He was sure that was what she'd asked. It was a question he'd posed to himself more and more often as Kyle reached the age to start attending school.

Not for the first time, Eli thought about the burden he'd placed on Kyle. Though Eli was scrupulous in making time for Kyle to be a *kind*, sometimes, like when they went to a store, he found himself needing the little boy to confirm a total when he was checking out or to explain where to find something on the shelves. If he didn't agree to Miriam's help, he was condemning his nephew to a lifetime of having to help him.

"All right," Eli said. "You can try to teach me to read lips."

Miriam seemed so confident she could teach him. He didn't want to disappoint her when she was going out of her way to help him.

Kyle threw his arms around Miriam and gave her a big hug. He grinned, and Eli realized how eager the *kind* was to let someone else help Eli fill in the blanks.

Don't miss
THE AMISH SUITOR by Jo Ann Brown,
available June 2018 wherever
Love Inspired® books and ebooks are sold.

www.LoveInspired.com

Inspirational Romance to Warm Your Heart and Soul

Join our social communities to connect with other readers who share your love!

Sign up for the Love Inspired newsletter at **www.LoveInspired.com** to be the first to find out about upcoming titles, special promotions and exclusive content.

CONNECT WITH US AT:

Harlequin.com/Community

 Facebook.com/LoveInspiredBooks

 Twitter.com/LoveInspiredBks

LISOCIAL2017

First Lieutenant Ethan Webb brushed past the startled aide standing in Colonel Masters's outer office.

"The colonel is—"

"Waiting for me," Ethan snapped. "I know." Lt. Col. Terence Masters, Ethan's former father-in-law, was always a step ahead of him. He led Titus, his German shorthaired pointer, into the office, found Masters seated in his leather chair.

"You're late," Masters said. "And I don't want your dog in here."

"With respect, sir, the dog goes where I go, and I don't appreciate you pressuring my commanding officer to get me to do this harebrained job during my leave. I said I would consider it, didn't I?"

"A little extra insurance to help you make up your mind, Webb."

"It's a bad idea. Leave me alone to do my investigation with the team at Canyon, and we'll catch Sullivan." They were working around the clock to put away the serial killer who was targeting his air force brothers and sisters as well as a few select others, including Ethan's ex-wife, Jillian.

"Your team," Masters said, "hasn't gotten the job done, and this lunatic has threatened my daughter. You're going to work for me privately, protect Jillian from Sullivan, draw him out and catch him, as we've discussed."

"So you think I'm going to pretend to be married to Jillian again and that's going to put us in the perfect position to catch Sullivan?" He shoved a hand through his crew-cut hair, striving for control. "This is lunacy. I can't believe you're willing to use your daughter as bait."

"I'm not," he said. "I've decided it's too risky for Jillian, and that's why I hired this girl. This is Kendra Bell."

The civilian woman stepped into the office and Ethan could only stare at her.

"You're…" He shook himself slightly and tried again. "I mean… You look like…"

"Your ex-wife," she finished. "I know. That's the point."